Beard Gang

Chronicles

Beard Gang Chronicles

Blake Karrington, Genesis Woods,
Johnni Sherri, Sherene Holly Cain
and Shantaé

www.urbanbooks.net

Urban Books, LLC
300 Farmingdale Road, NY-Route 109
Farmingdale, NY 11735

ISBN 13: 978-1-60162-902-9
ISBN 10: 1-60162-902-8

First Trade Paperback Printing March 2019
Printed in the United States of America

10 9 8 7 6 5 4 3 2 1

*This is a work of fiction. Any references or similarities
to actual events, real people, living or dead, or to real
locales are intended to give the novel a sense of reality.
Any similarity in other names, characters, places, and
incidents is entirely coincidental.*

Distributed by Kensington Publishing Corp.
Submit Orders to:
Customer Service
400 Hahn Road
Westminster, MD 21157-4627
Phone: 1-800-733-3000
Fax: 1-800-659-2436

Beard Gang Chronicles

Blake Karrington, Genesis Woods,
Johnni Sherri, Sherene Holly Cain
and Shantaé

Beard Gang

by

Blake Karrington

Chapter 1

From the first piece of "evidence" that was sent to me in the now-familiar plain-looking brown envelope, I kinda figured I was dealin' with a client who either had a whole lotta time on her hands or had been reading way too many of those *Fifty Shades of Grey* wack-ass romance novels. But when the shiny silver object fell with a heavy thud on top of the rustic dark wood kitchen tabletop that I had paid almost $4,000 for, I knew I wasn't dealing with a normal broad.

"What in the entire fuck is this shit?"

A small yellow sticky note with the hand-written words "Use me carefully," was on a very expensive-looking pocket knife. This shit was custom engraved with the letters "J.P." on a brass-like plate on a full gunmetal finish. I thought that she'd want it back when I was done with the job.

I put the knife back where it came from and added it to its other family of plain brown envelopes full of the other weird-ass shit she wanted me to use for this latest job. First was the black ski mask that came in the mail last week on a Monday with zero instructions. But it's not like I didn't know how to use a ski mask. Hell, I got caught red-handed wearing one tryin'a run and hide from that damn ghetto bird blasting all kinds of lights through the streets of that old perfect-ass rich neighborhood me and my then-patna Jo-Jo was trying to escape from. If we had been in the hood attempting to rob somebody, a helicopter would have been the least of our worries. But that's what happens when you try to put a "not-so-smart-ass nigga" from the hood on some gettin' money type shit and he fucks the plan all up. Don't think I didn't do my time for that shit either. Nineteen fucking years on a twenty-five-year prison sentence. I should have taken the plea bargain, but the hood got zero chill for snitches or niggas who make deals with the Feds. So there it was.

Then came the wooden ruler delivered by FedEx on Wednesday. There was a blue sticky note attached to it with the words "Don't break me." The cell phone and charger came on Friday. There wasn't any service on it though, because curiosity had me plugging that bitch up thinking I would get some free use out of it before the job, but that shit was deader than that nigga Rob, my old cellie, who made that backdoor parole a reality when he hung himself overnight. I guess he couldn't hang with that life sentence he was handed down for murdering an undercover cop on some robbery shit. Price you pay when you go undercover though, and the price you pay when you on some fucked-up hood foolishness because your kids gotta eat, and you murder the wrong damn person. Now they couldn't be fed from his hand behind some steel bars, and we all felt that way at one point or another, but to take your life was on a whole other type of deep level.

There was another sticky note with the cell phone though that said, "Make sure I'm charged fully," and I had that mug already plugged up for the job. Check. Other aspects of the job I was already fully prepped about. I checked the time on the Custom Diamond Yacht-Master $18,000 yellow-gold Rolex that my boss loaned me for this latest job. Nic wanted me to look the part to a T, and the watch along with the rest of my outfit would definitely do the trick. It was better than those prison orange duds that I unfortunately grew accustomed to these last years.

Staring out on the windy streets of New York City from my thirteenth-floor loft of this bougie-ass apartment building did bring me a sense of accomplishment. From living inside of that cramped, dirty, disgusting cell to a place of my own with exposed brick, exposed pipes in the ceiling, and brand new everything. Those people walking around below me, hurrying along their merry little lives, had no clue what kind of hell I had lived for most of the past nine years.

Well, at 43 years old, I was in the prime of my life thanks to years of lifting weights and muscle-isolation exercises in the yard and in my cell. Hell, at one point when they had us on lockdown for weeks, I lifted food trays stacked up to stay ripped. That shit was crazy. But now I had 25-year-old young-ass niggas asking me about my eight-pack and bicep muscles at the gym.

I took all the items my client had sent me and stuffed them into my brown leather Michael Kors messenger bag along with some specialty black leather gloves I wore to mostly all of my jobs. My clothes were all laid out across the king-sized bed, with the exception of the one piece of clothing that I always picked out last.

I had about two hours until the deed was going down. I went to the walk-in closet and stepped in front of the floor-length mirror and caught the reflection looking back at me. I knew my body was a thing of admiration. J.P., the initials on the knife, made me wonder what it stood for. Who was J.P., and just what exactly was I getting myself into tonight? This was the only part of the job I didn't feel entirely comfortable with. It almost felt like I was back on the streets, breaking and entering, even if this time I was given a key to each client's house by the usual messenger who was always waiting in my apartment's foyer entrance on the nights of my jobs. But I never knew what, or better yet who, was waiting for me behind that door after I turned my key ever so quietly in its slot.

The last but most critical piece of tonight's wardrobe was still hanging over one of the many wooden hangers in the closet, next to many others like it in different brands and textures. I chose a nice, thicker pair of Nike jogger-style gray sweatpants that hugged every muscle in my lower body like that glove that was supposed to fit O. J. Simpson. The bulge my dick print made in them whenever I wore them was overstated, and I honestly felt bad for any female who had to walk past me with their man. I saw 'em doing that "quick look," and I would smile 'cause I knew they wanted all this dick. Most women wanted a man who had a nice-sized piece and knew how to command what they wanted in the bedroom.

I grabbed the sweatpants and laid them on the bed next to the brand new all-black Jordan Retro 9s, still in the box, a black fitted V-neck T-shirt, silver link chain with a diamond cross pendant on the end, and black diamond stud earrings for both ears. I checked my watch one more time before heading toward the shower and didn't really think too much about this new client or this new job. I only had one thought: time to get this money.

I was well into my hot shower when I heard the cell phone that was sent to me on Friday ring. *What the fuck?*

Chapter 2

"There's an additional package that needs to be picked up along the way to the client," the familiar melodic voice said on the other end. I had only heard the phone ringing because one of my favorite jams by Chris Brown, "Tempo," had just ended on my play list. "When We (Remix)" was next up. I had jumped out of the shower, soapy and wet, and didn't even have a chance to grab a robe or towel. I just slid my right hand across the bed to pick up the phone. My fresh fade, waved up enough to make bitches seasick, goatee, and full, dark, curly beard were dripping wet, as I instinctively rubbed my left hand across my face, caressing my facial hair in a southern direction.

I had done a lot to keep my shit groomed up, using the best products out there on the market. It had paid off, because I got so many compliments and got invited to every Beard Game private group out there on most social media sites. When they saw my fine-ass profile pic—me with my shirt off and my jeans fitted around my waist, showing off my hard-earned V stomach taper—the ladies went crazy. They acted like I was some famous-ass nigga like Idris Elba or Michael B. Jordan or something. My beard was what had helped me to secure the bag these last years, so I did and would continue to do whatever I needed to keep these coins coming in.

"This job sounds like it's different from any other ones I've had before. Is there a reason why?" I asked my boss on the other end, the dripping water now forming a small pool around my pedicured feet.

"You can handle more. I'm sure that you already know this, Doulah. It's time that you, let's say, switched up the tempo a little bit. Address to follow. Don't speak when you pick the package up until you are fully inside the client's home."

And just like that, the conversation was over, which I should have been used to by now. My boss was not a lot for words, but she was a hell of a businesswoman, that was for sure. She didn't play with her bag, and I liked that, because when I got out of the joint, I needed some quick and legal coins.

Jumping back into the shower to rinse off, I closed my eyes and held my head under the hot water pouring out of the shower head, enjoying the light caresses the water gave my glistening brown skin. My muscles were still sore from the extreme leg and upper body gym workouts I had started doing twice a week trying to keep my body tight for any potential job I could get my hands on. This work was very different from any other job I had ever had, and while most brothas would love a slight chance to do what I got paid very well to do, it still was both mentally and physically demanding.

Nic could be a real bitch sometimes, especially when it came to me questioning her about the ins and outs of the business. She didn't realize I had my own future plans for upping my coins, and trying to understand how she created this company of hers off the backs of a bunch of grimy-ass street niggas confined in dusty jail cells was beyond me. But I would definitely figure that shit out sooner rather than later. But right now it was time to get this money.

I turned the shower back on as Tory Lanez's "Shooters" was coming through the speaker. I still had a little bit of time to hear the rest of my banging play list. *Time to get my head in the game,* was the last thought I had closing the glass door and allowing my thoughts to drown under the shower head.

I grabbed the brown envelope from the messenger waiting around in the foyer of my apartment building after I strolled casually out of the elevator, peacing out the light-skinned man as I pushed past him to open the glass doors and went out into the crispness of the New York evening air. The black Cadillac sedan was waiting for me at the curb. Nic always thought of everything, I swear. I couldn't wait until I was running my own shit. As I got in the car, the mystery cell phone buzzed again, this time with a text message showing an address.

"Hey, my dude, I need you to swing by this address before my final destination," I yelled from the back seat, handing the driver the cell phone so he could see the address information. He handed it back without a word and made a quick left turn. Guess he didn't need GPS.

The streets were buzzing with the beginnings of a typical New York City Friday night. Nightclubs, bars, and restaurants were lit up with the promises of a good night's pay. Even the prostitutes were out early. The driver finally pulled up to a somewhat massive home on a quiet street filled with similarly styled houses. Another incoming text buzzed against the inside of my pants pocket, where I had stuffed the cell earlier. Damn, this phone though.

The message read: Just wait in the car. Package coming out. Don't talk anymore until you both are inside the client's home.

Just when I was about to say something crazy about Nic's newest text message, my ears turned to the sounds of a lady's heels methodically clicking on the outside pavement, growing closer to the car door. The door opened, and one of the sexiest, most beautiful women I had ever seen in my life climbed in the rear passenger seat next to me. She glanced at me, reached one black-gloved hand over to my face, and caressed my glistening black beard slowly and deliberately. Her gloves were silky and felt good.

My dick began to grow a bit inside my gray sweatpants, and I had to work a little hard to keep it in check. That didn't happen much. She smirked at me and turned her head to face the front of the car. She had honey brown skin, almond-shaped eyes, and a short Chinese bob framing her face. She had two beauty marks, one above her lip and one under the outside corner of her right eye. The perfect pouty lips underneath the red matte lipstick she was wearing smiled at me a little bigger when she noticed my admiration and showed off her perfect white teeth. She smelled amazingly sweet. She had on a belted trench coat, but I couldn't see what was underneath, just the smooth, shapely legs that were bare besides the pair of candy-apple red stilettos.

I took off my black leather gloves and stuffed them in my jacket pocket. My instincts took over, and without looking at her, I put my large left hand on her right knee, underneath her coat, and caressed the pretty skin slowly. I moved it up slightly, still feeling skin and nothing else. I wondered what exactly she had on underneath the trench. Her thigh muscle twitched a bit underneath my hand as I increased my massage, my fingers slightly moving closer and closer to where I was thinking some type of clothing or the beginning of her dress would be. Still no fabric.

The driver made a quick right turn, and I was thrown a bit closer to her as I wasn't wearing my seat belt. My hand traveled a bit farther up and touched a mixture of lace, silk, and wetness. I heard the slight inhale when my fingers found my way around the panties and to the warm, slightly wet center of her soul. As my fingers slowly moved in and out, me looking out my passenger window, her hand moved to my wrist, trying to stop me from making her juices cum all over my fingers. I felt her pain, because my long brown fingers were playing a song all of their own, and I wanted her to hear the ending.

Her nails were now digging in my wrist, and I could feel the slight tremors of her orgasm around my fingers. My thumb was still rubbing her clit as I slowly pulled each finger out of her wet pussy one at a time. I turned around and looked her in the eyes for the second time since she got in the sedan. I brought the fingers of my left hand up to my mouth and sucked her juices off of three of the fingers, letting some of her juices run down my beard. The fourth finger I slowly brought up to her mouth, caressing her pouty lips with it and slowly parting them so she could taste her own honey-sweet juices. The driver could have been looking at us through the rearview mirror at this point, but I surely didn't give a fuck if he was, so I never bothered to check.

We exchanged a lustful glance while the sedan came to a stop at my client's house. While I still wasn't sure what role this woman played in my job tonight, I knew that I had not broken any of Nic's rules. She said not to speak to this beautiful package until we were safely inside the house. She never said that I could not touch her. And she damn well did not say I couldn't taste her.

The driver got out and opened the door. Ms. Mystery Package glanced back at me with that knowing look, took his hand, and exited the car, stepping to the side so I could get out as well. After thanking him for the ride, I proceeded to unlock the front door of the large house with the key from the door messenger's envelope. I held the door open for her while simultaneously putting one finger up to my lips to signal to her not to make a sound, and then I silently closed the door behind us. It was time to get this work.

Chapter 3

I took Ms. Mystery Package's hand and crept up the stairs quietly, as if I had been in the house a thousand times. Truth was, I had never even been here once, but the job was always the same. We snaked our way to the door that I was looking for. It had a single sticky note with the words "Open me" written in cursive. I glanced back at the girl to make sure she wasn't nervous. After all, I wasn't sure if she had actually been a part of any job of Nic's before, but she had a slight smile on her face, so my guess was more than likely wrong. Nahhhh, she was ready. *Good, easier for me,* I thought before turning the knob to open the door.

The room was lit by what seemed to be a hundred god-damned candles. I had to adjust my eyes for a minute to make sure my mind wasn't playing tricks on me. This was definitely different from any other job I had been on. Sitting directly on the massive office desk in front of me was a light-skinned honey with waist-length, amber-colored hair. Her plump ass was sitting on the desk, and both of her legs were spread wide open, her heels firmly planted on either end of the marble desktop. She was only wearing a red bow tied around her waist, and her nipples were pink and already hard. Damn.

There was another older lady in the corner sitting in a chair, smoking a cigar. She didn't have a bow tied around her waist, but she did have on one of those Chinese-styled robes. It wasn't closed, and she proudly was showing off some firm, chocolate brown double Ds with big, already-hard nipples peeking out of the fabric. She looked at me, uncrossed her legs so I could see that she had no panties on, pulled the cigar out of her mouth, slowly licked the brown paper, and put it back into her mouth. *Well, damn, ma. I see you.* There wasn't anyone else in the room besides me and Ms. Mystery Package. However, when I turned around to see if she was taking in all of this, the trench coat was now gone, and she was standing off to the side. Now I could see what was hiding underneath. The small, perky breasts were perfect for her athletic, petite frame.

She either was an athlete in her day or worked out a lot cause her toned body and abs looked amazing wrapped in the only thing on her body besides the red satin and lace panties I had felt earlier: another red bow tied around her waist. I chuckled. God, I loved my job. I put my bag down and took off my jacket, eyeing all the women in the room, planning my next move in my head. However, cigar lady was obviously in charge here and not me.

"Come over here," she said, laying her cigar in the nearby glass ashtray. I walked over to where she was, slowly pulling my white T-shirt off and tossing it to the side, allowing her to take in the chocolate eight-pack that I had worked on for the last nineteen years. She motioned at the full brown envelope near her ashtray. I reached for it and thumbed through about thirty hundred-dollar bills. Hiding my excitement about this payday, I casually walked the envelope over to my messenger bag and secured it in one of my zip folds. I went back over to where she was, ready to step my game up strong.

She reached down by the side of her chair and picked up a small bottle of massage oil, squirted out enough into her hands, and began to slowly rub them all over my stomach and chest, coating me with the warm oil. My full twelve inches started to grow inside the gray sweatpants, and that curve toward the end of it was about to get deadly in a minute. She grabbed my ass with both hands, pulling me closer to her face, and pulled down the joggers until they were around my ankles. I reached down, pulled off my loose boots, slid the joggers off, and put my shoes back on. I was going to need some grip for this work I was about to put in on these bitches.

I stood back in front of cigar lady, and she continued with her oil massage, now extending it to my rock-hard, huge thighs, legs, and ass. Lastly, taking my thick dick head and putting it into her mouth, she began to rub the shaft slowly, allowing the fingers of both her hands to intertwine as she continued the movement. Her lips, tongue, and mouth were doing a slow two-step on my head, and my snake started coming alive. I instinctively tilted my head back, allowing her to take more of my dick in her mouth, putting my hands in her black curls, helping her control the movements.

After getting me nice and hard, she pulled back on the D, got up, and walked over to Ms. Mystery Package. She put the bottled oil in her hand and whispered something in her ear. Ms. MP slowly walked toward the woman on the desk, our obvious hostess returning to her chair and her cigar to enjoy the beginnings of the show. MP stood behind the woman still spread-eagle on the desk, squeezing the bottle of warm oil directly on the woman's body. The oil fell like a waterfall all over her breasts and stomach. MP reached around with one hand and started to massage the oil slowly into each breast, tracing her nipples with each satin-gloved finger. With the other hand, she gently placed it around the lady's neck, pulling her head back onto her own chest. The lady started to moan quietly as she reached her nipples and started gently massaging each one of them slowly between her fingers, teasing her.

"Did you bring the items from the envelopes, Doulah?" the hostess asked me from the corner. I went and picked up my bag and took out the ruler, ski mask, and J.P.'s pocketknife, whoever that was.

"I have all your things. However, one quick question for you. What does J.P. stand for?" I said, tracing the outline of the letters on the knife slowly, waiting to see if she would give up her true identification.

"Well, I guess that depends who is asking. It could stand for Juicy Pussy, but you would have to taste it for yourself and tell me if I'm accurate, baby. Now, give the mask to little Miss Sunshine with the oil. We certainly can't cover up that nice full beard of yours, now can we? You've got a lot of work to do tonight with that tonight," she chuckled.

I walked over and handed the pretty lady the mask. She stopped what she was doing and put it on, covering the Chinese-styled bangs. Now I could see only her beautiful eyes and pretty red lips.

"Get my pocketknife out and open it up," she instructed me. At least I now knew that she was J.P. Maybe I would find out what it actually stood for, but I doubted it. Clients never used their real names for privacy's sake. I guess she was a borderline dominatrix or something, but I was down for that too if that's the way she wanted to play it. I guessed this was what Nic meant by me stepping up my game or whateva. I took out the pocketknife and opened it up, hoping that she wasn't going to have me stabbing no bitches up in here today. I wasn't tryin'a violate my probation for some pussy, however good it tasted.

"So, miss lady, what am I doing with this knife here? You know I'm not trying to go back to jail, right?"

"Doulah, you're quite a character. Walk slowly to the desk and get on your knees in front of my pretty ladies," she ordered. I did exactly that, getting on my knees while looking up at MP still rubbing oil on her friend. She was leaving a litter of red lip marks all over her neck and ears, kissing and licking them through her mask.

"Now, gently, take the tip of the knife and slowly, very slowly, run the knife over the skin of her thighs. Kiss her body as you're working that knife, baby. Show her what that beard do. And please don't break her skin. I would hate to leave a lasting mark on her."

Did she think I was a fucking killer or something? Dammit. The paycheck for this job was fat, but now I had to make sure I didn't accidently cut this light, bright chick now. A'ight. I had this. I just needed to make sure I didn't cut her. Easier said than done in my book.

I laid the knife against the lady's right thigh on the flat side, grabbing her other thigh with my free hand. I pulled her closer to where my head was, gently rubbing my full beard against the inside of her thighs, still slowly moving the knife back up and down against her skin. She started to shiver against my face. I was about to turn *Fifty Shades of Grey* black up in here. MP had slightly moved to her right side and lowered her masked face onto her chest, sucking her breast, and licking and sucking her nipple, leaving more lipstick marks all over her. I had taken my face and begun to rub my beard up and down her bare pussy, and her quiet moans started growing a bit louder. She inhaled sharply as I laid the knife flat against her oiled stomach, moving it ever so slowly so that I didn't pierce her. This shit.

"Cut both of their bows off with that knife, baby," our hostess instructed from the corner.

I lifted my head up and saw that she had completely put the cigar out now and had her robe fully open and her fingers inside of her dark pussy, playing with herself. Her stomach was flat, but she was thick as hell, with some curly, dark hairs left on the outside in a design outside of her shaved pussy. I reached up and did as I was told, placing the knife under the ribbon and pulling quickly to cut the satin fabric. I reached around the back of MP and sliced hers loose, as hers had slid almost to her ass. I instinctively smacked MP's ass and pulled her face to my own to kiss those pouty lips behind the ski mask. After tasting her sweet tongue, I laid little Miss Sunshine, as J.P. called her, fully down on the massive desk and began to kiss her other breast slowly, licking and gently biting her nipple. MP was working on the other breast.

I took the knife and rubbed it across her lips. She stuck her tongue out and licked its flat side. I brought it down against her neck while rubbing my beard down her flat stomach, careful not to even place the tip of it against her skin. My tongue found its way to her pussy, and I let the knife hit the floor at that point so I could have the full use of both my hands. Fuck what the hostess had said. I had had enough of the knife play anyway. I spread her legs even wider on the desk, as it was almost the size of a full-sized mattress. I parted her pussy lips with my tongue, gently licking and teasing her slowly, allowing my beard to tickle the insides of her thighs and ass.

"Mia, ride her face," J.P. said from the corner. At least now I had Mystery Package's name. She climbed on top of the desk, positioning her pussy over the face of our obvious sex victim, and sliding her panties to the side. The girl on the table cupped Mia's ass with both hands and began to eat her pussy like it wasn't her first rodeo. Mia's moans came rather quickly.

"Just like that. Don't stop," J.P. barked, continuing her military-style orders from the chair, fucking herself with her fingers, moaning as well on occasion. The thighs in my hands started quivering from the tongue-lashing I was giving out, my beard getting wetter and wetter as I sucked harder on her clit with my lips and tongue. I knew she was about to give her soul to me. I felt the orgasm before the falsetto screams started. Her pussy squirted all over my lips, and I lifted up slightly to rub my beard all over her pussy to soak in her juices and drive her crazy some more with the ticklish feel of my hair in between her thighs. Mia had cum at the same time as the girl on the table and had both hands around the girl's breasts, back arched, making sure she got all her juices in her mouth. Her pussy was still quivering as the white liquid oozed down the girl's neck. Damn. I heard that.

"Get the ruler and follow me now," J.P. said. The ladies and I got up to follow her out of the room, down a long hallway to a large bedroom, heavily decorated in a white accent. The room was warmed from the heat emitting from the fireplace, and four wine glasses sat atop a small coffee table alongside an already-opened bottle of vodka. What I assumed was orange juice was already splashed in each of the glasses She walked over to the table and poured us each a glass. We gathered around the table to collect our drinks.

"To the night, all this sexiness in the room, and that beard you got going on over there, Doulah. I need to see exactly what it feels like against my own skin," she stated, holding her own glass up and clinking it with the others. I downed my drink, walked up to the hostess, and took her almost-finished drink out of her hand and placed it on the table. I firmly but gently placed one of my large hands around the base of her neck, tilting her head to one side, licking and placing small kisses on her until I got to her ear.

"You wanna see what this beard do, huh, miss lady?" I whispered in her ear, licking on her ear lobe and caressing her neck with my beard. I peeled the Chinese robe off her and picked her up, cupping my hands around her fat ass.

"Hold on to my neck," I instructed, carrying her over by the bed. I could tell by the look on her face that she was surprised that I could carry all of her thickness with ease. I dropped her down onto the bed and then pulled her lower body toward me, placing a firm grip on each of her chocolate thighs with my hands. That design she had cut into her pussy was turning me on, and her wetness had added to it.

I put my head down and slowly began licking and kissing her stomach, letting her feel the softness of my beard between her legs. I could feel her already beginning to wet me up, and she tasted sweet once my mouth made its way down in between her legs. I inserted two thick fingers into her pussy, slowly fucking her while my tongue made her clit its latest victim, sucking it until her hands gripped my ears and pushed my mouth farther onto her clit. She then reached down and spread open her pussy, opening her legs wider so I could get all of her juices in my mouth once she came. And she was about to give up that ghost real quick as I was giving her that royal treatment. Finger fucking her, my mouth softly sucking her clit, twirling my tongue all around it, and moving my beard around the bare smooth skin down there as well. She was moaning like a baby, her toes pushed up against my hard thighs, trying her best to hold on for her life. She ain't even had this dick up inside her yet, and I already had her like this.

"Baaabeee, I'm finna cuuuum," she moaned, toes pushing at me harder.

"Wet this beard up, mama," I lifted my head up slightly and said to her. Her thighs clenched, and she squirted all over my mouth and lips. I rubbed my beard against her pussy, soaking it with her juices. I got up from the bed and went over to the sitting area, pouring me a straight shot of vodka. I looked around the room at all the ladies, and casually said in between swallows, "Now what we about to do with this ruler though?"

Chapter 4

As if on cue, the other two ladies who had been patiently waiting got up from where they were sitting and went toward the bed. Mia lay back on the pillows, spread-eagle, while Miss Sunshine lay in front of her, face down, ass up, just how I liked it. She was close enough to lick the wetness growing inside of Mia's smooth pussy. Grabbing the ruler, I walked over to the white-sheeted bed, eyeing both of the sexy ladies.

"Get that ass higher in the air," I ordered Miss Sunshine, and once she was positioned just right, I brought that ruler down firm on that ass. She arched her back a bit and looked back at me as if to say, "More please."

"You like that, ma?" I said, leaving a red mark on her light skin from my next two smacks, rubbing her ass cheeks with my hands in between. I kept the ass taps from the ruler coming.

"You want some of this shit too, don't you, baby?" I said to Mia and went toward her on the bed. I brought the ruler down firmly but gently on her pussy lips. She moaned. I gave it to her again, and again, until I saw the wetness creaming out from inside her. I pushed the other girl's face into her pussy so she could lick her sweet juice.

I grabbed a rubber from a nearby candy bowl conveniently sitting on the nightstand, slipped it on my hard dick, and proceeded to get in Miss Sunshine's ass. She was tight as hell, which I liked, and my long, deep strokes began to produce her rhythmic screams. She was eating the hell out of Mia's cookie again, as her back was arched and her moans were getting louder.

The hostess had lit a new cigar, put her robe back on, and was walking around the bed, surveying our porn scene. She puffed out some smoke and reached down to suck each of Mia's breasts. She took the ruler off the bed and gave each of her nipples a gentle smack, which made a deep, "Pleeeeeaaassseee," come out of her mouth. I had a feeling that she had been a victim of the hostess's before tonight and knew just how much pleasure/pain she could give and take. That was turning me on even more, and I pulled out of Sunshine's pussy and went straight in her ass. She tensed up for a minute, and the hostess grabbed her ass cheeks, smacking them with the ruler, and opened them wider for my dick to go in deeper.

"That's a good girl. Take all that dick," she said. And even if she didn't take all of it, I was planning on giving it all to her anyway. She arched her back some more and spread her legs wider, giving me all that ass to work with. My hand smacking her cheeks replaced the ruler, and I felt her about to give up the ghost when her ass and thighs started to quiver. As she started to cum, she had her face buried on Mia's stomach, stifling her moans. Mia pulled her face up to hers and tongue kissed her deeply, placing her hand slightly around the base of her throat.

"Give him that cum, baby," Mia whispered in her ear, licking and kissing her earlobe and neck. I pulled out of her and pulled the condom off, tossing it to the floor. I was still hard though and wanted to put my nut in Mia's sweet pussy instead. I grabbed another condom and slipped it on.

"Your turn, sexy," I said to Mia, grabbing her by both of her slim ankles toward me and pinning her knees to her chest. I had a feeling her pussy would be the icing on the cake. As I leaned closer to her to kiss her lips, she grabbed my beard, gently using it to pull it to her own mouth. Her tongue tasted good against my own, and she reached down to take the condom off my dick before I could put it inside her.

"Come up here so I can taste you, daddy," she said, her eyes never leaving mine. I crawled up toward her face, unpinning her legs along the way. She pulled my dick toward her, slowing licking my shaft and sucking my head softly and deliberately. Sucking, licking, and massaging my dick with her mouth, she slid down a bit and put my balls in her mouth one at a time, twirling her tongue around each one and gently sucking them. She went back up to my dick and laid her head back a bit to fully swallow my full hardness, grabbing my ass and pulling me closer to her. She was gagging on my shit but taking all of it like a champ. She made Tiffany Haddish in that scene from *Girl's Trip* when she was fake giving head on that banana look like a damn amateur. I was starting to become more impressed with Mia, and that didn't come too easily.

"Damn, baby, yes! Take all that dick," I moaned. As I grew rock hard, I was ready for some more pussy. I took my dick out of her warm mouth and got a new condom and slid it on. Pinning her pretty thighs back, I put my head in only, letting her small frame get used to its thickness, and then I slowly slid the rest of my inches in her. She reached out to her sides and clenched the sheets with her nails, holding on for dear life while I gave her that back blowout treatment.

The hostess was loving the way I was giving her this D, and she had little Miss Sunshine on her knees in front of her, getting her some head while she was still smoking her cigar, eyeing my chocolate, hard frame and the stroke of my long dick. She was holding up the girl's hair in a ponytail, pushing her face into her fat pussy, parting her legs wider when she saw me looking. I picked Mia up from the bed, her legs wrapped around my waist, and walked her around to where the hostess could get a better view. I put my dick inside Mia and gripped her ass, pulling her down on me so she could ride these inches as I was standing up. I knew her small coochie was going to be sore the next day, but I couldn't stop now. I was going to cum all over these bitches before too long. Mia began to scream bloody murder, her grip almost slipping, and I put her down and ripped off the condom. I turned Miss Sunshine around and held my dick to her face, so she could suck the cum out that was getting ready to bust outta me. Mia got on her knees as well, them both licking me and taking turns sucking my dick. I put my head back and deeply moaned and let the cum squirt out in Miss Sunshine's mouth, and then put it in Mia's mouth to let her finish swallowing the rest. They continued to lick and suck on me until I couldn't take any more. I grabbed my dick away, let out a quick laugh, walked back over to the bed, and fell backward with exhaustion. Gotdamn, a nigga could get used to this tempo switch-up shit. Fa sho.

"Bathroom?" I asked the hostess, pulling on my gray joggers.

"Mia, can you show him where to go please, hon?"

Mia had donned a robe from the hostess's closet and got up from the casual girl chat they seemed to be enjoying, smiling at me while simultaneously grabbing my hand. This house was really a piece of work, and we passed up several areas to finally make it to the bathroom. I went to one of the double sinks and grabbed a face towel off a freshly displayed stack sitting in a basket atop a corner table. The water was warm and felt good as I washed my face and pits and scrubbed down my dick a bit. Mia was leaning back against the vanity, eyeing my body, my beard, and my lips, in that order. I was curious about her as well, I had to admit. There was just something about her. How the hell did she get caught up in this sex game anyway? And was she on Nic's payroll, or the hostess's?

"So, Miss Mia, you put on quite a performance back there," I stated, putting the towel in an obvious dirty clothes bin.

"How long were you locked up for?"

"So, you just gonna hit me straight in the ass, no Vaseline, huh? Nah, I'm playing. I'm strictly a pussy kind of guy, no offense to anybody who's not though."

"You didn't use any Vaseline on Lana earlier, so I figured you were a straight-to-the-point kind of guy. Plus, I know that the guys we usually are paired with have a prison background, no offense," she stated, letting out a cute giggle on the last part.

"What makes you think I'm not a Wall Street investment banker who just likes to fuck pretty girls like you in my spare time, miss lady?" I asked her in a whispered tone, moving my body closer to hers. Now we were almost face-to-face, and she moved farther against the cool marble top, to an almost-sitting position, gripping it on either side to steady herself.

Looking her in those beautiful almond-shaped brown eyes, I kissed her full lips and said, "Nineteen years," through our kisses. She pulled my gray pants down, and I quickly turned her around to face the mirror. She braced her hands on the wall mirror in front of her, and I put my already fully erect dick inside her pussy again. What the fuck was I doing? I raw dogged Mia, but I knew that I had to keep a clean test on record with Nic for any diseases. I prayed to God she had to as well because I hadn't thought about using protection with her. She was different, and I think we both knew it. It was too fucking late anyway because this was a quickie and I was covering her mouth up with my hand, so nobody heard her while she and I both were cumming again. Everyone had to be on birth control, and that I did know, so I wasn't worried about any of my seeds growing sprouts inside her. Her pussy was just so damn good though. It was like lobster compared to the rest of those bitches in the room. We quietly finished up and quickly dressed, trying to act as if nothing just happened.

"She's going to kill me if she finds out we did this, and I won't even know your last name before I die," she whispered quietly, pulling her robe closed. I didn't know if she was joking or if she was serious, but she wasn't smiling.

"Jackson," I said, holding both her hands and looking down at her in her beautiful eyes. "How do I find you after I leave here, Mia?"

"You don't," the familiar stern female voice came from the door. We both turned around, and the hostess was standing there, brandishing a shiny Glock in her hand next to her side with a look on her face that I couldn't read. Fuck. Mia bolted past her, almost afraid of her, and I was starting to realize that she was really her sex slave on a whole other level of slavery that I didn't even know still existed.

The hostess had dropped my messenger bag along with the rest of my belongings near the bathroom opening, and she turned and started walking away. I didn't know what the hell I had just witnessed, but I wasn't trying to start a war with my money, not right now.

As I was putting on the last of my things, she turned around quickly and said, "Oh, and I deducted five hundred dollars from your pay for your unauthorized use of my bitch. Now get your shit and get the fuck out of my house," she spat out angrily.

I quickly found my way down the stairs and out of her maze of a house, and I closed the front door behind me. The black sedan pulled up to me as I was walking toward the darkness. As the driver got out to open the door for me, I looked up and found the window to the bedroom I was just inside of. Mia was staring down at me, but she quickly turned around as if someone was calling to her.

Everything inside my head was telling me to keep it the fuck moving and not try to be no Captain Save-a-Ho. But she was different, the voice inside my head chimed out to me. Something was very wrong with this picture. I got in the car, and the driver started going back in my direction. I was silent the whole car ride, trying to figure out how I had lost an extra $500 on some pussy. And some quickie action at that. I guess I went against some "don't fuck anyone without my permission" code of some sort, but damn, that lady was lucky I was about staying out of jail because she almost got fucking dealt with on some real shit.

The driver pulled up to my place, and as I was getting out and handing him a nice tip for the ride, he grabbed my wrist and pulled me closer toward him.

"My man, that pretty girl from the car is in way over her head. She didn't come back out with you for a reason. I saw that you all had a connection going on back there on the way over. I can put you in contact with her if you want, youngblood," he stated. He was an elderly black man, about 70 years old if I had to guess. I wondered how long he had been driving for her, but he must have liked it. Shit, this dude had on a gold Rollie with small diamonds encrusted inside the face.

"My good man, that's wassup," I said back, giving him a hood handshake with some dap and ending with my fist against my chest showing my earnest appreciation.

"But it's going to cost you," he stated back, getting inside the car. "I'll be in touch. I know where you live."

If there was one thing I learned in the pen, everything had a price. Damn. This old-ass nigga wasn't shit.

Chapter 5

Being trapped on the inside of a federal prison was nothing but some straight-up bullshit, and don't let anyone tell you different. Especially when you were given a long-ass sentence. Shit. I was young, dumb, and full of cum when that judge handed me them twenty-five years in front of my moms and my grandparents. I was her only child, and unfortunately she had to kiss goodbye any opportunities of me having her some grandbabies as the officers led me away in the orange duds in handcuffs with my head down. I couldn't even look their way because I felt their disappointment from across the room.

When I had first arrived, I tried my best to stay in my own lane, keep my head down, and find a group to be a part of in case some foul shit went down. I was told I needed some people to have my back, and eventually, after a couple of run-ins with some cats over some beef as simple as turning the channel on the rec room's TV, I had found the cats who would help me survive in that bitch and turn me into the man I was today.

I had become an angry li'l nigga because there was so much going on outside in the real world, and I felt like I was just missing out on my whole life. All these hard bodies, no women to look at except an occasional fat-booty female prison guard, no real food, no real TV shows, my gear consisted of these fucked-up prison clothes, the mattress was a basic piece of thick-ass cardboard, and I was basically working for less than a dollar per hour if you did the math. And that was just to earn some noodles, other snacks, or toiletries.

That all changed forever on my thirty-fifth birthday when Puncho came into my life. I had been in my cell writing another letter to my moms when a couple of cats came to my cell saying this legendary dude was requesting my presence. All I really knew about him was that he had access to some serious dough, but he was very well protected on the inside so I really never knew how he got his cash. He had a couple of older brothers apparently on his payroll as well, because they were doing better than most other cats in here, including me. I didn't have a girl on the outside who could help me out by putting money on my books, and my mother had been diagnosed with breast cancer a few years back, so every dime I earned inside here I sent to her to help her with her bills while she went through her treatment.

When I got to his special table out in the yard, his so-called bodyguards moved away and made room for me to pass through. The one thing I did notice about him and his crew was that they all had these beards. I knew that had been the fashion trend on the outside now, but it was hard enough trying to keep my long, curly hair braided so I didn't look all the way crazy. The last thing on my mind was a beard.

"You asked to see me, old man?" I asked him, looking directly into his eyes. I had learned that you had to look these cats in the joint eye to eye at all times so they didn't think you had no kinda punk in you. I didn't know what he wanted anyway. This could be a setup or anything, and I stayed on ready.

"I been watching you over the last few years. How's your moms doing with her treatments?"

"Look, old man. I don't know who you been talking to or what you think you know about me, but I'm not afraid of you or your goons. And my moms is not your concern at all. Ever," I said, walking up on him where he was positioned. He never flinched though. But his bodyguards did step closer to me, which made me back up a bit so to not alarm the corrections officers who were always watching.

"Calm down, son. I have a proposition for you is all. I know you need some money, and a sorta 'job opening' if you will came up to work for me on my team. I would have to get you ready for the job, but you ain't that far from what I'm looking for."

"Why would I want to work for you? I'm not doing no foul-ass shit that's going to get me caught up in this hellhole any longer than I have to be," I said, and I meant every word of that shit too. Some of the laws had changed with regard to my prison sentence, and my lawyer had been working to reduce my time. It looked more favorable than not, and I had a chance to get out of here in five years or less.

"Look at these brothers around me. Do they look like they on some foul shit, nigga? Or do they look like they being taken care of? They shining, fool. They getting this paper on the inside, and you know what else? They getting pussy, too. Good pussy. In order for you to cross over to where they are, there are some things you have to do. These good brothers will not only beat the living snot out of you if need be, but they will educate your monkey ass while they are doing it. These cats are what I like to call 'educated thugs.' And horny women with money pay good to get broke off by a handsome, buff, educated nigga, somewhat like yourself, and then go to they little corporate jobs all satisfied and shit. I used to be one of the head niggas fucking these bitches, but I got too old, so now I run the business from the inside, finding cats who about to leave these prison walls who will need a job once on the outside. Things are a lot different than when you came in. Social media has taken the money game to a whole other level, and niggas are securing the bag however they gots to."

"So how much does your job pay, old man?"

"Well, it's levels to this shit. You not ready yet, but I can get you ready if you think it's something you want to do. Plus, I gotta get you approved by my boss. Her name is Nic. It's a lotta people on her payroll inside this joint who make this shit work. But I can guarantee you that you will make a pretty nice li'l coin for every job you do. Once on the outside, I'm talking a minimum of a G per job. And you usually only have to do two or three jobs per month. So you stay under the radar. But there are some conditions."

"Like?" I asked him. I had to admit, I was curious at this point. Hell, my moms needed the money, and if there was a way for me to secure some cash like that when I got out of here and it didn't involve drugs, guns, or stealing shit, then I was in.

I had no idea what the fuck I was supposed to do when I got out anyway to make some money. That's why cats got locked back up all the time. How you gonna lock someone up like a damn animal for ten years or more, let them out, and expect them to fall right in line with society? Hell, it's at least been a decade since they were out on the streets before. It was damn near impossible. Prison was a gotdamned revolving door, big business, and the government knew it. I wasn't trying to become a statistic, and I would do what I needed to do to keep myself from coming back here once I did get out early. If I even got out. 'Cause at any time some foul-ass shit could go down that could cause a nigga to have to shank another inmate and stay here longer, maybe even for life. Like Puncho. This nigga was going to die in this bitch, but that was his own doing.

"You gotta keep your body in top condition. And gay-ass niggas in here talk, so I hear you gotta horse package up in there. No homo, young blood. It's necessary for the job, so I gotta confirm it. Also, have you ever heard of the beard game?"

"Beard game? Nah, not really. I don't really keep up with TV like that."

"Nah, nigga," he said, and they all started laughing, which kind of made me feel some type of way, and I wanted to say, "Fuck y'all niggas," and walk away, but the promise of money and pussy made me continue standing there.

"It's a fucking movement. These bitches out here are falling on their hands and knees and basically selling their damn coochie to niggas who got full blown beards. They even got a whole line of products dedicated to maintaining your beard. Oils and moisturizers and shit. And women love the feel of the man's beard on their pussy. They say it tickles them down there and they love that shit. They giving they whole damn wallets away, man! I make so much money on the inside with my niggas on my payroll it's not even funny. So you gots to grow a beard, my dude. That's the main thing these women are looking for, and you have gots to be willing to eat the pussy, too. If you don't wanna do either of those things, this job ain't for you."

"Man, being around these hard bodies all day, I could go for eating some pussy right now! As long as it was clean and shit. And I could grow a beard with no problem. It may take me a couple of months to do it though. My hair grows pretty quickly. Could I keep my braids though?"

"For now, yes, you can keep your braids. If you sign on once on the outside with Nic, well, she has her own rules, and she don't tell me shit about 'em. I don't ask her either. She's pretty cutthroat though. And all the ladies get tested. You already know they keep a test on us up in here. Shit. And Nic tests all her clients every two weeks. I have access to all their records. I can work out all the details. But you start on the inside. The guards sneak the bitches into a room, and one of my employees goes and handles his business with her. Some of them just want sex a certain way, but all of them want the feel of that beard on their pussy lips. When the job is done, you got immediate access to money on your books, or you can choose to direct deposit it to an account on the outside. Or you can do both. Before you actually get released from this hellhole though, you gotta sign a contract with myself and Nic to do a year on the job on the outside. If you choose to stay on with her, that's on you at that point. I don't have anything to do with it. So, youngblood, you in or out?"

This was definitely an opportunity that I couldn't pass up. I needed that cash, if not for myself, for my moms. Plus, I could use his crew's protection. Niggas sometimes tended to get crazy once they found out you could possibly get out sooner rather than later. I didn't see how I could lose.

"So basically I'm signing up to be a male ho, right?" I asked him with a smirk on my face.

"If you wanna look at it like that, yes," he replied, giving me the look of a man about to sign a lucrative business deal.

"Fuck it. I'm in."

"Welcome to the beard game, my nigga." He reached his hand out to shake mine. There was no official paperwork to sign yet. But a word given by a prison handshake that was broken was deadlier than any piece of paper anyway. Especially when you gave your word to a nigga who got life.

Chapter 6

The next morning I had an early knock at my door. I kicked the purple satin sheets off of my body and jumped out of my king-sized bed after the third knock. Looking through the peephole, I didn't necessarily like who I saw waiting for me on the other side of the door, but I did expect her to come over eventually after last night's fiasco.

"Good morning, Nicole. Excuse the morning breath. I was still asleep," I stated, moving out of her way as she strolled quickly past me, red bottoms clicking on my hardwood floors. She was definitely in a mood. Guess I couldn't blame her after last night's performance.

"Do you have a seltzer, Doulah?" she asked, removing her expensive shades and taking off her coat. She settled in one of my armchairs and put one leg over the other, staring at me with a look I had never seen before.

"Yes, ma'am. No problem." I padded over to the side-by-side fridge and pulled out a seltzer water. I only kept that shit for women anyway. Bougie bitches loved to drink some damn mineral water for some reason. I pulled out a tall glass, threw some ice cubes in it, and let the carbonated fizz work its magic. Handing her the drink, I excused myself to my bathroom so I could splash some water on my face and brush my teeth.

When I came back out to my living room, Nic had walked over to one of my large windows, staring down at the daily people-walkers of the New York City streets.

"Great view, isn't it? One of the main reasons why I love living here." I said, walking over to where she was. Nic was about five feet three inches tall and had a very nice, curvy, thick build for a 48-year-old woman. She was light skinned with deep dimples, and she wore her hair in the latest stylish pixie cut that all the black women were wearing these days. It suited her well. Today she had on an army green velvet-like jumpsuit, with black piping running down the side of it, and matched it with gold accessories and her signature red bottom black pumps. She knew how to dress, that was for sure.

"It is. So why would you jeopardize it with your little extra performance last night?" she asked me, turning around on her heels and looking up at me with her hands on her hips. "The deal is to do exactly what the clients ask for, Doulah. You have been doing this long enough to know how this works. What was it about this girl that you needed to have sex with her after your job was well over with?"

"I don't know, Nic. It just happened. I wasn't planning on it at all. You know me. There was something about her that was, I don't know, kinda special I guess. I think she's in trouble though. The lady pulled her piece out on us, and I thought she was working for you until she ran back in the lady's bedroom like she was her massa or something. It was like something out of a movie, I'm telling you. Something's up with that. I feel like I should do something. Or maybe we can do something."

"Don't take this the wrong way but, negro, what that lady does is not either of our fucking business. For all I know, she is her damn sex slave, whatever that means. She's an adult, honey, and she made whatever choices she did when she decided to work for her. All I know is that she pays well and is one of my best clients, no matter how much of weird-ass dominatrix she is. She likes toys and whips and knives and shit like that. However, I have watched her in action, and what she does is very safe. So I knew no matter how freaky the shit got last night on your job, you were safe. Until you fucked one of her girls, that is."

"Mia. Her name is Mia. And yes, I stepped out of line for a minute, but that doesn't give her the right to pull out a fucking Glock on a nigga. Damn. I am more refined at my age, but I almost ran up on her, piece or not, and busted that fat bitch upside her head. She don't know me like that, Nic."

"First of all, I don't give two cents about what that chick's name is. Secondly, the damage you caused not only cost you five hundred dollars, but it also cost me an earful, and I had to do some serious damage control and assure her that you would never be on a job of hers again."

"Well, I guess I should have expected that. I do apologize. And it won't happen again," I promised her, and although Mia was still on my mind, I had no plans of messing up any further jobs and risk losing everything I had worked hard to build.

"Good. I appreciate it. So are you ready for your next job?" she asked, giving me a mysterious look on her face.

"I stay ready. You know that," I replied.

"Good," she stated, clicking her heels back across my floor to where her belongings were. She picked up her bag and pulled out an envelope and took out seven Gs from it and walked back over to me.

"I'm your client, and I have what you lost last night, plus a couple extra hundred, Doulah. I need to make sure your head is in the right space. So show me what that beard do, baby." And with these last words, she walked over to my bed and started to undress, never taking her eyes off of me.

I had only thrown on some black joggers earlier, so I walked over to where she was and took them off. I had some massage oil in my nightstand by my bed, and I pulled it out. She had undressed down to the candy-apple red lace strapless bra and pantie set. She had a full leg tattoo that made her look sexy as hell, and her bowlegged ass knew it, too. I grabbed her hand and led her over to my off-white plush rug that lay in front of my fireplace. I laid her down on the rug and walked over to light us a fire. She lay back on the rug with her red bottoms still on.

"Get on your hands and knees," I stated, crouching down by her with my oil in hand. The fire was starting to crackle. This was the kind of massage oil that grew warm once you rubbed it on your body. That shit was fire. I poured some out and rubbed it between my hands. I laid both hands on her back and rubbed in a downward motion toward her ass. She was shaped a little bit like Kanye's ex, Amber Rose, and I knew exactly what I was gonna do with all this ass and titties in front of me. I then took some of the oil and held it over her ass and squeezed the bottle. Before the oil could drip off her ass to my rug, I got behind her and rubbed my beard over her ass, layering her with kisses and small bites along the way. It was like eating a fucking peach.

"Damn. Okay, baby. Your beard feels so soft. I like it," she said over her shoulder at me.

"You haven't felt anything yet, love," I said, smacking her on her ass and flipping under her where my face was right under her lace panties. I grabbed her oiled ass in both my hands and pulled her toward my face, blowing my warm breath into the center of her panties, licking through the holes in the lace fabric, my beard tickling her thighs. After soaking her panties with my tongue, I parted the fabric to the side with my teeth and worked my tongue inside her warm center. After a little while, I eventually replaced my tongue with two of the fingers on my left hand and focused my lips on her clit. My remaining hand on her ass found her other hole, and I worked one of my thick fingers inside her, gently at first, then both fingers grew faster. That double penetration sent her into a moaning frenzy, and she opened up her legs more so I could put all of her in my mouth more easily.

"Mmmmmmm, your hands feel so fucking good inside my pussy. Damn." She managed to get a couple more moans out before I took my fingers out of her and pulled her up to stand in front of me, sliding off her panties. I got on my knees behind her and started kissing all over her ass, sliding my tongue between her ass cheeks. I reached up inside her with my fingers once again, holding her hips down against my strong hand, still fucking her ass with my tongue. Her knees buckled under my fingers, and I turned her around to finish the job with my mouth.

I spread her pussy lips open and put my whole mouth on her center, alternating between gently sucking her clit to sticking my tongue in and out of her. She had her hands in my hair, and because a nigga stayed in the gym, I got on both knees and scooped her ass up in my arms and leaned slightly back, as she figured out what position I was going for, and she instinctively wrapped her legs around my neck and shoulders. I leaned back some more and moved my face up and down her pussy so that she got the full feeling of my lips coupled with my beard.

Her moans grew louder, but my hands couldn't cover her mouth, so I guessed the neighbors was gonna know my name this morning. Her ass and her thighs started to shake, and I knew she was about to squirt all over my face.

"Give me that cum, girl. Give it all to me." I slightly moved us where I could lie all the way back on the rug, her pussy still sitting on my face. She reached over me to grab something, but there was nothing in front of her, so she dug her claw nails into my broad shoulders instead. That was cool, as I was used to this reaction. Maybe she would start paying me even more now that she knew what I was worth.

"Here it comes, baby. It's coming. Ohhhhh myyyyyy dammmn. Doulah Doulahhhh Doouuuulllahhhh!"

All of my female neighbors would definitely be trying to come over here to borrow some sugar or some shit now, I was sure, thanks to her performance. Her juices came out hard on my face, creaming my beard. I reached up and unstrapped her bra with one hand, pulling it off of her and flinging it across the warm room. I flipped her around and crawled up toward those titties.

I rubbed my face and beard all over her nipples, sucking each one at a time while fingering the other one in between my fingers. I pushed them both together and put both her nipples in my mouth at the same time, licking and sucking until she moaned deeply, raking her nails up and down my back. I didn't stop until she was damn near begging me to, and I got up off of her to get a condom from out of my nightstand drawer. After all, she was a client, she said. And this was what my clients eventually all got. That D.

"This is what you want, Nic, right?" I asked her, gently ripping the package and pulling out the extra-large piece of latex.

She slightly laughed. "Hell yes, honey. Let me get my money's worth. You're back on the payroll so far. Don't fuck it up now."

My dick was already rock hard, so it was easy to slip the condom on. I walked back over to where she was lying, dropped down on my knees, and pulled her toward me. She rubbed her hands over my chest and abs, admiring every chiseled chocolate muscle.

I put my fingers in her pussy, making sure she was still wet from my beard bath earlier. I then held both of her legs straight up in the air by her ankles, making her pussy lips plump up to their fullest from that tight squeeze. I wasn't in the mood to take it lightly on her just because she was my boss, and I gave her all of this dick with my first thrust. She moaned like I knew she would and grabbed her full breasts, pulling on both her nipples. I continued to give her what she came for, the sound of my dick slapping against her pussy making me harder and harder. I pulled my dick out, adjusted the condom, and turned her around and had to see what Nic was truly made of since I probably wouldn't get this opportunity again.

"You gon' give up this ass today?" I asked her, trying to be somewhat considerate before I attempted to just take it. But for real, all pleasantries were over with when her pussy was in my face.

"You think you can handle all this ass on your dick, nigga? Let's see," she said. She then got off her hands and knees and laid me down on my back. She got on top of me, facing the other direction as if to ride me backward, and slowly inserted my dick inside her ass. She grabbed onto my thighs, and slowly began to grind against me, building up her tempo. She was a bad bitch. I saw why she was in charge, and she did that shit with no lube.

"Damn, Nic. That ass feels good," I told her, putting my hands around her waist and holding her down a bit more to get all my dick up inside her. She kept riding me like I was a fucking horse and she was trying to win the damn Kentucky Derby or some shit. Her moaning was off the chain, and I put two fingers deep in her mouth so she could suck on them instead of screaming when she started cumming. I knew I was about to bust all in this bitch next. I pulled her from on top of me and ripped the condom off, turning her around on her back. I jerked my hand back and forth on my dick, putting it in her mouth just in time to swallow all my cum.

"Uhhhhhhhnnnnnnn!" The neighbors was gonna know what I sounded like when I came too, I guessed.

I pulled my dick away and rolled over next to her, both of us breathing heavily. She sat up quickly next to me, her reaching for her nearby underwear, and reached out her hand and gave me the signature Wakanda hand dap.

"Girl, you are a straight-up fool," I told her, laughing my ass off. She started laughing as well, putting the rest of her clothes on.

"Doulah forever. Boy, you handled your business. You are definitely back on the payroll. You earned every red cent with that damn beard. I'll be in touch," she stated, putting her heels on last, and gathering her bag and coat in her arms. She had got dressed as if she was used to getting in and out of places quickly, I noticed. As her heels were clicking their way toward the door, she took one final glance back at me.

"You were definitely worth the investment. Thanks for the trial run, honey," she said, winking at me and opening my front door. She crouched down instead of continuing to walk out, and she grabbed something with her free hand and turned back around.

"Got a package, D," she said and threw it on the nearby armchair.

"Thanks, Nic. Talk to you soon."

I was exhausted. Between last night and this morning, I needed a full day of recovery, which usually included a full-body massage, manicure, pedicure, and a good steak dinner.

I walked over to where Nic tossed the envelope, and I looked at the sender. There was none listed, but my full name and address were written with a black marker. I took it over to one of the kitchen counters and grabbed a large Fiji water from the refrigerator. I opened the bottle and took a long swig, downing at least half of the refreshing liquid.

Putting the drink down, I tore open the envelope and frowned at its contents. I pulled out several eight-by-ten photos of a lady in different scenarios with a lot of different people, men and women. And it wasn't just any lady, but it was Mia. One photo showed several people dressed up for what looked like to be some sort of dinner party, but the lady wasn't at the table with the other guests. She was actually lying on the table spread-eagle with a bunch of food on her body. Another picture showed her lying in the fetal position across a bed as if she was crying or sad or something, with a small framed photo in her hand. Another picture showed her doing a line of cocaine with another girl. And a last photo showed her being carried up a flight of stairs by what looked like to be a pretty muscular man. However, her head was back as if she was either asleep or on some type of medication perhaps. There was a handwritten note inside the envelope as well, and I got it out and read it out loud: "I'll be in touch, youngblood. I told you she was in over her head. All money is not good money."

Damn. I was glad I didn't open this shit when Nic was here. I was back in her good graces and didn't have time to get involved with this *I Spy, Mission: Impossible* rescue shit anymore, once I had really thought about it. My money was way too important.

Since my mom had passed on last year from cancer, I didn't have anyone who needed my immediate help, and I eventually wanted to buy a house. I was saving. New York City was hella expensive. Maybe me and Mia did have a connection, and maybe I could have been just wanting to fuck her another time before I left. Who the fuck knows?

Nah, old man. You wasn't finna get me caught up in this shit. And neither was some pussy.

I went and got my lighter and the smaller metal trash-can from my bathroom. I looked at the pictures one last time and gathered them all back inside of the envelope, lit that shit on fire, and dropped it in the can. I walked away from it and started cleaning up the mess that Nic and I just made. I picked up my cell and called my massage girl to see if she was available for a quick rubdown. Lucky for me she was. I walked over and looked inside the trash can. The paper had almost burned completely down by now. Good. Now I could continue with my normal life. No more drama, and no more Mia. Or so I thought.

Chapter 7

Damn.

"Old man, why are you knocking at my door at two in the morning? Either you had better be dying, or you had better already be dead and you are haunting me or some shit," I yelled at the old black man looking back at me from across my condo door. He looked scared as shit, and he rushed into my place, wringing his old brown driving cap between his hands.

"I have been trying every which way to get a hold of you, young blood. You have dodged my every attempt. And now I need for you to come downstairs with me immediately!"

"What are you smoking on? I barely know you, and you could be leading me to my death. I'm not ever trying to go back to the pen, so whatever is waiting downstairs for me, you need to spit it out and tell me what it is right now. 'Cause, old man, I'm not going nowhere with you based on what you have said so far!"

"Mia is in my car! She passed out in my back seat on my way to that house, and I brought her here instead. I need you to help her. Now, please! Come with me!"

The old man was almost in tears. He acted as if Mia was his damn daughter or something. I was not even trying to get myself involved in her life again after what happened between us on the job I did a few months before. Especially after Nic's warning.

I quickly put on the red Nike slides that were by my front door, and bare chested, I followed him out into the

summer night's warm New York air. The familiar dark
sedan was parked across the street from my condo, and
he walked slightly faster than me over there to open up
the back door.

There Mia lay in an awkward position across the back
seat, damn near looking like she wasn't breathing. She
had on a tight midnight blue spaghetti-strap dress and
matching heels. However, one of them was off, and you
could see her perfect pedicure. She looked like a broken
dressed-up china baby doll, the way she was lying. I remembered that I almost could have loved her once upon
a time.

"What the hell, man?" I said, looking in the old man's
eyes for some kind of explanation.

"I have no idea if she took something while she was
in my car or what, but she was talking like she normally
does when she got in. All of a sudden, she was out and
lying across the seat," he stated.

"We have to call 911 or something, dude."

"We can't, man! She is a highly paid prostitute. And we
are two black men, and they are going to think we had
something to do with it, or even worse, if she dies on us,"
he said.

He had a point. Damn! Reaching into the car, I first
looked around me to make sure no one was out lurking
about, and I grabbed her out of the back seat, scooping
her into my arms.

"Grab her shoes and all her stuff she had and follow
me," I told the driver.

I quickly got her into my building and passing the door-
man, mumbled, "My new girl can't handle her own liquor,
man. You know how women are," and got on the elevator.
Once inside my place, I laid her on my bed and called my
go-to massage girl. She knew everybody and everything
and would always answer for her boy.

"Hey, Doulah, what's wrong? It's late."

"Jordan, I have a pretty crazy situation at my place right now. Can't go into detail right now, but I have a girl over who may have taken something, and I don't know if she did. She passed out, but she is breathing. I need some help or some direction."

"Wow. Okay. Look in her purse or bag and see if there is an empty bottle or something first."

Grabbing her purse, I emptied its contents out on my dining room table, and a medicine bottle half full of white pills came rolling across the table toward me. Grabbing the bottle up, I read its contents. Sleeping pills. What the fuck?

"Jordan, there is an almost empty bottle of sleeping pills prescribed to her."

"Is there a number showing how many pills were originally in the bottle, D?"

"Damn, girl, you are good. Yes! There were ten pills, and now there are seven left in the bottle."

"Damn. Okay. So, it probably is safe to assume that she took three pills a little while ago. She is probably not in any real danger where you will need to call 911, but you do need to keep a cool towel on her head and watch her breathing until she starts getting groggy and begins to wake up out of her sleep state. But you should be good, Doulah. But I'm here if you have any more concerns."

"Thanks, Jordan. That is a big relief. Will do. I thought I was going to have to come up with a web of lies for the po-po. Call you later."

"All right, D. Be careful. Bye," she said, and she hung up.

I went into my bathroom and got a small washcloth and wet it with warm water. After gently brushing her hair out of her face, I placed it across Mia's forehead and just stared down at her, watching her labored breathing. Whatever it was that she was dealing with had become so bad, apparently, that she wanted to maybe kill herself just to escape. I had witnessed first-hand the crazy lady she worked for pulling her gun on me once already. So I couldn't imagine what Mia had to go through. But then we all have a choice. If Nic started getting dangerous as a boss, I always feel I would just leave. But why wouldn't Mia do the same? I was determined to get answers when she finally woke up. But that was not my only problem. What was the mistress going to do when she found out Mia hadn't returned to her home?

"So, old man, looks like we just have a case of Sleeping Beauty on our hands. She didn't take enough pills to do any damage, and she can sleep it off here. But what are you going to do when that crazy lady finds out you had something to do with her escape?"

The elderly driver had already had his belongings in hand and was walking to my door. "She's in good hands," he stated. "I'm not worried about her honestly. That crazy lady is actually my sister. But she tends to take her business way too far for me anymore. I'm out of this game. My bags are packed. Your place was my first stop, young blood. I have a plane to catch. Take care of that girl. She's pretty special, and she shouldn't be in this game."

And with that he walked out, gently closing the door behind him. I turned off all the lights and climbed in the bed next to Mia, adjusting the washcloth. She was still one of the most beautiful women I had ever seen, and even with her in a deep sleep, she made my dick start throbbing with the memory of being inside her warm and sweet pussy once before. I wanted to pull her dress up and see if she had on any panties, but I wasn't trying to catch a case. Instead, I curled against her body and listened to her breathing steadily, looking at her beautiful face until my own eyes closed.

Chapter 8

Mia

I felt like my eyes were almost playing tricks on me after I was able to fully open them. They were so heavy. "Doulah?" I whispered in disbelief, remembering the sexy bearded man who had rushed out the house after Miss Danni had confronted us in the bathroom. He was sleeping right next to me, and I had a moment to look around the spacious loft and take in my surroundings. He had expensive taste. And it looked like he lived alone. I guessed he had to if I was in his bed, or maybe his woman was out of town. He must have heard me moving in the massive bed.

"Hey, Sleeping Beauty. You were out for quite some time," he said, staring down into my eyes with his own sexy ones. I couldn't see all of his rock-hard chest muscles because of the sheets, but I'd never forget what they looked like.

"How did I get here?"

"The old man brought you here after you passed out in his car. My guess is that you took one too many of these," he said, reaching over to his nightstand and shaking the small bottle of pills in front of me. He looked slightly disappointed.

"Doulah, I can explain. I have been in this crazy nightmare with Miss Danni that never ends for me. She met me at a network marketing conference in Las Vegas and invited me to New York under the guise of doing business with her. The money was good, but it was way more than just marketing, as you saw. I had plans to leave and get my own place after I had lived with her for about six months in her home. She became almost obsessed with me and started drugging me slowly, and every time I planned to leave, she would find ways to keep me there. Threats, drugs, guns, whatever. Anything I grew to love, she grew to hate and threatened its very existence. That's why she pulled a gun out on you. To scare you away because she saw something between us, despite our small interaction with each other."

"Was she lying? Do you feel something for me, Mia?" he asked, caressing my hair with one of his hands.

"No, Doulah. There is something about you that I just can't explain. My mind has been craving you ever since I saw you in the car that day. And when we had sex, despite the other people in the room, I felt like it was just me and you. Honestly, I took the pills as an escape from her. I didn't think they would put me out like they did. I wanted to not deal with her that night, and I figured someone would drag me up to her house and throw me in my bed in my room there. But now I'm here. With you."

Doulah grabbed my face in his hands and kissed me slowly and deeply, his tongue exploring my mouth. I knew my breath had to be slightly bad, but obviously this man didn't have that on his mind. His actions were speaking a different language. And I was willing to give him not only my body, but also my mind, heart, and soul. He scooped me up out the bed in his strong arms and carried me to the bathroom, placing me on the massive countertop, which brought back a delicious memory.

"Hold your arms up, baby."

I did as I was told, wriggling my ass from side to side so he could get the dress up and over my head. My pussy was slightly wet from his deep kiss, and all I wanted right now was his dick inside me and his bearded face in between my legs. Like Rihanna's hit song, I had been having wild thoughts about this man since our very first encounter, and I was about to make them my reality, if only for a short time.

Doulah's lips met mines again for a small, slow kiss. He took my hand, and I eased off the sink's countertop and followed him into the massive walk-in shower. The heat of the water only paled in comparison to the unseen heat between Doulah and me. He had a variety of shower gels and found something neutral that we both could use, and he gently washed my body down, kissing me on my ears, neck, and shoulders along the way. I then returned the favor, the shower sponge lingering against his caramel chiseled body.

After we were all rinsed off, he dropped on his knees in front of me, and grabbing my ass in his hands, he pulled my small frame toward his waiting mouth. His beard felt so soft against my thighs, and I thought I would faint when two of his thick fingers found the deep insides of my pinkness. I instinctively grabbed the back of his head when he put his mouth on my clit, sucking and swirling his tongue around it until I was moaning in pure ecstasy. Just when I was about to squirt all over him, he stood up, kissed my wet mouth, and turned me around. I placed both hands on the shower wall and lifted my hips slightly forward, allowing him to enter me from behind.

"You about to get all this dick, girl," he said, pulling me into him so that he could get a better grip.

"I want it all too, baby. Just like that," I moaned. He felt so damn good, better than I had even remembered. His touch was firm but gentle. His hands around my waist were getting tighter and tighter, and I could feel his rock-hard thigh muscles tensing up. Doulah was about to cum all inside me, which was a good thing because the shower water was growing cooler and my pussy was growing more impatient.

"I'm finna cum all over your ass, Mia. You ready for that? You straight?"

"Yeah, daddy. Bring it home to mama," I said, and with that statement, he shot all his juices inside of me, pushing his dick up fully inside of me. When he finally released me, he put his head down where it was fully under the shower water. He squeezed his beard out with one hand and turned off the water with the other. Doulah quickly jumped out, grabbing two thick, large chocolate bath towels out of a nearby basket on the floor.

"Here you go, Ms. Mia," he said, wrapping the massive towel around my athletic, petite frame. I reached up to kiss his lips in a thank-you gesture, wondering what I was going to put on since I had no clothes at his house. He led me to his closet, where he had a decent pair of joggers that could fit me and a small T-shirt, which would have to do. I guessed I could still rock my red bottom heels from last night. I quickly dressed in the clothes and threw on one of his baseball caps.

"I like you like that. It's actually pretty cute."

"Boy, please. I look kinda crazy, but I will be okay. It's lunchtime now, and I need to figure out what I'm going to do about this situation, you know. It's not going to fix itself, Doulah. Plus I can't just stay over here forever. You do have a job and a life."

"Well, let's juggle one thing at a time for right now. We will figure something out. I promise you," he said, looking at me very sincerely. "Really, Mia. I'm going to help you get out of there," he added, selecting clothes from his closet to put on.

As he threw on some gray sweatpants, a white V-neck, and a ball cap himself, I rummaged through my bag, gathering a few items to put on some light makeup.

"Okay. All ready," I said and walked toward the door where he was waiting for me. We headed out the door and patiently waited for the elevator to open up. Neither of us had to speak about the oversized-ass elephant that was inside of the small space with us. We both knew that this whole situation still had one big problem, and a dangerous one at that: Ms. Danni. But we didn't have to wait long to come to that conclusion.

I noticed her as soon as we opened the door leading out to the slightly warm New York City air, even if Doulah hadn't. He had taken my hand and was trying to lead me in the opposite direction up the busy sidewalk, but I had stopped dead in my tracks. That bitch was leaning against her crimson BMW Z4, hair intact, shades on.

"Mia, what's wrong? There's a great café right down the way and . . ." He didn't even get to finish his sentence because his eyes started to travel in the direction I was firmly staring at and he finally saw what I had already seen. But he was too late. He hadn't even noticed me going through my purse to retrieve my .22.

I walked toward her quickly and drew my piece. "I am done," I yelled to her, my weapon gleaming as passersby started running in different directions. "I will kill you and myself before I ever work for you again. So, looks like you have a choice to make, miss lady. And I'm giving you ten seconds to make it. Ten, nine . . ."

Doulah started backing away, trying to get me to give up my gun. It was too late now. I guessed the police would be getting involved pretty soon.

"Little girl, you are making a huge mistake," Ms. Danni said very calmly, not moving a muscle.

"Six, five, four . . . If I am making a mistake, then you had better get right with God, lady," I stated.

I didn't get a chance to finish counting. Doulah moved toward me too quick and got in the way trying to get the weapon. Wrestling with Doula, all I saw was Ms. Danni rushing toward me as well, pulling something out her bag. Damn Doulah! I needed him to get out of my way so I could get a clear shot at her.

He didn't move, and next thing I heard was screaming and the sounds of gunshots ringing out in the air. I couldn't tell if I had been hit, but looking at the body crumpling down around my feet, I knew that someone had been shot, and pretty badly. I immediately got on the ground and started mouth-to-mouth. And the only thought ringing through my head was that I just made a grave error and had to try to save the one person who had treated me like family, because the other person was clearly dead.

Chapter 9

"Baby girl, Mia, I'm so sorry. Really. I know how much he meant to you, girl, even if the world didn't. Nothing is going to happen to you. I promise. The police and your lawyer will figure everything out, and they will see that you were acting in self-defense."

"How is that, Shantel? I pulled out the gun first! It was my own fault and . . . and there would be no white sheet covering that man's face in that hospital bed right now if it weren't for me and my stupid actions! Ms. Danni is the one who should be dead right now, not him! Not now! He had my back, front, and both sides so many times that I cannot even keep track. And he truly loved me unconditionally! Ms. Danni didn't realize how close we had gotten because she was too busy being an *I Spy* on all of us girls who worked for her. But he was working to help me get out. To be free from under her thumb once and for all. And me and my gun ended all that. How could I be so stupid? Let me know what happens, please. You have to keep in contact with me now that I'm locked up in here on these charges. You're one of the only people I can trust right now and who knows why I actually did what I did."

"Girlie, you don't have to ask me twice. I got you. Keep your eyes open, and your head up in there and remember who you used to be to get you through this test. You got this. Call me soon. Love you, girl."

"Thanks, boo. I hate to bring back the old Mia, but I know where she lives if she needs to come out to play up in here. Damn. Hopefully that won't get me in more trouble, though. I have some things to live for now. Love you too, boo. I will call soon."

And with one more look into my best friend Shantel's eyes, I hit one end of the phone to the heavy plastic partition and put my right palm out to meet hers. A good man was dead, and I was in fucking jail. All I wanted to do was leave a bad situation, and the old Mia, with all the old battle scars, came back through with a vengeance.

"Are you done? Some of us do have visits waiting too, ya know."

That had to be Joiey, or "Joey" as everyone called her in the joint. This bitch was going to get on my fucking nerves before it was all over. She had caught a drug case running a drop for her boyfriend. He was a big-time behind-the-scenes dealer in Queens, and the Feds had been watching them for a while. I guessed they figured if they could get her and some of his runners, she would drop the dime on him for sure. They were wrong. This bitch was built for prison, and she didn't have any problems letting anyone know.

"Damn, girl. I just got done. Wait in line like everyone else. Fuck outta here." Joey had been starting shit with me since my first night in here. I wasn't about to take any more of her shit. She had no idea what I had been going through, plus I was carrying a bigger secret that I had to try to protect until I could figure out a way out of this mess.

She wasn't that much bigger than me, brown skinned, long, curly hair that she wore in a high ponytail. I could see that outside of here she was gorgeous. But inside here, beauty faded quickly when you couldn't use the standard beauty products. I guessed she felt like she had to play the tough-girl role so she wouldn't become someone's bitch. Well, she and these other chicks in here would get introduced to the old Mia real fucking quick if they wanted to. She was a person who I had buried a long time ago on the last day I had walked out of a five-year prison sentence. Maybe that's why Doula and I had had such a strong connection from day one.

I missed him so much right now. There were so many things I had to tell him, wanted to share with him. Walking back to my cell, I had to fight back the tears that threatened to tell my story and cause me more trouble inside these unforgiving walls. And that was the last thing I needed. Doula was now my past. He would be buried in my memory like all the good things that ever happened to me. Maybe Miss Danni was right when she said I was like a bad omen and would never amount to anything but a pretty face and a pair of open legs.

Balled up like a small child on the paper-thin cot they wanted us to think was a decent replacement for an actual mattress, the scene outside of Doulah's loft crept back inside my mind. When that bitch Ms. Danni came toward me, all I could think of was all the negativity that she had fed my spirit the last four years. It had begun to eat at my soul to the point that I thought I would choke on it eventually if I didn't get out of her game. I gave negative zero fucks about trying to put her into the ground if it came to that, because I would be damned if she was going to take me away from a man who I knew loved me and cared about me. I could feel it. He was like a magnet to my soul. I just saw red when she ran up toward me. And then when Doulah started wrestling with me and her, the gun went off.

But the problem was the other person who came into the picture trying to always protect her, even against his own will. Why was the old man constantly trying to protect everyone? Damn! He came out of nowhere. I didn't see his car at all because he had followed Ms. Danni back to Doulah's place and parked around the corner when he saw that she was posting up in her car. He couldn't warn me or Doulah because she would see that coming. What she didn't see coming was my gun. The old man saw it and ran up from outta nowhere and jumped on top of the pile of us just as the gun was going off. My mouth-to-mouth wasn't going to save him. Nothing was. The man who had grown to treat me like his own daughter had been a victim of my rage. He was always trying to protect me from her rage. Always trying to get me to get away from her. And finally when Doulah got into his car one night before one of our jobs was to start, and he saw my immediate attraction to him, he knew he could possibly be my way out. But the key was to really get Doulah to see that I was in potential danger.

So he started sending photos, calling him with details, leaving messages with him about my situation. I personally didn't think he would care as much as he did, but the old man finally got through to him. And then he got in the way. And I was arrested when the police got to the scene of the crime because I had the gun, and I shot him. It wasn't self-defense. He wasn't supposed to be there. I couldn't hold my tears back any longer because I truly had loved him like a father. Ms. Danni's screams of rage at me when he drew his last breath didn't help either. Doulah pulled me off of him, because I wasn't going to stop trying to bring him back to life. This just couldn't be how it was supposed to end.

Those last thoughts eventually put me to sleep until the loud banging occurred right outside my cell, jerking me wide awake. It was a security guard dragging Joey down the hall. Whatever she had done, they were attempting to take her to solitary confinement, and she had grabbed one of the security guard's black billy clubs and ended up dropping it on the ground right outside my cell as he reached for her hands and stopped to cuff her. This bitch wasn't going to make it out of here alive, I swear. But I was. I needed to. If not for me, for the child living inside of me now.

Doulah's child. The old man was the only one who had kept my almost-three-month-old secret, and now I had killed him. I had to get out of this place. I just had to. And more importantly, I had to see Doulah.

Chapter 10

Doulah

The knock on the door jarred me from my thoughts of Mia's face behind a set of steel bars. I had been calling in all kinds of favors from lawyers and people I knew on the inside to see if anything could be done about her case. I still couldn't believe she had just pulled out that piece like that and gotten off one shot.

"What do I owe the pleasure of this visit to?" I asked Nic, my extremely irritated-looking boss lady.

"Doulah, we have to stop meeting like this. Do you remember when the earlier days were much more, ahem, simple?" she asked, but I wasn't sure if she actually wanted an answer, so I just took her coat and ushered her to my living room. As her heels clicked across my floor, she proceeded to finish her statement.

"There were no bathroom trysts with clients, no gun showdowns, no falling in love with anyone you just happen to fuck for money, and definitely no murders."

"Nic, that's not really how it went down though," I answered, defending myself even though it was a lie and we both knew it.

"Lies, Doulah. It was just a good, old-fashioned, drama-free, modern-day 'Boyfriend Experience.' I'm not understanding if you are just trying to get your fine self fired, man. Because at this rate, you are going to be unemployed soon if you don't start keeping your good name

out of these client's messy lives. What the hell happened
to that old man, Doulah? I think it is about time that you
told me what was really going on."

"Look, Nic, I had nothing to do with that man getting
shot. But I did have something to do with Mia being over
here."

"Mia, as in the girl from that job?"

"Yes, same girl. Long story short, the old man has been
trying to rescue her from Ms. Danni for months. He sent
me photos, has been texting me, calling me, leaving me
messages, stalking my damn place. All until I finally listened. She was really in danger, Nic. And well, I suppose
I sort of fell for her in the process. I won't lie. I never mix
business with pleasure, but there was something different about her, Nic. And I wanted to find out just what
that 'different' was exactly. I don't plan to leave my job
anytime soon, and I have made her aware of that. I will
just have to figure this out.

"Anyway, I was taking her to get a change of clothes
after she woke up from a drug-induced state that she was
in when the old man brought her to my place. I called a
friend in the medical field, and they instructed me what
to do to get her to eventually wake up. I didn't even know
she had the gun when we walked out of my place to go get
some clothes for her, and I guess when she saw her boss,
she sorta flipped out and went renegade all on everybody.
But now she is down at the jailhouse, hoping that her
lawyer will be able to pull some magic out of a hat. Same
jailhouse I was in so I know what she is going through. I
just hope that I'm able to help her in some way. That old
man meant a lot to her, and he came from out of nowhere.
If something doesn't change soon, she will end up rotting
in that jail cell. And that's pretty much the story, Nic," I
stated, giving her a chance to soak up everything I told
her. I wondered which hand she would play next.

"That sounds like a lot of drama, to be honest. I hope that she's worth all this trouble. On another note, my main goal is to satisfy my high-paying clientele. That said, you have another job. I mean, unless you're not up to it. It's not like your girl will know. She is in jail after all for murder, Doulah. Just keep that in mind."

"Another job, another day. I can separate the two. Trust me. I have to be able to."

"Yes, you do, and you also have to stay ready."

"Nic, I stay ready. You already know it."

"Good, because I have a job for you tonight. If you blow this, Doulah, we are finished with you."

"I completely understand, but I've got this. Where is the information?" I asked.

Nic clicked over to her purse and pulled out a small brown padded envelope and handed it to me. "You know the drill. This one is pretty simple. No fancy gimmicks or tricks required, just bring the heat, that beard, and that body, and you will do fine. Cool?"

"Yep. Thanks, Nic. I'll keep you informed of the other situation. Guess I will start getting ready for tonight."

"I'll show myself out, D. Have a good night, and uhm-mm, good luck with that other little messy situation," Nic stated, closing the door behind her.

The last thing I needed right now was this job, but it was my bread and butter so what other choice did I have? "Time to make the donuts," as the catchphrase used to go.

It was eleven o'clock in the morning. It was almost time for me to go to visit Mia. Glancing at the job details, I saw it was for nine o'clock tonight. Plenty of time for me to do bobage with a change of clothes that would not need ironing for my job later. I grabbed my keys and headed out the door, ready to see the only girl who mattered at the moment.

Chapter 11

"Place your belongings in the basket, sir, and I just need your ID. You did say you had an appointment, correct?" the female officer asked me, writing all my information down and checking it against the inmate visitation information. She was looking me up and down like I was the latest popular snack.

"Yes, ma'am. Booked it online."

"Oh, okay. I got you here. So I see you are a part of the Beard Gang, hmmm? Well, if you ever want to grab a coffee or something you know where I am," she whispered so that her coworkers couldn't hear her, sliding me my appointment confirmation information.

"Thanks. I will keep you in mind if I ever want to grab a coffee or something." I charmingly smiled back at her. Maybe she could help me with making it easier on Mia someway. It paid to be nice up in here. I knew first-hand.

I made my way to the phone visitation booth that she assigned me, and I waited patiently to see her walk through the door. About ten minutes later, I recognized the petite, athletic frame sort of semi-swallowed in the jail orange duds. She was still gorgeously sexy even with no makeup, and I wanted to just create a vortex to take her away from all this once and for all. Why hadn't I done a better job of checking to make sure she didn't have a gun? But damn, why would she even have a gun in the first place? I waved her over and picked up the phone once she sat down.

"Doulah, I'm so sorry I got you into this mess," she began, looking at me with tears rimming her eyelids but willing them away. No time for tears behind these walls. That was for sure.

"Baby. It's okay. I said that we would get through this, and I meant it. What is the latest from your lawyer?"

"I have to pay him some more money to continue his representation, but they are trying to get it reduced to self-defense if I can prove that Ms. Danni put me in danger and threatened my life before. You were there when she pulled the gun out on us, Doulah, so you may be able to testify on my behalf if it comes to that."

"Yeah, that's a lot. I'm sure your lawyer will let me know if that is what it comes down to. How are you holding up in here though? Is anyone messing with you? Do you have enough cash on your books to get the little stuff that you can get to make it a little more 'human' in here, if there is such a thing?"

"Yes, you have been very generous, and I appreciate it, Doulah. You are so handsome. I miss your face so much. I need to tell you something though. It's really important, and it's not the best way that I could have told you. But present circumstances dictate that I need to make you aware of another situation that could get worse in here."

What the hell was she talking about? What could be worse than jail? "Go ahead, pretty lady. I'm listening."

"Doulah, I know there is just no perfect time to say this. Especially now. But I'm pregnant. Three months along. I believe that it is yours, but honestly, I'm not so sure." Mia was looking down at the table with an almost-embarrassed look on her face.

Of all the really fucked-up things that she could have told me, this had to be in the possible top five. It wasn't so much that she was pregnant. It was just the "I believe that it is yours" part that was kinda hard to swallow. But

I had accepted Mia for who she was in my mind, and she had done the same for me. We both had jobs that were not conducive to raising a child, but maybe there was a way we could figure out how to make the same money we both made and still have a baby. "Maybe" was the key word here though.

"Wow. I really am just . . . Wow. First, let me just say that I know how hard it is for you right now. I have been there and done that, and I know that you can do it as well. You have to. Especially now, Mia. Does anyone know that you are pregnant? Do the COs know?"

"No one knows yet. I have hidden it well, but soon enough I won't be able to any longer. I just need to know that you have my back through this, Doulah. I mean, after I find out if it's yours. I have no idea how I'm going to be pregnant and in jail. This is the worst feeling ever. I did talk to my lawyer the other day, and he is almost sure that I could use the self-defense argument. I don't know if it will work, but I'm going to try my hardest. I gotta get out of here and soon by any means possible."

"Baby girl, don't worry. Despite you being in here, I am happy about the pregnancy. You work on staying positive in here, Mia, for your sanity and for the baby's health. And depending on the lawyer's time line he gives you, you may have to tell someone. Your boy got you. Don't worry. We will come up with something."

"That means a lot, Doulah. It's been okay in here. I'll manage one way or the other."

"Look, I know our time is up. I'm going to put some more money on your books after this visit. You mean a lot to me, Mia. Really."

"I'll see you again soon?" she asked, not really wanting the visit to be over.

"Sooner than you think, babes, and remember what I said." I got up to replace the phone in its cradle. I placed my hand on the glass, and she did the same, placing hers right over mine. Looking each other in the eyes was almost painful. But I manned up and got through it for her. Besides, I had a job to do, and I didn't want to fuck up my contract with Nic. I was definitely going to need it now more than ever.

Chapter 12

The gold key easily turned in the large red door. This house looked like it could belong to someone either very rich or very famous. It looked like something out of *MTV Cribs,* complete with an eight-car garage. This was already seeming to be an unforgettable night. Everything was dimly lit with rose-colored scented candles, and there were pink and white rose petals lined across a spiraling staircase.

I followed the rose petals to a bedroom door that was slightly open. I pushed it open very gently, and there laid out on a massive king bed dressed in nothing but bare bronze skin and long, flowing, curly hair was a gorgeous exotic-looking woman with large breasts with nice-sized nipples. She motioned with the fingers of one hand to come over to her.

I dropped my messenger bag and walked over to her, my all-black Timberlands being the only noise in the room. She had some play list going and Chris Brown's "Hope You Do" was currently in rotation. She got on her knees and pulled my midnight blue V-neck T-shirt over my head and tossed it on the floor. She rubbed her hands all over my dark, muscular chest and grabbed the back of my head, pulling my face to her waiting lips. She tasted like she had been eating peaches, because her tongue was still slightly sweet from their lingering juice. I went deeper with my kiss, sucking her tongue and putting my hands in her hair to pull her closer.

"Dang, baby, you taste—"

"Don't speak. Just feel," she interrupted. I guessed this was going to be a silent session, which was fine by me. I was up for any challenge, but once she got this D and this beard between her legs, I had a feeling that she was going to be breaking her own rule.

I kicked off my shoes, and she instinctively started pulling down my jeans and my black Tommy Hilfiger boxer briefs. She started gently sucking my chest, leaving small bites in random places. So I returned the favor. I cupped one of her full breasts in my hand, sucking the skin and the nipple, biting it gently at first, then harder as her moans grew deeper when I did that. I grabbed her around her neck and slightly pushed her back onto the bed. She was about to get this work.

Her pussy was shaved like I liked it, and I alternated kissing, sucking, and biting down her smooth belly until I came to the insides of her thighs. I began to caress her inner thighs with my beard, holding her legs apart. She reached down and started playing with her clit, making herself extremely wet, which turned me on and instantly gave me a hard-on. I started sucking her pussy softly at first, but knowing that she liked it rough, started kissing and sucking her clit harder and harder, putting my tongue fully inside her pussy.

I turned her over on her belly and rubbed my beard all over her nice, full ass cheeks, parting them so I could suck all her juices out. Her moans were taking over the music, and when my tongue began dancing inside her ass, she almost ripped the sheets apart from her grip. She obviously had never had it like this before. Well, now she knew what this beard do. It was time for me to show her what this dick could do as well.

I opened up her ass wider, and grabbing a condom, worked my way inside her ass, using her own juices as lube. She felt good, and I needed the release that great sex only could provide. After I felt she had had enough in that ass, I flipped her around and changed condoms, taking her left leg and throwing it up against my shoulder. I put her right leg under my legs so she couldn't escape and I could go deep inside of her without any hesitation. She was loving this shit, and her pussy showed it by all the cum that was dripping off my dick each time I switched positions.

Sometimes I couldn't believe women actually paid me for servicing them. And these were some of the most eligible, well-off beauties at that. It was crazy to think about it, but I guess when you got to a certain level, it was hard to get what you actually desired and deserved without someone trying to use you for your money. I didn't know what I would do if this baby were mine actually, but I needed to try to stop thinking about it and focus on the job at hand.

This beauty was doing a great job of not speaking actually. Now moaning, on the other hand, was a whole other story. I had found her spot, my dick was going deeper, and the way her thighs started quivering showed me that she was at the point of no return. I grabbed both her wrists and held them down as I plunged even deeper inside her drenched pussy.

"Baby! Oh, myyyy sweet Jesus! I'm cumming again!" she screamed, arching her back.

Damn, I guessed some rules were meant to be broken. I knew she wouldn't last long with her silent treatment. I just looked at her and grinned, letting her go and gently caressing her hair. She rubbed her fingers through my beard, and I caught one of them in my mouth and sucked it slowly.

I would find a way to either separate my work from my personal life if Mia was to be in it, or I would have to find another means of income that could match what I was earning now. I just hoped that I could find a way to help Mia get out of jail before this baby was born. But right now, I had to put in this work to stack money for her lawyer. A nine-to-five wasn't going to help me do that. But this beard, my chiseled, dark body, and this long dick would.

"Ready for round two, ma?" I asked, knowing the answer already. I was already ripping open the condom. This was going to be a long night.

Chapter 13

I didn't even notice that my fists were both balled up and each placed at opposite ends of the small, square, plain table when I heard the booming familiar voice in front of me that immediately made me look up once at him then down at both my hands as I slowly uncurled them.

"Who you finna fight, D? It ain't like you gotta be up in here no more sleeping on these brick-hard cots, waitin' on a nigga to act up and get his head busted to the white meat!"

The old man smiled and held out his hand for some dap. Puncho looked good, despite knowing that he would never experience freedom as the majority of the world knows it again. His choices at a younger age had made sure of that.

"What up, my nigga? You are looking well, old man. You must be still running shit from the inside, huh?"

"Young'un, I'm running shit on the inside and on the outside. You should know. You are making me look good. All that work you puttin' in. I have heard some other bull-shit, though, about a girl, a gun, and some dead nigga." Puncho said the last two words in a whisper while taking a quick glance around the room as if someone were actually sitting somewhere taking notes on our conversation. Prison talk. No one wanted to be implicated for "some dead nigga," no matter the circumstances. I didn't miss it at all.

"Well, that's why I'm here, Punch. I kinda got myself in this situation with this girl."

"Always some bitch getting in the middle, huh? You got some pictures?" he asked, doing his leaning in, whispering thing again.

"Nahhh, man. Listen up. I need to talk to you about that whole situation. Shit has gotten ugly, and the 'bitch' is now in jail, but I love her, and I need to find a way to help her at this point."

I began to tell Punch the quickie version of the tale, knowing our visitation time was running out. I needed two things from him: some help trying to see if Mia could beat this rap somehow and get out of jail before this baby was due, and some help figuring out how I could start running my own show from a business perspective, like him and Nic. Surely they had room for another partner.

"Man, that's a tough one there," Puncho said, rubbing both his old but strong hands over his bald head. "I think there may be some technicalities that your girl can get off on, plus it's a few lawyer peoples who owe me favors on the outside. I'll let you know what I find out.

"Now the other thing. Doulah, I'ma be straight up with you. You are one of our top moneymakers on the outside, man. You have to determine if you really want to give up all that you're doing just to focus on being with this girl. You can do both if you want. Have your family and still do what you need to maintain it. And for you, that's hittin' these wealthy bitches' pockets up so we can get all they coins, as the young people say. How long can you hold out? I mean, she ain't getting out tomorrow. She at least will have to do six months, I can tell you that upfront. That's the system. She gonna do some time for attempted murder, but she probably can get a plea deal or something 'cause she pregnant and it's her first offense. But you gotta give me and Nic some time to discuss some options and come up with something. I can't guarantee that you will be able to keep your nose clean in the months and years to come after your girl gets released, but I can probably keep the late nights you have fucking these bitches to a minimum. I'll let you know."

"That's all I can ask for, my nig. Be easy, man. Be in touch soon," I said, giving him some more dap and a brotherly embrace.

"A'ight, bitch. Go get my money."

"Pretty soon it will be our money, Punch. Remember that," I said, smirking and hoping that Nic would be as understanding as he was about possibly cutting me in on their bosses' share of the pie. I knew she wouldn't be though. Not by a long shot.

His Muse

by

Genesis Woods

Chapter 1

Siyah

I looked at the time on the stove and shook my head when the loud knock on my door thundered throughout my apartment. I had a little over an hour to get ready for my girls' night in shindig that was being held inside of my home tonight, and I was already behind schedule. I should've gone with my first mind and stopped by the bakery at the corner to buy a few treats to satisfy these greedy heffas' appetites, but leave it to me to wanna show out my exceptional culinary skills and try to make from scratch the spread that I wanted them to enjoy.

When the loud knocking sounded on my door again, I threw the spatula I was holding into the sink and ran toward the front of my apartment. With my tattered purple terry-cloth robe lightly pulled around my body to hide the lace bra and boy shorts set that I had on, I turned the knob to let my guest in.

"Hey, Juan," I said, turning my back to the door. "I know it's super late and past your normal work time, but my damn stove went out again, and I have guests coming over in about an hour. I tried calling your phone but it was disconnected, so I had to call the emergency line. I hope you brought whatever you did last time to get this thing working again." I didn't even give Juan enough time to answer. I was already back inside of my kitchen switching the pot on my hot plate to a skillet and trying to sauté some onions for the brie and caramelized onion tartlets I was making.

"Aye, Juan," I called out when I didn't hear his footsteps behind me. I assumed he was checking out some of the new paintings on my wall that I put up the other day. His appreciation for art was somewhat similar to mine, and he seemed to always notice when I got a new piece. "How you been, man? I haven't seen you walking the property in a while. Does the office have you handling stuff over at the other site again?" I yelled over my shoulder.

Another minute or two passed by without Juan answering any of my questions, and my instincts began to kick in that something wasn't right. Turning the hot plate down to a medium temp, I turned around and headed back to the front of my apartment. When I got there, I stopped dead in my tracks when my eyes connected with a set of deep chestnut irises that belonged to one of the finest men I'd ever seen in my life. He was dressed in a one-piece green maintenance suit that did little to hide the outline of his sculpted frame.

I was caught up in a daze before he cleared his throat, capturing my full attention. "You . . . you aren't Juan," hoarsely came from my mouth as I exhaled the breath I'd been holding since I looked at his face.

The dents in his cheeks deepened when he smiled, and I gasped like a starstruck groupie. "Nah, I'm not Juan. And I was hoping you realized it before I walked into your home unannounced. I didn't want to scare you when you turned around and saw that I wasn't him."

I nodded my head because for some reason my throat was dry as hell all of a sudden. I tried to open my mouth and formulate some type of response, but I started coughing instead.

"You good?" his seductively sweet voice asked, causing that electric current thing to zap right to my clit. The soothing cadence in his tone had the butterflies in my stomach dancing to its rhythmic beat.

"I'm good. Just need a little water, that's all." His cheek hiked up when he smiled at me.

I blushed for some reason. "If you don't mind me asking, who are you and where's Juan?" I tugged at the center of my robe and tried to tighten it around my body when I noticed the way his eyes kept roaming up and down my plus-size frame.

"Juan was given sort of an extended vacation, so I was hired on to fill his position. My name is Weyland by the way, Weyland Michaels. And I'm your new maintenance man."

He extended his hand to mine, and I gave it to him. I didn't know if he could feel the sexual energy radiating from my body to his through our touch, but I was hoping he did.

I cleared my throat and returned his greeting when his grip on my hand tightened. "Uhh, nice to meet you, Weyland. I'm Siyah. Siyah Daniels."

"Siyah, huh?"

I slowly nodded my head, caught up in his rapture again.

"Pretty name for a pretty face."

"Thank you," came out a little more sex kitten than intended. I almost didn't recognize my own voice. Embarrassed by my reaction, I tried to steer our conversation back to our original topic. "So, you're the new handyman? How's that going?" I internally rolled my eyes. *That was so freaking corny, Siyah.*

Weyland drew his bottom lip into his mouth and bit it. The look on his face was one I couldn't quite read. There was a mixture of curiosity and interest, but also one of hesitance. It seemed like he wanted to say something to me but didn't know if it was cool to say it at that moment.

I shifted my weight from one leg to the other and looked down at the floor. His intense gaze didn't have me feeling uncomfortable, but I did feel a little timorous. When I lifted my head back up, Weyland's thick tongue slid across his lips, wetting them just a bit before he answered my question, a conning smile covering his face.

This sexy asshole could sense my sexual attraction to him. I knew he felt it.

"So far working here has been okay. Maintenance isn't my first love, but it's what pays the bills when my other job is moving a little slower than I want."

Weyland finally let my hand go, and for some reason, I was already missing his touch.

"I've been here for about a couple of weeks now, and I must say, this is the first time I actually don't mind getting an after-hours call on the emergency line." His smoldering eyes roamed over my face for a few seconds and then my body again. "This job just keeps on getting better and better."

I reared my head back. Not because I was offended by what he just said, but because I wasn't sure if he was really flirting with me. I shook my head. Nah, he couldn't be flirting with me. How could he be? I answered the door looking a hot mess, not expecting this fine-ass man to be standing here. Juan was used to me looking all kinds of crazy ways whenever he stopped by to fix something, so I knew he wouldn't trip about me being in the middle of getting dressed. I mean, besides the frayed robe I threw on after I got out of the shower, my hair was still wrapped up under my bonnet, the only type of makeup I had on was my cocoa-butter lip balm, and I just applied this homemade exfoliating mask ten minutes ago. I knew if he couldn't see the small chunks of papaya mixed with raw honey on my face, he sure as hell could smell it.

"Well." I clapped my hands together, trying not to make the moment any more awkward than it was. "I'm so glad you're enjoying your job. And I totally appreciate that comment, but do you think you can fix my stove real quick? It's not coming on again, and I have a little get-together happening in about an hour that I'm trying to have food ready for."

At that request, Weyland finally stepped over the threshold of my door. The sound of his boots scuffing against my hardwood floors followed him. I watched as his eyes inspected every inch of my living room and dining area. His gaze lingered on one of the Black Rain paintings on the mantle above the fireplace.

"Nice place and nice choice of artwork. How long has your stove been cutting off?" he asked once his gaze landed back on me.

"Thanks, and I love that painter, but my stove's probably been tripping for a few months now. I told Juan I thought I needed a new stove, but he said that he could fix whatever was happening to it. Some shit about a shortage in the wiring." I shrugged my shoulders when his face twisted up in confusion. "I don't know."

He chuckled. "Juan's ass was lying. He should've ordered and installed a new one for you about two months ago. All of the other apartments have been upgraded, except yours, the apartment next door"—he raised the top sheet of paper on the clipboard that was in his hand—"and the vacant one across the hall."

Now it was my turn for my face to twist up in confusion. "Upgraded? Juan never mentioned anything about me getting a new stove."

"I'm not surprised by that," he replied with a small smirk. His eyes squinted a little as he looked at something behind me. I cleared my throat. He continued, "Yeah, but the stove model you have right now was recalled weeks ago. Management thought everyone had been changed out already, but apparently Juan dropped the ball on that."

"Wait," I began to say, but the smell of my onions burning began to fill the air. Turning quickly toward my kitchen, I abruptly ended our conversation, leaving Weyland where he stood. I went to try to save the main ingredient I needed for my tarts.

"Shit," I swore to myself when I saw that the bottom of my pan was coated with burnt Vidalias. I took the skillet from the hot plate and threw it into the sink. The cold water from the faucet caused a huge cloud of smoke to cover my kitchen once it hit the sizzling pan. The loud and annoying sound of the smoke detector going off had me grabbing my head in frustration. It seemed like everything that could go wrong was starting to go wrong, and I literally had a little less than an hour before my girls arrived.

Taking a deep breath to get myself together, I grabbed a couple more onions from the grocery bag and placed them on the cutting board. When I turned around to try to fan some of the smoke away from the detector so that it could stop, Weyland was already reaching up to do it for me. The biceps on the underside of his arm flexed a little, and I could see the end markings of some kind of tattoo that I hadn't noticed before.

"Thank you for taking care of that. It probably would've taken me forever to fan all of this smoke out of here."

Weyland walked over to my kitchen window and opened it. The cool air whipped through my apartment and cleared the air. "I figured I could give you a hand since you already had a situation with whatever was burning." His eyes scanned my cluttered countertop, stopping on the wooden display stand holding my Senshi Dual Knife Set. "You're a chef," was said more like a statement.

"I'm a caterer," I corrected as I began to chop up more onions. "I took my love for food and eating and turned it into a business."

"That's what's up." Weyland shimmied my stove from its space and started messing with some of the wires in the back. "What's your favorite dish to cook?"

I stopped chopping the onions and turned to him, only able to see the dark and deep black waves at the top of his head. "I don't really have a favorite. I just love to cook. However, if I had to choose, I would say my chicken piccata is my best and most favorite dish to prepare. It's been known to make the strongest man fall to his knees and beg for seconds."

"Is that right?" he asked, pushing my stove back into place and wiping his hands against his pant leg.

I nodded my head and turned back to getting my tarts ready.

"Maybe I can get an invite one day to try it out. I don't have a problem with falling to my knees if the meal is worth it."

Oh, shit. Weyland's ass was flirting with me. If I didn't fully believe it before, I totally knew it now. The way his voice dipped when he said that last statement told me that there was more than one meaning behind it. Instead of turning back around and risking the chance of him freaking out from the goofy-ass smile on my face, I shrugged my shoulders and replied, "Maybe we can make something happen."

His chuckle sent that zap through my body again, this time hitting my nipples as well. I could only imagine how good his tongue would feel circling my pebbled nub and then pulling it into his mouth to suck on. Those enticing full lips, that long and thick tongue. I was pretty sure he'd dished out plenty of mind-blowing orgasms with that delectable combination.

The clicking noise my stove made when turned on, followed by the swooshing sound of the blue flame igniting, broke me from my freaky thoughts. Pleased with the small interruption, I finished prepping my food with a clear mind, and I set everything to the side. After washing my hands, I had every intention of expressing how grateful I was for Weyland swooping in and saving the day. But before I could turn around to thank him for fixing my stove, I felt the heat of his strong body covering the back of mine. We weren't necessarily touching one another, but if I had stepped back even half an inch, I was sure my ass would be sitting right on that bulge I noticed earlier.

When he lowered his lips to my ear, my body stilled and tingled at the same time when his warm breath hit my skin. "The next time you need something fixed, feel free to call me anytime. And whenever you're ready to feed me, you got the number."

I wanted to say something in return, but by the time my tongue untwisted and my body stopped with the small tremors, he was gone. The only thing left to remind me that he was even there was his scent and the wetness in my boy shorts that I didn't even realize was there until now.

Chapter 2

Siyah

I took a long pull from the tightly rolled blunt nestled between my fingers, and I laid my head back against the small pillow I placed on the armrest of my couch. The potent smoke filled my lungs, and I smiled. Smoking weed wasn't something I did daily, but whenever my girls and I got together, we always matched a couple and threw back a few shots to try to relieve some of the stress in our lives and to just shoot the shit like we always did. It had been a couple weeks since our last girls' night in, when I'd met Weyland. We wanted to meet up to vote on a new book to read this time as well as talk about the upcoming girls' trip I unfortunately had to back out of at the last minute.

"Has anyone heard from Jalisa?" Taren asked from my loveseat directly across from me. Her feet were propped up on my coffee table as if she didn't have a lick of home training. Her nose was deep in her phone.

I rolled my eyes and threw my pillow at her. "First of all, get your shit off of my table. Secondly, Jalisa texted me thirty minutes ago and said she was going to stop by the store to grab our snack request and then she'd be on her way."

"Well, she needs to hurry up." Taren stood up to stretch her long limbs and rubbed her flat belly. "I got the damn munchies." She turned her attention toward my dining room table where my other friend, Dawn, was sitting. "Hey, Dawny, where you get this weed from? That shit fiyah as fuck."

I nodded my head in agreement as I took the blunt back from Taren and slowly took another pull. "This shit is fiyah. I'm high as fuck right now."

Dawn laughed. "I bet your ass will sober up real fast though if your maintenance bae knocked on that door right now."

I flipped her off and took another puff before passing the blunt back to her. I couldn't help the smile that formed on my face though by the mere mention of Weyland's fine ass. The girls hadn't seen or met him yet, but they'd heard plenty about him.

Ever since the night he came and fixed my stove, I'd been telling anyone who would listen to me about my attraction to his chocolate, sexy, and fine ass. If we weren't bumping into each other in the parking lot or around the property, he was in my doorway, trying out a new recipe I was working on at my request or sometimes just hanging around looking at shit that didn't really need to be fixed. I mean, the sexual chemistry and genuine interest between us was there like crazy, just like it was the first time he came to my house, but for some reason, Weyland hadn't tried to take it there yet even though I could tell he wanted to. The way he would look at me sometimes had me rubbing one off as soon as he would leave. The orgasm I would have was good, no doubt, but it would've felt so much better had it been his hands dipping in my treasure box and massaging my clit.

"Damn, bitch. You over there drooling and shit. That freaky flashback must've been good," Taren yelled while laughing, bringing me back from my thoughts.

"Yeah, Siy. Your ass zoned out for a minute or two," Dawn added. "Who got you over there moaning and shit just from thoughts alone?"

"I hope it wasn't Chris's triflin' ass." Taren rolled her eyes. "I know you said the dick was cool and everything, but I could never fuck with a nigga who thinks it's okay to still be living with his baby mama while he's damn near in a full-blown relationship with someone else."

Before I could respond to her, the front door of my apartment opened, and Jalisa walked in. She was carrying a plastic black bag filled with our goodie request from the liquor store, her big-ass duffle bag purse she carried all the time, and a look on her face that had me sitting up in my seat instantly. I didn't know if she was scared or in shock, but whatever it was had my high immediately coming down. After dropping the bags on the floor, she hurriedly closed the door and looked out the peephole before turning back to us. All our eyes expressed the same thing. What the hell was her problem?

"Bitch, why you didn't tell us you had a new neighbor across the hall?" she asked, looking out the peephole again. "That nigga and whoever his friend is helping him move is fine as fuck."

"What new neighbor?"

She pointed behind her. "The fine-ass neighbor I just saw in the hallway carrying a shitload of boxes and other shit up and down the stairs. I almost offered their asses these cold and refreshing Sprites Dawn wanted, but I didn't. Instead, I gave them my sexiest hello and a flirty wink."

Taren laughed. "Leave it to your ho ass to try to get the scoop on the fresh meat before Siyah has a chance. You know she needs a new cuddy buddy. Her shit has to be drier than a fat bitch's throat after a one-mile run. Pussy probably choking and everything trying to get a little wet."

These bitches snickered at my expense, but I was used to it. It'd been a minute since the last time I got a taste of some grade A certified dick, but I was too focused with trying to get my business going to be concerned with any of that. I had a few niggas I could call if I was really desperate for some, but I didn't have the time or patience to deal with them or their shenanigans.

I needed—no, scratch that—I wanted a man who could satisfy me in every way possible, mind, body, and spirit and honestly I hadn't met anyone who did that for me. Well, I hadn't until I met Weyland. I didn't know what it was about him, but his whole being spoke to me in so many different ways. Although our encounters had been brief, something deep inside was telling me that he could possibly be the one to knock me off my square and be the man I'd always wanted.

I got up from my place on the couch and hurried over to the door at the same time as Dawn and Taren. After a few tugs, pulls, and hip bumps between the three of us, I was finally able to get enough elbow room to allow myself a quick peek at the new neighbor moving into the complex.

"Oh, shit. That's him," I whispered. My hands instantly went to my hair to make sure my shit was straight. "That's freaking him."

"Him who?" Taren asked as she took her turn looking through the peephole.

"That's Weyland."

"Wait. Who's Weyland?" Dawn asked.

Taren moved back from the door and popped Dawn in her titty. "The maintenance bae, dummy. Siyah's ass has only said his name like a million times in the last two weeks. Fifty times since we been here. Almost fucked up my high talking about how she wants to take him down. Your slow ass needs to keep up."

I looked out the peephole again when I heard the door across from me open and close. Some brown-skinned brother, who reminded me of an older Bryson Tiller, walked into the middle of the hallway first and then came Weyland. Dressed in nothing but a wife beater, some loose-hanging jeans, and his usual black steel-toed boots, his ass was a sight to see. The beard that lined the lower part of his face was trimmed low and lined to perfection. His bushy eyebrows were perfectly arched, and his smooth, dark skin was glistening with sweat. Sorta gave him that super sun-kissed skin look.

I felt my heart start to beat a little faster, my nipples start to grow a little firmer, and my clit start to thump a little harder. I tried to regulate my breathing, but my body was reacting like it always did whenever he and I were in the same space. And as if he could sense the change happening in me behind the barrier between us, Weyland's low eyes glided over to my door and right to the small hole I was looking through. I tried to move just in case he could see me, but my feet weren't fast enough. The loud knock that rattled against the door vibrated on my forehead before Taren pulled me back from my spot and placed her hand on the knob.

"Bitch, get your shit together," she whispered through clenched teeth. "Don't let this nigga see you sweating him like that or he's going to think you're crazy."

I absentmindedly nodded my head and stepped farther away from the door, trying to calm my nerves. I accidently bumped the back of my thighs into my end table, knocking over the ashtray with our blunt roaches in it, but I didn't care. Looking down at the strapless jersey jumpsuit I was wearing, I prayed that this casual but comfy look still warranted that bottom lip tuck and look of appreciation from Mr. Michaels. He seemed to enjoy me showing any ounce of skin. Stretch marks and all.

So consumed in my thoughts, I didn't see or hear when Taren opened the door and greeted Weyland and his friend. Nor did I realize she had invited them in. It wasn't until I felt a nudge in my rib cage from Jalisa that I snapped out of my stupor and finally spoke. "Hey."

"Hey," he returned. His eyes swept over my entire frame from head to toe. He walked farther into my apartment, stopping directly in front of me. When that bottom lip was pulled into his mouth, and that lustful glint appeared in his eyes, my insides started to go crazy. "You look beautiful as always." His finger caressed my bare shoulder, and I shivered.

"Thank you. You don't look so bad yourself."

He nodded his head and then turned his attention back to my friends, but not before letting his gaze linger on my body for a few seconds longer. "Ladies, sorry for coming in and not properly introducing myself. I had to speak to the lady of the house first. But I'm Weyland." He shook each of their hands. "And this is my buddy Phelix."

We all waved and said hello.

Weyland turned back to me. "I was stopping by to hear how the new stove is working out for you and to see if you finally figured out when you would let me take you out on a date."

"Pardon me, ladies, but my boy came about a date," Phelix interrupted. "However, I came to see who wanna match one with me real quick. I've been smelling that fiyah the whole time I've been helping my boy move in, and I finally convinced him to let me take a smoke break."

My eyes grew twice their size when the words Phelix just said registered in my head. "Wait. You're moving in across the way?" I damn near yelled. Surprise was all in my tone.

Weyland's cheeks lifted, and those cute dimples started to show. "I am. The owners offered me the spot across the hall in addition to the salary they are already paying me. Something about wanting twenty-four-hour maintenance service on the property. My old place was getting a little too crowded, so I decided to move into this one."

I didn't know why I smiled so hard and wide. But I did. "That's cool."

He licked his lips. "Indeed it is. And now that you know where I live, how about carving out a little time in your busy schedule so that I can take you out?"

"Um, I would love to go out with you, Weyland. It's just—"

Jalisa cut me off. "It's just nothing. Siyah will be more than happy to take you up on that dick . . . shit," she swore and corrected herself. "I mean, date offer."

Weyland laughed at my friend's slip-up and turned his inquisitive eyes back to me. "So this Friday, we have a date?"

I nodded my head. "I guess we do. It'll just have to be an early one because I have a rehearsal dinner that I have to prep—"

Jalisa cut me off again. "No. Don't worry about prepping. I'll come over and help you get everything together. I got you."

I opened my mouth and shut it and then opened it again. "Well, I guess it's a date."

While Phelix and my girls sparked up another blunt, Weyland and I made plans for the dinner he offered to make at his home instead of going out next weekend. Once we agreed on a time and the choice of wine I would bring, we sealed the deal with a hug that had my whole body melting into his as soon as he enveloped me in his arms. The tantalizing scent of whatever cologne he had on was fucking up all of my senses. And when he pressed his soft lips to my temple and again on my cheek, I damn near melted into putty.

I can only imagine how it would be when we finally fucked. I made a mental note to stop by Victoria's Secret sometime next week to pick up a cute little set to wear underneath my clothes at dinner. The appetizer and entree were yet to be determined, but the dessert was going to be hot, ready, and definitely enough for him to get seconds of.

Weyland's Interlude

I didn't know what it was about Siyah, but the girl turned me on like no woman ever had. I didn't know if it was her smile, her scent, the way her hair framed her chubby face, or the way her body looked in the lace get-up she had on under the robe the first day we met, but I couldn't stop thinking about her ass for nothing. It got so bad with me having to see her that I would knock on her door every day when I would pass by just to update her on the stove or any maintenance situation.

We would chat for a few after the updates and end with promises of seeing each other in passing again. A couple of times she prolonged our little encounters by asking me to sample whatever new recipe she was working on, and I was always up for that. I mean, I loved every second of whatever it was going on between us, but I wanted something more. I needed something more.

My dick and tongue craved her essence, and I hoped she wouldn't have a problem allowing them a little taste. I wanted to do something special for her with the dinner I offered to cook for her this coming weekend. I just hoped all of my hard work would pay off and she would actually enjoy herself. The way that this night ended would determine where we went in the next phase of friendship: fuck buddies or an actual relationship. Either way, I was open to both if it meant having her for myself.

Chapter 3

Siyah

"Girl, would you stop stressing over your hair and out-fit? You look good," Jalisa expressed over my shoulder as she ran her fingers through my loose curls. "I don't know why you're tripping. Weyland's ass is already smitten with you."

"Smitten?" I shook my head and laughed. "Girl, what are you talking about?"

"Yes, smitten. The way that man looks at you . . ." She shook her head and groaned. "I would give anything to have someone as fine as him look at me in that way."

I applied another layer of my smoked purple matte lipstick and pressed my lips together. "How does he look at me?" I questioned, standing in front of the mirror and admiring the Versace-inspired shirt dress that hugged my curves and left very little to the imagination. I went to slide my feet into my flat gladiator sandals, but Jalisa kicked them out of the way and handed me the peep-toe thigh-high platform boots. "I'm not going to wear these to go across the hall. The sandals are more casual."

"Girl, trust me when I say the boots are a better choice. They lift your ass more and make your legs look hella long. You'll thank me later," she murmured as she fluffed my curls again and left my room.

Going with her suggestion, I slid the boots on and then looked at myself one more time before heading to the front of my apartment. Jalisa and I had been prepping food all day for the catering event I had scheduled for to-morrow. It wasn't until a couple hours ago that I started to get ready for my date with Weyland. I wanted to go over there with a nice pair of jeans and one of my off-the-shoulder sweaters, but Jalisa told me she'd kill me if I did. So here I was dressed for a night on the town just to go across the hall and eat whatever takeout Weyland ordered for the night.

When I walked into the kitchen, Jalisa was placing the tops on some of the plastic containers that had the gar-nishes in them and putting them in the fridge.

"So how do I look?" I asked, doing a 360 so she could get the full view.

A slow smile formed on her face. "Like a muthafucking snack. If that nigga doesn't try to dick you down tonight, something must be terribly wrong with Weyland's ass."

"Ummm. Ain't nobody said anything about getting dicked down." I popped a piece of pineapple in my mouth and moaned. I'd been eating these damn things all day. "I'm just going over there for a nice dinner and to get to know my neighbor a little more."

"Girl, stop playing. You better get to know that nigga while his face is in between your thighs or his tongue is down your throat. We all seen the chemistry between the two of you last week. That sexual attraction was so thick we could cut it with a knife." Jalisa pointed at the time on the stove, letting me know that it was time for me to go. "If that man offers you some dick instead of a five-course meal, Siyah, you better take it. I know you ain't hard up for the D or anything like that, but have a little fun for me and yourself, okay?"

I grabbed my keys off of the counter after eating anoth-er piece of pineapple and headed for the door. "See, this is why I don't hang around with you like that. Your ass always trying to offer up someone else's pussy and not yours."

Jalisa had been celibate for the last three years. After she divorced her cheating ex-husband and kept running into the same trifling-ass niggas while she was dating, she decided to take a break from sex and committed relationships all together. Something about wanting to find and love herself first before she tried to love another.

"Quiet as it's kept, I might be offering up some of this good good in a minute."

"With who?" I stopped in my stride and turned toward her, my eyes wide and my mind running with who she could be possibly thinking about giving it up to. I raised an eyebrow, hoping she would continue, but she waved me off and pushed me out the door.

"We'll talk about my love life after you call me tomorrow morning with all of the juicy details of your night with Weyland. Tell him I said what's up, and your ass better not try to find an excuse to turn in early. We prepped all the food for tomorrow and packed all of your shit in your truck already." Jalisa grabbed my keys from my hand and locked the door. "Siyah, just enjoy your night. And don't overthink anything. I know how you get when it comes to someone you like."

"But I don't—" I tried to protest, but she raised her hand, cutting me off.

"Bitch, don't even try it. As much as you talk about him, you like this nigga. Plus I heard the feeling is mutual. Phelix said Weyland talks about you a lot too. We both agreed that this date between y'all was well overdue."

I nodded my head in agreement until what she had just said registered with my brain. "Wait, you talked to Phelix? When did that happen?"

Although Jalisa's skin was the same mocha tone as mine, I could still see the blush that rose up on her cheeks.

"Like I said, I'll tell you about my love life later." She stepped around me and knocked loud and hard on Weyland's door. "Right now, I need you to get ready to give this maintenance man something to fix." And with that, her tall, lanky frame ran down the hallway, disappearing as soon as she hit the corner.

I only had about fifteen seconds to get my whole attitude together before Weyland opened the door, and when he did, my knees buckled, and my throat went totally dry. Because of his busy schedule and mine, we really didn't get a chance to see each other much in the last week. A few quick glances and waves, hi and bye, were the extent of our interaction. Now he was standing in front of me, looking like the Beard Gang president himself. He was dressed in a black wife beater that hugged his muscled chest and showed off his well-defined and tattooed arms.

I nervously licked my lips at the energy I could feel emanating from him to me. My eyes scanned down to his narrow waist and then down to the gray joggers he had on that did little to hide the thick bulge lying against his thigh. His normal footwear was replaced by a pair of Nike slides with the Nike crew ankle socks.

Weyland cleared his throat, and my eyes immediately went back to his face. His beard was a little thicker than the last time, but it was still neatly trimmed and cut to perfection. That bottom lip was pulled into his mouth as he scanned me from head to toe as well. He swung the dish towel in his hand over his shoulder and stretched his hand out to me. Just like the missing piece to a puzzle, I placed my palm in his, and the fit was just right.

"You look beautiful as always," he whispered in my ear before pressing his soft lips to the back of my hand.

At that moment, I had already made up my mind that I was going to be fucking his fine ass tonight.

"Dinner is almost ready." He removed the wine I forgot I had brought from under my arm. "Let me go get two glasses so we can open this up and have a few sips before we get started. Come on in and make yourself at home. I'm still in the process of moving in and turning this into a suitable living space, but you're in good hands."

I crossed over into his apartment and didn't know what to expect. But once my eyes landed on the open loft floor plan and the ginormous chef's kitchen, I totally fell in love. "So this is how the new lofts look on the inside? This is nice. Wish they had this option when I moved in."

With my hand still intertwined with his, he pulled me farther into his home, where he took me on a little tour of the open space. "This is actually just how my loft looks. The others aren't as swanky as this one. After knocking out a few walls and redoing these walls with the brick overlays to give it that Upper Manhattan vibe, I think I get the feeling of home."

"Home being New York, right?" I remembered from one of our conversations.

"That's correct. Harlem to be exact."

I nodded my head and continued to follow him, taking in the emerald green, wheat, and gray color scheme that surprisingly didn't clash with the burgundy in the brick wall overlays.

"Oh." I stopped when we made it back to the living room area, where I noticed a stack of canvas paintings against an end table. "You're a fan of Black Rain? I love his work. I have a few of his pieces on my wall right now."

"I know. I saw them that night I came to fix your stove."

"I wish I could get the second painting for the *Torn Heart* piece that he did. But I heard he hasn't created it yet. Something about not having the right muse."

Weyland let go of my hand and walked into his kitchen, where he checked on something in his oven. I couldn't tell what it was, but it did smell heavenly. As I bobbed my head to Ella Mai's song "Boo'd Up," I continued to thumb through the rest of the paintings, stopping on a blank canvas.

"You paint or something?" I asked over the music.

Weyland's eyes caught mine, and he smiled. "Why do you ask?"

I pointed to the blank canvas. "Because you have this. I don't know too many people who have these in their home if they don't paint. I mean, unless you're—"

"Aren't you supposed to be here to have dinner?" he questioned, cutting me off. A mischievous look was on his face. "I promise we can talk about Black Rain and anything else you like once I fill that stomach." He held a glass of the Moscato out. I walked over to where he stood, and I took it. When I tried to look at what was inside of one of the pots, he hurriedly put the lid on. "Not yet. I wanna see how good that palate of yours is while we're eating."

"What do you mean?"

Weyland spun me around so my back was to his front and pulled my body into his. All thoughts of whatever we were just talking about got pushed to the back of my mind. His arm snaked around my waist. His large hand fanned out on my belly in a possessive manner. When his nose grazed my neck, I moaned. The soft hairs of his beard tickled my skin as he made a trail from my collarbone to that sensitive spot behind my ear.

"God, you don't know how bad I wanna bend you over this center island and feel how tight and warm your pussy is. I promised myself that I'd pace myself, so I'm going to try my hardest to do that. I just need you to stop moaning like you just did or else I'ma say fuck this dinner and give you a real reason to make that type of sound."

The levee between my thighs broke at his words, and I could feel my panties dampening by the second. "I . . . I'm sorry. I'll try not to moan like that again."

I could feel his smile against my neck. "I didn't say you couldn't make that noise. I just want you to hold off on it for right now. Can you do that for me?"

I feverishly nodded my head and finally swallowed the lump in my throat, silently responding to him.

"Now I need you to take a seat for me right here and close your eyes."

I moved to walk toward the cute two-seater bar table in the corner of the kitchen when Weyland grabbed my arm and pulled me back. His strong hands went around my waist. He hoisted me onto the countertop, to my utter surprise, and positioned himself between my thighs. The gentle strokes of his fingers caused goosebumps to decorate my skin.

"Keep your eyes closed and open up for me."

Instinctively I opened my legs wider, and he chuckled. Weyland's hands moved to the middle of my thighs. His thumb skimmed over the crotch of my panties. "As delectable as I know this is, I was talking about opening your mouth." He kissed the top of my thighs. "We'll get to that later."

At that admission, my mouth dropped and in return was filled with something sweet, savory, and moist. Weyland's soft lips kissed away any crumbs that managed to fall onto mine as I chewed on whatever it was that he fed me.

"Oh my God. What is—"

He silenced me with a kiss to my lips. "Shhhh. Don't talk. Just taste."

With my eyes still closed, I nodded my head and opened my mouth for whatever was coming next.

"Good girl," he whispered in my ear after placing a second helping of the delicious appetizer in my mouth. I sucked his fingers after taking it all in, and he groaned. "Now can you tell me what I just fed you from only being able to experience the taste alone?"

For the next forty-five minutes, Weyland continued to feed me samples of the meal he prepared for me while I tried to figure out what it was. I enjoyed every second of the guessing game and damn near got every one right, too. From the peach and prosciutto crostini appetizers to the creamy lobster bisque soup and coconut shrimp with piña colada dipping sauce. Weyland surely outdid himself, and I was even more attracted to him now that I knew he could cook damn near better than I.

I was still sitting on his counter with my third glass of wine as I watched him wrap up the leftovers and then clean up the mess he'd made in the kitchen. My boots had already been stripped off courtesy of him, and my mood was on relaxed, full, and chill.

"So what do we do now?" I inquired, wanting to know what else he had planned.

Weyland placed the last dish in the dishwasher and then turned around to me. His arms crossed over his chest, and his legs crossed at the ankle. That bottom lip was pulled into his mouth, and his eyes were real low. I chanced taking a quick glance down at the front of his joggers, and just as I suspected, his dick was still lounging against his thigh but was far from being asleep.

"Come here," he demanded in a low whisper. When I didn't move, he stood from his relaxed state and walked over to me. He positioned his body between my legs. His dick was heavy and hard against my inner thigh now. I downed the last of my wine and placed the glass on the side of me.

Weyland's eyes went to the top of my exposed breasts. My chest was heaving up and down. He placed his hand over my heart, and instantly my breathing began to slow.

When his eyes scanned back up to my face, they locked in on my lips, and subconsciously I stuck my tongue out to wet them. Before I could retract it, Weyland gently grabbed it with his teeth and pulled it into his mouth.

The kiss started off slow at first, but after my knocking the wine glass over and not giving a fuck that it shattered over the floor, our connection deepened and so did my nails in his arms. Before I had a chance to suck in some air, my body was pushed back on the counter, and my shirt was ripped open. Buttons sounded like BB gun shots as they hit the different surfaces. With my head hanging over the edge and my legs up in the air, my panties were next to go. A low but masculine moan escaped from Weyland's throat as he nuzzled his face in my pussy, inhaling my scent. His big hands splayed across the back of my thighs, motioning for me to open up.

"Good girl," he praised once I did. I took in a deep breath and closed my eyes, ready for what I knew what was about to happen next. His cool breath blew against my clit, and my body shuddered. When the tip of his thick tongue began to snake its way through my folds, I knew I would be in for the fuck of my life.

As soon as he found my clit and pulled it into his mouth, my back arched and my eyes shot open. I stared at the ceiling. Horseshoes, moons, stars, and purple balloons began to blur my vision as he gently bit, sucked, and licked my pussy until I came in his mouth and on his beard three times. His tongue was still assaulting my shit when that tingly feeling started to build at the tip of my toes and travel through the rest of my body. This orgasm was going to be big and well deserved.

Weyland's tongue didn't stop thrashing against my clit for a second. He wanted it, and he was going to get it. His arms circled my thighs tighter, trapping me in his hold. His grip on my inner thigh dug deeper. I raised my hips to feed him more, and he took it all in, lapping up every ounce of juice that dripped on his chin and lips. My heart rate picked up, and my body started to tremble. My back arched and my hands grabbed whatever I could hold on to anchor this orgasm.

After a few more pulls and twirls of his tongue, my body ascended higher into the air, and I released every month of pent-up sexual frustration that was inside of me. The second I felt my eyes getting wet and the tears falling down the side of my face, I knew that I was going to fall in love with this man. I blacked out for a few seconds and came back to after my body began to descend. When I opened my eyes, I was greeted with the sexiest sight I'd ever seen. My essence was all over Weyland's face, accompanied by a small smile. His dimples went in and out every time his lip twitched.

I opened my mouth to say something but gulped in a large amount of air instead when the head of his dick pressed against my entrance.

"Now that that craving has been satisfied, let's move on to the next," he unabashedly said, his large frame hovering over mine. That intoxicating scent of his added to the deliriousness I was already experiencing.

"You . . . you don't want to take a break or move this to your bed?"

He chuckled. I could feel his chest against mine. His heart was beating just as wildly as mine. "We'll eventually get there." It was all he said before pushing inside of me and burying his dick to the back of my throat.

Chapter 4

Siyah

"Ahhhhhh," I loudly moaned. Pure bliss rummaged through every part of my body. Weyland was by far the best sex I'd ever had, and I was already thinking of where I wanted to get his name tatted. "Damn, baby. Right there. Keep hitting that spot right there."

Both of our bodies were covered in sweat. The ceiling fan above his bed was on, but the raw heat between us would not allow any ounce of the coolness flowing from it to touch our skin. Weyland gently pushed my hips down onto the mattress. His strong, wet, and muscular frame now covered my whole back side as his dick slid into my pussy from behind.

My walls instantly clung to his shit, not wanting to let go. Weyland's stroke in this position started out slow and sensual as he sank his teeth into my shoulder blades with every thrust, but the hornier he got, the faster his hips started to move. When he placed his hands on the dip in my back to balance himself and began to kill my pussy with his hard and deep plunges, I could feel a gush of my juices saturating his dick and balls. The smacking sound our bodies made as they collided together mixing with the smooth beat of Mila J's song "Friend Zone" was music to my ears.

I tried to lift my hips to allow him more access, but instead, I was pushed back into the mattress with a swift strike to the ass. The sting did something to me, causing another tidal wave of juices to release from my gates.

"Fuuuuuck," Weyland moaned in my ear. "Your pussy is golden, Siy."

I didn't know why my heart started to flutter, but it did at his words. The raw passion in his tone let me know that he was enjoying my feel just as much as I was enjoying his.

Without breaking our connection, Weyland rolled to his side, landing on his back and placing me in reverse cowgirl. This wasn't my favorite position, and I kind of felt he sensed it when my body stilled and my hips barely began to roll.

"Relax baby." He patted my ass. "Just move your body to the beat."

I closed my eyes and rolled my head back. My arms stretched out and gripped his strong thighs. Chanel Sosa's "Dig That" now flowed through the speakers:

> Come a little closer if you're nasty
> Make you wanna rub right on this fatty
> Put it on your tongue like a shot of that D'usse
> A couple more shots, got the boy getting loose
> (God damn)
> We ain't gotta talk about, when I get you in the room we gone work it out
> Bell ring, knock ya down

I slowly started to wind my hips. The music was flowing through me as if I were a part of the actual composition. A low, throaty moan followed by fingers digging deeper into my love handles let me know that Weyland was loving the way I bounced my ass to the rhythm. When I doubled down and bucked my ass to the drum machine's pulsation, Weyland grabbed my waist and held me down on his dick. The fat mushroom head of his manhood was throbbing against my walls as he filled the condom with his third round of nut.

He smacked me on my ass after a minute or two of getting himself together. "Don't ever doubt yourself, baby. You got this."

"Yeah?" I inquired as I reversed my position on the bed so that I was lying next to him face-to-face.

Weyland smiled, and I couldn't help the silly grin that formed on my face. He tapped my nose with his finger and then kissed my forehead. "You hungry? I can go whip us something up real quick."

I looked at the time on his TV and shook my head. It was already a little after two in the morning. "I think I need to be heading home. I got an early morning and only a few hours to get some sleep."

His face turned serious. "You can always just stay here. I don't mind sharing my bed with you, and anything else I have for that matter." Weyland's eyebrows furrowed as he stared down into my face. "Did I say something wrong? Why did your facial expression change?"

It was funny how he could read me so easily now that we had been intimate with one another. Although I felt as if I could tell him anything and not scare him away, I still wanted to tread lightly with what I did say, just in case my intuitions about him were wrong.

"No. You didn't say anything wrong. I just—"

"You just what?"

"I . . . I just didn't want to overstay my welcome, that's all. I mean, although we just had sex, we're still getting to know each other." I shrugged my shoulders. "I don't know if you like to cuddle after fucking my brains out or want to be left alone to collect your thoughts."

Weyland snorted, and a low chuckle followed. He licked his lips and pulled my body closer into his. One arm was securely wrapped around my neck, while the other was desirously gripping my side.

"If I didn't want you here, I would've never invited you," he whispered into my neck. "And now that I have you here, I don't know if I want to ever let you leave again."

I giggled uncontrollably as the fine hairs of his beard tickled my skin the same way his tongue did as he licked the delicate spot between my shoulder and neck.

"As much as I wouldn't mind being held captive by you and"—I reached down between us and gently started to stroke his semi-erect dick—"my new best friend right here, I have to go handle some last-minute prepping and then get ready for my day."

"But I thought Jalisa helped you with all of that earlier," he said as he sat up on his side of the bed. The muscles in his back flexed each time he moved to slip back into his joggers. When he stood up to finish getting dressed, I couldn't help but to take a sneak peek at the rest of the tattoos that covered his chocolate frame. Weyland noticed what had my attention when I didn't respond to his question, and he smirked when our eyes connected. He cleared his throat and then flopped back onto his bed, pulling me into his strong arms again. "So you just gon' stare at me and not answer my question?"

I wiggled out of his hold. "I was going to answer. I just became a little distracted."

He kissed the lower part of my back and stood back up. Grabbing his phone off of the dresser, he scrolled through his missed calls and texts. After a few seconds of looking through his messages, he pressed a few buttons and then placed the phone to his ear.

"Yeah, man, what's up?" He nodded his head. He looked my way. "Sorry about that. I was kinda in the middle of something, and it was hard for me to get away." Weyland winked his eye at me, and I blushed. "Nah, did he say if it came back on?" he questioned, walking over to his kitchen and grabbing two waters out of the fridge. His joggers hung low on his waist, revealing that sexy-ass V shape and his slightly defined abs. He opened one of the bottles and handed it to me. "Okay, well, I'll call his number on file and see if he still wants me to come now or wait until later in the morning. Oh, okay. Thanks, man, I'll see you in a few."

After releasing the call, he went to his closet and pulled out his work shoes and a T-shirt.

"Emergency call?" I asked. I grabbed my boots from his couch and my keys from his counter, avoiding the broken glass still on the floor.

He nodded his head. "Yeah. One of the new tenants downstairs has been having problems with his pilot light going out and the outlets in his master bedroom not working. It wouldn't be so much of an emergency if he didn't need the hot water and outlets to be working properly for his elderly father he takes care of. So I'm gonna go down there and check it out after I walk your sexy ass home."

I laughed as I headed for the door. Weyland was right on my tail. "I only live across the hall. What could possibly happen in three steps?"

Weyland grabbed my arm without warning and spun me around. My back pushed roughly yet playfully against his door. With a light grab of my neck, he placed his lips over mine and kissed any words that I had left out of me. Not wanting him to break our lip lock any time soon, I grabbed his beard and pulled him deeper into my hold. My body was already responding to his and welcoming his soft touches on my breasts and ass. The shit was just getting better when the sound of his vibrating phone broke the spell that we were both in, ending our kissing session. Weyland rested his forehead against mine and kissed the tip of my nose before pulling me into one last hug and unlocking his door.

"I already know that's the owner calling my phone to tell me that the tenant called again. Let me get down here and handle my business." He pecked my lips. "Can I see you later today?"

I slowly nodded my head against his. "Yeah. I'll just call you when I get home."

He opened his door and let me walk out first. "You do that." After locking his shit up, he turned and watched me unlock my door. "You get some rest and text me when you get to where you're going. I wanna hear about your day and everything, okay?"

I bit my lower lip and nodded my head. "Okay. I guess it's good night then?"

"Good night."

"See you later."

Those small indents formed in his cheeks. "Indeed you will. Same place, same time."

With one last look, I waved bye to Weyland and walked into my apartment. His intense gaze was still lingering. I closed and locked the door behind me and pressed my forehead gently against the frame.

"Jesus," came out in a whisper as I released the breath I'd been holding since we walked into the hallway. "That man, that man, that man."

When I thought enough time had passed for Weyland to be gone, I stood on my tiptoes and looked through the peephole just to make sure he had left, but to my surprise, I looked right into his smiling face as he blew me a kiss and finally turned to leave.

I shook my head and smiled. *His arrogant ass surely can and will be the death of me,* I thought as I made my way to my bathroom to shower and then go to bed.

***

"So start from the top, and your ass better not leave anything out." Jalisa's loud voice rang through the Bluetooth speaker in my truck.

"There's nothing to tell, Lee. We ate dinner, had a little conversation, and got to know each other a little better," I mused as I turned into the busy lot of the event location that I was about to cater at.

"Wait, wait, wait, wait. Do you mean 'better' in the horizontal sense or 'better' as in you sat up all night talking each other's ears off and no tapping of the ass took place?"

I laughed at Jalisa's crazy ass. "I mean 'better' as in it's none of your business. Especially since you're being so tight-lipped about you and Phelix hooking up."

There was a slight pause before she responded, "First of all, Phelix and I are just talking. We did go out for drinks a few nights ago, but that was it."

"And?"

"And what?"

"And what else happened?" I pressed the key fob to open my trunk and got out of my car. Two of the facility's waiters were waiting for me at the top of the stairs and came skipping down to help once they saw me unloading my things.

"Nothing else happened. He and I are just getting to know each other. That's it, that's all."

I wasn't going to push her for more information because I definitely wasn't going to give her any more than what I did when she asked about my night with Weyland. After promising to meet up for drinks sometime during the week along with Taren and Dawn, I grabbed the rest of the things I needed from my truck and headed into the establishment. I was in the middle of garnishing the large platters of fruits and vegetables when my phone dinged with a text from Weyland.

Him: Hey, beautiful. Can I get a rain check on our plans for meeting up tonight? Something came up. I promise to make it up to you later.

I didn't know why, but after reading his message, my whole vibe seemed to change. No longer was I floating on cloud nine like I was earlier, but it felt more like I was just coasting at ground level now. I was so looking forward to spending more time with Weyland tonight and getting a few more rounds of that dopeness he had between his legs. However, I understood that things happened, and in this case, I had to be okay with spending time with him on another day. After going over what I wanted to say in return, I finally typed out my response and sent it to him.

Me: It's cool. Just know that my rain checks come with an expiration date, so you better come correct with your makeup game.

It seemed like it only took a second for him to respond.

Him: I always cum correct. If I'm not mistaken, you just got a front-row seat witnessing that a few hours ago.

Me: I did.

Which is why I don't want no muthafucking rain check for tonight, I thought. I wanted to add that but decided not to.

Him: I hope you're not mad.

Me: I'm not. Just a little disappointed. I enjoyed myself last night and had a lot of fun. Was hoping we could eat some of those leftovers and talk about that Black Rain collection of yours. How long have you been collecting his stuff?

I was impressed by the catalog of paintings he had. Some I'd seen before and some I never knew existed. I really needed to see about getting his Black Rain hookup. There were a few pieces that caught my eye and would have looked good on my walls, too.

Him: Still on that Black Rain thing I see. What if I told you I knew him personally?

I didn't know why I became so geeked.

Me: STFU. Do you know Black Rain for real? Please say that you do. I need a few of those pieces. I swear, I would give you anything for that hookup.

Him: Real shit? Anything?

I thought about that question for a second. This could go left real quick.

Me: Ummm, just about anything.

It took a few minutes for him to respond, but when he did, I let out the loudest laugh, causing some of the client's guests to look over at me.

Him: Go in the bathroom and send me a picture of those lace panties I know you have on. Give me something to fantasize about while I'm handling this business.

Everything in me wanted to take my ass into that bathroom and give him what he wanted, but the fact that I wore my regular comfy cotton panties today stopped that sext from happening.

Me: Maybe next time. I still got some setting up to do.

Him: Well, what about an audio clip of you moaning my name? I swear to God I could sit and listen to that sweet sound all day. The shit making me hard just thinking about it right now.

I blushed at that text and tried to steer the conversation back to a nonsexual one. I was still at work, for Christ's sake.

Me: I'm flattered and all that my moan makes you feel that way, but uh, let's get back to that Black Rain hookup.

Him: We can, and we will, after you sit on my face and feed me what I've been craving since you left. I can still smell you on my lips and taste you on my tongue.

Me: Bye, Weyland.

That was all I responded before placing my phone back in my bag. I had to end that conversation before I was walking around this joint with some wet panties and some sticky thighs. I'd for sure be using one of my vibrators when I got home tonight. I wasn't going to have Weyland there in the flesh to aid me in releasing this orgasm, but that didn't mean I couldn't imagine that he was.

Chapter 5

Siyah

"Stooooop, babe," I playfully hummed as Weyland turned me over onto my back and nuzzled his face into my neck. The heavy weight of his body was a comfort I'd missed since the last session we had about two hours ago. "I gotta get up in the morning to drop the girls off at the airport, if you forgot."

He stopped his assault on my neck. A mischievous grin was on his lips. "It's only one in the morning, Siyah. You aren't leaving until four, right?"

I tried to turn over to hide the smirk on my lips, but I was pinned down in my position once he dropped the rest of his weight on me. I could feel the thick head of his dick massaging my lower lips, causing a low moan to escape from my mouth.

"Umm hmm. You know you want me inside of you just as bad as I want to be inside of you." His soft lips kissed my chin and then made a slow trail of kisses down the nape of my neck. "Just open up for me for a few minutes, baby. Please. I promise I won't take too long."

Oh, shit. His ass was begging, and the good Lord knew how much I loved a begging man. However, as much as I adored it, I still wasn't going to give in. Weyland would have to say those magical three words to get me to forego these last few hours of sleep and let him pound my shit into the early morning.

"Is that how you ask for some of this pussy?" I ca-joled, turning the seduction on him. My legs were now securely wrapped around his waist. My arms were loosely draped around his neck. When he rose up to try to push into my love box, I arched my back, causing his dick to slide between the fold of my ass. The invasion of his girth was foreign to that part of my body, but it felt good as it lay there.

Weyland chuckled at my swift movement. Remnants of my essence were still on his breath from the last time we tangled in the sheets.

"You better stop playing before I take that hole back there. I like to dabble in a little anal from time to time." The seriousness in his tone let me know that he wasn't ly-ing, and although I'd never done anal before, I wouldn't mind trying it with him.

Instead of responding to what he just said and start-ing a whole conversation on ways to enjoy backshots, I pulled Weyland's face down to mine and pressed my lips softly to his. My fingers massaged the lower part of his chin underneath the silkiness of his beard.

"Tell me what I want to hear," I said between kisses. A small smile formed on my lips. "Say the words that let me know you really want this pussy."

Our kiss deepened, and somewhere in between our lips locking and tongues dancing with one another, Weyland managed to whisper those magical three words.

"I need that," flowed softly through my ear. His tenor was the sweetest melody I'd ever heard. As if on com-mand, my legs and pussy opened to Weyland, granting him access to his new favorite place.

"Shiiiiiiiiit."

"Bitch, if you don't stop daydreaming and wake the fuck up . . . It's your turn to play," Taren yelled. She snapped her fingers in my face and pulled me from my nasty dream.

"Girl. That nigga must've put it on your ass real good. You over here zoned out and shit. Moaning that nigga's name and giggling."

My face fell. "No, I was not."

Jalisa poured some more wine in my glass. "Yes, you were. We really weren't paying attention until it was time for you to play. When you started moaning and your hand started moving down toward your pussy, that's when Taren started yelling your name."

"You guys are lying."

Taren smacked her teeth and rolled her eyes. "What do we have to lie for? Your ass was straight about to have a full-on jack-off session right in front of us. What's up, maintenance man ain't hittin' it right anymore?"

I didn't know if I should answer that question. Yes, I ended up admitting to my friends that Weyland and I had some incredible sex, but what I didn't tell them was that it had been almost two weeks since we spent any intimate time together or just kicked it. I mean, I'd caught glimpses of him around the property or when looking out of my peephole after I heard his door open and close, but we hadn't spent any real time together since the night he made me dinner. We kicked it for a few hours that following Monday after, but that was about it. Even when I hit him up to come and sample a new recipe I was working on, he either was super busy working on a unit in our complex or at one of the other properties doing work there. I didn't want to believe that what we experienced together was a "hit it and quit it" situation, but something was definitely off, and I didn't know how to approach him on the matter.

For the next couple of hours, my girls and I enjoyed our game night playing Tonk, Pitty Pat, and a few board games while we caught up on each other's lives. Taren's crazy ass was the first to leave because she had to go to work super early, and Dawn left shortly after when she received a phone call from the new dude she's been talking to. I thought Jalisa would make her exit soon after that, but she ended up staying around and had a few more glasses of wine with me while we watched episodes of *Star* on Hulu.

"So what's really going on with you?" she asked, plopping on the couch across from me after using the bathroom.

"What do you mean?"

"I mean just what I said. What's going on with you? I can tell that there's something bothering you. You haven't been the quirky Siyah for some days now." She took a sip of her wine and then looked me dead in my face. "This change in attitude wouldn't have anything to do with Weyland, would it?"

I wanted to lie to her and say no, but Jalisa was the one friend out of the three who knew me better than anyone. "I haven't really spoken to or seen Weyland in almost two weeks. Besides the little sightings here and there, I'm starting to feel like he's purposely avoiding spending any one-on-one time with me."

"And why do you feel that way?"

"Because before we had sex, I would see him all the time. He was always at my door at my request or his, and it seemed like he always made a way to run into me whenever I was on my way to the parking garage or laundry room. But now?" I shook my head. "Nothing."

"Honestly, Siyah, I don't think it's any of that. From what Phelix tells me, Weyland is very into you. He talks about you more now than he ever did."

"It doesn't feel that way." And it really didn't. I knew all I had to do was open my mouth and ask him if we were good, but I wanted him to be the one to do it first. *Show some type of love toward me.*

Wait. Did I just say love?
Nah. Nope. My bad.
I obviously used the wrong word. I didn't love him. I couldn't. It was too early.

"Um, Siy. You okay?" Jalisa asked, and I nodded my head. "Did you hear what I just said?"

"No. What did you say?"

She gave me a weird look and then shook her head. "I said Phelix did mention something about Weyland working on something at night. Did he ever tell you about a second job or anything like that?"

I thought over the conversations Weyland and I had had and didn't remember him mentioning a second job. "No. I just know he does the after-hours emergency thing for maintenance, but that's it. Phelix didn't say if it was that, did he?"

She gulped down her wine and poured herself another glass. "Nah. I don't think it's that. Whatever it is, he's real secretive on the subject. I tried to ask him about it. Even offered to cop him a feel or two in exchange for the info, but he wouldn't give it up. Said when Weyland wants you to know, he'll tell you himself."

Now that right there really got my mind to wondering. What the hell was Weyland doing other than maintenance that he had to be so secretive about? *And why the hell does it seem like Jalisa knows more about my man than I do?*

Wait. Did I just say my man?
Again, wrong choice of words.

"Well, look, I gotta get out of here. I need to finish packing for our trip, and I need to stop by the store to get some things for my mom." She stood up from her seat and walked to the door. I followed slowly behind her. "Siy, before you completely write him off—because I know you—talk to him first. If you can't catch him outside, go knock on his door when you think he's home. I don't think he's trying to avoid you. I just think he may be real busy with work."

I smiled at my friend and gave her a hug. "I will. I mean, it's not like he doesn't text or call me. That hasn't changed too much. But this not spending time together thing, it's—"

"It's nothing. Like I said, just talk to him. I'm sure if you express your concerns, he'll do what's necessary to make you happy."

I nodded my head and gave Jalisa one last hug before opening the door and watching her walk out.

"Oh, and before I forget—" she started to say, but stopped when Weyland's door opened.

Both of us turned our attention toward his direction. A big smile was on my face, ready to see his fine ass block the doorway. However, that smile instantly turned into a frown when a chick who looked like Sanaa Lathan walked out of his apartment first, followed by a smiling Weyland. When his eyes landed on me, his whole expression changed.

The woman who was oblivious to our eye war turned around and kissed him on the cheek after giving him a tight embrace. "Okay, Wey. Are you sure you can't do that for me? I mean, I am the only girl in the world that you love."

He cleared his throat, his eyes still on me. "Uh. Nah. You already know I can't."

She pouted and hit him in the chest. "Why, Wey? See, you gon' make me call your mama in a minute. You know she's always been on my side. Oh, and speaking of mamas, you still going home in a couple of weeks right? Did you buy my ticket too? I haven't been to New York since the last time we were there. I'm so ready to go back. Even with the snow still on the ground and all."

Little Miss Sa-Not Lathan laughed and grabbed Weyland's arm. When she noticed his attention was not on her and on something else, she followed his line of vision and looked over at me.

Her eyebrow quirked. "Oh. I'm sorry. Were we being too loud? Wey and I tend to get like that when we go days without seeing each other." She patted his chest. "This man here. All work and no play. I don't even see why he does this maintenance job because with the—"

Weyland cut her off before she could finish. "All right, Trace. I think it's time for you to go."

"But I didn't get a chance to meet your new neighbor," she whined as Weyland gently pushed her down the hallway. "The way you two were looking at each other . . ." was the last thing I heard her say before she disappeared around the corner.

Jalisa turned her concerned gaze to me. "It may not be what you think, Siy. Phelix never said anything about Weyland having a girlfriend."

I rolled my eyes and chuckled. "What homeboy has ever ratted on his friend about having another woman? It's cool though. His relationship status should've been something I inquired about when I first agreed to go on a date with him. Now I see why our interaction with one another has decreased and our phone calls and text messages are done at booty-call hours."

"Siyah," Jalisa pleaded, but she stopped short when Weyland returned.

"Hey, Jalisa." He nodded at her and came to stand in front of me. "Hey, beautiful."

"Beautiful?" I smacked my lips. "Nigga, you can't be serious."

"Look, Siy, I'm about to let you guys talk. Call me if you need me," Jalisa said as she made her way down the hall.

Weyland stepped closer to me and tried to touch my face, but I moved it out of reach and stepped aside. My back hit my slightly closed door and pushed it open. I crossed my arms under my breasts. The spaghetti-string tank top I had on was doing very little to shield my pebbled nipples. My flannel pajama shorts rubbed between my thighs. If I rubbed them together any harder, I was sure I could start a fire. Against my better judgment, I turned my attention back to the man standing in front of me. When he pulled that bottom lip into his mouth and grunted, I knew that he could see my body's reaction to his closeness. My nipples pushing through the thin cotton fabric was pretty evident of that.

"Your scent is so intoxicating and alluring. I don't know whether I should fall to my knees right now and push that moist little pussy in my face or take you in my apartment right now and have you for dessert like last time."

I scoffed. As much as his words turned me on, I wasn't going to fall like putty into his mouth. This nigga just had a whole bitch come out of his shit. Her hair and makeup were still intact, but ain't no telling how long she'd been there to fix it.

"So who was that?" I questioned, jerking my head over to his door.

Weyland licked his lips and smirked. "I never pegged you for the jealous type, Siyah."

"I'm not." That was a lie.

"Then why ask who that woman was? You don't think you've made a lasting impression on me physically and mentally enough that I would still need to see other women?"

"I don't know what I've done, Weyland. However, according to your actions, I don't think it was much."

He tsked and shook his head. "You need to be more confident in yourself, ma. You have the key in your hands

already and you don't even know it." His slight New York
accent came out.

"The key?" I reared my head back. "The key to what?"
I blew out a frustrated breath. "Look, I thought we were
building something here. That night you had me over was
earth shattering and heart moving for me. I thought the
only thing that would change would be whose apartment
we spent more time in, but for some reason, it seems like
you've been pulling away. I haven't seen you since damn
near two Mondays ago. My calls and texts go unanswered
until late in the evening or ignored all together, and then
when you do decide to hit me back, it's during booty-call
hours. I mean, what am I supposed to think?"

It was his turn to rear his head back. "You're supposed
to know that I'm not ignoring you. You're supposed to
understand that I just might be busy at the times you hit
me up and I can't just stop what I'm doing and I'll call
you right back. You're supposed to perceive that I've been
feeling you ever since the first time I laid eyes on you.
Even with the face mask, no makeup, and an old robe
on. Hair still wrapped in a bonnet. You literally took my
breath away. I didn't even know the type of determined,
loving, funny, and caring woman you were until maybe a
week or two later, and still I was captivated by you." He
pulled my arms from under my breasts and intertwined
his hands with mine. "I'm not saying that I fell in love
at first sight, Siyah, because we still are getting to know
each other, but I am feeling the fuck out of you, and I
hope you're feeling me too."

Y'all, I was speechless like a muthafucka. Every part
of my skin was covered in goosebumps, and my heart,
pussy, and stomach had butterflies wildly dancing about.
Maybe I did have him all wrong, and maybe I should've
just asked him what was up like Jalisa said before assuming that he was pulling away. And maybe, just maybe, the

girl who walked out of his apartment was just a friend, and I had nothing to worry about.

I swallowed the lump in my throat and looked up into Weyland's eyes. Those beautiful brown irises were trying to tell me something, but my attention was momentarily taken away when ol' girl came rushing back down the hallway.

"Oh, Weyland. You forgot your underwear, deodorant, and toothbrush when you spent the night a couple of days ago. I forgot I had them in my purse to give to you, which was my reason for stopping by. Oh." She stopped talking when she realized the moment she interrupted. I couldn't read the expression on her face, but her eyes kept going from me to him. "What's going on here?" she asked, walking slowly toward us.

I didn't know why, but something in me broke a little after hearing that he had spent the night over at another woman's house. Another woman who looked like she was kind of hurt that she almost caught us kissing.

"There's nothing going on here," I reassured her after pulling my hands away from Weyland's. "He's all yours now."

"Siyah," he called, but he was met with my door slamming in his face.

Weyland called my name a few more times and even knocked on my door for a couple minutes trying to get me to come back out. But after realizing that I wasn't going to open up for him, he finally walked across the hall and went back into his spot. I wanted to look out the peephole so bad to see if Sa-Not went in too, but I decided to go take a nap instead. I needed to tune the world out for a bit. Hopefully, when I came back, Weyland would be out of my mind and life for good.

Wayland's Interlude

I stood on the outside of Siyah's door for a few more moments waiting to see if she would come back, but she never did. I didn't think Tracy showing back up would be a problem, especially after I had just finished expressing to her how I felt. But I could understand why she reacted the way she did. I should've just introduced the two of them to one another, instead of assuming that Siyah would see that there was nothing going on between Trace and me. Especially since Tracey was my little cousin. The only reason I spent the night at her house a couple days ago was because she needed my help setting up her new entertainment center and vanity mirror in her bathroom. By the time I finished everything it was kind of late, so instead of driving all the way back home, I went and got my gym bag from the car and stayed at her house.

I blew out a frustrated breath and finally turned toward my apartment.

Siyah's ass had a lot of learning to do when it came to me and the way I was when I was invested in someone else's time, feelings, and heart. She didn't even give me a chance to explain what had been going on these last couple of weeks and why I hadn't been communicating or spending time with her as much as I wanted to.

Believe me when I say I was feeling shorty something crazy. She was constantly on my mind. Her smooth brown skin, round, cute face, pouty, soft lips, and thick, curvy body would make any man weak at the knees, but it was that quirky laugh, giving heart, and strong ambition that attracted me to her the most. The way her face lit up whenever she talked about her catering business made me smile. The way she was so focused on building her brand and name made me want to invest in our future. I'd never met anyone as driven, funny, beautiful, and chill as Siyah, and I wanted her to see and know that what I was feeling for her was real. In my mind, she was the perfect package for me. My good one. My muse. I just hoped she allowed me to explain everything to her once she had enough time to calm down. I knew the task of getting her to listen to me was going to be a hard one, but I didn't care. To continue seeing that smile every day in her apartment or mine was definitely worth it.

Chapter 6

Siyah

I didn't know how long I was asleep, but when I woke up, the sun had been down for a few hours and the cool afternoon breeze had my whole apartment feeling like an icebox. I pulled my robe down from the corner of my bedroom door and threw it over my shoulders to try to get a little warm. After handling my business in the bathroom, I headed to the front of my apartment to turn on the heat.

Although I slept for at least five hours, I was still kind of tired and thought about turning back in for a few more hours. Not only was my body tired from the hectic week I just had, but all of this shit going on with Weyland was still weighing heavy on me.

For the first hour of me trying to get some sleep, I actually didn't. I lay in my bed, tossing and turning, trying to get his ass off of my mind, but every time I closed my eyes, those sexy lips, thick beard, bedroom eyes, and magic tongue kept popping in my head. Yeah, I was mad at him and hopefully over his ass, but I'd be lying if I said I wasn't missing him and the dick already. I had to be strong though and not give in to temptation and get over his ass. It was going to be hard with us living right across from each other, but as long as he respected my decision and space, I thought we'd be cool.

I was roaming around in my kitchen and had just dropped my peppermint tea bag into my favorite mug when there was a soft knock on my door. My first thought was to ignore it and let whoever it was try again tomorrow or another day, but something on the inside was telling me to go answer it. When the knock sounded again, I placed my spoon down on the counter and walked to my front door, tightening the strap around my robe a little tighter.

I looked through the peephole and didn't see anyone at first, but after a few seconds passed, a head full of salt-and-pepper curls came into view. Opening the door slowly, I made sure to keep my hand on the knob just in case I had to block whoever it was and slam my shit in their face.

"Good evening, ma'am," I addressed the older woman, who had the brightest smile on her face. "Uh, I think you may have knocked on the wrong door." Looking over her features, I didn't remember seeing this woman around the complex at all.

"Hey, deary. Sorry to bother you at this time of the evening, but I wanted to let you know that there was a big package at your door earlier. I knocked for about five minutes, but when I didn't get a response, I dragged it over to my house so that no one would take it."

I opened the door a little wider. "There was a package for me?" I didn't remember receiving an email stating that I had a delivery on the way. I did order some new travel containers online yesterday, but they were not due to be here for another couple of days. Maybe they shipped early.

She nodded her head and turned to walk down the hall. Her red knitted sweater matched the ruby red coat of lipstick on her lips. Small pearl earrings in her ear were identical to the string of pearls around her neck. I watched as she slowly shuffled her kitten heels toward the apartment next to me and opened her door. Two gray cats jumped out and began to purr at her ankle as soon as she pushed through. What I thought was going to be a small box that FedEx must've dropped off, unbeknownst to me, actually turned out to be a large-ass rectangular package that covered more than half of the old woman's body. She struggled to bring it out of her apartment, so I left my spot at my door and went and grabbed it from her.

She blew out a low breath. "I told you it was a big one."

I looked at the brown butcher papers and neatly tied rope around it. "I surely wasn't expecting this." I placed the package on the ground and leaned it against the wall. "Thank you so much for getting this for me. I owe you big time."

She shook my extended hand and then waved me off. "Oh, dear, you don't owe me anything. I hope you would do the same for me if I missed a delivery. By the way, my name is Nadine Ross."

"Hey, Ms. Nadine, I'm Siyah Daniels. It's a pleasure to meet you."

"You as well. I've seen you around a few times, but never got the chance to introduce myself."

I was shocked by that, because I'd never seen her before. Weyland told me that I had a new neighbor, but I always assumed it was someone young like me who worked a lot.

"Oh. Okay. Well, I'm glad we finally got the chance to meet. Thank you again for picking up my package."

She nodded her head. "No problem."

I turned to leave but stopped when she called my name. "Yes, ma'am."

She waved for me to come closer to her, and I did. Her small, beady eyes darted over my shoulder and then back to me.

"I may be a little overstepping my bounds here, but I think you should give that nice young man across the hall from you another chance. I've talked to him on many occasions, and whenever I bring up introducing myself to you or gushing about how beautiful I thought you were, his whole face would light up." I opened my mouth to say something, but she raised her hand to shut me up. "Now, he's never divulged the extent of y'all's relationship to me and didn't really have to, because the way you two look at one another told Ms. Nadine all she needed to know." She looked around her and then lowered her voice. "Don't you miss out on a good thing because you aren't willing to hear the man out, Siyah. Take another couple hours to get out of your feelings and then go get your man."

After her little speech, I didn't know what to say, so I just nodded my head, smiled, and headed back to my apartment. Once I closed the door, I shook my head and chuckled at her little feisty ass. Ms. Nadine was all right with me.

Placing the package on my dining room table, I went and reheated my tea, grabbed a few of my honey-butter cookies, and decided to open the small white envelope that was attached to the butcher paper. My name was scribbled on the front in small, neat lettering, and the back was sealed with a gold sticker. After ripping it open, I took the small notecard out and read the message that was written on it.

For you, my muse.
B.R.

"Muse? What in the . . ." I said to myself as I ripped open the wrapping paper, not caring that I had just created a big mess on my floor. The faint smell of turpentine got stronger the closer I was to opening my gift. When I finally discarded every shred of wrapping paper and turned over what seemed to be a canvas to face me, the air in my lungs stopped, my eyes bugged out, and I could feel moisture forming in my tear ducts. There in front of me, in my home, was the second piece of Black Rain's *Torn Heart* painting. I knew this much because the oil paints he used in the first were an exact match to this one. The shades and depths. The intensity in the stroke. The emotion in the woman's facial matched the ones in the broken-hearted . . . *Wait a damn minute.* I stepped back and really looked at this picture.

"No fucking way," I squealed after observing the beautiful painting a few seconds longer.

I didn't notice it at first, but the longer I stared at the naked woman holding a man's patched-up heart in the palm of one hand while a chain that kind of reminded me of a rosary with a key at the end hung from the other, I noticed that some of her features were similar to mine. The pouty, heart-shaped lips. Bright, almond-shaped eyes. Round, chubby face with the small scar above her right eyebrow.

Holy shit. This painting wasn't a similarity of me. It actually was me. My large breasts, wide hips, and thick waist. The pudginess of my stomach, the birthmark on my left thigh. He even captured the small blemishes on my skin from years of dealing with bad acne and the small tattoo of three hearts that I had behind my ear. *What in the entire fuck? Who could've done . . .*

"Nooooo. No." I shook my head in disbelief. "Noooo. He can't be."

I looked at the painting one more time and then placed it on my table. There was no way Weyland could've painted this. No freaking way. He must've called in a favor to someone who knew Black Rain and was lucky enough to be one of the first to purchase it. Yeah, that had to be it. Nothing about him screamed painter to me. Then again, nothing really screamed maintenance man either, but he was a damn good one.

I grabbed my keys and phone off the couch and rushed out of my home, stopping right in front of Weyland's door. Without thought, I started to bang on the hard wood with all of my might, hoping that he was home so that I could get some answers.

"Weyland," I called out after a few moments had passed. "Weyland, open up. It's me."

I stood there for another few moments, waiting for him to answer, and he never did. Just when I started scrolling through my contacts to call his phone, the locks on his door started to twist and turn. When he opened the door with nothing on but some stained cargo jeans that hung low on his waist, bare feet, and the sexiest scowl on his face, I literally died for two seconds and came back to life. "Chances" by Exit 21 was faintly playing in the background. The lights in his apartment were dim, and the smell of some floral fragrance filled my nose.

My eyes scanned his entire frame from head to toe, zeroing back in on his jeans. The same oil stains were embedded in the fabric of the canvas, mirroring the splotches on his pants.

"So you do paint," I finally said more as a statement once my eyes connected to his.

Weyland held up the paintbrush he was holding in his hand. "I do. But It's only a hobby."

"Only a hobby?" I shrieked in disbelief. This man's work was known all over the world. "Why didn't you say anything?"

He stepped out of his apartment, closing the door behind him. His large body invaded my space.

"Because I didn't want you to know at the time. Would you have really given me the chance to get to really know you if I told you off top who I was?" I opened my mouth to respond, but he laughed, cutting me off. "The answer is no. And you know it. As much as you talk about the paintings, our whole conversations would have been filled with questions about Black Rain and his work. But I didn't want that. Not from you."

"What do you mean?"

He wiped his hand over his face and licked his lips. One arm crossed over his chest while the other tugged gently on his beard. "I wanted you to get to know me, Siyah. I wanted you to get to know Weyland and not the artist whose work you adore, Black Rain. I wanted you to see my heart through my eyes and not through his."

I didn't know what to say or do. I was flattered, speechless, and excited all at the same damn time. I understood that he didn't want my love for Black Rain to overshadow my like for Weyland the maintenance man, and I was going to respect his wishes and not cloud him with questions right now. However, I did have one that I really wanted him to answer.

"The painting? Whe . . . when did you do that?"

A boyish grin formed on his face. His dimples peeked out. "I actually started on it about two weeks ago. Hence the reason we haven't kicked it in a minute. Once I get in a zone, it's usually hard for me to break out of it. I would do my regular job in the day and come home and paint the rest of the night. I knew it probably seemed like I was pulling away or distancing myself from you, but that was totally not the case. To make up for my absence I tried to send a text or call you whenever my mind would tap back into the real world, but I guess my efforts weren't as effective as I thought."

So that's why we hadn't been together since the last time. He was busy, in his element, painting a portrait of me. The one he saw as the healer of his broken heart. His muse. I swear, at that moment, I wanted to jump in his arms and kiss the shit out of him, but after the blowup earlier, I didn't know whether to thank him for the painting and go on with my life or take my chances and see if he was still into me as much as I was him.

Weyland must've sensed my apprehension, because before I could even form the correct words to say, he pulled me by the lapels of my robe into his hard chest and pressed his lips down on mine. It took only the tip of his tongue to trace the outline of my mouth for me to allow him in, and when I did, I swear every doubt I ever had in my mind about him disappeared in that kiss.

Not wanting to ruin the moment with frivolous conversation, Weyland continued to tongue me down with his intoxicating kiss as he pushed his door open and slowly led me into his loft.

My robe was pushed from my shoulders, as well as the spaghetti straps of my shirt. The only break in our lip lock happened when he peppered my jaw, neck, and chest with butterfly kisses until he reached my breasts. Weyland lightly brushed his lips against my nipple before drawing it into his mouth. The warmth mixed with the roll of his skilled tongue made my shit harder than what they already were.

"Wait," I moaned, caught up in the rapture of Weyland's masterful touch and feel. "Wha . . . what does this mean?"

"What does what mean, baby?" His deep voice vibrated against my skin. His mouth still lapped my erect nipples.

"For . . . oooooh, shit. For us. What are we?" I knew this probably wasn't the right time to have this conversation, seeing as people tend to say whatever sounds good in the heat of the moment, but I had to know.

Weyland's low, grunted laugh rumbled in his chest before he raised his head and whispered in my ear, "I can show you better than I can tell you. Stay right here." Our bodies parted, and I was already missing the building heat. His soft lips pressed against my forehead and then both of my eyes, causing my eyelids to fall. "Keep these closed."

I wanted to object, but I remembered the last time I was at his home and he told me to close my eyes. I smiled at the memory.

"Good girl," he said against my lips after pressing another kiss to them. I shook my head and smiled. Those damn goosebumps and tingly sensation zipped through my body.

I stood in the open area of Weyland's living room for what felt like two minutes before the sound of something being stirred rang loudly in my ear. The smell of chocolate invaded my nose, and the closeness of his body caused my body to react. Weyland kissed me on the forehead once more, followed by a sweet kiss to my nose. The tips of his fingers lightly caressed the areas of my frame his tongue would soon explore. I stepped out of my shorts and the rest of my clothes with his help. Completely naked now.

"What are you up to?" I asked when I felt him kneeling before me.

"You will see," was the only response I got before the cool feel of something wet being brushed against my body had me standing motionless. "Relax, baby," Weyland said in between kisses to my thighs. "I'm in my element right now and need you to be as still but relaxed as you can be. Can you do that for me?" I nodded my head, eyes still closed, ready for whatever was next. "Just a few more strokes and then I'm done."

Strokes? Was he painting on me?

My question was quickly answered when I felt the heat of Weyland's body on my backside, his lips low on my ear. "You remember when you asked me a few minutes ago what are we?"

I breathlessly answered, "Yes." Chest heaving up and down. Pussy thumping like crazy.

"Open your eyes."

I lifted my heavy lids, trying to focus on the mirror Weyland had to have placed in front of me. My heart was rapidly beating, and my palms were starting to sweat. Once my eyes were able to see straight, they immediately went to the white chocolate brush strokes neatly placed all over my body. The word "Mine" was written over and over from the tip of my chin to the top of my feet.

"Does this answer your question, baby?"

I angled my head to the side, admiring his work. "I'm yours?"

"Yeah, Siy. You're mine and have been since the first time I laid my eyes on you. The night we shared each other's essence with one another only solidified the connection I felt with you the second you opened your door and invited me in, but you've always been mine since day one."

Weyland licked some of the chocolate off of my shoulder, and I moaned.

"Can I have some of my pussy now?" he asked as he kneeled before me again, this time tracing the letters of his chocolate words with his tongue. When Weyland's lip reached the top of my love box, I fell into his arms.

"You don't have to ask if it's yours."

With a slick smile on his face, Weyland laid me down on the floor and made sweet love to me for the rest of the night.

Never in a million years would I have ever imagined that a switch-up in maintenance men would lead me to the love of my life. Although I adored the work of Black Rain and was super geeked about being his muse, I loved the heart, attention, love, and sex of Weyland Michaels even more.

The End

Meeting Noble Shaw

by

Johnni Sherri

Chapter 1

Imani

"Shit," I muttered, grabbing the yellow piece of paper off of my front door. I looked down at those dreadful words, FINAL EVICTION NOTICE, stamped in big black letters.

After being taken off the night shift at Miss Ruby's diner, I'd been struggling like hell to make ends meet. My rent was now ninety days past due, and I knew no matter how much I earned in tips this week, it just wouldn't be enough.

I folded up the piece of paper and stuffed it into my purse before jogging down the steps of my apartment. As soon as I stepped out into the cold, I zipped up my coat and began my daily walk to the bus stop. I lived in one of the roughest parts of Baltimore City over on the west side, but Miss Ruby's diner was way downtown. My car got repossessed sometime last year, so at this point, the bus was my only means of transportation.

I arrived at work exactly four minutes past eight, and as soon as I clocked in, I heard Big Will hollering from the back. "You're late, Imani!"

Rolling my eyes, I headed straight for the kitchen. As I grabbed my white smock off the hook, I could feel Big Will's eyes burning a hole through me. He was a short, burly-looking man, standing just over five feet tall but weighing nearly 300 pounds. He was dark skinned with a widespread nose and always walking around wearing a greasy apron. To some, he might have appeared intimidating, but to me, he was more of a nuisance. Since he was our "so-called" day-shift manager and the part-time cook, he was always threatening to have me fired. But I'd been there long enough to know that he handed out empty threats as often as he changed his funky drawers.

"You've got one more time to be late, Imani, or that's your job!" he warned as I brushed past him to head up front.

As I stood behind the front counter, looking at all the ticket orders, I heard the doorbell suddenly chime. As a burst of cold air entered the room, I looked up to see a tall man, with a rather long beard on his face, stepping through the threshold. My eyes carefully observed him as he came in looking to be seated. He first removed the cashmere scarf from around his neck before removing each of his black leather gloves. He wore a navy blue fitted suit with a black lapel and a pair of slick black shoes. Along with his height, his big, boxy shoulders and elevated chin made for a very powerful, formidable presence.

Karen, one of the other waitresses on my shift, was quick to greet him. She put an extra arch in her back to push out her full-sized breasts and even added an extra switch in her hips as she sauntered toward him.

I shook my head, seeing how desperate she was for a man, but as I allowed my eyes to roam over him once more, I couldn't blame her. The bearded fellow was more than fine. From the deep-set waves on the top of his head to the long black beard on his chin, he was easy on the eyes. His skin was a warm shade of caramel, and his sleepy eyes were low as if he were coming down off of some sort of high.

He followed Karen with his shoulders pulled back, striding as if he owned the joint. After being seated in a booth in the rear and placing his order, he sat reading the morning paper.

Karen hurriedly came back up and put his order in before coming over to me. "Girl, do you see how fine that nigga is?" she asked, trying to whisper. She leaned on the counter with her back toward him and her hand cupped around the side of her face, as if he were actually paying her some mind.

"Who?" I asked knowingly.

"Mr. Blue Suit in the back is who. I think he's the one who just bought that nightclub down the street," she said.

I gave a nonchalant shrug before grabbing a hot plate off the metal counter behind me. While delivering a plate of steak and eggs to Mr. Rooney, I allowed my eyes to wander to the back of the restaurant. I was only able to see the top of Mr. Blue Suit's head before Mr. Rooney caught me off guard and said, "And a cup of hot coffee, baby. If you have it."

Feeling like some sort of stalker who had just been caught, my eyes widened before I cleared my throat. "Ah yes, sir, Mr. Rooney. I'll be right back with your coffee."

As I walked back up to the front counter to get Mr. Rooney his coffee, I heard Big Will holler from the back, "Order's up!" followed by the customary ding. I looked down at the overstuffed omelet on the plate before grabbing the ticket from underneath. This was Karen's ticket, but as I searched around, of course she was nowhere to be found.

"Goes in the back corner," Big Will said, pointing from behind the kitchen window.

My eyes followed his stubby finger that sure enough led to Mr. Blue Suit in the back. "Oh, that's Karen's table," I quickly said, trying to get out of it.

"Go ahead and take it for her. She's on an important call in the office," he said.

Releasing a deep breath, I tucked my shoulder-length hair behind my ears then smoothed down my apron. After grabbing the hot plate off the metal counter, I reluctantly headed toward the back. As I came near, I could see that whatever Mr. Blue Suit was reading had him perplexed. He was stroking that long black beard of his with one hand while his low eyes studied the paper intently, moving from left to right.

"Ahem," I said, clearing my throat. Leering down, I patiently waited for him to look up at me, but he never did. Instead, he kept his eyes trained on that darn newspaper. *Who still reads the newspaper in 2018?*

"Steak and cheese omelet, sir," I said, trying once again to gain his attention.

Rather than acknowledging my presence, the arrogant bastard actually had the nerve to tap his finger down twice on the table. His head was still down, and his eyes were still engrossed with whatever he was reading. I didn't know why that got under my skin so bad, but it did, and before I knew it, I had plopped the hot plate down on the table and taken off.

As promised I went back and got Mr. Rooney his coffee and ended up serving one other table before Mr. Blue Suit finally left. The entire time he was there I didn't go back to check on him, not even once, which was totally unlike me. Although I hated my profession, I was actually good at waiting tables. The patrons who came in all loved me. So for this arrogant son of a bitch to pull me out of character pissed me off. However, when I finally did go back to clean off his table, I noticed that under the salt shaker there was a crisp fifty-dollar bill.

"Damn, he left?" Karen came up and asked. She made a little pout with her lips as she looked back at the corner booth that was now empty. She had been gone for nearly forty minutes.

"Where have you been?!" I asked a little louder than I had intended to.

"Girl, Andre's school called and said he's sick. I've been calling all around to see if I could get someone to go pick him up for me, but of course no one wants to answer the damn phone," she fussed.

"So what you gonna do?" I asked, continuing to count the money in the register.

"I ain't got no choice. I gotta go pick him up," she said.

All of a sudden she got quiet, which caused me to look up at her. She had her hands pressed together under her chin as though she were about to pray. "Pleasse," she begged, almost in a childlike manner. Her big green eyes just batted away as she swayed from side to side.

"Unhun!" I shook my head. "No, I'm not working your second shift, Karen," I told her firmly, already knowing what she was about to ask. Sure, I needed the money, but catching the bus late at night wasn't safe. Working the night shift was all good when I had my car, but now I just wasn't feeling it.

"Pleasse, Imani. You always talking about needing money, well, here ya go."

I thought back to that yellow eviction notice that was taped to my door this morning, and I sighed. "Fine."

"Yesss! Thank you, thank you, thank you," she said, giving me a hug. She took off so fast without giving me a chance to even say, "You're welcome." I figured she just didn't want to give me any extra time to change my mind.

At the end of the night after pulling a double that day, my feet were tired, and I was beyond ready to go home. Somehow keeping busy throughout the day allowed me to forget that I would have to walk four blocks at one o'clock in the morning just to get to the bus stop.

"Night, Big Will," I hollered in the back just as I was zipping up my coat. Big Will actually pulled a double with me and stayed to close up the place just so I wouldn't have to be there by myself.

As I stepped outside, the late January wind was whipping something fierce. I pulled my winter hat down tighter on my head and tucked my hands deep in my pockets to feel for my keys. After securing my satchel purse around me, I began trekking down the block, hearing loud music thumping from the new place on the corner. I looked up and saw a bright blue neon sign that read THE HEAT.

Suddenly I heard a man's voice coming from a nearby alleyway. "Aye, shorty, let me holla atchu for a minute."

I craned my neck to look down the alley, but it was so pitch-black that I couldn't see anyone. I could only hear the sounds of several men murmuring and laughing in the darkness. Petrified, my heart rate picked up speed, and I began walking faster. I was trembling from both fear and being cold at the very same time. Just as I was about to cross the street, I heard a car loudly honking its horn.

I turned to see some black spaceship-looking sports car with dark-tinted windows pulling up next to me. If I wasn't before, I was more afraid now than ever. Unfortunately, the light at the intersection had abruptly turned red, and I could no longer cross the street without getting hit. I stepped up, frantically pressing the crosswalk button as if that would magically make the traffic disappear. That's when the car rolled up a bit more beside me, and I could hear the buzzing sound of the window being rolled down. However, I dared not to look, keeping my eyes fixed across the street. My hands were tucked deep in my pockets, squeezing at the fabric as I rocked back on my heels in an attempt to keep calm and warm.

"Excuse me, miss," I heard a deep male voice say.

Without even looking, I knew it was coming from the spaceship, so I refused to even look that way. I just kept silently praying that the light would hurry and turn green.

"Excuse me. Lady from the restaurant," he said, finally gaining my attention.

I turned to see none other than Mr. Blue Suit leaning across his passenger seat. His low, sleepy eyes were peering up at me as the musical sounds of his radio floated out into the night's air. *So now you notice me.*

"I'm just trying to offer you a ride, ma. It's too late for you to be out here walking alone," he explained.

Shaking my head, I turned back to see that the light had finally turned green. "No, thanks," I simply said before charging across the street.

To my surprise, he slowly followed me in his car to the other side with his window still rolled down. "Look, I own that club right there called The Heat. I'm just a businessman. I'm not trying to hurt you," he explained.

Stopping in my tracks, I released a breath so deep a thick puff of fog instantly formed in front of my face. When I looked again, seeing those dark, sleepy eyes staring back at me, I turned to look down the street. Noticing right away that I had another three blocks to get to the bus stop, and probably an extra fifteen- to thirty-minute wait for it to even come, I twisted my cold lips to the side, mulling over the idea of actually trusting this bearded stranger. And just as I was about to turn his offer down, for a second time that night, a lone snowflake drifted down in front of me.

"Ugh!" I groaned, finally making my way to his car.

After opening up the car door, I slid down into the soft leather seat, instantly feeling the heat and smelling that new car scent as I dropped my purse down to the floor. In almost a matter of seconds, I began to feel self-conscious, realizing that I probably looked like death and smelled like a dirty refrigerator as I removed my hat and smoothed down my hair.

I glanced over at Mr. Blue Suit, who was looking at me like I had two heads. With one of his thick eyebrows raised, he smugly said, "I see you changed your mind."

"Well, it's starting to snow," I said low, as if that were good enough reason to bum a ride from a complete stranger.

He extended his large hand for me to shake. "Noble Shaw," he said before running his tongue across his dark pink lips.

Reluctantly, I took my right hand out of my coat pocket and shook his hand. "Imani. Imani Williams."

Chapter 2

Noble

"Where we going?" I asked, keeping my eyes on the road.

When she didn't answer, I looked over to see her sitting up all stiff in the seat. Clearly, she was uncomfortable, and for good reason, I must admit. But I just couldn't allow a little lady like herself to be out there walking alone this time of night. Although I could tell she was probably in her late twenties, there was so much innocence about her. Perhaps it was her wide set of slanted eyes with the wing-like lashes or that single dimple in her right cheek that could be seen without her even cracking a smile. Or maybe it was her soft little voice that she believed carried so much attitude, when in reality it came out just the opposite.

"What's your address, ma?" I tried again, speaking up a bit louder.

She cut her eyes over at me and began blinking rapidly. "Um," she stammered, taking a deep swallow. "1575 Northern Parkway," she finally said.

Not yet knowing my way around, I quickly plugged her address into my GPS and navigated my way around the city. Most of the ride was quiet other than the soft music playing on the radio and the windshield wipers brushing off the flurries of snow. Every so often I'd steal glimpses of her, noticing just how nervous she was. If she wasn't twiddling her thumbs and bouncing her knee, I'd catch her tucking that hair of hers behind her ear. She was . . . cute.

When I finally pulled up to the slum apartments, I immediately knew why she was nervous, or rather, embarrassed. It was now going on two in the morning, and there were dope boys and junkies hanging out in the parking lot and in front of the building's door. The dumpster that sat right up front was filled to capacity, so trash bags were starting to collect all around it. To make matters worse, it looked as though the cats and rodents had torn through it, leaving behind the trash to spill over in the street.

"Is this it?" I asked, hoping that she would say no.

I looked over, seeing that her cocoa-colored skin was flushed. "Thanks. This is me," she said. Without so much as a goodbye, she hopped out of the car, slammed the door shut, and ran for the building in a hurry.

With my engine still running, I sat and watched as she jogged through the falling snow, first making her way past the crowd of rowdy young men, all the way until she'd finally made it inside. For just a minute I sat contemplating whether I should go up and make sure she'd made it in safely. But after realizing that I didn't know which apartment door was hers, not to mention I didn't want to make her more uncomfortable than she already was, I threw my car back in drive. I took off back toward the inner harbor where I had been living for the past two months.

After a twenty-minute drive, I entered my security code and pulled into the parking garage. It had been an extremely long and grueling day at The Heat, and I couldn't wait to get into my bed. Just as I put the car in park and cut the engine off, I looked down and instantly noticed Imani's purse sitting on the floor. Sighing, I grabbed it up and hopped out of my Bugatti. I was so tired I could barely lift my feet off the ground as I trudged toward the elevator. Preparing for the second Saturday after the grand opening at The Heat had been hard work. The nightclub was actually doing better than I expected. In fact, it was just as good as the others I owned upstate, so I really couldn't complain.

Taking the elevator all the way up to the top floor, I entered my three-bedroom apartment, which was quiet and mostly dark. However, as I stepped in farther, I could see a low light glowing from my bedroom door. When I reached my room, my eyes immediately fell upon my Monday appointment, Brittani. After taking Imani home, I had totally forgotten about her. She was already lying back in the bed, buck-naked, with her thick thighs crossed one over the other. Next to her on the nightstand was a wineglass, and from where I stood in the entryway, I could see her red lipstick stained around the rim.

"Nice of you to finally join me, Mr. Shaw. You're late," she said in a teasing manner.

I carefully tossed Imani's purse down on the lone chair in the corner and began removing my shoes. As I peeled off my suit, I watched Brittani begin to play with herself, bringing each of her full breasts up to her mouth one at a time before taunting her hardened nipples with the tip of her tongue. Her freehand leisurely found its way down to her center and gradually began plugging its digits in and out of her with ease. Her eyes suddenly closed and her back arched up from the mattress as soft, sensual moans seeped from her lips.

"I see you're not gonna wait for me," I said, lustfully looking her over. I licked my lips as I took in the scene.

As though she were in some sort of a zone, she didn't answer me. She just kept pleasing herself with her eyes sealed tight, methodically working her fingers in her core as her mouth hung slightly ajar. The more I watched her, the harder my dick became, so I knew I needed to hurry up and jump in the shower.

After just fifteen minutes in the bathroom, I came back out to my room to see Brittani still spread-eagle on my bed. With a white towel wrapped around me, I walked over to get a closer view. Her smooth dark skin was flawless like melted fudge and played nicely against the smudged red lipstick on her lips.

While she was still pleasing herself, looking as though she were coming down from a euphoric peak, I leaned down and grabbed a handful of her long, black, curly hair. With just enough force, I lifted her head up off the mattress. And with my free hand, I removed the towel from around my waist, allowing her to come face-to-face with my long erection. Before I could even guide it in her mouth, she opened up and took in all ten inches, swallowing me whole as she snaked her wet tongue up and down my shaft.

Feeling that tightness already stirring in my groin, I grabbed the other side of her face and thrust my hips harder against her. "Shit, ma," I hissed.

Hearing me grunt and groan must have added to her motivation, because without warning she began humming and sucking on me faster. She twisted her hands around the base of me until she came to a steady rhythm, and my knees grew weak. I wasn't sure if it was because she just wanted to taste me or if it was because she'd already gotten hers, but either way, she was trying to make me cum faster than I liked. I needed to be in control at all times, and she knew that.

Grabbing the base of my dick, I pulled it out her mouth and slapped her hard across the cheek with it. "Slow the fuck down," I commanded.

"I'm so sorry, Mr. Shaw," she whined, batting her dark brown eyes. She stuck out her pink tongue and wiggled the tip of it as though she were desperate to have me back in her mouth.

"Nah, turn over," I ordered.

She turned around, and before she could even balance herself on all fours, I grabbed the sides of her hips and plunged myself deep inside her, punishing her in a sense.

"Ahhh," she moaned out loud, clenching the sheets.

Wrapping her long hair around my hand, I yanked her head until it was fully cocked back. I picked up speed, hearing our slapping flesh come to an unchanging beat. Gradually her moans turned into pleasurable screams until she abruptly went mute. Her muscles locked and contracted all around my dick at once, and within a matter of seconds, her legs began to quake. I slowed my pace, feeling the abundance of moisture collect between us.

"Ahhh fuck!" she moaned.

Leaning down, I softly kissed her back, allowing my beard to lightly graze the surface of her skin as she shuddered beneath me. Gently I reached under her, wrapping my hand around her throat and whispered in her ear. "Come ride this dick, ma."

I knew she was spent, but I didn't give a fuck. Slowly she nodded her head and got up from underneath me. When I lay back in the bed, she hurriedly climbed on top and slid down onto me with ease. It didn't take her long to start rocking her hips and moaning all over again. And before I knew it we were both cumming hard together.

After Brittani cleaned herself up and got dressed, I walked her up to the front of my apartment. I kissed her on the forehead with the promise of seeing her next week before seeing her out the door. I didn't do relationships, nor did I fuck random broads. I just needed one freaky woman who could be dominated and knew her place.

Currently, Brittani was that for me. She was one of the associate partners at the law firm I contracted with, and since our first encounter, she hadn't missed one Monday appointment.

That night as I lay in bed underneath the heavy covers, my mind drifted back to little Miss Imani. I'd already made up my mind that I would return her purse first thing the next morning before going in to work. For some reason the mere chance of seeing her face again made me smile, which was rare. After closing my eyes, I quickly dismissed all thoughts of her, allowing much-needed sleep to finally take over.

It was a quarter past eight the next morning when I entered Miss Ruby's diner. Thank goodness the snow from the night before had cleared, so I was able to get there with ease. With the purse in hand, my eyes immediately began to scan the sparse setting. There were only three customers seated, and from where I stood, Imani was nowhere to be found. But then I thought perhaps she was just working in the back. Of course, the short, busty girl from the day before was the first one to greet me. She was all smiles as she switched over in a flirtatious manner. She was a round little thing with big, pretty green eyes. However, her skin was much too light for my taste.

"That omelet must have been good. Came back for another?" she asked with a toothy grin.

"Is Imani here?" I asked, cutting straight to the chase.

Subtly, her neck jutted back, and her eyes widened with surprise. I assumed it was because I'd referred to Imani by her first name. "She didn't show up today," she said with a questioning look.

Straightaway that got my attention, and thoughts of me pulling off last night without seeing her to her door suddenly flooded my mind. "Did she call?" I asked, feeling my brow wrinkle with worry.

"No, but I think her phone is off. I'll probably stop by there toni . . ." Cutting her own words short, she cocked her head to the side and narrowed her green eyes. "Wait! How do you even know Imani?"

"Here," I said, reaching down into my pants pocket for a business card. "Give her this and tell her to call me when she comes in."

I walked back down the block with Imani weighing heavily on my brain. When I reached my office upstairs over the nightclub, I sat down at my desk and tried my best to get some work done. But it was tough. Throughout the entire day, I just kept staring at my phone, hoping that she would finally call, but she never did. And before I knew it, it was five o'clock and almost dark outside.

Before I got in my car to head home for the day, I made sure to pop back into the diner. The short, green-eyed girl was long gone, but the little squatty fellow in the back told me that Imani never showed up that day. After getting in my car and cranking up the engine, I pondered over the idea of swinging back by Imani's place. Not only did I want to return her purse but I also wanted to make sure she was okay.

I pressed on the gas, and before I knew it, I was headed back over to the west side. When I finally arrived at the Linden apartments, darkness had completely seized the sky. Right off the bat, before I could even get out, I noticed someone's entire life sitting out on the curb, from their living room furniture to all of their clothes and shoes. I was born and raised in the Bronx, specifically the Millbrook Houses, which was smack dab in the middle of the hood. So this scene was nothing new to me.

After getting out, I hit the alarm and headed toward the building I'd seen her go into the night before. Not only was the same rough crowd playing dice and talking shit out front, but the loud sounds of police sirens flying up and down North Avenue could also be heard.

Small clouds of smoke dissipated in the air and the potent smell of kush grew stronger as I came near. When I finally approached the building, all eyes suddenly turned to me. I was sure I stuck out like a sore thumb in my tailored gray suit, black peacoat, and black leather shoes, not to mention Imani's brown satchel purse that I was carrying in my hand, but I didn't give a fuck.

"Yo, you in the wrong neighborhood, ain't you?" one of them asked, causing a few others to snicker. They couldn't have been no more than 19 or 20 years old.

"Nah, B, I got the right one," I casually said, easing my way through the herd.

When I looked up the stairwell, I suddenly realized that I didn't even know what door to go to. Without giving it any thought, I turned back around and asked, "Aye, do any of y'all know Imani?"

Dude who had spoken up before cracked a sly grin. "Don't even waste ya time on that one, yo." He shook his head. "She ain't coming up off the pussy, I done already tried," he explained.

I let out a light snort before shaking my head. "Nah, I just need to find her."

"Her shit got set out today so . . ." he said, letting his voice trail off as the others around him all laughed again. "So if she ain't out here roaming these streets, she might be over at Nikki's."

Hearing that Imani was actually the one who got evicted and that people were laughing at her expense immediately pissed me off. I didn't know why I got angry, being that I really didn't know her at all, but there was something about this woman that compelled me. I just wanted to see her face to make sure she was okay. I wanted to be there for her.

"And where does this Nikki live?" I asked through a clenched jaw, trying my best to ignore the wannabe thugs who were turning her hardship into a joke.

"Apartment 17B," he said, pointing up the stairs.

Just as I turned to head for Nikki's, he hollered out behind me. "Aye yo?"

I craned my neck back around, seeing that same stupid little grin on his face.

"If you hit, make sure to let me know how the pussy is, a'ight," he said, chucking up his chin.

Shaking my head, I climbed the rusted metal stairs and looked for apartment 17B. When I finally found it, I tentatively knocked because I wasn't exactly sure how Imani would react to me being there, knowing that I'd seen all her shit lying out in the streets and that I'd hunted her down like some sort of stalker. But I had to see her face.

After one more hard knock, I heard the clanking sound of the door finally being unlocked and then unchained. When the door pulled opened, a wide-eyed Imani appeared on the other side.

"Noble?" she said with her voice slightly elevated from shock. "What are you doing here?"

Chapter 3

Imani

"What are you doing here?" I asked, completely caught off guard.

I looked him over seeing that he was standing there, dressed like the prince of Zamunda in his fancy black dress coat and gray suit underneath. While I, on the other hand, looked like hell. I had on an old purple sweat suit, and my shoulder-length hair was pulled back into a small straggly ponytail.

"You left your purse in my car, ma," he said, licking his lips. When I didn't respond, he said, "I swung by the diner on my way in to work, but they said you didn't come in today."

Suddenly, I got embarrassed when he mentioned my job, because I didn't even call out like I should have. Although I didn't have a phone, it was no excuse because I could have just used Nikki's or one of my other neighbors.

I swallowed, nervously tucking a straggly piece of hair behind my ear. "Oh, thanks. I was wondering about that," I said, reaching for my purse.

After he handed it to me, he just stood there, staring as if there was something else he needed to say. "Was that it?" I asked.

Stroking his long black beard, he tilted his head to the side and looked in the apartment behind me. "So you straight? You gon' stay here?" he asked, alluding to the fact that he was fully aware of my eviction.

My eyes instantly narrowed. "What are you talking abo—"

Before the untruth could even roll off my tongue, Nikki hollered out from the back. "Hell nah! You can't stay here. Lamont's gonna be home soon, and you already know I don't allow no other bitches around my man."

Rolling my eyes, I released a deep groan. "I know I can't stay here, Nikki," I turned around and said.

"Long as you know." She plopped down on the couch and began picking at her nails.

Although I appreciated Nikki allowing me to stay in her apartment that day, I'd be lying if I didn't say that she was as ghetto as they came. Her long blue weave had been left in beyond its expiration date, and her pointed nails were at least three inches long. Whenever she would talk, she'd use her nails as some sort of wand or tool to add emphasis. Not to mention she drank and cussed like a sailor.

When I looked back, Noble was still on the other side of the door with a sympathetic look on his face. "You got any family you can stay with?" he asked.

Hating that he pitied me, I sucked in a deep breath and allowed my shoulders to hike up. "I got one sister in Connecticut, but we don't talk like that," I said.

"I'm gon' put you in a hotel for the night."

My neck whipped back. "A hotel?" I asked rhetorically with my eyes suddenly constricting.

"Look now, y'all letting out my heat!" Nikki yelled from behind me.

Releasing a heavy sigh, I said, "Look, thanks for bringing my purse, but as you can see I gotta go." I tried closing the door on him, but he blocked it with his hand.

"Well, wait! Where you staying tonight?"

"I don't know. I'll find somewhere."

Before I could even attempt to shut the door again, Nikki came up behind me with her cell phone in her hand. "Look, Mani, I'm sorry but you gots to go. Bae just sent a text saying he 'bout to pull up," she said, putting the tip of her long nail between her teeth.

Closing the door in Noble's face, I walked back into her apartment. "Can't I just stay on the couch for just one night? You know I don't have any family."

She shook her head and patted her blue weave. "Sorry, boo, but you already know the rules. What about your girl? You know, the one from the diner?"

"Karen's got four kids and barely enough room for all of them," I explained.

After seeing the unconcerned look on her face, I quickly gathered up my things. It wasn't much, only a cardboard box that housed a few of my prized possessions and a black trash bag full of as many clothes as I could collect.

As I was headed to the door, Nikki had the nerve to shout out, "Call me and let me know you're safe."

I rolled my eyes and exited the apartment, letting the heavy door slam behind me. I saw Noble still standing there, waiting off to the side as I attempted to ease right by him.

"Give me that," he said with authority, grabbing the trash bag from my hands.

He followed closely behind me as I went down the apartment steps. As we walked through the crowd of knuckleheads loitering in front of the building, all eyes were upon us.

"Hey, how you doin', Imani?" one of the young guys named Peanut flirted and asked. No matter how many times I told him that I was too old for him, he never stopped shooting his shot.

"Hey, Peanut," I casually said, making my way toward the parking lot.

When I didn't see the black spaceship from the day before I spun around on my heels. "So where's your car?"

Noble clicked the alarm on his key fob and automatically ignited the engine of an all-white Range.

"Another fancy car I see," I muttered.

After opening up the car door for me, he took my belongings and threw them in the trunk. Once he got in the driver's seat and leaned back with just one hand on the wheel, he drove off with no questions asked. Things were quiet between us for most of the ride, just as they'd been the night before. But when we stopped at a red light down on Pratt, I turned in my seat to look out of the front windows, quickly observing that we were back downtown.

"I can't afford to stay at a hotel down here," I said. Noticing the red light reflect off of his handsome face, I waited for a response.

"It's already handled, Imani," he firmly said. His deep voice was emotionless as he kept his eyes ahead, focused on the road.

Discreetly I twisted my lips to the side after hearing him reference my name as though he actually knew me personally. Since I only had a total of $200 until my next pay, who was I to argue with the man? I mean, if he wanted to put me up in a fancy hotel for the night, then so be it. But as I mulled over the idea in my head a bit more, realizing that this man didn't know me from a can of paint, I knew I had to pose one question.

"Why are you doing this for me?" I looked over to him and asked.

He appeared to already be deep in thought as his fingers tapped against the wheel.

"I mean, I know nothing in this world is free. So exactly what you do want in return?" I continued.

Running his free hand down his jaw, he let out a deep sigh. "I don't want shit from you. I'm just trying to help."

I decided to leave it alone for the moment, thinking that perhaps, just maybe, I'd stumbled upon a kindhearted Samaritan. That thought lasted for all of five minutes, up until I noticed we were pulling up to a parking garage of an apartment building I didn't recognize.

With my hand on the dash, I sat upright in my seat. "Where are we? Where are you taking me?" I asked in a panic.

"Calm down. This is my place," he said calmly as if it were no big deal. After entering the key code, he slowly pulled in, whipping his car into a parking space with the one hand as his dark eyes remained forward.

My mouth fell open, and my eyebrows gathered together in confusion. "Your place? I thought you were taking me to a hotel."

Instead of answering me, Noble hopped out of the car and popped the trunk.

Feeling totally confused, I immediately got out behind him. "Why didn't you just take me to a hotel?" I asked again, seeing that he now had all of my things in his arms.

Since his hands were full, I pulled the trunk closed and followed him through the dimly lit parking lot. Although his long legs were moving at a fairly normal pace, it seemed like I had to speed walk just to keep up.

When we finally reached the elevator doors, he looked back at me and said, "Press the button."

I hurried around him and pressed the button just like he ordered, then I turned back to face him. "Why are you just ignoring me? Why did you bring me here?"

As if he'd been saved by the bell, the elevator suddenly opened, and he stepped in. Releasing a groan of annoyance, I got in as well as and pressed the number ten as he instructed. Now, I realized that at any given moment, I could've left of my own free will. I could've gotten a hotel room for at least three nights with the money I had. But

I'd be lying if I didn't admit that there was something about this Noble guy I trusted. Although his presence was commanding and powerful, his dark eyes were kind. And even though he always spoke in such an authoritative tone like he was daring me not to follow his lead, I could tell that he actually cared.

While riding up to the tenth floor, I allowed my head to just fall back against the wall. I kept thinking, *how did I let it come to this?* From the time I was 17 years old, I had been on my own, working one meaningless job after the other. I moved from Connecticut all the way down to Baltimore before I even turned 21, thinking that I was in love. When that all fell apart and my parents both died, I found myself with no one to turn to. And now as I stood here at 28 years old without a pot to piss in, nor a window to throw it out of, I couldn't help but cry. I began to sob uncontrollably, shielding my face with my hands from being caught totally off guard by my emotions.

"Imani," Noble said, speaking so low that I barely heard him over my own weeping. "Imani," he said again, only this time a little louder than before.

Wiping the wetness down my face, I looked over at him standing on the opposite side of the small space.

"Everything's gonna be all right, ma," he said, raising only his chin because his hands were so full.

Although he hadn't said much, his words somehow comforted me in that moment. I sniveled back the last of my tears and wiped my face once more before taking a deep breath. When the elevator finally chimed and the doors opened, he stepped out ahead of me. But when he realized I wasn't following him, he turned around, instantly seeing that I was still planted in the same corner I'd been in for the entire ride up. He said, "Come on," motioning his head in the opposite direction.

Just as all the other times he spoke, I followed his lead, and I walked through the carpeted corridor behind him. Along the way, I took in all the fancy sconces and mirrors hanging on the pearlized walls. When we reached the door, he tilted his head down and said, "Reach your hand in my pocket and get the keys."

Not giving it much thought, I slipped my hand down into his pocket, immediately feeling the warmth of his skin and firmness of his thigh. When my hand brushed against his long dick, an instant pulse thumped inside my groin, causing my skin to grow hot and flush all at once. Although I didn't think he even noticed, I felt ashamed of my physical response. Taking a deep swallow, I retrieved his keys and handed them over to him.

"Here, just give me the box while you open the door," I told him.

Instead of giving me the box, he set it down on the floor and proceeded to let us in. While he walked in ahead of me, I discreetly fanned my face because within the past five minutes I had gone from crying hysterically to being horny as hell. As soon as he hit the lights and I took my first step inside, I noticed just how nice his place was. From the exposed brick walls and bold color palette, all the way down to the slick mahogany floors, everything appeared to have been carefully chosen.

After dropping my things down, he took off his coat and hung it up in a small closet. "Let me get your coat," he turned to me and said.

I removed my jacket and passed it to him before allowing my eyes to further inspect his place. From where I stood, I could see the open kitchen, which had the prettiest white stone counters and most sparkly clean steel appliances. Then there was a long, dark hall in which I could see a bright light glowing from one of the open doors.

"Follow me," he said, loosening the tie around his neck.

As we walked down the hall, we came to a room on the right. He walked in and flipped on the lights, allowing me to see a queen-sized poster bed centered in the room.

"You can stay in here," he said, turning around to see that I was still apprehensively standing in the doorway. "Come on in, Imani," he said, summoning me with his hand.

As I entered the room, I looked around, noticing the purple bed linens and all the nice wooden furniture.

"You have your own bathroom here." He pointed toward the adjoining bath. "And there's fresh towels and soap in there already," he said.

"Thank you," I said sheepishly, feeling ashamed that it had ultimately come to this.

Chapter 4

Noble

It was Friday morning, and Imani had been staying at my place for the past four weeks. Although she tried her best to convince me that she'd be moving out soon, I knew she'd be here for a while. Truth be told, I actually liked having her around. Slowly but surely I was becoming very fond of her charming personality. Some nights she would binge on reality TV and talk to me about the cast as if they were her friends and enemies. Then other nights I would hardly see or hear from her at all because she'd be wrapped up in a good book and just wanted to read.

Another perk that came with her being here was her amazing skills in the kitchen. She would get up early each morning while I was at the gym and have a hot breakfast waiting on the stove when I returned. While I was used to eating takeout most nights, Imani made sure I now had a home-cooked meal after work. And not just any old meals. Her cooking was award worthy. In fact, the happiest I think I'd ever seen her was when she was working in the kitchen. It was definitely where she found her peace.

For the past three weeks, I'd even canceled my regular appointments with Brittani because I didn't want to make Imani feel some type of way. But after hearing the distress in Brittani's voice the last time we talked, I broke down and promised to see her this upcoming Monday.

Hell, I was a man after all, and I figured Imani would just have to understand.

After jumping in the shower and getting dressed, I walked over to Imani's bedroom. I knocked on the door, and since it was partially cracked, it creaked open, allowing me to look inside.

"Imani," I called out to her, but she didn't answer.

Entering her room, I immediately heard the shower water running. I glanced over in that direction and noticed that the bathroom door was also slightly ajar. Even though I would never admit it out loud, I had been attracted to Imani since the first day I saw her in the diner. I loved the creamy color of her brown skin and those thick lips of hers that I would sometimes imagine being wrapped around my dick. Not to mention her figure was banging. She was stacked like a Coca-Cola bottle with her curves in just the right places. So while I knew I should have turned around and walked out the door, curiosity got the best of me.

Stepping lightly, I walked up and gazed through the crack that was maybe three inches wide. Even through the fog, I could see Imani standing naked through the glass shower door. My eyes instantly began to travel down her mocha-colored frame, first taking in her apple-sized breasts and stone-hard nipples, which were a deeper shade of brown. As I took in her small waist, which led down to her large, round ass, I instantly felt myself becoming hard.

Slowly she poured liquid soap onto her sponge and gave it a gentle squeeze, allowing the thick white lather to cascade down the curves of her body. Oblivious to being watched, she gradually slid one of her hands down between her thighs and began playing with herself. It must have felt good to her because little by little her head dipped back into the water and her hand picked up speed.

Steadily, her mouth began to form an O as though she was right on the verge of an impending orgasm. It was faint, but even over the water I could hear her soft little moans. At that point my dick was throbbing so badly it literally hurt.

Then all of a sudden my iPhone started buzzing in the pocket of my pants. Completely startled, I jumped a bit before pulling it out. As I walked back over to exit her room, I declined the call in a hurry. After making my way down to the kitchen, I sat up at the bar and began scrolling through all of my notifications. First I saw a missed call from my brother, whom I left in charge of my other two nightclubs, and then I noticed a bunch of emails from work and IG requests.

After responding to a few emails, I heard Imani say, "Good morning, Noble."

I looked up, seeing that she had already begun busying herself around the kitchen again. She was wiping down the counters and washing the dishes from the mess I previously made. Grabbing up my glass off the bar in front of me, I got up and walked around into the kitchen.

"Good morning, Imani," I said, coming up behind her from where she stood at the sink. "Here, let me get that," I said, dropping my glass down into the suds. The last thing I wanted her thinking was that I brought her here to be my maid.

"No, it's the least I can do since I can't afford to pay you rent."

"Imani," I said. When she didn't look at me, I gently grabbed her arm and spun her around, flinging bubbles and droplets of water on the floor.

When her wide set of slanted eyes gazed up and connected with mine, an undeniable jolt of something was felt inside my chest. Of course, even before today, I felt the attraction between us, but this here was something different. It was like we were two magnets being drawn together by an unknown force. And as I stood there staring at her, taking in her understated beauty, I found it hard to even breathe.

"What were you saying now?" she asked, breaking me from my thoughts.

"Um," I stammered, swallowing hard, trying my best to remember what I was even saying. "Um, let me wash those dishes while you finish getting ready for work."

Her full lips curled up into a semi-smile, exposing that lone dimple in her cheek. "Are you sure?"

Releasing a breath, I ran my hand down my face. "Imani, I didn't bring you here to be my maid. I appreciate the help, ma, but you really ain't gotta do all this," I explained.

"Oh," she said softly as though I'd hurt her feelings. "I was just trying to help."

With the tip of my finger under her chin, I lifted her face, which seemed to have fallen just a bit. "You are helping. Now go get ready for work."

She nodded slowly before easing her way around me and heading out of the kitchen. While she finished getting ready, I cleaned up the rest of the dirty dishes. Less than an hour later we were in my car and on our way to work. Thankfully, she was allowed to keep her job, so for the past few weeks, we'd been driving into work together.

When I pulled up to the diner and parked the car along the curb, I looked over at Imani. "I want you to come out tonight."

"You mean to the club?"

"Yeah. You can even bring your friend," I told her, referring to Karen.

She shook her head. "No. I don't have anything to wear, and besides, I really should be saving my money, not spending it at some club."

Pursing my lips to the side, I narrowed my eyes. "You really think I'd invite you out to a club I own and expect you to spend a dime?"

"Well, I mean—"

"Look, go home after work and be ready by ten, a'ight?" I told her, cutting her off.

She let out a light snort of laughter. "We'll see, Mr. Shaw. We'll see," she said.

As she got out of the car, my eyes unconsciously raked over her ass, which was poking out of her black uniform pants. I watched her intently until she finally made her way inside, then I headed down to the end of the block. When I got up to my office, I immediately went to work, making calls and checking emails to ensure everything set for that night.

Suddenly the phone on my desk rang, and I hit the speaker button. "Yo," I answered, only partly engaged as I continued to read an email.

"Noble." Right off the bat, I knew from the all-too-familiar sound of his voice it was my little brother, Kells.

"What's going on, Kells?" I said with my eyes still ahead on the screen.

"Yo, I've been trying to reach you. How shit looking down B-more?" he asked.

"Things are good. Business is booming, you know. What about up there?"

When he didn't respond right away, I released a deep sigh and ran my hand over my face. "Nigga, speak the fuck up! Tell me what's wrong!" I barked.

"It's just the money done came up short for the second time this week and—"

Before he could even finish, I cut him off and said, "I'll be up there tomorrow morning."

"Nah, B, let me handle it. Rashad's already on it, checking all the security cameras and shit. We can handle it. I was just trying to keep you in the loop, ya feel me?"

"In the loop," I muttered evenly.

"Yeah."

"All right. I'll let you handle it, but make sure you do, because if you don't, that's your ass," I warned.

"I got it, bro. Don't worry," he assured.

Just as I killed the line, there was a sudden knock on my door. "Come in," I said.

My assistant, Kingston, appeared with a D&G catalogue in his hands. "Red or black?" he asked, tilting it down for me to see.

I allowed my eyes to scan quickly across the page before looking back up at Kingston. "Red," I said.

"Size?"

"Eight."

"Red bottoms?"

"Of course, size seven. Now, is that it?" I asked.

He nodded his head. "Yes, that'll be it, Mr. Shaw."

Chapter 5

Imani

"Oh my God, girl! This how you been living?" Karen asked as she looked around the place.

She agreed to go to the club with me that night since Noble wouldn't take no for an answer. After swinging by her place after work to grab her clothes for the night, she came over so that we could get dressed together. As I set my purse down on the chair and began taking off my coat, Karen walked around the place, her fingers lightly skimming the furniture as she observed every detail in awe.

"Come on, let's go back to my room," I said.

"Your room? Girl, you getting mighty comfortable up in here, ain't ya?" she said.

I rolled my eyes. "No. I'm moving out soon. Just waiting on a call from the housing authority."

"You moving back to the projects? After living like this?" She waved her hand around the room.

"I can't afford to live like this, Karen. Hell, with the financial situation I'm in, I don't have a choice but to move back to the hood."

"Hmm," she murmured with a devious little grin.

"Hmm, what?"

"You could always make this your permanent home you know."

"And just how could I do that?" I asked, rolling my eyes and already preparing myself for the foolery about to spill from her lips.

"Just sit on that black dick a few times. I'm sure he'll let you stay."

I laughed. "Karen, you crazy. You know I don't even get down like that."

"Well, you already I know I do. Four kids, four baby daddies, and four child support checks," she said, snapping her fingers.

I shook my head. "Come on here, girl," I said, motioning my hand down the hall.

"What you wearing tonight?" she asked, following me.

"I don't know. Probably just jeans and a shirt. You know half of my clothes got thrown away," I told her.

When we entered my room, the first thing I noticed was a large white box sitting on the bed with D&G stamped on top in black. "What's this?" I muttered, taking the box in my hand.

I opened up the top to reveal a red mid-length bodycon dress with a deep V. As I picked it up, feeling the expensive fabric against my fingers, I noticed the tag. Dolce & Gabbana.

"Oh my God, bitch!" Karen shrieked over my shoulder. "Do you know what that is?"

"Well, apparently it's a Dolce & Gabbana dress," I said as though I were unimpressed. Meanwhile, on the inside, I was more excited than she was. I'd never seen such a costly piece of clothing in real life, let alone had the opportunity to wear it.

"You got this nigga over here buying you all types of expensive dresses and letting you live in this fancy-ass apartment." She cut her eyes over at me and twisted her lips to the side. "You sure you haven't sat on his dick?"

I was offended by her accusation, and my jaw dropped. "Hell no, Karen!"

She held her hands up in surrender. "Girl, don't get all bent out of shape. I was simply asking a question. Now, what shoes are you going to wear?"

"Ugh!" I groaned, realizing that the only pair of heels I now owned was a faux leather pair of black pumps. They were so old and cheap that all of the scuff marks on them were white and the heels had been worn down to a lean. "I don't have any shoes to wear with a dress like this. Fuck it! I'll just wear my jeans," I said, tossing the dress back on the bed.

"Shidd! I'll rock that bitch with the shoes I just got from Rainbow last week," she said, causing me to laugh.

I walked over to the closet that now housed every single piece of clothing I owned, and I carefully pulled it opened. As I looked down to the floor where my only four pair of shoes sat side by side, I noticed a new shoebox. "What's this?" I mumbled.

Lifting up the box, I immediately noticed the words Christian Louboutin in fancy cursive writing. Slowly I began opening it up, but before I could even pull out the nude-colored pumps, Karen let out an ear-splitting scream. Damn near jumping out of my skin, I turned to look at her. My hand was over my heaving chest as I saw her green eyes all lit up with excitement.

"Bitch, that nigga done bought you a pair of red bottoms!" she exclaimed dramatically.

I looked back down into the box and saw a small gift bag and white piece of paper folded in half. I opened up the note and read:

Dear Imani,
Please accept the dress along with the shoes and jewelry as a small token of my appreciation for all you've been doing around the house. I really didn't know your taste, so I took a chance by selecting something I'd like to see you in. See you tonight at the club.
Noble Shaw

"Jewelry," I whispered through a blushing smile. Reaching down into the small gift bag, I pulled out a beautiful pair of fourteen-carat gold dangly earrings with matching bangles. "Wow," I breathed.

"And you sure you didn't sit on his dick?" Karen said from behind me.

After getting into the car Noble sent for us that night and heading back downtown, we arrived at the club at exactly 10:33 p.m. There was no standing in line, nor did we even have to cut in front. Noble made sure that from the time we arrived curbside, someone was there to personally escort us in.

As I entered the club, I must admit that I felt sexy. The red dress he'd chosen fit my body to a T, and I felt a sense of empowerment walking in such high-priced heels. Luckily Karen did my hair for me, smoothing it out into a nice, sleek bob and even trimming the edges. I wore just a little bit of makeup and accentuated my full lips with a bright cherry color. Karen, on the other hand, looked sexy in an all-black catsuit and leopard-print heels from Rainbow. Her shoulder-length brown hair was fixed in big, loose curls, and her mouth was painted a soft shade of pink, complementing her big green eyes.

Walking over to the bar, I scanned the dance floor, which was completely packed. The DJ had the whole room moving while strobe lights flickered throughout the entire space. I noticed a few glances from the opposite sex as we sauntered over. Although I wasn't used to dressing up like this, I was still known for turning a head or two. Men hit on me daily at the diner, either telling me just how pretty I was or complimenting my figure.

Once Karen and I sat up at the bar, I leaned over and asked the bartender for a pinot noir, which he immediately told me was on the house.

"Wine?" Karen questioned with her eyebrow raised. "Girl, I see you really trying to play the part tonight." She shook her head.

I couldn't help but laugh at her. To be honest, Noble had been introducing me to all different kinds of red wines. Each night he and I would have a taste right before bed, allowing my palate to explore some of the finest wines from all over the world. It seemed as if there were two sides to this man: one with that New York accent who just didn't give a fuck, and the other who was this rich, well-spoken businessman who cared for only the finer things in life. The blend of the two made for the sexiest man I'd ever encountered.

After the bartender poured me a glass of wine and made Karen her lemon-drop martini, a tall, dark-skinned man approached us.

"Ms. Imani, is it?" he said, extending his hand.

I could feel my eyebrows instantly scrunching together. "And who wants to know?" I asked over the music.

The tall gentleman leaned over and whispered in my ear. "My name is Kingston, ma'am. Mr. Shaw would like me to escort you upstairs."

When he pointed his finger up, my eyes followed until they landed on Noble Shaw. He was standing there, up on the balcony, leaned over with his elbows resting on the rail. His legs were cocked in a wide stance as he took in the entire scene below him, completely unaware of just how commanding his presence truly was, even from afar.

"Uh, Karen?" I spun around on the stool to see her grinning in some guy's face. I watched as she sipped through the thin black straw in her martini glass before leaning into him with that kittenish giggle of hers. Rolling my eyes, I tapped her on the shoulder and said, "Hey, I'm going up to talk to Noble for a minute. I'll be right back down."

With her flirtatious eyes still on the guy in front of her, she said, "Take your time, honey. Please, take your time."

I got up and followed Kingston through the crowd until we reached an elevator that was somewhat concealed. For some reason, as we rode up, I began getting nervous. For the past four weeks, I had seen Noble every single morning and every night, so I had no earthly idea why I was feeling that way. But with each second that passed, I found it harder and harder to even breathe.

When the elevator dinged and the doors opened up, I expected Kingston to step off first. But instead, he turned to me and politely smiled, gesturing with his hand for me to exit. Inhaling deeply, I ran my hands down the front of my dress before stepping out. As the elevator doors closed behind me, I looked over to my right and saw Noble still standing by the rail.

After lowering my shoulders, which were hiked from nerves, I put an extra arch in my feet before strolling over toward him. "Good to see you, Mr. Shaw," I said, leaning into him with a playful nudge of my shoulder.

He took a step back, allowing just enough room for his eyes to travel the entire length of my body. Subtly taking his bottom lip between his teeth, he let out a low humming sound. "Good to see you as well, Ms. Imani," he said.

I swallowed hard because I'd never seen his eyes filled so much lust. And from just the way he said my name, an unexpected moisture began to shamefully gather in the seat of my panties.

"You summoned me?" I asked, tucking my hair behind my ear.

"I did. You look very nice," he said, still looking me over.

Tucking my hair behind my ear once more, I silently prayed he couldn't see me blushing. "Thank you for the dress, Noble. Oh, and for the shoes," I said, sliding out my foot for him to see. "You shouldn't have."

While I was speaking to him, I noticed that his sleepy eyes weren't even on my face. He was still slowly observing each and every inch of me while stroking that long beard. Feeling nervous, I cleared my throat and awkwardly adjusted my posture. It was like all of a sudden I felt tense and didn't know exactly what to do with my arms and legs.

He let out a little snort of laughter. "You're so fucking beautiful," he said, licking his lips.

This time I turned my head and tucked in my lips to hide my growing smile. I couldn't believe that Noble was actually checking me out. Even with his arrogant ways, I'll admit that I'd been attracted to him since the first day I saw him walk into the diner. But not once since that day had I seen him look at me like this.

"Come take a walk with me," he said, offering his arm for me to hold.

Feeling privileged, I took his arm and began to walk with him. He led me to his office, which was just as stylish as his apartment. All-black leather furniture and mahogany wood furniture filled the four stone-colored walls. As he locked the door behind us, I could smell the hint of a fresh cigar lingering in the air.

"You smoke?" I asked, taking a seat.

"Occasionally when I work late nights," he said, sitting next to me. "Do you smoke?"

"No. Never," I stated matter-of-factly, causing him to let out a light chuckle. "What's so funny?" I asked.

"Nothing."

"No, tell me." I looked over at him, seeing that he was trying to carefully select his words.

"How do I say this?" he started, while stroking his beard. "You're a good girl. A sweet girl who just fell on hard times, I guess."

"And that makes you laugh?" I asked with my eyebrows pinched.

He released a small snort as he shook his head. "No, absolutely not. It's just, I always see you as being so innocent, but when I saw you tonight"—he waved his hand in front of my body—"looking like this, I just . . ."

"You just what?" I asked, needing more.

"Excuse my language, but you just look so fucking sexy. Like a . . . like a bad girl."

Suddenly the percolating between my thighs intensified into its own tempo. And before I could stop myself, I said, "I am a bad girl."

Noble's eyes widened before the left corner of his mouth turned up into a sexy smirk. "Then kiss me," he said.

Chapter 6

Noble

Little Ms. Imani was attempting to put on her big-girl panties tonight, and I was going to make her eat her words. After I told her to kiss me, her mouth practically hit the floor, and within a split second, she found herself at a loss for words.

"Get over here and fucking kiss me," I said again, this time with a little bit more dominance in my voice.

Even with space between us, I could feel just how hard her heart was starting to pound. Sucking in a deep breath, she tentatively leaned into me. Her eyes were already closed with her lips slightly parted, as though she were about to receive her very first kiss. When her lips finally landed on mine, I didn't waste any time. I immediately took in her tongue, tasting the sweet noir, then softly suckled on her bottom lip.

As we kissed, I grabbed one of her hands and put it up to my chest, seeing if she would explore. But her hand simply stayed put, letting me know right away that she liked to be guided. With my hand already on her knee, I grazed her soft, buttery skin. My inquisitive fingers began to move, playing just at the hem of her dress before they gradually slid up her thighs.

"Ahh." With her eyes still closed, she let out a miniscule moan as though she were holding back. That silvery sound only goaded me.

I removed my tongue from her mouth and slowly slid it down her cheek into the crook of her neck. All the while my hands moved freely up the sides of her smooth, thick thighs until her dress was almost at her waist.

"Noble," she breathed, sounding almost as if she wanted to fight against her own sexual urge.

"Take this shit off," I demanded, causing her eyes to pop open wide.

She looked at me with skepticism at first, but after seeing just how serious I was, she stood up in front of me. Bit by bit, she slowly began removing her dress, raising it up over her head. As she pulled it off and tossed it to the floor, I took in just how perfect her body was. Her mocha-colored skin glowed under the pot lights, favoring a shiny shade of bronze. Spilling out of a black satin bra that appeared to be a size too small were her full, perky breasts, each jutting out and begging to be licked. And directly in front of my line of vision was her pussy, hidden behind the same satin fabric.

"Come here," I told her, signaling with my finger.

Sheepishly, with her hands nervously clasped together, she took a few steps forward, closing the space between us. Although it was faint, I could smell her essence mixed in with the sweet scent of her perfume. After scooting up to the edge of the chair, I grabbed hold of her ass and pulled her pussy in close to my face. Gently, I nibbled the outside of her moist panties, allowing my beard to prickle the tops of her thighs.

"Ahh," she moaned.

With the tip of my tongue, I swiped up and down the fabric, giving just enough to taunt her sexual desire. As I snaked my tongue, I could feel her hips beginning to squirm from anticipation. I slid my hands around from her bare backside to the front, allowing my fingers to slip under the edges of her panties.

"Pleassee," she whined softly, letting her hands run over the top of my head.

With my fingers still under the elastic, I gradually slid her panties down over her waist. She was clean-shaven with only a sliver of hair parting each of her lips.

"Mmm." I inhaled her essence, allowing her panties to finally slip to the floor.

As soon as she stepped one foot out, I raised her leg and propped it up over my shoulder. I buried my face and beard between her thighs as she held on to me for support. At the very moment my tongue slid between her wet folds and connected with her clit, I glanced up to see her head fall back from nothing but pure pleasure.

"Ohh, Noble," she moaned.

Gently, I sucked on her pearl, as she rocked her hips against me. "Come put that pussy on my face, ma," I muttered.

"Are you sure?" she asked with an airy breath.

Without warning, I lifted her other leg up off the ground and threw it over my shoulder, immersing my entire face between her thighs as I cupped the side of her ass to hold her in place.

"Noble, wait, don't drop me," she said, holding on to my head.

Little did she know I worked out every morning just so I could do shit like this. Completely ignoring her, I went back to work, eating her pussy like it was my first good meal in months. I could hear a series of moans fleeing her lips just before she went mute and her legs began to quake.

"Ahhh, wait. Ahhh, ohhh, fuck!" she wailed out in a release.

After a few last tender kisses to the front of her clit, enough to send tremors down her spine, I put her back down to the floor. After swiping my hand down over my wet beard, I stood up and began removing my clothes. But before I could even get my shirt undone, Imani surprised me by dropping down to her knees. While I removed my shirt and tossed it to the other side of the room, she hurriedly unbuckled my pants and slid them all the way down to my ankles.

I looked down, seeing her in a sexy squatting position with the red bottom heels still on her feet. Dark, innocent, catlike eyes were already peering up at me as though she were waiting for her next set of instructions.

"Go ahead and taste me," I told her, giving her the green light.

As soon as she licked the tip of my long erection, a low moan launched from the back of her throat. She sounded as if she were tasting her favorite dish for the very first time. My hardened dick twitched in her mouth as soon as she slid her red lips down to the base.

Feeling eager, I grabbed hold of each side of her head before thrusting myself a bit deeper. "Shittt," I hissed, as her tongue slithered against me.

As I worked my hips in a circular motion, I began grinding in and out of mouth until we both came to a nice, steady pace. I heard nothing but the sounds of her wet mouth colliding against me and the bass of the muted music playing just outside the door. Suddenly my toes began to curl, and a tightness started to develop in my groin.

"Oh, myy fuckk!" I groaned, pulling her up from the floor. With a little force, I grabbed her chin and pulled her face into mine for a kiss.

"I swear I love your mouth," I said low. Our bodies were so close her soft breasts were pressed up against me.

"I love yours too," she whispered, looking up into my eyes.

With both of my hands, I reached down and grabbed her ass before lifting her in the air. With her legs wrapped around me, I took a step back and sat down on the couch. As we deeply kissed, she eased her tight walls down onto me, causing me to grunt inside of her mouth. Rolling her hips, she began taking charge for the first time, and oddly enough, I actually liked it.

"Fuck, ma," I breathed, sliding both of my hands up her back to go even deeper.

For the next thirty minutes, Imani rode me into oblivion. She danced on my dick so good there were actually times I found it hard to even breathe. And when we both came, we came hard, so fucking hard that even several minutes later we remained in that same position on the couch. Our sweat-covered bodies were glued together as our lifeless limbs draped heavily from being completely spent. We tried to catch our breath as we came down from the most extraordinary high.

The next morning Imani was in my bed rather than across the hall. I hadn't woken up beside a woman in over three years, and that was with my ex-wife, Sarah. Sarah still lived up in New York, and although we both knew we could no longer be, we somehow remained good friends.

As Imani squirmed underneath the covers, struggling to wake up, I took the time to take in her natural beauty. Even without makeup, her brown face was flawless in the morning's sun. Careful not to wake her, I traced my fingers along the edges of her hair, actually liking the fact that her roots puffed and curled when she sweated. And then there was her long neck, which led down to her smooth, coppery shoulders. Although I'd never admit it out loud, I was taken with Ms. Imani.

"Good morning," I said, finally seeing her eyes start to open.

"Good morning," she said softly, raising the covers to hide her beautiful smile.

I dove under the covers and immediately attacked her naked body with dozens of light kisses while she squealed. Being so close to her caused my dick to instantly rise. I slid from beneath the covers and hovered over her, preparing to kiss her lips.

"Kiss me," I said.

She grabbed the sides of my face and gently pecked my lips, but before we could even take things further, my iPhone started to ring. I sat up on the edge of the bed and grabbed it from the nightstand, immediately seeing Rashad's name flash across the screen.

"Yo," I answered.

"Noble, what's going on?" Rashad said.

"Yo, you tell me. Did you find what you were looking for?" I asked, cutting straight to the chase. Ever since the last call I got from Kells about someone stealing money from the club, I hadn't heard a word, so I was expecting an update.

"Look," he said, letting out a deep sigh. "I know Kells doesn't want to bother you with this because he wants you to trust that he can handle the business, but honestly, I'm getting worried. We took another major hit last night. Fourteen Gs came up missing whereas last time it was only five. Whoever the fuck this is getting bolder, and nothing's turning up on the cameras," he said.

"Say no more. I'll be there in a few days," I said, killing the line.

Suddenly feeling pissed, I shot up from the bed and started walking over to my adjoining bath.

"Is everything all right?" Imani asked. I turned around to see that she was now sitting up in the bed. The white sheet was wrapped tightly around her breasts as she wore a look of genuine concern.

"It's just business, ma. Look, I've got some shit to handle down at the club today before I head out of town next week. You gonna be good here by yourself, right?" I asked.

She nodded her head, and although she tried to disguise it, there was a sudden sadness in her eyes. "Yeah, I'll be fine," she said.

Even though I didn't have time to deal with her emotions, or anyone's for that matter, I walked back over like a gentleman and briefly kissed the top of her head. Last night with Imani had been fun, no doubt, but now after talking to Rashad, it was time for me to get back focused. I needed to prepare myself for this upcoming trip to New York, ensuring that my club in Baltimore would run smoothly while I was away. Not only that, but I was determined to find whoever was stealing my fucking money, because when I did, there would be hell to pay.

Chapter 7

Imani

"So, girl, tell me what happened with you at the club last night. You just dipped on a sister," Karen said, making me laugh.

I was sitting across from her in the back-corner booth at the diner. Since Noble rushed into work this morning, saying little to nothing to me before he left, I decided to take the bus down to the diner on my day off. I knew Karen was working, so I was gonna catch up with her on her lunch break.

"Oh, Noble just showed me around is all," I said, scratching behind my ear before looking out of the window.

"Mm-hmm. Lying ass."

I was finding it harder by the second to hold in my smile. "What?"

"What," she mocked. "You know what. You fucked him, didn't you?"

Shrugging my shoulders, I said, "I mean, well, I might've sat on his big black dick."

Karen's eyes doubled in size and her jaw suddenly dropped. "Girl, shut up!" she said loudly, drawing attention from the other patrons nearby.

"Shhh," I said, holding my finger up to my mouth before looking around. "Yes, up in his office. Last night."

"How was it?" she asked with a goofy grin, her green eyes already lit up with anticipation.

"It was . . . hmm, how should I explain it?" I asked myself, pressing my finger up to my chin.

Karen rolled her eyes. "Look, you are not Nia Long, so don't give me that bullshit about how his dick just spoke to you, all right?"

I laughed then leaned over the table a bit so she could hear me speak when I lowered my voice. "Let's just say I'd never been handled that way before." Closing my eyes, I slowly shook my head. "By far the best sex I'd ever had. I swear," I said, holding up my hand in a promise.

"Damnnn, girl! It was like that?"

Biting down on my bottom lip, I nodded my head to confirm. "Like that."

"So what now?" she asked.

"Honestly . . ." I hiked up my shoulders, allowing my voice to trail off to give it some thought. "I really don't know. I mean, I'd hate to be overzealous and think we're in an actual relationship."

"Overzealous?" Karen's eyebrow shot up as she gave a little smirk. "Girl, that nigga's got you sounding all bougie and shit. I love it!" she teased.

I waved her off and rolled my eyes. "Shut up, Karen."

She laughed. "So then you really like him?" she asked.

"Yeah. I really, really like him," I confessed.

Karen pursed her lips to the side. "Well, if this ain't some rags-to-riches bullshit, then I don't know what is. I knew I should have gotten to him first," she mumbled under breath as though I couldn't hear her.

"Really, Karen?"

"What?" she asked, raising her voice an octave. She shrugged her shoulders then let out a laugh. "No, but seriously, I completely understand what you're saying. If you really like him, then just talk to him and find out where his head is at."

"Yeah, I think I will. I'll talk to him tonight."

***

That Saturday night I waited up for hours for Noble to get home until my eyes just couldn't stay open anymore. He wasn't there to invite me back into his bed, and because I didn't want to make things more awkward than they already were, I returned to the guest bedroom. The next morning when I woke up, he still wasn't there, and the only reason I knew he'd even come in was because he'd made a small mess in the kitchen.

All day that Sunday I cleaned his entire apartment, hoping it would calm my nerves. I kept rehearsing in my head exactly what I was going to say him as soon as he walked through the door. First, I wanted him to know that although I'd only known him for a month, I really, really liked him. I wanted him to know that I felt a true connection between us and that the things he did to my body this past Friday night were . . . unforgettable.

Now, I didn't want him to think I was rushing or forcing him to be in a relationship, but I at least wanted to know if my feelings for him were mutual. Could we possibly grow into something or was it just one night of fucking at the club? Did he still see me as the young woman from the slum apartments with her shit set all out on the curb? Or did he now see me as being a woman worthy to be on his arm? Did he see me as the aspiring chef I wanted to be, who for the past year just fell on hard times? Did he see me as a young woman who, thanks to him, now had almost $6,000 in the bank and wanted better for herself? I desperately needed to know what this man thought of me.

All of a sudden the house phone rang. I ran, sliding across the floor to grab it, already sure that it would be Noble on the other end. "Hello," I answered.

"Hey, girl," Karen said. Other than Noble, she was the only one who called the house phone, and that was only because I still didn't have a cell.

"Hey."

"Why you so sound sad? You don't wanna talk to me?" she asked half jokingly.

"No, I just thought you were Noble is all."

"You still haven't talked to him?"

"Talk to him? Girl, I haven't even seen Noble since Saturday morning when he rushed out of here."

"Damn," she muttered. "Well, it's Sunday. I'm sure he'll be home at the normal time tonight. What you cooking?"

"Shrimp scampi with diced garlic and tomatoes. I may add some arugula, I don't know."

"Is that Noble's favorite dish?" I could hear the smile in her voice.

"One of them."

"Well, good, you got the right idea. Sex is always better on a full stomach," she said before we both laughed.

After hanging up with Karen, I looked around, seeing that the entire house was clean. I went right into the kitchen and began cooking to get inspired for the night. After everything was completely done, I went and jumped in the shower. I didn't have any sexy lingerie, but I did still manage to have a few nice bra and panty sets, so I made sure to put on one of those. The matching set I chose was red lace, so I painted my lips a bright shade of red and threw on my new red bottoms to complete my look.

It was a little after seven when I went in to set the table. "Okay, let me just light these," I said to myself as I lit two white candlesticks in the center. I pulled out a bottle of Chateau Margaux 1983 from the wine cooler, hoping that it would pair nicely with our meal. And with just my undergarments on, I took a seat at one end of the table and just waited.

I waited for almost an hour before I decided to call Noble's cell. When he didn't pick up, I called the nightclub for him, something I had never done. When Kingston told me he'd have him call me back as soon as possible, I immediately felt a little bit better. I mean, at least I knew for sure that he was there and that he knew I was wanting to talk to him. But after another hour of waiting and the melting wax from the candles dripping down onto the tables, I got discouraged.

Finally feeling defeated, I kicked off my high-heeled shoes and got up from the table. I blew out each of the candles before putting the food away. Although it wasn't a planned date, somehow I felt like I'd been stood up. For a second night in a row, I was disappointed that I wouldn't get a chance to see the sexy man I was living with. After the entire kitchen was cleaned, I slipped into a frumpy pair of pajamas and got back into my bed. It was almost eleven o'clock. Just as the night before, I tried my best to wait up for him, but sleep ultimately took over.

Since Noble left for the club that Monday morning before I even had the chance to wake up again, he sent a car to take me to work.

"How nice," I muttered sarcastically, sliding in the back seat as the driver held open my door. Here I was in my dingy work uniform, getting driven in some sleek black SUV that looked like it transported nothing but A-list celebrities.

After a twenty-minute drive in rush hour traffic, we made it to the diner. When we passed by the nightclub on the corner, I looked over to see Noble's white Range sitting in the parking lot. My stomach instantly started to twist. Taking a deep sigh, I got out and entered the diner before the time clock had even changed to eight o'clock.

"You know, ever since you hooked up with the nightclub owner you haven't been late for work once," Big Will hollered from the back.

"Ugh!" I groaned lowly. "Morning, Big Will."

"Morning. Now, I got two orders almost up, and Karen's gonna need your help."

"Sure thing, Big Will."

I didn't waste time getting right to work that morning, seating people and waiting all the tables I could. Luckily, being able to handle things around the diner quickly took my mind off of Noble. Before I knew it, it was noon and time for me to take my break. All morning long Karen tried to convince me to go down to the club and just talk to him. But since he hadn't returned any of my calls or at least made an attempt to speak to me at the house, I didn't think that was a good idea. At this point, I'd pretty much chalked it up to the idea that I was just a one-night stand for him. I was someone he'd pitied and temporarily brought into his home out of the goodness of his heart.

"Come on, girl, you ready?" Karen asked, grabbing her coat off the hook.

"Ready for what? Where we going?" I looked at her and asked.

She pursed her lips as though I already knew the answer then put her hand on her hip. "Down to the club, where else?"

"No, I'm not going down there to harass that man. I mean, he's made it pretty clear that he doesn't feel the same way about me. And I may be down right now, but I'm not that damn desperate."

"You're not going to look desperate, Imani. I promise. Just go in there real casual and say something like, 'Hey, I haven't seen you in a few days, and I was wondering if you wanted to have lunch and catch up.' Girl, you just gotta know how to work it," she explained.

I guess when she said it, it didn't sound so bad. I mean, the worst he could do was say no, right? "Fine, I'll do it but . . ." I paused, narrowing my eyes, "Wait, why are you going?"

"I just want to see that fine-ass assistant of his. Kingston," she said, fanning herself.

I shook my head and laughed. "Come on, girl, let's go."

After stepping out into the cold, Karen and I walked down to the club. When we entered, I noticed right away that it looked completely different at this hour than it had last Friday night. I could actually see the dance floor and all the nice features of the space. The entire nightclub was decorated in black and silver, from the leather barstool with chrome legs and feet all the way to the shiny black marble floors that had hints of sparkles in them.

"Hey," I said to the guy I quickly recognized as the bartender from a few nights ago. He had his back toward us while he stocked the shelves.

"Hey, how's it going?" he turned around and asked. His eyes were reduced to slits as he tried to recall where he knew us from. However, since he served different folks night after night, I wasn't surprised he didn't remember us.

"I'm Imani, Noble's friend. Is he up in his office?"

"Oh, yeah, I believe he's up there," he said, looking me over. I guess I didn't exactly look like most of Noble's friends as I stood there in my frumpy work uniform.

"And where's that fine-ass nigga Kingston?" Karen boldly asked.

The bartender chuckled before pointing across the room. Kingston was sitting at one of the pub tables, fervently focused on a laptop in front of him. In fact, he was so wrapped up in whatever he was looking at that I doubted he even saw the two of us come in. While Karen sashayed in his direction, I headed over toward the elevator doors. Up until this point, my nerves had been kept in check, but they were slowly resurfacing.

Leaning back against the metal wall as the elevator ascended, I inhaled a sharp breath. I shook my hands up and down in an attempt to release my last-minute jitters before stepping off.

With my heart beating faster by the second, I began walking to Noble's office. From a few feet away, I could already see that his door was slightly cracked. As I continued on my path, I began to hear a low grunting sound that seemed to grow louder as I came near. While I knew I should have knocked first, my natural instinct was to peek inside.

When I looked in, I immediately saw Noble sitting down on the couch at the back wall. His pants were down around his ankles with his button-up shirt and tie still on. And there squatting between his naked thighs was a dark-skinned woman with long, black, curly hair. His head was thrown to the back of the couch, and his eyes were closed as she bobbed up and down in his lap.

My heart instantly sank to the pit of my stomach as I stood there watching her give him head. And on the exact same couch we'd fucked on just three short nights before. Noble wasn't my boyfriend by any means, nor had he made me any promises, but in that moment my eyes started to water. I was crushed.

"Imani, wait!" I heard someone yell out behind me. I turned to see Kingston jogging toward me with a fretful look on his face.

"Imani?" I heard again, but this time my name was being called from inside the office. When I peered through the slightly opened door, Noble was staring right at me.

Chapter 8

Noble

For the past two mornings, I'd rolled out of bed early, spending at least one hour in the gym before driving into work. Ever since I got that call from Rashad the other day, my sole focus had been ensuring that The Heat would run smoothly without me for the next few weeks. Well, that and finding out who was stealing my fucking money. I'd been so busy that not only was I leaving before the sun had its chance to rise, but I'd also been coming home fairly late, slipping into a cold, empty bed well past the midnight hour.

Although work had certainly consumed me, Imani was still very present in my mind. That's why I made sure she had transportation to work this morning. Mentally, I'd even made plans to speak with her tonight before I left for New York the following day. I definitely needed to see where her head was at after our little situation the other night at the club, and I also wanted to make sure she'd be okay spending the next few weeks alone in the apartment.

With my sleeves rolled up to my elbows, I sat at my desk, scrutinizing our accounts payable log on the screen. It was almost lunchtime, and although my stomach was hollow, I refused to leave without completing my work. Just as I was making another data entry, my telephone abruptly began to ring. Letting out a deep sigh of annoyance, I hit the speaker button. "Hello."

"Um, sir. I tried to stop her but—" Kingston said, clearly unnerved.

"Stop who?"

Just as the name, "Brittani," came through the speaker, a soft double knock was heard at my office door.

"Fuck, Kingston! Not now," I groaned intensely.

"I'm so sorry, Mr. Shaw. She slipped by me while I was getting some work done," he explained.

Exhaling slowly, I pinched the bridge of my nose. "All right, Kingston, all right," I said, hanging up the phone.

Already feeling irritated, I pushed away from my desk, hearing the wheels of my chair roll against the hardwood floors. Loosening the tie around my neck, I got up and trudged over to the door.

"What's up, Brittani?" I asked, holding the door only partially open.

Brittani stood there before me with her long khaki-colored trench coat already open, exposing her dark, flawless brown skin and pink lace undergarments while giving the most seductive smile. She knew what she was doing.

"Our Monday appointment, Mr. Shaw. Or did you forget?" she said.

Brittani somehow managed to squeeze past me, the sweet scent of her perfume wafting in the air. I craned my neck, watching her from behind as she leisurely sauntered in. Her high heels clicked against the wooden floors before she finally took a seat down on the leather sofa and crossed one smooth leg over the other.

Letting out another deep sigh, I softly shut my door and followed her inside. "Not today, Brittani. I'm gonna have to take a rain check, ma."

Brittani stood up in front of me and slowly peeled back the coat off her shoulders, allowing it to fall to the floor. Planting her hands on the sides of her waist, she pushed out her large breasts and stood erect like a model. Her body was undeniably a composition of art. And although I needed to get back to work, my dick instantly sprang to life at the sight of her. *Fuck.*

After she removed a single pin from the bun in her hair, her long black curls fell down to frame her pretty heart-shaped face. "You look tired, baby," she cooed, seductively strutting toward me.

I shook my head and held up my hand to stop her. "I said rain check, ma."

However, it seemed as if Brittani was on a mission. She kept walking until she was up close and personal, so close that her soft breasts pressed against me and her manicured hands palmed the muscles of my chest.

"Please, Mr. Shaw," she said low, her voice dripping with full-on desperation and desire. Removing one of her hands, she boldly slithered it down to the crotch of my pants. "Well, he surely doesn't want a rain check," she said, biting the corner of her lip.

Instinctively I closed my eyes, enjoying the feel of her hand massaging me. Now, it wasn't like me to follow someone else's lead, to be influenced or under a woman's spell, but I was so exhausted in that moment. All of the fight in me had suddenly diminished, and truthfully I was in need of a good release.

"Fuck it!" I growled. "You want the dick?" I said low, pushing her down to her knees. "I'm gon' give you this dick."

Before I even had the chance to, Brittani hurriedly unbuckled my pants, eagerly stripping them down to my lower legs and freeing my erection. She was trying to take control again, so when she wrapped her hands around the base of me and widened her mouth to take me in, I yanked her head back, grabbing a handful of her curly hair.

"Nah, this my show," I told her, slapping her hands away before slowly feeding my dick to her one inch at a time.

As we made our way over to the sofa, with her hair still clenched in my fist and me still lodged deep in her throat, I could hear the subtle sounds of her gagging. It was a sound of mutual pleasure. When I sat down, I immediately tossed my head to the back of the sofa. Closing my eyes, I finally allowed her to do her thing, only guiding her down my shaft with one hand at the back of her head.

"Fuck, ma," I groaned. I bit down on my bottom lip as that tingling sensation began to settle in my groin.

Suddenly, I heard the echoes of someone shouting, "Imani!" from outside of my office. My eyes instantly popped open wide and traveled over to my door. Through a crack no more than three inches wide, I could see the side of someone's face. Someone who looked just like Imani.

"Imani?" I asked low in surprise.

Immediately her head turned, and I could see her eyes peering at me through the gap of the entryway. Eyes that, even from a distance, struck me as being pained.

"Fuck," I mumbled under my breath. Brittani must have thought that I was talking to her because she began to pick up speed, sliding her wet mouth up and down my pole while moaning. I quickly pushed her off of me and yelled, "Imani, wait!" while pulling up my pants.

I rushed to the door, and right away I could see that Imani had left. When I stuck my head out into the hall, I saw that she was just about to step onto the elevator with Kingston.

"Imani, wait! Kingston, hold the fucking elevator!" I barked.

As I watched Imani proceed to step inside, Kingston stood out and held the doors open for me. Thankfully that gave me time to zip up my pants and fix my clothes. When I approached, Kingston grabbed the back of his neck, allowing a contrite expression to cover his entire face.

"You're fucking up big time today," was all I said before stepping onto the elevator. At the very moment my eyes landed on Imani, seeing that the rims of her eyes were slightly red and that she wouldn't even look at me, I turned to Kingston and said, "Give us a minute."

The moment the elevators doors closed between us, I filled my lungs with a deep breath of air. Tentatively, I turned back toward Imani and stared at her, seeing that her sexy little frame was covered in a thick winter jacket with her work uniform on underneath. Her cropped hair was smoothed down neatly, and her brown lips were coated in what appeared to be a sheer layer of gloss. Truth be told, her understated beauty intrigued me. I could tell she was getting a bit nervous under my intense gaze, because she tucked her hair behind her ear. It was an idiosyncrasy of hers that I'd caught on to early on.

After allowing a few more seconds of silence to pass between us, I finally spoke. "Are you okay?"

"I'm fine, Noble," she responded softly with her eyes cast down to the floor.

Running my hand down my beard, I asked, "Imani, do we need to talk? Did you come to talk to me?" I needed clarification, any indication at all of what or how she was truly feeling.

For the first time since I'd crossed the threshold of the elevator doors, she looked up at me. "I just wanted to know if you were hungry. I haven't seen you in a couple of days and . . . just thought you might want to have lunch."

Hearing her soft, innocent tone of voice, I briefly closed my eyes and felt a sudden sense of guilt, something I hadn't felt in years. "Imani," I breathed. "About what you saw up there—"

As if on cue, the elevator abruptly stopped on the first floor and dinged.

"It's fine, Noble, really. I mean, it was just one night of fun between us, right?" she asked with a forced smile on her face.

When I didn't answer, she attempted to skirt past me and exit through the doors. Without delay, I grabbed her by the arm and drew her body back into mine. "Are you sure that's all it was?" I leaned down and whispered in her ear.

Almost instantly I could feel the connection between us as her back rested up against my chest. It was the same powerful force I'd felt that night in my office. The same one that seemingly carried over into my bed until the wee hours of the very next morning.

"Just one night of fun, Noble. That's all it was," she whispered. After she gently pulled away, I watched her walk out the front door with Karen chasing behind her.

"Shit," I muttered, pressing the number two to take me back upstairs.

When I entered my office, Brittani was now lying fully naked on the couch. "Put your clothes on. It's time for you to go," I said.

Brittani's mouth dropped as though she were offended. "And just who was that?" she asked.

"None of ya business. Now put your clothes back on so I can finish up my work." I snapped my fingers twice so that she would get the point before I made my way back over to my desk.

After Brittani unhappily left, I tried to get my focus back on work but I just couldn't. The image of Imani's teary eyes kept coming back to haunt me. If there was anything I needed to accomplish before leaving for New York the next morning, it would definitely be to talk with her. Over the last month, I had grown to truly care for Imani, so the last thing I wanted to do was hurt her.

The next time I glanced up at the clock on the wall, I saw that it was five minutes past three. Although I had fully intended on staying until five, I was no longer able to just sit at my desk. After getting up and throwing on my coat, I made my way downstairs. Braving the cold, I went out and cranked up my Range. Even though I could've just walked down the block to the diner, I wanted to be ready in case Imani accepted a ride home from me.

Minutes later I walked into Miss Ruby's diner, seeing that they were completely packed. My eyes immediately went to searching for Imani, but from what I could see she was neither behind the front counter nor waiting tables on the floor. However, I saw Karen, and as soon as my eyes locked in with her bright green ones, she started making her way over toward me.

"Is Imani around?" I asked right away.

With a tray in her hand, she looked over each of her shoulders in an attempt to look for her. "She's around here somewhere. Now, what happened between you two earlier? She's been in a funk ever since we left the club."

Scratching behind my ear, I let out a deep sigh and said, "I think you should talk to Imani about that."

Just as Karen opened up her mouth to finish our short conversation, I saw Imani darting toward the kitchen. "Excuse me, Karen," I said, leaving her slightly confused.

Not really giving a shit about the EMPLOYEES ONLY sign that hung on the swinging double doors, I entered the kitchen in the back.

"Hey, you can't be in here," the short guy named Big Will said. He was standing in front of the hot plate window wearing a dirty white smock around his neck and a white chef's hat on his head.

Completely ignoring him, I looked around the chaotic space until my eyes finally landed on Imani. She was a little farther back, talking to one of the cooks by the stove.

"Imani!"

Chapter 9

Imani

I'd seen Noble as soon as he entered the diner, but I just wasn't ready to face him. I was too ashamed. The fact that I almost cried over a man I'd only barely known for a single month was embarrassing. Noble made me no promises or commitments, even after the passion-filled night we shared. And if I'm being completely honest, I was a fool to even think he'd consider taking a woman like myself seriously. While he was a successful nightclub owner who wore thousand-dollar shoes on his feet, I was a simple waitress making a measly $4.25 an hour, plus tips.

"How much longer on that burger, Don?" I asked one of the cooks.

"Imani!"

Over the past month, I had committed Noble's voice to memory. Recognizing it almost instantaneously, I turned back to see him standing there not too far from Big Will. Gradually my heart rate began to pick up speed.

"Imani!" he said again, walking toward me.

After taking a deep swallow, I somehow found my voice. "Noble, what are you doing back here?"

"Take your guest out front, Imani," Big Will said.

I rolled my eyes and sighed. "You can't be back here, Noble."

"Then come talk to me outside, ma," he said, licking his lips.

Tucking my hair behind my ear, I proceeded to follow Noble out of the kitchen, all the way until we got outside. It was only thirty-nine degrees in Baltimore that day, so I was freezing standing there on the sidewalk. Noble must have noticed me shivering because he immediately took off his coat and wrapped it around me. I almost closed my eyes feeling its silky lining against my skin and smelling the familiar scent of his cologne.

Standing tall in front of me with his big, broad shoulders all squared, he looked down into my eyes. "I'm leaving for New York tomorrow," he said.

"Okay." That was all I could think to say.

"Just for a few weeks. I got some business I need to handle with one of my clubs."

"I see."

He let out a little snort and shook his head. I could only assume it was because I seemed to be preserving my words. "You gon' be all right at the house by yourself? I mean, I'll make sure you have transportation and all."

"Oh, me? I'll be just fine. As a matter of fact, I should be getting a call from housing any day now."

Gliding his tongue to the roof of his mouth, he stroked his hand down over his beard. He took another step forward to close the space between us, and surprisingly he took hold one of my hands. "You know you don't have to go, right?" he asked. His voice was faint but deep enough to send chills down my spine.

Feeling an instant surge of flutters in the pit of my stomach, I said, "Noble, I can't live with you forever. I've already outstayed my welcome as it is."

"Says who?" he quickly asked with another lick of his full lips, interlocking our fingers as he peered down at me with those hooded dark brown eyes.

From just that single touch, and the look of intensity in his gaze, I could feel moisture starting to gather in my panties. *Lord, why?*

I immediately removed my hand from his. "Look, Noble, I've got to get back to work, so . . ." I said, letting my voice trail off.

"Well, then I guess I'll see you at home tonight. Can I give you a ride?"

"Thanks but I've already got a ride," I lied. "And yes, I guess I'll see you back at *your* place tonight."

After returning his coat, I made my way back into Miss Ruby's diner without so much as a goodbye. I could barely take one step into the back kitchen without Big Will biting off my head.

"Imani, you know we don't allow patrons in the back. If the company you keep can't follow the rules, you may need to find another job," he warned.

Twisting my lips to the side, I cut my eyes over at Karen, who was also standing there. She and I were close enough that she could always read my mind. He was such a pain in the ass.

"Won't happen again," I muttered.

Just as I grabbed the next order off the counter and headed back out into the restaurant, Karen was quick on my heels. "What did he say? What happened between you two back at the club?" She rattled off one question after the other.

"He's leaving for New York tomorrow and will be gone for a few of weeks. He just wanted to make sure I'd be straight," I told her, only providing a partial story.

"Oh, wow. Well, are you gonna be all right?"

After delivering a hot plate with an artificial smile to table number five, I turned back to her and said, "I'll be fine, Karen. Besides, I'll probably be gone by the time he gets back anyway."

"So where will that leave the two of you? Did y'all talk about that? Did he even mention the night you sat on his big black dick?" She was trying her best to whisper as she followed me back up to the register.

I shook my head. "It was just one night. I need to move on."

Her neck whipped back as she widened her eyes. "Just one night? Is that what he said?"

"No, but it's the truth. Look, I'm trying to get into this culinary school, and really that's where my focus should be anyway. Not on some nightclub owner," I said, unintentionally downplaying his obvious appeal.

She held up her hands, foregoing any further interrogation on the subject of Noble and me. "Well, if you need a ride home tonight, just let me know."

"Thanks." I headed over to the kitchen window and grabbed the next order off the counter.

Later that night I entered the apartment, expecting it to be just as quiet and empty as it had been for the past two days. However, to my surprise, I could hear the TV down the hall coming from Noble's room. I didn't want to have another meaningless conversation with him. As fine as he was, I didn't want to have to look at him and face the fact that I was just one of many women on his sexual roster. I didn't want to acknowledge that my fast-blooming feelings for him were much stronger and more prevalent than what he'd felt for me.

Fleeting straight to my bedroom, I flipped on the lights and shut the door behind me. After removing my coat, I quickly stripped down out of my clothes. I was so overwhelmed by today's sequence of events that I knew a nice, hot shower would help clear my head. I grabbed a fresh towel and washcloth before reaching in and turning on the shower. And once the water temperature was just right, I eagerly stepped inside.

Following my normal routine, I washed my hair first before lathering my entire body with suds. And just as I closed my eyes to step back under the water and rinse off, I heard the shower door suddenly open. I immediately unsealed my eyes and saw Noble standing before me.

"Noble!" I shrieked before my eyes roamed the entirety of his naked frame, skipping over his handsome face to go right to his muscular pecs and travel all the way down to his long, meaty dick. I swear this Noble Shaw was a chocolate dream.

"What are you doing in here?" I asked, trying to cover myself with the small rag in my hand.

Noble didn't speak. He just kept coming closer, causing my heart to race inside my chest. "Noble?" I said again, but he just ignored me.

He reached out, latching his hands to the sides of my waist before pulling me into him. "Kiss me," he said, staring fervently into my eyes.

"Noble," I breathed weakly. I suddenly felt faint from his touch. I found it harder and harder to resist his demand as his face drew near.

"Kiss me," he said again.

It was like we were two opposing magnets in that moment. No matter what type of resistance I tried to put up, it was of no use. The powerful attraction between us was too strong of a pull. I reached up and grabbed the sides of his face, feeling his beard lightly prickle the palms of my hands. "Noble," I whispered in one final plea of desperation before crashing my lips against his.

Noble parted my lips with his tongue and kissed me so deep that my limbs went limp. I was literally like putty in the man's hands as my knees buckled beneath me. His large hands gradually wandered down to my ass for a firm squeeze, and I could feel his heavy dick pressed against me. My body began betraying me right away, responding to his touch. My core throbbed as uncontrollable moans passed from my mouth into his.

Unexpectedly, Noble broke from our kiss, and without warning he spun me around, forcing me to the shower wall as hot water poured over both of us. He slid his hands down between my thighs and parted my legs in preparation.

"That's right, ma, open up for me," he said, leaning down to whisper in my ear.

Closing my eyes, I did exactly what he'd ordered. I felt both the cool marble tiles beneath my spread fingers, and the hard muscles of his chest pressed up against my back. My body suddenly went stiff as I mentally prepared for what I knew was about to come. However, to my surprise, Noble began placing tender kisses to my left shoulder. His lips traveled all the way up the curve of my neck until he was able to softly suckle on the lobe of my ear.

Just as my body relaxed, melting into his, he plunged into me with ease. "Ahhh shit," I cried, suffering through the satisfaction of just how deep he was buried inside of me.

"This pussy, Imani, fuckkk," he breathed, gliding in and out of my soul.

Although his strokes were slow, they were also hard and deliberate. It was like he was on a mission, journeying to a place only he had ever been, a place that only he could reach. And with each shot as he thrust into me, he was starting to succeed. Our labored breathing joined forces all at once, becoming one united sound.

Skillfully he reached around and slithered his hand up my stomach until it latched on to my breast. "Ohh, Noble," I moaned, feeling him tease my nipple between his fingers as our bodies steadily slapped against one another's beneath the water.

As soon as his hand snaked up and wrapped around my throat, he began grinding into me with a stir of his hips. His grip was a little tighter with each forceful push inside. "Ahhh," I whimpered, literally feeling like I was about to implode.

"Nah, take that shit," he muttered, still grinding hard, traveling so deep inside my walls as he hit against the core.

When his strokes began to pick up speed, I felt my body start to quake. "That's right, cum for me, Imani," he said. And just like that, I did.

My body, all of a sudden, went into a seizure-like frenzy only to release in the most orgasmic gratification. "Ahhh, Noble," I cried.

As I came down from my high, I slowly worked my hips in a circular motion, matching his steady rhythm to a T. Then suddenly his dick swelled inside of me and I could hear his soft grunts and groans gradually turning into a loud roar. "Arghh. Fuckk!"

When he pulled out to release in the stream beneath us, I could feel the beat of his heart vibrating through my back. "Shit," he hissed.

I turned around to see him holding his long dick in his hand for one final stroke. The instant we locked eyes, he reached out and pulled me in for a kiss. Originally I thought I would have felt guilty for giving into him so easily and angry at myself for submitting to my own sexual needs, but instead, I found myself going with the flow. I naturally kissed him right back just as passionately while being held captive by his allure.

After we got out of the shower, he delicately towel-dried each and every inch of my body. He picked me up and carried me bridal style to his bed, where he held me close in his arms. He spooned me in the dark while making pillow talk beneath the sheets like only true lovers do. Eventually, that turned to more casual conversation.

"So which culinary school are you trying to get into?" he asked, recalling one of our previous conversations. "Was it Stratford?"

"Oh, God, no," I said, shaking my head. "I mean, I'd love to go there, but they're way too expensive, and I won't even get financial aid. I'm trying to get into the HCAT."

"But that's out in Glen Burnie."

I let out a little laugh before looking back at him over my shoulder. "And? The bus goes out to Glen Burnie too."

"Funny, funny," he said, draping his heavy leg over my thigh as his fingertips lightly brushed up and down my arm.

All of a sudden, things got quiet, and I could only hear his soft, rhythmic breathing. "Are you asleep?" I asked.

"No, I'm still up."

Tucking my lips inward, I briefly closed my eyes, thinking of just how I was going to broach the topic. "So umm . . ."

"Yes, Imani?" he said, still softly rubbing my arm.

"What exactly is this?" I turned around to face him, touching his chest then mine. "You know, between you and me?"

From the light of the window, I could see Noble staring intently at me as a few seconds of silence passed between us. "What do you want it to be?"

Ughh!

"Well, apparently you're a ladies' man with quite a substantial body count—"

His deep, guttural laugh cut off my words. "So now you assuming shit?"

"Well, am I wrong?"

"Everybody has a past, Imani."

I sat up in the bed, already not liking the way the conversation was going. "But we aren't talking about your past, Noble. I'm talking about just twelve hours ago," I said, looking down at him with my arms folded across my chest.

He laughed again and sat up in the bed next to me. With his back resting against the headboard, he said, "And correct me if I'm wrong, but twelve hours ago is still considered the past. Isn't it?"

Smart ass.

"Look, I'm too old for someone to be playing with my feelings. If this is just casual sex, then—"

Before I could even finish my statement, Noble leaned in and kissed me. With his hand at the back of my head, he practically stole my breath away. And when he pulled back, with one final suck to my bottom lip, I was truly at a loss for words. So much so that I couldn't even remember what I was saying to begin with.

"It's not just casual sex for me," he said, gently stroking his finger against my cheek.

"It's not?" I whispered, feeling both of my eyebrows raise.

He let out a light snort before he shook his head and said, "No, Imani, it's not. I'm feeling you, and I definitely wanna see where this goes."

I folded my arms back across my chest. "And what about ol' girl? You seeing where things go with her too?"

His wide grin cut through the darkness like a crescent moon in a pitch-black sky. "Nah, I'm done with that because I'm solely pursuing you, remember?" he said with a hint of amusement in his tone.

"Is there something funny?"

"It's just . . ."

"What?" I asked, confused.

"You know you're cute when you're jealous, right?"

My jaw slightly dropped as I blinked rapidly. "I am not jealous! I just don't want community dick."

He chuckled again, further irritating me. "Nah." He took hold of my hand then reached down beneath the covers to grab himself. "This here is definitely not for the community, ma."

"Well, I would hope not," I said softly, feeling that warm tingle resurface between my thighs as I stroked his shaft.

"So stop pouting and just give me a kiss . . . umm," he hummed, closing his eyes. His head collapsed back against the headboard as his dick swelled in the palm of my hand.

Enjoying his physical reaction to my touch, I smiled. I leaned in until our lips met, and I wrapped my arms around his big, muscular shoulders. Our lip locking gradually turned into another round of hot, steamy sex that left my body both sore and satisfied all at the same time.

I slept so hard that night that I didn't even remember Noble leaving the next morning. There was only a faded memory of him pecking me gently on the cheek.

Finally rubbing the sleep from my eyes, I looked over at the digital clock on the nightstand and saw that it read 8:04 a.m.

"Shit, shit, shit!" I muttered, realizing that I was beyond late for work.

I shot straight up in the bed, but before my feet could even plant themselves to the floor, I saw a white envelope with my name on it. Grabbing it off the nightstand, I instantly noticed that it was lumpy and that there was some weight to it. I tore it open in a hurry, seeing a simple white folded sheet of paper along with a set of keys.

Imani,
Stop panicking, beautiful. I've already called Big Will and told him that you wouldn't be coming in today. If he asks tomorrow, you were severely

sick in bed with a twenty-four-hour stomach bug. The keys are to the all-white Mercedes GLC parked next to my Range. I know you're too prideful to just accept it as a gift, so please consider this to be our temporary arrangement. I don't want you on that bus at all, and I do mean just that. Also, I got you a cell phone.

My eyes glanced back over to the nightstand where, sure enough, a brand new iPhone was placed on top.

You can call me day or night, and I promise I'll do my best to answer. But if there's ever more of an immediate need, Kingston knows to be available. I've also deposited some funds into your account, and yes, before you even ask, you're free to pay me back. I take cash or late-night shower sessions as payment. The choice is yours, ma.

Lastly, when I get back, I think I want to take you away somewhere. So be thinking of a place, preferably somewhere warm. Kingston knows to help expedite your passport. I'm already envisioning you walking along a white sandy beach, wearing nothing but a string bikini. Hint, hint.

I blushed.

> *Yours Truly,*
> *Noble Shaw*

God, this man!

Chapter 10

Noble

I'd been in New York for almost a whole week, and nothing seemed to be turning up. In fact, this past Friday and Saturday night, the club profited more than ever before. Right away, I knew that there could only be one explanation for that. Whoever was stealing my money knew with certainty that I was in town.

As I sat in the back table of Pearl Diner, reading the *New York Times*, I heard the door momentarily chime. Expecting to see my brother Kells, I quickly lifted my eyes from the paper. Surprisingly, he was strolling in with Rashad and my ex-wife Sarah behind him. Instantly, I narrowed my eyes in confusion, wondering why he decided to bring an entourage when he knew I wanted to discuss business.

In typical lawyer fashion, Sarah looked sharp in her heather gray pantsuit and heels, while on the other hand, Rashad and my brother wore jeans, hoodies, and Tims. When they all approached the table, I somehow managed to relax the grimace on my face.

"The whole gang's all here I see," I said, widening my eyes at my brother before standing up to greet Sarah. I hadn't seen her since I'd been back home.

"Now I know you weren't going to come home and not see me, Noble," she said, giving me a hug.

"Of course not." I wrapped one arm around her shoulders to reciprocate her affection.

Despite going through a divorce after three tough years of marriage, Sarah and I remained good friends. Growing up in the same Bed-Stuy community, my mother helped to practically raise her as a child, and because of that Sarah would always be like family. However, during our years together it seemed that Sarah was just as ambitious as I was. With her working twelve-hour days to become partner at her law firm and me opening up two nightclubs at the very same time, we naturally drifted apart.

After dapping up my brother and Rashad, we all sat down at the table. While they all looked over the menu, my cell phone started buzzing in my pocket. I pulled it out to see an incoming text from Imani flash across the screen. I bit back my smile as best I could, but apparently Sarah had me under deep observation.

"Well, obviously there's someone who can make you smile," she said.

With my eyes still cast down on the screen, I let out a little snort.

My Imani: Good morning, Mr. Shaw

"It's not your Monday appointment, is it?" Sarah asked with a little giggle. It was one of the few things I had told her about my social life since moving to Baltimore.

I shook my head. "None of your business, Sarah."

"Since when?" I didn't even have to look at her to know that she was pouting.

"She must be special, 'cause Noble's keeping this one under wraps," Rashad cut in and said.

I grinned before quickly looking up at the both of them. "It's none of your business either," I told him before typing back my response.

Me: Good morning, Imani. Where are you?

My Imani: Still at home in bed. I'm working the night shift.

Me: Back to work at night I see.

My Imani: Well, yeah. My sugar daddy loaned me a brand-new car, so back to the night shift it is.

Me: Sugar daddy?

My Imani: Just joking, Mr. Shaw.

Me: You better be. What are you wearing?

"Are you gonna sit here and text all morning or are you going to eat with us?" Sarah whined.

"Jealous are we?" I asked with a hint of humor in my voice. Sarah and I played back and forth like this all the time with one another. In fact, over the years we both admitted that we were actually too good of friends to have ever gotten married in the first place.

She rolled her eyes. "Yeah, right, Noble, you wish. If the poor girl knows like I do, she'll turn the other way and run like hell."

I shook my head.

My Imani: I'm wearing my birthday suit. You know, the one you seem to love so much.

Me: That I most certainly do. Can I get a picture?

My Imani: (Smiley face) I'll call you before I go into work tonight.

Releasing a low snort of laughter at the way she dodged my request, I sent one final text.

Me: Do that.

After the four of us all ordered and ate our breakfast over casual conversation, Sarah left for work. However, with club business still to discuss, the three of us stayed behind.

"Why'd you bring Sarah when you knew we needed to talk about business?" I asked my brother. Bringing Rashad along was one thing, but inviting Sarah was completely another.

"Last night she and Monica were on the phone, and she told her you were in town. Then she asked when I was going to see you again, and Monica told her about our breakfast plans," he explained with a shrug. "I guess she wanted to surprise you."

I never did care for his motormouth girlfriend, Monica. She was always butting her nose into shit where it didn't belong, and this little stunt here only reinforced my opinion of her.

"After two years, I see you still don't have her ass in check," I said.

"Man, she's just like Sarah. Ain't no checking a woman like that, B."

"And that's why the fuck Sarah's ass is alone now," I countered with a serious tone, causing Rashad to laugh. I glanced down at my watch, seeing that it was almost nine o'clock. "I have a meeting in an hour, so where are we on the stolen money?"

"We've interviewed security and the rest of the staff at the club, but no one seems to know anything. And you already know that the internal surveillance cameras didn't show shit," Rashad explained.

"And how about the cameras on the street? Did you check those?"

"Nah, but I got a guy who can look into it for us," Rashad said.

"Let's make it happen." I paused. "And, Rashad, make sure I see every bit of that footage myself, understand?"

"You got it, boss."

For the next thirty minutes or so, the three of us put our heads together, thinking of who the thief might possibly be. Although a few people came to mind, no one really stood out because the motive just wasn't there. Of course everyone needed money, but this just felt all too close to home. It felt personal.

Once I left the diner, I went to meet with the marketing exec I'd hired to run my club's promotional campaign.

While my two clubs were the hottest in New York City, I wanted them to be the hottest clubs on the entire East Coast. And the only way to do that was to pour more money into the business. Getting A-list celebrities to make frequent appearances and making sure that the club's name was flashed across every billboard on the I-95 was what I needed. I needed advertisements to be heard on every national and local radio station known to man.

After a long day at work, I returned to my quiet SoHo apartment. It was seldom used, only when I came back home for business or to visit my family. But being that it was my first major purchase after having a profitable year in the nightclub industry, I refused to let it go. It was one of my many symbols of success. Once I got out of my coat, I went over to my minibar and poured me a glass of cabernet. That instantly made me think of Imani.

Looking up at the big wooden clock above the fireplace, I saw that it was now a few minutes after seven. I immediately reached down into my pocket and took out my cell to see if I'd had any missed calls or texts from her. But when I didn't see any, I instantly began to get worried. She went into work today at three and promised to call me beforehand. I quickly dialed her number, hearing that it only rang twice before she picked it up.

"Hello," she whispered.

"Imani?"

"Hey, Noble. I didn't forget to call. My cell phone died."

"You at work?" I assumed, which was why she was whispering.

"Yeah. I get off tonight around midnight. Will that be too late to call?"

All of a sudden, I heard Big Will barking in the background. "Imani, no personal calls out on the floor, ya hear?"

Within a split second, I could feel my fury boiling up inside of me. That little fat fucker was getting on my last nerve. It seemed like he was constantly on Imani's back about one thing or another. And although I didn't want to cause her any further conflict on the job, I was just about this close to saying fuck it and bashing the nigga's head in.

In an attempt to calm myself, I took a deep breath and ran my hand down my face. "Imani, just call me on your way home, all right?"

"Okay, I'll call you then."

"Don't forget."

"I promise I won't."

Chapter 11

Imani

"Giirrll, you must have put something serious on that nigga," Karen said, her green eyes scanning over the white Mercedes that I'd been driving as we stepped out that night from work.

Laughing, I gave her a dismissive wave. "Girl, you're crazy."

"Now tell the truth. What exactly did you have to do to get everything this man has given you?" she pressed.

Releasing a puff of air into the cold atmosphere, I rolled my eyes. "It's just a loan, Karen. Trust me, it's all temporary."

"Even if it is a loan, you had to have done some special trick. Some freaky position in the bedroom perhaps?" she asked, shooting her eyebrow up toward the sky.

I shook my head. "No, Karen. There's no special trick, I promise," I said, laughing at just how serious her expression was.

"Mm-hmm," she muttered with her lips pursed to the side. After slipping her blue knitted hat on her head, she began walking off toward her car. "See ya tomorrow, girl," she said over her shoulder, throwing her hand up in the air.

"See ya tomorrow."

After clicking the alarm, I opened up the car door and slid into the cold leather seat. As soon as I cranked up the engine, I dialed Noble's number so that I could speak to him on Bluetooth. However, after just three rings, a wave of disappointment quickly washed over me, hearing his voicemail message on the other end. I knew it was extremely late, but all day long I'd been looking forward to talking with him.

After turning up the heat, I cupped my hands over my mouth and blew hot breath into them for warmth. And once I ensured the car was heated properly, I threw the gear in drive, but before I could press on the gas my cell phone started to vibrate on the console.

Tapping the glowing screen on the dashboard, I answered. "Hello."

"Imani," Noble said groggily.

"Hey, I was just calling because I promised to call you when I got off, but go back to sleep. You sound really tired."

I could hear him shuffling around as he cleared his throat. "Nah, you're good, ma. I'm up."

I smiled. "Well, I'm driving home from work now, if you wanna talk to me on the way." I gently pressed on the gas to begin my drive home.

"Yeah, I can do that." Noble momentarily paused, then out of nowhere he said, "Hey, have you ever thought about getting another job? You know, one where you don't have to work nights or deal with that fat little fuck . . . What is it that y'all call him? Big Will?"

"Noble!" I squealed, covering my mouth in laughter.

"What?"

"I mean, yes. Of course I've thought about leaving the diner, but truthfully I make decent money there. And Big Will, well, he's not all that bad."

It sounded like Noble sucked his teeth before he said, "Well, he's got one more time to talk to you like he's crazy. So either you find another job, or else he and I are gonna have some serious problems."

I scrunched my nose up at his words. While I was happy to have Noble defending me, I couldn't in good conscience allow a man I'd only know for a couple of months to dictate the ins and outs of my life. Well, at least no more than Noble already had. "Noble, I'm not quitting my job. I need money for school, remember?"

"Well, how about this? I'm starting a happy hour at the club a few days a week, and with that, I want to start serving appetizers. Why don't you come work for me? Come be a cook over at the club?"

"A few days a week?" I shrieked, coming to a halt at the red light. "I can't live off of that."

Noble gave a little snort of laughter at my expense. "Three days a week. I'll work around your school schedule, and I'll double what you're already making," he said with a bit of arrogance.

"No, Noble, really. You've spoiled me enough already."

"Imani," he said like he was trying to gain my attention. "I haven't even begun to spoil you like I want."

As if he could see me, I tucked my lips inward to hide my blushing smile. I was truly taken aback, and briefly, I found myself at a loss for words. "Noble," I breathed.

"What? I'm serious. Let me spoil you, Imani."

As I navigated the streets of downtown Baltimore, Noble and I chatted along the way. Even after I'd made it home safe and sound, it seemed that neither one of us wanted our conversation to end. After making sure to secure both the top and bottom locks, as he adamantly instructed, I removed my coat and plopped down on the living room sofa.

"So you'll at least think about it, right?" he asked, going back to his proposal.

Sighing deeply, I flung my head to the back of the couch. "Noble, you don't understand. I was just twenty years old when I came down to Baltimore all the way from Connecticut solely based on the empty promises of a man. He was my first boyfriend, my first everything, and he vowed to give me the world."

"And? Exactly what does he have to do with me?"

"The point is, Noble, I moved too fast with him. I trusted everything he said and ended up with nothing. No family, no real job, nothing! And now . . . now that you've helped me get back up on my own two feet, I just want to make moves on my own, ya know? For once, I want to be my own woman."

"Hmm, I see," was his casual response.

Confused, I asked, "Are you upset?"

"Upset? Why would I be? I swear, you just don't know how sexy you are, Imani."

"Sexy?" I asked, feeling the corners of my lips turn up slowly into another smile.

"Absolutely, ma. This independent woman shit you on right now, I can't even lie, it's sexy as fuck. Just don't forget to need me sometimes."

I didn't know why, but the vulnerability in Noble's last statement caused an unexpected throbbing between my thighs. "How could I? I'm practically living off of you right now. But it's only temp—"

"Temporary," he said, finishing my sentence. "I know, I know."

Noble and I talked for another thirty minutes before we hung up and finally called it a night. Once I got in the shower, memories of Noble's heavenly body and sexual techniques flooded of my mind. So much so that I found myself suddenly getting aroused. And before I knew it, I was toying with my clit beneath the water, wishing like hell that he was here to handle me himself.

After bringing myself to a subpar orgasm, I stepped out of the shower and dried off with one of his plush white towels. Using my imagination, I put lotion on every inch of my body with his large, masculine hands in mind. And within a matter of minutes, I found myself buried beneath the thick covers of his bed, smelling the faded remnants of his cologne before slowly drifting off into a deep slumber.

Late the next morning, around eleven thirty, I was eating a bowl of Frosted Flakes in the kitchen when the house phone began to ring. With my mouth still full of food, I hopped up from the barstool, scurried around the counter, and picked the phone up off the hook.

"Hello," I answered with a swallow.

"Yes, may I please speak with Imani Lewis?" the caller asked.

No one besides Karen ever called the house for me. With a slight arch in my brow, I replied, "This is she."

"Hi, my name is Debbie Austin from Stratford University, and I just wanted to congratulate you on your recent acceptance into our culinary program."

"Stratford?" Wondering if I'd heard her correctly, I temporarily pulled the phone away from my ear and looked down into the receiver. "Culinary program?" I asked.

"Yes, ma'am, we're excited to have you," she said with a chipper peal in her voice.

Tucking a loose strand of hair behind my ear, I nuzzled the phone tighter against my shoulder. "But, ma'am, I didn't apply to the Stratford Culinary Program. I believe you've somehow made a mistake."

"Well, you are Imani Lewis, aren't you? Date of birth, November 6, 1989, and your address is . . ." I heard her shuffling through some paper. "200 International Drive, unit 2108?"

My jaw dropped simultaneously with the phone, as it struck against the floor. Hurriedly, I reached down and picked it up before placing it back up to my ear. "Uh, hello. Hello, Ms. Austin, you still there?" I asked, trying to recover.

"Yes, ma'am, I'm still here. So like I was saying, we have all your information and will be expecting you at the start of the summer semester. You should be getting your enrollment packet in the mail any day now."

"Uhh, okay," I stammered, still in a partial state of bewilderment.

"You know, it's not every day I see people move to the top of the applicant list of our program. But Dean Roberts says you come highly recommended from one of our board members."

"Board members?" I whispered, bringing my fingers up to my lips.

"Ah, yes, a . . . a Mr. Noble Shaw."

Well, I'll be damned!

Within a split second, a cheesy grin extended across the width of my face. Hearing Noble's name and learning that he was the one who'd actually pulled this off made my heart instantly flutter. It seemed that every day for the past two months I was being schooled on the ways of Noble Shaw. He wasn't just some nightclub owner working down at the other end of the block. He was a man of influence, one who made things happen. And as hard as I had battled against playing the role of sad old Cinderella, it certainly had been a challenge not to when it came to Noble Shaw. I was starting to believe that he was truly my prince, my knight in shining armor who left little to no room to protest his rescue missions or even his excessive generosity.

"Miss Lewis?" Ms. Austin said, regaining my attention.

"Ah, yes."

"So as I was saying, all semester fees have been paid in full, so I'll see you at the beginning of the summer."

After ending the call, I rushed back around the kitchen island and dialed Noble on my cell. From all the excitement, my heart was beating wildly in my chest, and I could barely contain myself as I waited for him to answer. But after just a few short rings on the other end and getting his voicemail message, I became discouraged. I was almost to the point of leaving a message for him to call me back, but something in my mind told me to try just one more time.

Wasting no time, I went back and dialed him again. In the middle of the second ring, I heard the phone pick up followed by the sounds of a woman's laughter growing near. My ears perked up right away, and the excited energy I had coursing through me slowly began to fade, turning into anxiety and fear.

"Hello," she said, laughter still somehow resonating in her voice.

"Ah, yes, can I please speak with Noble?"

"Give me my phone, Sarah!"

Sarah?

A lump immediately formed in my throat as soon as I heard Noble's voice booming in the background. Hearing that he was with another woman, I abruptly ended the call and clutched the phone against my chest, suddenly finding it hard to even breathe. I knew I needed to speak with Noble firsthand and not make any assumptions, but in that moment I couldn't even think straight. An all-too-familiar feeling of jealousy and mistrust came over me, and within a blink of an eye, I had lost all control of my sensibility.

When Noble kept calling back to back, I didn't even pick up. I couldn't, for fear of hearing some bullshit lie or excuse spew from his lips. I'd been so hurt by my past relationship that in that instant I could only imagine the worst. And no matter how much I was starting to fall for this man, I just couldn't allow him to send me back to my former state of heartbreak. It would just be too painful to bear.

Chapter 12

Noble

"Give me my phone, Sarah!" I barked, looking at her as she grinned. She was teasing me almost in a childlike manner, shaking it from side to side in her hand.

But when she noticed the grimace on my face, her goofy smile faded into a frown. "Fine," she said, tossing the phone at my chest. "She hung up on you anyway."

One failed attempt after the other, I tried calling Imani back only to get her voicemail in return. "Shit," I mumbled under my breath, feeling frustrated that I was unable to immediately explain, because God only knows what Imani was thinking.

"Oh! I see what it is now," Sarah said. I looked up at her, seeing that her head was cocked to the side and a silly smirk was plastered on her face. "She's special to you, isn't she?"

Monica, who was sitting on the couch, let out a half-suppressed laugh.

With my jaw clenched, I gave Sarah a blank expression before turning around and heading back down the hall. Although she was right, I would never give her the pleasure of knowing it, especially this soon in my relationship with Imani. Sarah would only get a kick out of trying to mess with Imani's head. Under any other circumstance I probably wouldn't have even cared, but when it came to Imani, I knew that I could only tolerate but so much.

As I walked farther away, I could hear the juvenile sounds of her and Monica's snickers, fading until it was no more. I was actually over at my brother's place that morning going over the footage from outside the club. It just so happened that Sarah stopped by to see Monica on her lunch break. Even after Sarah and I went our separate ways some years back, she and Monica seemed to remain joined at the hip. I was cool with that, because again, Sarah was like family.

When I got back in Kells's home office, I returned to my seat behind the desk and carefully observed the screen that would show footage of each date in question. I had plans already etched in stone to look at every single person who'd both entered and left the building those nights.

Just as I was about to select the next date of footage, something caught my eye. It was Monica going in the building. Now, Monica was no stranger to the nightclubs I owned, but what caught my attention was that she was entering alone. Her usual entourage of girlfriends wasn't traipsing beside her, and from what I could see on the screen, Kells was also nowhere to be found.

"Since when does Monica come to the club by herself?" I asked, looking over at my brother.

Kells was sitting in the lone leather chair in the corner, pulling from a Belicoso cigar. With a swirl of smoke escaping his lips, he shifted in his seat. "Sometimes I'll have her meet me there. Or sometimes her and her girls will come separately to meet up in VIP."

While that made good enough sense, my intuition was telling me something different. However, I didn't say anything. I just kept going through the film quietly with a fine-tooth comb. On four out of five tapes, I witnessed Monica both entering and leaving the building by herself, each time with a large purse over her shoulder.

Now I was never one to make assumptions, so I didn't say anything to Kells, but I did cut my eyes over sharply at Rashad. Although Rashad was more of the muscle of the crew, he was both business and street smart like me. Upon receiving the message my eyes were sending, he gave me an obscure nod of his head.

After going over the footage a few more times, I got up from my chair, ready to leave. I first walked over to my brother and dapped him up before approaching Rashad, who was standing by the door. With a brotherly merge of our hands, I pulled Rashad in close and whispered in his ear, "Monica."

The serious look he gave when we locked eyes was all the reassurance I needed to know he'd follow through.

Heading for the front door, I passed through the living room only to see Monica sitting on the sofa. She had one foot propped up on the coffee table, painting her toenails a bright shade of pink. Instantly my nose flared from both the toxic smell and her outright boorish behavior. Not that Monica wasn't a pretty girl, but other than her looks she just didn't have much to offer in my opinion. She didn't work and always stayed in the clubs. It seemed that over the years I had racked my brain over a thousand times trying to see what Kells saw in her.

"Sarah's gone?" I asked, looking down to where she sat.

"Yeah, she went back to work. You know her job here was done once she pissed your little girlfriend off," she said with a little giggle.

Not even responding, I walked out the front door and headed over to my car. As soon as I got inside, I tried calling Imani's number once again. However, the phone only rang one time before sending me to voicemail, indicating that I'd been blocked.

"Fuck!" I cursed, slamming my fist down on the wheel.

With the engine not even cranked, I sat in the cold car, pondering over ways I could reach her. Then suddenly a thought occurred to me. Imani was at work, and I knew that the best means of contacting her at this point would be to call Miss Ruby's diner directly.

Out of the blue, as I went to dial the number, an unfamiliar sense of nervousness overcame me. Shifting in my seat, my shoulders all of a sudden grew tense. I had prided myself on always being a confident man in everything I did, so it was rare when something put me on edge. Not only did Imani have me cuddling after sex and pillow talking late at night, but she was now pulling emotions out of me I thought had long ago gone extinct.

Taking a deep breath, I listened as the phone rang for the third time.

"Hello."

I immediately recognized Big Will's voice and clenched my jaw. "Yes, ah, is Imani there?" I asked through gritted teeth, forcing a cordial tone.

"Look, Imani's working, and we don't take personal calls here at the diner."

"Listen here, you fat muthafuc—"

Before my tirade of words could release into the phone, the annoying sound of the dial tone interjected.

Motherfucker!

After just three more days of dealing with my business in New York and several unanswered calls to Imani on the house phone, I knew it was time for me to head back to Baltimore. Rashad promised to keep me updated on Monica, as well as all other possible leads, saying that he'd have more information by the time I returned. We tightened security at all exit points of the club to ensure we were not only checking people coming in but also those who looked suspicious when leaving. Instead of only three security guards, we now had six, and I had more cameras installed, homing in on the areas of the club where money was either kept or exchanged.

After a four-and-a-half-hour drive, I arrived back at my apartment a little after noon. Since Imani was now working the night shift at Miss Ruby's diner, I was expecting to see her before she left. With the explanation of Sarah already on the tip of my tongue, I eased the key inside the door. Crossing over the threshold, I immediately felt a change of energy in the place that was undoubtedly different from before I'd left. The warmth, happiness, and laughter that had spread all over my home these past couple of months was now gone.

Knowingly, I charged down the hall to Imani's room. From her door being open, I could see the bare mattress and box spring of her bed. She'd stripped them of their linens. With a sudden tightness developing in my chest, I crept into the room and went over to her dresser. Each drawer came up empty as I frantically pulled open one after another. Then, with one last attempt, I trudged my way over to her walk-in closet. Other than the velvet hangers on the rack, the only thing inside was the red Dolce & Gabbana dress I'd bought for her. And as my eyes traveled down, I noticed the Louboutin shoebox strategically placed on the floor. I didn't even have to look inside to know that the shoes I gifted her were in there. Pulling the door closed, I released a deep breath of frustration. Could the woman really be this childish, not to even give me a chance to explain?

Teetering between a state of anger and dejection, I trudged over to the master suite. I sat down on the edge of my bed only to smell her sweet scent rising from the sheets. On the nightstand were the keys to the new car I'd given her to drive, as well as the cell phone. No note, no

nothing. Suddenly my mind began to go haywire thinking of all the ways I could reach her. Even with all the
drama, something in the back of my mind kept telling me
that Imani was worth it.

Now don't get me wrong. I had a peaceful life before her,
successful with a nice place to come home to. But there
was something about her entering my life that ignited the
desire to have more than just casual sex. At 32 years old
I had already been divorced and had fathered not one
child. Even in the short amount of time I'd known Imani,
she reminded me that once upon a time those were the
things I had wanted: marriage and children.

Rubbing my hand over my face, I pulled out my cell
phone and dialed Kingston's number.

"Hello, Mr. Shaw," he answered, obviously recognizing
my name and number on his screen.

Foregoing any niceties, I got straight to the point.
"Kingston, do you know where Imani is?"

"Oh, yes. I dropped her off at her new apartment yesterday."

With my eyes bulging from my head, I felt my face burn
with anger. "Dropped her off? At her new apartment?"

"Well, yes. She said you knew that she was leaving,"
he replied low. Confidence faded in his tone as he now
spoke with uncertainty.

"And why did you have to be the one to drop her off?" I
wasn't accusing Kingston of anything, but I had so many
questions overlapping each other that it probably came
off that way.

"To bring your car back, sir. I'm the only she knows
who has the key code to enter the secured parking garage," he explained.

I briefly pinched my nose then allowed my hand to
travel down my jaw. "Send me the address," I said before
ending the call.

As soon as I got the text with Imani's new address, I was in my car and on my way. Apparently she was living just outside the inner harbor on Lombard Street, and it took me less than ten minutes to get there. Expecting to see another rundown neighborhood like the one she'd stayed in before, I was happily surprised when I pulled up. It was such a stark difference from her former place that I even glanced down at my phone to double-check the address.

After parking curbside, I stepped out of my car and admired the tall, historic red brick structure that sat on the corner of the block. It was just steps away from some of the most frequented bars, shops, and restaurants that Baltimore had to offer. Suddenly, I began to wonder how she was even able to afford a place like this.

I stepped up on the curb and jogged up the five brick steps of her building. Once inside, I found myself climbing a flight of stairs as I looked for her apartment number along the way. That's when I saw it: a painted green door with the numbers 242 plated in brass at the top. Taking a deep swallow, I approached the door and lifted my fist, prepared to knock. But that's when I unmistakably heard her laughter on the other side. Something about her being happy at a time when I was damn near falling apart instantly pissed me off. But that wasn't the only thing to stop me in my tracks. The sound of a male voice and his laughter was like salt being rubbed in my open wound.

Without hesitation, I pounded on the door hard like the police. "Imani, open up this goddamn door!"

Chapter 13

Imani

When the housing authority called me back last week and told me that the only apartment available was back down in the hood, I started to panic. Then on top of that, Noble had some other woman answering his phone the other day. I knew right then that I had to get out of his place, but the only question was how. Unless I wanted to go back to living in the slums, I had to start making moves.

It just so happened that Ms. Milly, who comes into the diner, was subletting her apartment down on Lombard Street. I wasn't even going to call her at first, but being that I now felt backed into a corner, I decided to at least see how much she was charging for rent. Thankfully, since Ms. Milly had known me for a few years, she said she would only charge me half of what she was going to charge a normal tenant. Typically, downtown apartments rented for no less than $1,500 a month, so when she told me $500, I jumped at the opportunity, signing a one-year lease for a place I hadn't even seen.

After moving in what little I owned, I called Peanut from the old neighborhood to come help me shift some things around. My furniture had been delivered earlier that morning, and I knew I'd need a nice set of muscular arms to get things placed just right. It wasn't much, just a queen-sized bed, a couch, and a small dinette set, but it was enough to me started.

"No. Put the couch over there," I told Peanut, pointing toward the corner of the room.

Being that this would be his third time moving the couch for me, Peanut let out a deep sigh. "This the last time, Imani," he said, bending over to get a good grip on the couch.

"Okay, then wait." With my hands clasped together under my chin, my eyes scanned across the living room.

"Dang, girl, you indecisive as hell," Peanut complained. He stood up and removed the workman's gloves from his hands before reaching around to his lower back, grimacing as he gently massaged the problematic area.

"Peanut, you're way too young to be having back pains," I told him.

"Come rub right here for me," he said, causing me to narrow my eyes at him. Peanut was always flirting, so I never knew if he was playing or serious at times like these. However, after seeing that he was truly in some discomfort, I went over and massaged his lower back through his T-shirt.

After a minute or so, Peanut glanced at me over his shoulder. "You know, just 'cause my back is a little sore doesn't mean I can't put in work," he said with a little wink.

I slapped him on the back of his head. "Boy, shut up and move this damn couch!" I said, causing Peanut to double over in laughter.

As soon as he reached down to lift the couch again, I heard someone banging loudly at my door. "Imani, open up this goddamn door!"

Hearing Noble's fury on the other side of the door, I looked over at Peanut.

"Don't look at me," he said, shrugging his shoulders.

I rolled my eyes and walked over to the door, hearing that Noble's pounding was nonstop. Feeling myself get angry, I unlocked the door and yanked it open hard. "Would you stop knocking on my damn door like that?"

With his dark eyes enlarged to the size of quarters, Noble's chest heaved up and down. He pushed past me into the apartment as if he was looking for something specific.

"Nigga, what the fuck are you doing here?" Noble spat, looking right at Peanut.

As if he were being held at gunpoint by the Baltimore City police, Peanut threw his hands up in surrender. "Yo, she just asked me to come help her move," he quickly explained, realizing that Noble's fury was nothing to play with.

"Well, you can excuse yourself," Noble told him. He was so angry that his fists were balled up at his sides.

I sucked my teeth. "Peanut, you don't have to leave," I said, watching him gather up his things.

Noble turned to me with the deadliest glare.

"You can't just come up in my house like you run things, Noble," I said.

As Peanut started for the door, I heard him mumbling under his breath. "Damn. Pussy must have been fye."

"Aye, fuck you say?" Noble asked with a harsh tone. He walked up behind Peanut like he was ready to ring his neck. I grabbed his arm to stop him.

Peanut let out a snort of laughter and shook his head. "Nothing, yo. Y'all two lovebirds have a good day."

After Peanut left, letting the heavy door slam behind him, Noble turned to me. "What the fuck is this, Imani? You just up and move out and don't tell me shit?"

"Look, it was never a secret that I was moving out, Noble. You've known my plan all along."

He moved in so close that I literally felt the heat of his anger radiating off of him. "Stop. Fucking. Playing with me. You blocked my fucking calls for the past few days, and now you've moved out. For once, act like a fucking adult and tell me what's wrong!"

Both his words and the intense glare he now had me under made me feel small. "I'm not going to be sitting around in your apartment, waiting for you while you out gallivanting with a bunch of different women, Noble," I said weakly, realizing that it had come out much stronger the last time I'd rehearsed it in my head.

"What women, Imani? I told you, I'm only pursuing you!"

I released the breath I had been holding and briefly closed my eyes. "The woman who answered your phone," I admitted.

"I'm not fucking Sarah or any oth—"

"Sarah is it?" I asked, raising my brow and instantly feeling jealous at the mere sound of her name.

Noble reached down in his pocket and pulled out his cell phone. His fingers skimmed lightly across the screen before he pressed down hard. Then suddenly I could hear the phone ringing from it being put on speaker.

"Noble, what are you doing?" I asked.

He held up his finger to quiet me. "Hey, Noble," a woman answered.

"Sarah. When was the last time we fucked?" he asked straightaway, making my eyes grow wide, and a lump instantly formed in my throat.

"I don't know, Noble. It's been what, shit, almost four years?" she said.

I opened my mouth to speak, but he put his finger back up to stop me once again. "And when I come home to New York, do I make any attempts to fuck you, or do you ever try to fuck me?"

Flabbergasted, she gasped. "Oh my God, Noble! Why the hell are you asking me this?"

"Just answer the question, Sarah," he demanded.

"No. Never."

"I'll call you later," he simply said before ending the call.

You could have bought my ass for ten pennies in that moment. I was so embarrassed, and the grimace on Noble's face as he glared at me wasn't making me feel any better. He walked up close, and without warning, he wrapped his hand around the front of my throat. I flinched at first and closed my eyes, until I realized that his grip was soft.

"You've been a bad girl, Imani."

My eyes instantly popped open, hearing the lust trickle from his voice. With his fingers still gently around my neck, he pulled me forward and pressed his lips against mine. His tongue teased my lips just before snaking its way inside, its sweet flavor instantly drawing me in like honey to a bee. As his hungry mouth began to overpower mine, I felt my arms reaching for the sides of his abs to draw him near. It was all I could do to hold on as his kiss nearly seized my breath.

The pounding between my thighs had now magnified tenfold, creating a wet mess in my panties. Being this close to him had me feeling lightheaded, and my skin had grown hot to the touch. It was like all of a sudden I was high. My heart was thumping so loud in my chest that I could practically hear it between my ears, and I was so caught up in his rapture that I could no longer tell my left from my right. All of these, I knew, were physical symptoms of missing Noble's touch. My body craved this man like never before, and the only thing I wanted was to feel him inside of me.

Noble reached down between us and gently stroked my pussy with the front of his index finger. Even beneath the thin fabric of my yoga pants, that simple gesture alone was enough to make me shudder. My center was now throbbing so badly it ached, and without even thinking I found myself tugging and pulling on his shirt, trying desperately to yank it from his pants before grabbing hold of his belt.

Removing his hand from around my neck, Noble broke free from our kiss and looked at me. It was the look that told me that he was in charge. "Take this shit off, Imani. Now!" he demanded.

I didn't waste any time wiggling out of my pants until they were sitting on the floor. After pulling my shirt over my head and flinging it across the room, I stood in front of Noble in a blue lace bra and matching panties. His gaze, as he looked over every inch of me, was so intense that I was finding it harder and harder to even breathe.

All at once, Noble reached back for my throat, causing a yelping sound to rise from my lungs. As I panted, he brought his face in close to mine, and with a whisper without bass against my ear, he said, "You wearing this shit for another nigga, Imani?"

Although his grip around my neck was tighter than before, it was turning me on in ways I'd never experienced. "No, no," I breathed, shaking my head from side to side.

Noble removed his hand from my throat and reached around my back to unclasp my bra. When my taut nipples were exposed, he leaned down and swirled his cool tongue around each of them, one after the other. I gripped his shoulders for support and let my head fall back in delight.

Slowly, he began to glide the tip of his tongue down my stomach until he was squatted in front of me. With his lips against the front of my panties, he looked up at me with dark, lust-filled eyes. "Don't give my pussy away, Imani." When his warm breath tickled my clit, it was all I could do to keep it together.

"Never," I whispered, panting like a dog in heat as I shook my head.

Noble deeply inhaled my scent before slipping his fingers beneath the edges of my panties, bringing them down vigilantly over my hips as he kissed the tops of my thighs. His beard lightly prickling the surface of my skin as he sent what felt like zaps of electricity up and down my spine. And at the exact moment, I felt the lace pool around my ankles, his soft tongue dipped into my folds.

"Ohh, Noble," I moaned.

Noble pulled my leg up over his shoulder, burying the whole lower half of his face and beard between my thighs. Suddenly, I could feel his stiff tongue enter me over and over, dipping in a bit deeper each time. And when I could feel my muscles starting to contract, I grabbed hold of his head.

"Ohh, Noble, pleasse," I begged, feeling my eyes roll to the back of my head.

However, my pleas fell on deaf ears, because Noble didn't let up at all. His tongue just continued to stab into me repeatedly. It was as if he was trying to figure out just how many licks it would take to get to the center of me. And just when I felt like I couldn't take anymore, like my body was about to explode, Noble pulled back and gave one single suck to my clit. I lost it.

"Ahh, shiitt!" I wailed out in pleasure. I felt one giant release as an abundance of wetness seeped out of me.

Noble rubbed his face and beard between my thighs, wasting no time to lick me clean. He stood up, and in one fluid motion, he hoisted me in the air, wrapping my legs around his waist.

"Bedroom?" he asked, making his way down the short hall.

"On the right," I stammered, still trying to catch my breath.

As soon as we entered my room, Noble tossed me on the bed and began removing his belt. The entire time

I watched him undress, my body burned with desire. I was so anxious to have him inside me that I could barely contain myself. My mouth started watering, and the pulsation in my center had returned.

Once Noble was stripped down and fully naked in front of me, my eyes roamed the entirety of his muscular physique, from his strong arms and chest down to the six hard mounds of his abs. And between his big, beefy thighs hung my special friend. It was a long, thick saluting pole that was begging for my affection. I licked my lips at the sight.

When Noble approached the bed, I crawled over to the edge and eagerly took him in my mouth. I slid my lips down as far as I could go before slithering my tongue up his shaft.

"Shit, Imani," he hissed, grabbing me by the hair.

I looked up at him with wide eyes when he pulled me off of him. "Turn over," he said.

"But I wanted t—"

"I said, turn the fuck over, Imani!" he demanded in a stern tone of voice.

I hurriedly turned around and got on all fours just like he'd instructed. With a grip of the sheets, I closed my eyes, preparing to feel his girth. But when I felt his hands spreading my thighs apart, I looked back at him.

Smack!

He slapped me so hard on the ass I knew he'd left a mark. "Turn back around!"

If I weren't already hot for him before, I damn sure was turned on and ready for him now. Without further delay, he clutched the sides of my hips and pushed what felt like every bit of his length inside of me.

"Aargh, fuckk!" I wailed, simultaneously feeling both pleasure and pain as I gripped the sheets with both of my hands.

Noble tugged at my hair, making my chin lift to the ceiling and my back dip in at an angle. "Take that shit," he said, thrusting deeper from behind.

"Ohh, Noble," I moaned.

The way he drilled into me, with so much force and so much passion, there was no mistaking that he was punishing me. Punishing me for leaving his place and punishing me for acting so jealous without good reason. With clenched teeth I held on for dear life, just riding the wave. That was until my body felt like it was about to erupt. Noble must have felt it too because he said, "Cum for me, Imani."

"Wait, I . . . No . . ." I stuttered, feeling his strokes come to a steady pace. With only the sound of our flesh slapping against one another's stirring around the room, I held on as best I could.

"Fuck," he hissed, tightening his grip on my hair as he continued to buck against me. "Let that shit go, ma," he demanded.

And just like he'd ordered, I did. "Noooble!" I cried, releasing all over him so hard that my body jerked and my legs trembled beneath me.

As Noble continued to slowly pummel me, bringing me down from my high, I could feel him beginning to swell up inside of me. "Catch it for me," he said through a strained whisper.

Hurriedly, I crawled back around and opened up my mouth, impatiently watching him as he gave his throbbing dick a few more strokes with his hand. And as his hand went from base to tip, he leered at me intently, biting down on his bottom lip.

"Arrgghh fuckkk!" he groaned, squeezing his eyes tight as his thick cream spurted out everywhere. On impulse, I covered him with my mouth and suckled out the remains until he collapsed back on the bed.

"Shit, baby, I made a mess," he panted, his chest rising and falling fast as he attempted to control his breathing.

"And these were my only sheets," I whined with an artificial pout before laying my head down on his chest.

"I'll buy you some more sheets, Imani."

"But you don't need to."

"Let me buy you some damn sheets, woman!" he fussed, making the muscles of his chest flex.

I let out a little laugh before wrapping my arm around his torso and snuggling closer against him.

"You promise to stop acting so jealous, Imani?" he asked low, shifting the conversation back to a more serious one.

When I didn't answer, he reached down and lifted my chin so that I could look up at him. "I told you, I'm only pursuing you, okay?"

Absorbing his words, I cautiously nodded my head. "Okay," I whispered.

He leaned down and kissed my lips one final time before we dozed off in each other's arms. I knew that I was punishing Noble for the hurt I'd experienced in my past, but I couldn't help it. I promised myself long ago that I would no longer play the victim. I may struggle to make ends meet on my own, but I would no longer allow a man to build me up so high that he had the sole ability to make me crumble.

For now, I was just going to follow my heart, casting all cautions to the side, in hopes that Noble and I were building something real.

Chapter 14

Noble

It had been five days after I barged in on Imani at her new place, and we were now holding hands on an airplane, descending into Sangster International Airport. She never did let me know where she wanted to go, so I took the liberty of booking us a trip to Jamaica. Luckily Kingston had gotten her passport expedited, and since I already owned a house in Montego Bay, it was an easy decision.

I glanced over at Imani, seeing a frazzled look on her face. Her shoulders were hiked up high, and her chest was puffed as though she were holding in her breath. This was her very first time on an airplane, and as expected, she was a huge bundle of nerves. Gently, I lifted her hand that I was holding and kissed the back of it. "Just breathe," I told her.

Just as she exhaled and nodded her head, the wheels of the plane landed on the strip. "Ahh!" she screamed, as we shook and bounced up and down.

Inwardly, I chuckled at her dramatics, but still, in an effort to comfort her, I pulled her close and wrapped her in my arms. "Calm down. We're here," I said, kissing her on the forehead.

Once the plane came to a complete stop, I helped Imani up from her chair. She was shaking like a leaf, so I held her by the waist to support her. Being that we were in first class, we were first to exit, and as soon as we made it down to the baggage claim, I saw my driver, Dominic. He was holding up a white sign that read Mr. Noble Shaw.

I went over and greeted him with a handshake. "Dominic, my man."

"Mr. Shaw, it's so good to see you again," he said with a bright smile. Dominic was a tall, slender fellow, with midnight-colored skin. Like always, he stood before us in a simple black suit and tie, ready to take us to our destination.

"Dominic, this here is my . . ." Letting my voice trail off, I looked down at Imani because I wasn't exactly sure what to call her. Since we hadn't given our relationship a title, I didn't want to offend her either way.

"I'm Noble's good friend, Imani," she said, extending her hand.

Bowing his head, Dominic took her hand and kissed the back of it. "Beautiful Queen Imani," he said in his thick island accent, grinning from ear to ear.

"Ahem," I said, clearing my throat to gain his attention. Both he and Imani shared a little laugh.

Dominic arched his left brow and gave a cunning smile. "She's just your good friend, right, sir?"

I shook my head and let out a snort of laughter because Dominic knew good and well that Imani was more than just my friend.

We each grabbed a piece of luggage and followed him toward the exit. As soon as the doors automatically slid open, I could feel the warm tropical breeze brush past my face. I glanced over at Imani, whose eyes were already filled with excitement, and her hair was seemingly blowing in the wind. Right then, I knew all of her nerves had subsided and that she was finally ready to experience Jamaica.

Once Dominic let us in the back of the car, Imani rested her head on my shoulder.

"Are you tired?" I asked, placing my hand on her bare knee.

"No, I just wanna be close to you," she said, looking up into my eyes.

I leaned down and first pecked her lips then her nose while allowing my thumb to caress across her skin.

"Thank you so much for convincing Big Will to give me the whole week off. I just don't know how you did it," she said with a closed-lip smile.

With a downward stretch of my lips, I carelessly shrugged my shoulders, as if it were no big deal. Well, that was the only response I could come up with on such short notice. Unbeknownst to Imani, I told the fat fucker yesterday over the phone that she would no longer be working there. I knew she'd be pissed when she found out that I resigned for her, but I didn't want to get into all of that now. I just wanted her to kick back and enjoy Jamaica without having to worry about that damn job.

Now don't get me wrong, I did call into Miss Ruby's diner with the best intentions, and I asked Big Will if she could have the week off. I wanted to surprise her, you know? But when he started talking about how I didn't need to be the one requesting time off for one of his employees, I cussed his ass out and told him to take that damn job and shove it up his fat ass. Shit, Imani didn't need that job anyway. I would handle whatever expenses she had, and if she was that damn adamant about having a job, she knew that she could always come work for me. Either way, it wasn't a problem.

As soon as we pulled up to my villa, which sat right along Cornwall Beach, I watched Imani's eyes light up. "Wow. This is absolutely beautiful, Noble," she said, looking out the window in awe. Her eyes cast up to take in the exterior of my eight-bedroom estate.

Once Dominic drove around the circular driveway, which was lined with palm trees and colorful flowers, he put the car in park. While he hopped out to get our luggage, I helped Imani out of the car. With one hand in mine, she stepped out and covered her mouth, taking it all in. I must admit that it was a perfect Jamaican day at just eighty-four degrees. The sun was shining bright, and the sweet scent of hibiscus carried in the wind. Even the birds were welcoming us with a chirping song. It was as if everything had been flawlessly staged for Imani's arrival.

As Dominic rolled our luggage to the front door, Imani quickly kicked off her flip-flops and ran full speed around the house. Her bare feet trekked through the lush green lawn that I knew would eventually merge with sand. All I could see was the back of her and the white sundress she wore flowing in the air. I guessed she could hear the waves crashing against the shore when we arrived and just couldn't wait to see the blue waters for herself. I chased behind her, laughing at her playfulness.

Just before I reached the beach, I stopped to remove my socks and shoes. As I was kneeled down, rolling my pants above my ankles, I looked up to see Imani fully submerged in the ocean. Although she still had on her dress, it was as if she didn't care. In that moment she was a free spirit, flicking water up with her hands. In all my 32 years of living, I didn't believe my face had felt a bigger smile.

"Imani," I called out to her, walking through the sand.

She looked back at me over her shoulder with those innocent catlike eyes. Her beautiful brown face and short black hair were already dripping wet with water. "You coming in?" she asked.

I stepped in, feeling the cool water creep up to my feet. "It's too cold," I said, giving a little smirk.

"Pleasee," she whined, batting her eyes as a cute pout formed upon her lips. I shook my head and let out a little chuckle because I'd quickly realized that Imani already knew how to get to me.

Hesitantly, I stepped into the ocean to join her, feeling my jaw slightly clench as the cold water rose to saturate my Armani linen pants. As soon as I got near, I grabbed her from behind and tickled her sides. She squirmed and squealed in laughter before turning around to face me. The moment our eyes connected, it seemed as if the waters stilled. And as I pulled her into me, I could feel the beat of her heart sounding as if it were trying to break through her flesh.

"This is all like a dream," she said, putting her arms around my neck. "I just don't know how I'll ever repay you—"

Going in for a deep, passionate kiss, I cut Imani's words short. I didn't want to hear any nonsense of her paying me back. All I wanted was to be with her. As I savored the sweetness of her tongue, I reached down and cupped her ass beneath her dress. Under the water, my hands mindlessly slid up and down her silky skin. And even in the coolness, I could feel myself growing hard. Without warning, she jumped up and wrapped her legs around me.

As the waves plowed into us, I held her in place and continued to kiss her lips, loving the feel of her wet skin against me as she caressed the back of my neck. And when our soft moans and groans began to overpower the sounds of the ocean, I carried her over to the shoreline. I gently laid her back in the sand as I wedged myself between her thighs.

"Oh, Noble," she breathed as though she were trying to catch her breath. She looked into my eyes and stroked my beard with her hand.

It was at that exact moment that I felt something shifted between us. It was like my heart had literally begun skipping to a brand-new beat, a beat I knew with certainty could've only matched Imani's. And as a man who hadn't loved a woman in over four years, I found myself all of a sudden overwhelmed with foreign emotions. I mean, it was well beyond the basic "butterflies in your stomach" bullshit. This here was realizing, for the first time, that I'd never be the same me without her. I had a sudden desire to be everyone and everything to this woman so that she would never have to look any further when it came to matters of the heart.

"What am I gonna do with you, Imani?" I whispered, staring down into her beautiful catlike eyes.

"Oh, I'm sure you'll think of something, Mr. Shaw," she teased before pecking my lips.

After kissing her lips, I smothered her with more light kisses that journeyed into the crook of her neck. Her taste, both salty and sweet, was like caramel to my tongue. My hands roamed under her dress, searching for the edges of her panties, but before I could pull them down, she put her hands on my forearms to stop me.

"No, we can't," she said, looking from left to right. "Not out here."

"Move those fucking hands, Imani," I muttered in a low tone of voice, my lips still connected to her skin.

"But what if someone sees us?" she whispered.

Lifting myself, I hovered over her and peered down into her eyes. "I don't give a fuck. Let them look," I said, looking into her eyes. "I need you," I breathed, unable to wait a minute longer to feel her. I felt like if I didn't have her right then and there, I would just die.

As I pressed my lips against hers, I went back to exploring underneath her dress. Once I had a grasp on the lace, I gave one good yank and ripped her underwear completely off.

"Ahh," she squealed.

I anxiously slid my pants down just enough to free my throbbing dick before pushing her dress above her waist. And without any further delay, I gripped the sides of her hips and slowly plunged my dick deep inside her. My eyes instantly closed when I felt her body open up for me. Her legs wrapped themselves around my waist.

"Ohh, Noble," she cried, with her mouth adjacent to my ear. Her hands instantly clawed at my back from the force.

"Imani, this pussy . . . Shit," I hissed, stroking against her.

The pleasurable sounds of her moans made me thrust that much harder. I closed my eyes and stroked at a steady pace so that I could enjoy just how tight and wet she was. I traveled in and out, deeper and deeper while she softly cried my name.

"Oh, God. Noooble, pleassee."

And just as her walls started to contract around me and she began to tremble, I felt that tightness build up in my groin. I bit down on my bottom lip in hopes of detaining my own groans of pleasure.

"I'm cumminn'," she cried, sucking my body even deeper toward her core.

And within just that split second, I had lost all control. My eyes rolled to the back of my head, and the muscles in my ass squeezed tighter than the lid on a pickle jar. "Arrghh, Imani," I groaned, releasing inside her.

Feeling completely spent, I allowed my body to collapse down on top of hers. Both of our hearts raced frantically as we tried to catch our breaths. With our bodies still connected, I closed my eyes and laid my head against the sand. Somewhere between the sounds of the ocean, having Imani near, and that calm breeze that was relentlessly blowing over me, I had started to drift off to sleep.

Suddenly, I could feel Imani's hands softly rubbing my back in a circular motion.

"Noble," she whispered. "Are you asleep?"

"Hmm."

"You do know that your ass is completely out right now, right?" she asked with a hint of humor in her voice.

Hearing that snapped me out of the mini coma I was in. Not only was my bare ass exposed for all of Jamaica to see, but Imani was also lying in a very compromising position. Thankfully, the next house down was quite a ways away, but that didn't mean folks didn't stroll down the beach all the time.

"Oh, shit." I leaned down to get my pants before standing up

Although my body was tired, I found enough energy to pull Imani to her feet. I brushed the sand off the both of us, and when I saw that her legs were wobbly, I picked her up and threw her over my shoulder.

"Noble," she shrieked, laughing as I ran with her toward the house.

In Jamaica, the doors and hurricane blinds of the house always stayed open. So as I approached the downstairs great room, right off the pool, I didn't need any free hands or even a key to enter. When my sandy feet hit the cool travertine tile, I set Imani down. She and I both looked at one another and just laughed at what we'd just done.

"Ahem."

When I heard somewhere clearing his throat, I look past Imani to see Dominic across the room. He was standing behind the bar, doubling as my butler.

"So. You two friends want to go and get cleaned up for dinner?" he asked, emphasizing the word "friends." I knew from just the silly grin on his face that he'd seen us fucking out there on the beach.

I chuckled. "Yeah, man. What are we eating?"

"Katherine has prepared curry shrimp and chicken, and rice and beans with mixed vegetables for dinner," he said, referencing my Jamaican chef.

"Tell Miss Kathy we'll be back down in just twenty minutes."

As if she knew where she was going, Imani pulled me sexily by the shirt and led me up the stairs. We got halfway up before she looked back down and said, "Aye, Dominic, let's make it thirty, okay?" Then she gave a little wink.

He let out a small laugh and shook his head because he knew just like I did that Imani was yearning for another round.

Chapter 15

Imani

"Yes, that one," Noble said, swiping his thumb down one corner of his mouth. His thick, muscular legs gaped wide as he sat back in the chair, undressing me with his eyes.

I turned around so that he could see my backside. "You don't think it's too short? I mean, for a woman my age?" I said, feeling insecure that my ass was practically spilling out of the romper he'd chosen.

"It's perfect, Imani. Sexy," he said in a deep, sultry tone. He ran his tongue across his bottom lip as he allowed his eyes to linger.

My left shoulder hiked to my cheek in a bashful manner as I tucked my lips inward to hide my smile.

For the past three days, Noble and I couldn't keep our hands off of one another. Although each time was spontaneous, it seemed as if we'd been fucking morning, noon, and night. It didn't even matter where we were: in the shower, on the beach, and even in the back of the car on our way into town. I could barely contain myself when I was around this man. With each day that passed, my desire to feel his touch had intensified to a point I never knew existed. I had it bad for Noble Shaw.

After walking back into the dressing room, I changed out of my clothes and glanced at myself in the mirror. I had never felt more beautiful in all my life as I turned from side to side to admire my reflection. I took in my slim waist and wide hips, which had light tiger stripes across them. Even my full-sized breasts, which had been flawed by Noble's marks of passion, were beautiful to me.

My short hair was currently in its naturally curly state because I couldn't do anything with it. As much time as we'd spent in the pool or at the beach, there would have been no use in flat ironing it. But the way Noble would grab hold of it when we had sex, or the way he'd tuck a wispy piece behind my ear, made me feel so pretty. Rarely would I ever hear him say it, well, not outright at least, but the way he would sometimes look at me told me that he thought I was one of the most beautiful girls in the world.

I put my maxi dress and flip-flops back on before heading back out to where Noble had been seated. He'd taken me to Clutch, one of the most exclusive and expensive boutiques in Montego Bay. Apparently Noble was well-known around here, because they treated him like a celebrity. They'd shut down the entire store just for him, and when I came in, they already had racks of clothes for me to try on.

The entire time I was in the dressing room, the ladies from the store made sure to keep Noble comfortable. He sat on a blue suede sofa while being served flutes of champagne. He even had it where a tray of fresh fruit and cheese were just a finger snap a way. It was a bit odd to me that Noble could get this kind of treatment just from owning a few nightclubs back in the States, but then I had to remember that he visited Jamaica often. Each time he stayed, I was sure, he'd probably spent a shitload of money, and with most of its population being so poor, they did what anyone in their situation would do. They treated him like a king in hopes he'd spend even more the next time.

Before passing the romper over to one of the ladies in the store, I glanced down at its price tag. *$600*. "Noble!" I shrieked.

He looked up at me from where he sat in the chair. "What's wrong?"

"Did you know that romper is six hundred dollars?"

Casually, he took a slow sip of champagne before leaning over to place it down on the small table beside him. He reclined in his chair and looked up at me with a calm expression on his face. "What's your point, Imani?"

"Noble, I just don't want you to spend that kind of money on me. I mean, that's more than a whole month's rent."

Noble stood up from his seat, and with one arm he pulled me into him so that we were cheek to cheek. "You don't tell me how to spend my money. I work hard for my money. So if I want to buy this whole goddamn store, then that's what the fuck I'll do," he whispered sternly against my ear.

Although he didn't yell, his words were harsh, which had me feeling conflicted. On the one hand, I wanted to argue back and flat out refuse his gifts. I mean, shit, he couldn't force me to take them. But then on the other hand, I was suddenly hot and bothered, completely turned on from just the simple way he'd checked me.

"Fine," I said, rolling my eyes. I attempted to pull away, but Noble held me firm by the waist.

"Kiss me," he said.

"No, I don't want to kiss you right now, Noble," I said, turning my head away. Even with his hands at the small of my back, I managed to fold my arms across my chest, putting space between us.

"I said, kiss me, woman," he demanded.

Unintentionally, my lips curled up into a smile. When I turned back to look at him, I saw that his tongue was resting sexily at the roof of his mouth. His dark, hooded eyes peered into me, and just like that, I was back under his command. Leaning in, I submitted to his drawing power and softly kissed his lips. Noble held me close and dipped his warm tongue into my mouth. His hands leisurely traveled up and down my backside as though we were the only ones in the room. And when we finally broke apart, I looked over to see that the ladies in the store were all standing off to the side, smiling and staring at us with admiration.

"We'll take that one, and the first three dresses she tried on as well," Noble told them.

"But, Noble," I sighed, putting my hand on my forehead. He lifted my chin and quickly shut me up with another quick peck to my lips.

After we left Clutch, we walked the strip for another hour, just talking and holding hands. Noble was a strong a man, a boss, and even a bit arrogant at times, but boy was he romantic. He never seemed to forget the small things. He spooned behind me at night, blew lashes away that threatened to enter my eyes, and no matter where we were, he always held my hand.

It was around five o'clock that evening when Dominic drove us back up to the villa. We were hitting up a nightclub called Dirtee Gyal later on, and Miss Kathy promised to feed us before we left. Based on the name of the club, I asked him if it was a strip club, but he simply laughed and assured me that it wasn't.

When he told me that we'd be meeting some of his friends there, I instantly got nervous. I started wondering what they'd think of me. Had I'd been the only one of Noble's women they'd met? If not, how would I measure up to the ladies he'd presented in the past? Slowly but surely I started feeling uncertain about the whole damn night.

"Noble, I'm not feeling so good. Maybe you should just go without me," I said, looking at him from across the dining room table.

"What's wrong? Was it the food?"

As soon as Noble said that, Miss Kathy scoffed from the corner of the room. I glanced over, seeing her standing there like a statue with a white kitchen towel draped neatly across her arm. She was a heavy-set, dark-skinned woman, in her late forties I supposed, who wore a white turban on her head. She was supposed to be observing unless we needed her.

"Miss Kathy, everything was delicious. It's not the food," I assured her.

Noble cocked his head to the side and licked his lips. "Well, if it's not the food, then what's wrong?"

"I'm just not feeling up to it. My hair is a mess and . . ." My voice trailed off as I tucked a piece of hair behind my ear.

"So you're nervous about meeting my friends." His left cheek hiked into a smirk.

"I never said that I was nervous about meeting your friends, Noble."

Noble released a small snort of laughter. "You didn't have to." He stood up from his chair and looked back at Miss Kathy. "Is Della here?"

"Yes, sir, she's upstairs waiting."

"Imani, come with me," he said.

I got up from my chair and walked over to where Noble was waiting for me to take his hand. Together we climbed the stairs and walked down the hall to a room that was set up with a makeup counter. There were even flat irons, curlers, and other supplies to do my hair. And off to the side, I could even see the new clothes we'd just bought, hanging up right above a few pairs of high-heeled shoes.

"Come sit, Ms. Imani," a thin, dark-skinned lady with long dreads said, patting the stool in front of her. I looked over at Noble, slightly confused.

"Imani, this is Della. She's going to do your hair and makeup for tonight."

"But—"

"Go ahead, ma. Let her take care of you, and I'll come back to check on you in an hour," he said, kissing my cheek.

Tentatively, I sat down and let Della do her thing. After two hours my hair was flat ironed in a silky bob with a part down the middle. It had grown a bit over the past few months, so even after a quick cut it still fell level with my chin. Della was a true professional. She painted my face with just the right amount of makeup, allowing my natural beauty to break through.

Even after all the fuss I'd put up earlier, I decided on the peach romper Noble had chosen. He was right. It looked absolutely perfect on me. It made my legs look inches longer, and it complemented the gold high-heeled sandals I wore. I threw on a pair of gold hoop earrings and paired it with a bangle before grabbing my clutch.

As I walked down the stairs, I could see Noble standing by the bar, wearing simple blue fitted jeans and a white Armani T-shirt. Over the past few months I had never seen him dress so casual, but damn if he didn't look good. Even his scent was relaxed and easygoing as I came near. The fresh combination of soap and sandalwood had me practically drooling.

"You look beautiful, Imani," he said, stroking his beard as his eyes drank me in.

I walked over and wrapped my arms around his neck. "You don't look too bad yourself, Mr. Shaw."

After getting into the car and making it over to Dirtee Gyal in less than twenty minutes with Dominic behind the wheel, we were stepping into the club. The dimly lit place was completely packed and blaring Reggaeton from wall to wall. Normally I didn't dance much, but the vibe was contagious, and before I knew it I was moving to the beat.

"Mr. Shaw, let me escort you to your area," a short fellow approached us and said. He led us up the stairs to what I assumed was their VIP lounge. As we walked in, I could see two men and two ladies ogling us.

"Noble, my man," the stocky, light-skinned one said, standing up with his hand already extended.

Noble dapped him up and brought him in for a brotherly hug before the tall, dark guy stood up next.

"Imani, this is Bilaal," he said, pointing at the lighter one. "And this here is my boy Phillip."

His boy Phillip couldn't take his eyes off me. "It's nice to meet you, Miss Imani. Noble has told us so much about you," he said, taking me by the hand. I glanced over at Noble and arched my brow.

"Oh, and let me introduce you to their wives," Noble said, guiding me by the waist. He looked down at the white sofas that the two ladies were seated on and gestured with his hand. "This here is Bilaal's wife, Enid."

"Hi," I said, shaking her hand. She was gorgeous. She had sparkly hazel eyes and sandy brown locs that hung down around her vanilla-colored face.

"Hello. Nice to finally meet you, Imani."

I smiled. Noble had been mentioning me to his Jamaican friends.

"And this here is Robin. Robin is Phillip's wife."

She too was a beautiful woman. Obviously, she was much taller and thicker than Enid. Her skin was dark and flawless like melted fudge, and her long, silky black hair draped down the front of her ample bosom.

"So dis is her, huh?" she said in her thick Jamaican accent, standing up from her seat. I was right. Robin looked to be just a few inches shy of six feet tall, and her figure looked to be about a size sixteen. She could have easily been a plus-sized model, standing there in a blue sleeveless jumpsuit.

"Yes, I'm Imani," I said, offering my hand but she only stared at it.

I looked over at Noble, but he only smiled, which confused me. Then all of a sudden, Robin pulled me in for a hug. "Welcome, ma dear. You're stunning, just like Noble said."

Unsure of it all, I hugged her back before we took our seats. Robin immediately nudged Phillip and told him to order us a few rounds of shots. I tossed Noble a look, because other than wine, I didn't drink much. Noble kissed me on the shoulder before bringing his lips over to my ear.

"Drink up. I'm gonna take advantage of you tonight," he whispered. I felt my cheeks instantly warm, and my clit start to pulse.

"So what did Noble tell you about us?" Phillip asked.

"Well, nothing much really," I answered honestly.

"Damn, it's like that," Bilaal laughed. "The three of us met at that resort on Rose Hall some years back and made a drunken investment in this here nightclub. Remember?"

My eyes cut over at Noble, wondering why he didn't tell me that he'd owned this place.

"Well, we do know that you're a chef," Enid said.

With my eyes still on Noble, I shook my head. He was still wearing a sly grin on his face. "No, not yet. Maybe one day though," I said with a shrug.

"Well, he brags about yi all di time," Robin said. "So tell us, how did you two lovebirds meet?"

Lovebirds?

Resting my cheek on my shoulder, I bashfully glanced back at Noble. He was sitting back in the chair with his arms out wide like he was waiting for me to answer. "He just gave me a ride home from work."

"No, you're telling the story all wrong, Imani. I rescued her one day when she was walking home in a snow blizzard," he said.

"A snow blizzard?" I scoffed, pursing my lips to the side. "No, I was walking to catch the bus home, and I assure you that it was only a few snow flurries, you guys. Not a snow blizzard," I explained, causing his friends to laugh.

He shrugged his shoulder before cracking a smile.

As the drinks continued to flow, the conversation got a bit racier and eventually led to the topic of sex. "So, Miss Imani," Robin said in her island tongue, gaining my attention. "Yuh don gave Noble di pum yet?"

I could feel my drunken eyes stretch wide as a goofy grin spread across my face.

"Aw, don't be shy, Imani. I fucked Bilaal on the first night. And looka here," Enid said with a laugh, flashing her diamond ring.

"No, I fucked you on the first night," he corrected, making us all laugh. She smacked his shoulder, and he leaned over to give her a sweet kiss.

Noble gently rubbed my knee and sat up in his seat before he said, "Robin, how long have you known me?"

"Fah five years, mi bredda."

"All right then, so you already know that we've fucked."

"Noble!" I shrieked, smacking him on the arm.

He and Phillip slapped hands and laughed like some high school football players in the locker room.

"What?" Noble turned to me and slurred. With his hand still on my knee, eye still locked with mine, he licked his lips in a lustful manner. "And as a matter of fact, I'm fucking again tonight," he said with a wink. I was mortified.

His friends were all laughing like he'd just told the funniest joke in the world, but I was truly embarrassed. Without even thinking I hopped up from the chair, only to feel lightheaded and dizzy in the process. I'd had way too much to drink at this point, and I was just starting to feel its effects. Noble grabbed me by the arm and pulled me down in to his lap. I could feel his hardened manhood beneath me, and my body shuddered in response.

"Loosen up, ma. I'm just joking okay?" he said low. I could feel the warmth of his breath tickle the back of my neck. Although I was still angry at him, the velvety sound of his voice made my head nod up and down in agreement.

"Fine."

"Aw, you two are so cute," Enid gushed, snuggling up closer to Bilaal.

"Yuh, dey are," Robin agreed.

I couldn't help but blush.

"Come on, let's dance," he whispered against my skin.

Surprised, I looked back at Noble over my shoulder. I would have never taken him for the dancing type. He lifted me from his lap, and with his hand on my stomach, he staggered behind me all the way down the stairs. Once we reached the dance floor, everyone parted for Noble like he was a king. Although he was partially intoxicated, you'd never know it. He swaggered through the crowd with such confidence. His shoulders were pushed back, and his chin was slightly raised in the air as he led me by the hand. And then there it was: a semi-private corner that was designated just for us.

The music had suddenly slowed to a sexy reggae beat, and with our bodies wedged together, we began to dance in sync. He placed his hand on the front of my throat and rhythmically ground his hips into me. Lust dripped from his eyes and practically oozed from his skin like he wanted to fuck me right then and there. The way he was handling me on the dance floor felt all too familiar, and without warning, my body began to respond. I was literally burning from the inside out as my hips circled to the beat. My panties were soaking wet, and my center was throbbing like crazy. I knew the only thing that could relieve my symptoms was Noble. He was the only cure to the aching between my thighs.

"Noble, let's just get out of here," I said over the music. He cracked a knowing smile and nodded his head.

Chapter 16

Noble

Imani couldn't wait until we got back home, so she sank down to the floorboard of the car, unzipping my pants right there in the back seat. I knew she was drunk because she didn't even care about Dominic seeing us like she did the times before. She and I both were out of our element.

She lifted her head and focused in on my eyes. "I just want you so bad, Noble," she breathed.

"Tell me what you want, baby." I stroked her cheek with the back of my hand then ran my finger across her lips.

"To taste you."

"This?" I asked, massaging my long, hardened dick now standing right in front of her face.

Imani swallowed hard and licked her lips. "Yes," she whispered, nodding her head.

"Tell me," I said, attempting to pull it out of her.

"I want . . ." she panted.

"Tell me, Imani. Tell me you what you want, baby."

"I want your dick, Noble," she said, barely loud enough for me to hear.

She leaned forward, yearning to put me in her mouth, but I grabbed her by the shoulder to stop her. I needed to be in control, and for once, I was going to make her say it. "Where? Tell me where you want it, baby."

She closed her eyes, and I could see her chest heaving up and down. "I want it . . . in my mouth," she breathed out desperately. Passionately.

I smirked.

I lowered my length, first teasing her lips before grabbing the back of her head. She eagerly opened her mouth, allowing me to feed her slowly, one inch at a time. As I pushed myself to the back of her throat, I bit down on my bottom lip. It just felt that damn good. She began sliding her lips down to the base, and each time I could feel myself pulsing inside her mouth. Imani never gagged, as she gave herself short intervals to breathe. She worked me over like a true professional. Her innocent eyes watched me the entire time.

"Shitt, Imani," I hissed, tossing my head back against the seat. The way her wet lips glided over my head, each time with a little more pressure than the last, had me feeling like I was ready to burst. I lifted my hips and began thrusting into her.

"Mmm," she hummed, rolling her tongue up and down my shaft.

As the wetness spilled from her lips, I could feel it reaching every crevice I possessed down below. This woman was driving me wild. Before I knew it, I was plunging myself harder and faster. I met her lips stroke for stroke until finally, I felt that tight tingle in my groin. I could hardly breathe.

"No, wait," I panted, attempting to push her back. But she held firm, rendering me powerless against her.

Her lips slid down to the bottom of my length one final time, and in that moment, it seemed as if every muscle in my body locked up on me. "Aarghh, fuckk," I groaned. I clenched her hair between my fingers as I climaxed hard. After licking my head clean, she lifted her head from my lap with swollen lips, which curled up into a mischievous smile.

That night when we went back up to our room, Imani fucked me like the shit was going out of style. She'd already shown out in the car, and even though I loved to always be in control, I let her continue to have her way with me. After her third orgasm hit, I held her close in my arms with only the sounds of the ocean outside filling the room.

"You asleep?" she asked with her back facing me in the dark.

"Nah," I told her. I was lying there just thinking, thinking about my feelings for her.

"Can I tell you something?"

"Anything."

Her shoulders rose and fell from the deep breath she took in. "Noble Shaw, I think . . . I think I'm falling in love with you," she whispered.

I pulled her back in even tighter so that we lay flesh to flesh. And with our fingers intertwined, I tenderly kissed the nape of her neck. "I'm falling for you too, Imani."

We arrived back in Baltimore at exactly 11:05 that Saturday morning. I'd parked my Range at BWI, so we cruised back to my place in no time. During the flight home, I had convinced Imani to come back and stay with me. I even told her that I'd pay her lease up for the year. Surprisingly, she didn't even fight me on it.

As we walked through my parking garage, rolling our luggage bags, I felt my phone vibrate. I pulled it from my pocket and saw Rashad's name on the screen.

"Rashad," I answered, motioning with my hand for Imani to press the button on the elevator.

"Noble, we need to talk, man."

"What's wrong? Did you find my money?" I cut to the chase.

"Well, not exactly," he said with a deep sigh.

"Spit it out, B. I just got back in town, and I'm trying get in this house," I told him as I stepped onto the elevator behind Imani.

"I didn't find the money, but I found out for sure who was stealing it," he said.

My ears jumped at that declaration. "Is it who we thought?"

"Yeah. It was Monica," he said.

My jaw clenched, and my chest progressively burned with anger. "How do you know?"

"You know the extra security cameras we set up? They paid off. She's on the fucking tapes."

"Fuck!" I spat, crashing my fist into the elevator wall. "I'll be there tomorrow."

As soon as I hung up the phone, Imani grabbed my hand. "Is everything all right?" she asked sweetly. Her eyes were filled with concern as she observed the grimace on my face.

I let out a deep sigh then ran my hand down my beard. "It's fine. I just have some business in New York tomorrow."

Her eyes momentarily saddened. "You're leaving me already?"

The elevator chimed, and the doors slid open before us. "Come with me then."

She smiled and nodded her head as we stepped off the elevator together. "I guess I can. I mean, since I don't have a job." She rolled her eyes.

Our last night in Jamaica, Imani had called back home and spoken with Karen. Of course, the first thing Karen asked her was why the hell she quit her job at the diner. Imani blew up on me after she discovered it was I who gave her resignation. I had to explain that if she continued to work there, I was liable to kill that nigga Big Will.

Although she was still upset, she was at least talking to me.

After walking the long, narrow hall to my front door, I was stopped in my tracks by the sight of Brittani. With my eyebrows pinched, I called out to her. "Brittani?"

"Mr. Shaw, we need to talk."

I could feel Imani's eyes burning a hole in the side of my face. Walking up closer to where Brittani stood by the door, I said, "Look, Brittani, you can cancel all of our Monday appointments. The arrangement is finished." I was trying to be discreet.

"This is important, Noble. I need to speak with you."

Releasing the grip I had on my rolling bag, I pinched the bridge of my nose. "Look, ma, you doing too much right now. I'm in a relationship, so we're done. Finished. You got it?" I leaned in to see if she understood.

"For God's sake, Noble, I . . . I'm pregnant!" Brittani cried.

"Pregnant?" My head drew back at first because I had to have heard her wrong. Then my eyes fell to the slight bump in her abdomen.

"That's right. Seventeen weeks." Her voice was low as she bounced her eyes between me and Imani.

"Noble," Imani whispered. I looked down to see her fingertips pressed against her mouth. Her face was frozen from shock, and her eyes were filled with hurt.

"But how, Brittani? We used—"

"Not the last time we didn't." She shook her head adamantly.

Shit, she was right. The very last time we'd fucked, I didn't use protection. It was only that one slipup, but I guessed that's all it took. Grabbing the back of my neck, I looked at Brittani, who stood there by the door, twiddling her thumbs. I wasn't used to seeing her so passive, so muted. Usually, she was trying to rip my clothes off, waiting for me to put her in her place, sexually. But not today. Today, she stood there with her black curls gathered into a youthful ponytail and her pouty lips painted a soft shade of pink. She had a glow about her.

"Brittani, can we talk about this tomorrow?"

She released a soft snort and arched her left brow. "So I take it you'll be answering my calls now?"

I nodded with humility, because for a little while I'd been avoiding Brittani worse than suede on a rainy day. "Yes, tomorrow. I'll get up with you," I said, swallowing hard.

Brittani's eyes stayed on me for a few seconds longer before she ultimately walked away. Unsure of what else could possibly be said in the moment, Imani and I both stood there in stunned silence. Her eyes were cast down to the floor as though she was deep in thought, while I just stared at her, waiting. I was waiting for her to yell at me, fuss, cry, shit, anything at all, but instead, she just stood there expressionless.

I sucked in a deep breath and parted my lips to speak, but before I could even begin the conversation I knew we needed to have, she turned and meandered away.

"Imani!" I called after her, but just she kept walking. Her shoulders slumped as she headed back toward the elevator doors.

With long strides, I charged behind her until finally, she was within arm's reach. "Imani!"

She looked back at me then down at the grip I had on her arm. "Let's just forget it, all right?" she said, pulling away.

"Forget it?" I asked, narrowing my eyes. After the week we'd just shared, I was confused as to how she could even utter those words.

"Let's just face it! You and I obviously aren't meant to be, Noble. We need to just walk away now before someone gets hurt." Suppressing a sorrowful laugh, she shook her head. "I mean before I get hurt."

Absorbing the weight of her words, I briefly closed my eyes and swiped my fingers down the corners of my mouth. "Look, I don't even know if this baby is mine, Imani. And if it is, you already know that it happened before you and me. I . . . I just don't understand."

She held her hand up between us. "Please, Noble. I just need some time to process this. It's just too much," she let out weakly.

Imani started to walk away again, but I gently grabbed her by the shoulder. When she looked back at me with a glossy set of eyes, I could feel a tightness develop in my chest. "Stop fucking running from me! Every time something happens where you think you might get hurt, you run. I'm telling you right here and right now, I'm not gonna hurt you. Even if the baby is mine," I tried to explain.

As she closed her eyes and shook her head, I could see her body slowly start to cower into submission. Without a second thought, I grabbed her by the arms and pulled her into me. She sank her face into my chest and wrapped her arms tightly around my waist like a child needing comfort. And then she began to weep. Her body rocked against me as the emotions she'd been trying so hard to repress gushed out all at once.

Kissing the top of her head, I cupped her face in my hands and lifted her chin. "I promise you that everything will be okay, ma," I said lowly, pecking her on the lips. I peered down into her eyes with such intensity because I didn't want to leave any room for doubt. "You've come to mean so much to me in such a short period of time. I swear I could never intentionally hurt someone as precious as you."

With a subtle sniff, Imani nodded her head and allowed me to take her luggage from her side. As soon as we entered my apartment, we headed back to the master bedroom to unpack. Both of us were quietly moving about, deep in thought as to what a baby could possibly mean. Now, this thing I had with Imani was still very fresh, but my intuition was telling me that she was it for me. There was something about this woman's presence that forced me to acknowledge just how incomplete I was. In just a brief span of time, Imani had made my entire world feel whole.

Chapter 17

Imani

My stomach felt queasy as I climbed the steps behind Noble, approaching a beautiful brownstone in Brooklyn. This would be my first time meeting his mother, and I was beyond nervous. Noble kept saying that I'd be fine, but based on my sweaty palms, racing heartbeat, and nausea, I wasn't too convinced. When he finally realized I wasn't at his side, he looked back over his shoulder and gave me a handsome smirk.

"You'll be just fine, baby. My mother will love you," he said, offering me his hand. I laced my fingers through his and sucked in a deep breath before taking on the next brick step.

Once we reached the top stoop, Noble stepped forward and pressed the button to her apartment, producing a faint buzzing sound. I quickly glanced down at myself to ensure that everything was in place before smoothing my hand down the front of my dress. It was late spring and unusually warm this sunny day in the Bed-Stuy community, so I decided on a maxi dress with three-quarter-length sleeves. It was a muted shade of mustard that Noble said complemented my cocoa-colored skin. And with my hair being straightened, I gave it a neat part down the middle, allowing it to fall just above my collarbone.

"Noobie, is that you?" I heard coming from the speaker system adjacent to the front door.

"Noobie?" I whispered mockingly.

Noble looked back at me with pursed lips and his left
eyebrow hiked in a warning fashion. I giggled at that expression and couldn't wait to tease him privately.

"Yeah, Ma, we're here," he said. It was nice hearing the
way he referenced his mother. In fact, today Noble wasn't
the same stuffy businessman wearing a fitted suit, or the
"well-to-do" guy who could only drink expensive bottles
of red wine. Today he was "casual" Noble, dressed in a
plain white T-shirt that fit his muscular chest and arms.
He wore khaki-colored cargo pants with fresh Timbs on
his feet. He was just Noble from around the way, and I
had to admit it was refreshing seeing this side of him.

The next thing we heard was the front door automatically unlocking. As we walked up the next set of stairs,
Noble took my hand and tenderly kissed the back of it.
I guessed it was his way of calming me down. When we
reached her apartment door, Noble knocked twice, allowing me just enough time to take a deep breath.

He glanced over at me with a crooked smile. "Calm
down," he said then leaned over and pecked me on the
cheek.

Seconds after I could hear the bolts being unlocked,
the door swung open to reveal a short little lady with silver hair and skin just a tinge darker than mine. Although
this woman appeared youthful, there was no doubt in
mind that she was Noble's mother. It was her piercing
set of dark brown eyes and the great bone structure that
gave it away. She was beautiful.

"Noobie!" she squealed, not even waiting for us to fully
cross the threshold before she reached out to hug him.

While I stood there in the entryway, hands clasped together in front of me, I watched the two of them embrace.
They held on to each other as they rocked from side to
side like they hadn't seen each other in years before, fi-

nally breaking apart. When his mother's regard shifted over to me, I gave a sheepish smile, tucking my hair behind my ear. That's when I saw her arms open up for me.

"Miss Imani, right?" she said with a welcoming smile.

"Yes, ma'am." I stepped forward a bit and allowed her to enfold me in her arms, the same as she'd just done with Noble. I could now see why he held on to her for so long. His mother's touch was so warm and loving, matching the infectious aura around her.

"I'm Noobie's mother, Charlene. Now y'all two come on in here and sit down," she said, gently pulling me by the hand. I looked back at Noble over my shoulder and quietly mouthed his cute little nickname again before giving him a teasing wink. He let out a snort of laughter and shook his head.

As we walked into her living room, I took in the tan-colored furniture, Oriental rug, and various family pictures spread throughout the modest space. Everything was tidy but not overwhelmingly lavish like Noble's place. Instead of mahogany floors, she had plush off-white carpet, and rather than leather, her sofas had a basic knitted finish. Solely based on that, I knew this woman was down to earth, and instantly I felt right at home.

"So did Kelldon tell you about the barbecue he and Monica are having today? The one down at Prospect Park?" she asked, looking at Noble. The two of us sat side by side on the sofa across from her.

"No Ma, he doesn't know I'm in town."

His mother cracked a crafty smile. "Oh, he knows all right, 'cause I told him."

That's when a huge surge of air could be heard releasing from Noble's nostrils. He was irritated. "I'm only here on business, Ma."

"Oh, business schmisness," she teased with a slight roll of her eyes and dismissive wave of her hand. Then her regard fell to me. "How do you deal with this guy, huh?"

Beaming at her question, I glanced over at Noble, who was now staring intently at me with doting eyes. This was a new expression, one I'd never seen on him before. As his low, hooded eyes stayed connected to mine, awaiting an answer, I could feel his fingers making silver dollar circles on the small of my back. Still drawn to Noble's gaze, and with a shallow breath, I muttered, "With lots of patience, Ms. Charlene."

He flashed a sexy grin then ran the tip of his tongue across his bottom lip. *Sheesh!* Noble was making me fall deeper in love with him and turning me on at the same time.

"Ahem," his mother cleared her throat, gaining our attention. When I looked over at her, she beamed, "I must admit that you two are very cute together. Finally, just finally, I might get me some grandbabies," she said.

Hearing her say that caused my heart to sink to the pit of my stomach. I felt like I'd just dropped from the highest peak of a roller coaster.

"Too soon for that, Ma," was all he said. He provided nothing extra about Brittani or the baby, which somehow made me feel at odds. We hadn't talked about the possibility of this baby being his since the day we'd returned home from Jamaica. And now we were sitting here in front of his mother like some couple newly in love who had everything figured out. That was far from the truth. I tucked my hair behind my ear, and without even realizing it, I scooted an inch or two away from Noble.

"Hmm," his mother mumbled, closely observing the two of us. "Well, son, the barbecue is about to start. You gonna give your mother a ride. I made your favorite." She stood up from the chair and started making her way over to the galley kitchen.

"Did you really?" he asked, smiling like a kid on Christmas day. I didn't know why but that irritated me.

Ms. Charlene didn't answer him at first, but you could hear her opening up the refrigerator door. When she came back out into the living room, she was holding up a New York–style cheesecake that looked to be at least five inches thick. Mounds of strawberries were piled up on top while the red sauce dribbled down the sides. It was so pretty that it could have graced the cover of *Taste of Home* magazine.

Lifting my jaw, which had dropped from astonishment, I turned back to Noble. "You never told me that you like cheesecake."

"That's Noobie's favorite," his mother gushed.

"I mean, I know it wouldn't have been your mother's, but I could've at least tried," I told him.

Unconcerned, Noble hiked his left shoulder. "Ma will give you the recipe."

"I sure will, dear. Now let me get back here to comb my hair down and change my shoes," she said, taking off toward the back of the apartment.

Standing up from his seat, Noble looked down and offered me his hand. Hesitantly, I placed my hand in his, allowing him to lift me to my feet.

"Where are we going?" I asked with a little attitude. I wasn't upset by the damn cheesecake. It was this baby thing that had me so unnerved.

"Come," he demanded, pulling me down the same hall his mother had disappeared into.

As we neared the second door on the right, Noble guided me into a small, dimly lit bedroom. In the center was a full-sized bed, blanketed by a navy blue kiddie comforter. However, hanging on the wall was an aged poster of Melyssa Ford, modeling a two-piece swimsuit. My eyes danced further around, taking in the thin navy drapes that were designed with a sports-themed print. There were even medals hanging up on the walls and football trophies sitting on a nearby dresser. It didn't take me long to discover that this was Noble's childhood bedroom.

"Your room?" I questioned in a murmur. Letting go of his hand, I walked in farther to explore independently.

As my fingers skimmed over a few of his things, they stumbled upon a childhood picture sitting on his nightstand. Right away I could tell that one of the little boys in the photo was Noble because other than getting more handsome, he hadn't changed much over the years. If I'd had to guess, I would've probably said that he was around ten years old when that moment was captured. He had his scrawny little arm draped over a younger boy who looked similar to him, only the little boy was shorter and missing his two front teeth. I quickly assumed that was his brother.

With my eyes still cast down on the picture in my hands, I said, "Is this you and your little brother?"

Within a matter of seconds, I could feel Noble's warmth as he approached me from behind. His close proximity and virile scent immediately caused the fine hairs of my arms and neck to lift from my skin. Suddenly I could feel his big hands glide around my waist as he pressed his erection into my backside. When he positioned his cheek right next to mine, I instinctively closed my eyes and inhaled a deep breath.

"Yes, that's me and my brother Kells," he whispered low in my ear. I could hear a hint of lust dripping from his velvety voice as his beard whisked the side of my face.

Slowly, Noble's right hand traveling up to my breast where he began to massage it gently. With his left hand, he applied a firm grip on my waist while grinding his hardness against my ass. When he began kissing the curve of my neck, swirling the tip of that lethal tongue across my flesh, my body turned weak. My head fell back to his brawny shoulder as the picture in my hand dropped down to the carpeted floor. Just like always, I was feeling lightheaded and hot all over simply from Noble's touch. And just like that, all unsettling thoughts were cast aside.

Gradually pinching at the fabric, Noble gathered my long dress up around my hips so that my saturated panties were now exposed. All the while, he was kissing the length of my neck with care. With his hand still reached around in front of me, he slid his fingers between my legs. When two of his digits slipped just beneath the lace, I released a soft moan.

"Ahhh, please, I don't want to disrespect your mother's home," I stammered in a whisper. My eyes were sealed shut as I enjoyed the strumming of his fingers across the front of my throbbing sex.

Unexpectedly, he removed his lips from my neck and plunged two of his eager fingers deep inside of me. "Ohh," I breathed. I collapsed deeper into his chest as I reached around, grabbing the back of his neck for support.

I was so aroused that you could hear the sounds of my wet pussy echoing throughout the entire room. Noble, however, never said a word. He just kept sliding his fingers in and out of me with care. And without warning, he placed his thumb over my swollen bud, creating an intense amount of pressure in my core. Steadily his penetration began to pick up speed, and that damn thumb of his started working in a circular motion.

"Ohh, Noble," I cried, slowly bucking my hips against his hand.

"That's right, cum for me, baby," he whispered against my neck, still drilling those fingers inside of me.

Then out of nowhere, I heard his mother holler out his name. "Noobie!"

Oddly, it seemed that the sound of her voice only encouraged his activity, because his finger started to go deeper.

"Noobie!" we heard again.

"Ohh, Noble," I moaned, feeling like I was about to burst. I ground steadily against him all in an effort to match his fast, even pace.

"Shhh," he whispered.

"Noobie!" The sound of his mother's voice was louder this time, indicating that she was near.

"I'm coming, Ma!" he yelled out, still plowing those fingers of his inside of me.

Then, to my surprise, he pressed his thumb down over my swollen clit. "Oooh, shhii—"

Noble hurriedly clamped his hand down over my mouth, muting my vulgar cries as I exploded all over his fingers. With a fresh arch in my back, I squeezed the rear of his neck in an attempt to control my wild, jerky movements. But it was no use. All you could hear was the stifled sounds of my whimpers as his slick fingers dipped in and out of me with decreasing speed.

Once I was able to catch my breath, he gently removed his hand from my panties. And when I turned around to face him, I noticed that he'd already had them in his mouth, tasting the remnants of my release. Staring at me with low, drunken eyes, he pulled one finger from his lips at a time.

"Kiss me," he finally said.

I crashed my lips against his and immediately felt his sweet tongue enter my mouth. As we began sharing a passion-filled kiss, his large hands reached down and grabbed a handful of my behind. That caused another moan to slip out of me and his hardened dick to twitch in between us. At this point I was hot and bothered all over again, wanting so badly for him to take me.

"Noble!" his mother called out again, reminding us that she was waiting in the other room.

He pulled back and smirked right before smacking me hard on my ass. "We gotta go, baby."

Shit.

Chapter 18

Noble

As soon as we pulled up to Prospect Park, I could see a crowd of familiar faces in the distance. Some were sitting on the uncovered picnic tables, talking among themselves, while others were mobile, dancing in the grass to an old nineties' track that blared from undetectable speakers. Even from the confinements of the car, I could smell that sweet blend of charcoal and barbecue as smoke drifted up high in the air. I took in all the small children running around and playing, some blowing bubbles in the wind. And although I didn't like the circumstances that brought me back home, I couldn't stop the faint smile from forming on my face.

I glanced over at my mother, who was sitting next to me in the front passenger seat, while Imani sat in the back. "You ready?" I asked.

My mother nodded her head and unbuckled her seat belt before opening up her car door.

Just as I got out to open up Imani's door for her, I peered through the window to see my mother's heavy cheesecake in her hands. When she stepped out of the car, my dick uncontrollably leaped in my pants. It was a natural reaction to Imani that I still hadn't gotten used to. The woman was just that sexy to me, and the fact that I had just felt how tight and wet she was, not even a mere hour ago, didn't help. Right when she observed the lust in my gaze, as I raked over her curves in that damn maxi dress, she cut her eyes away. She tucked her lips inward in an attempt to hide her blushing smile.

"Mmm," I groaned lowly with a subtle bite down on my bottom lip.

"Are you two coming or what?" I heard my mother ask.

Imani let out a girlish giggle as I nodded my head and removed the cheesecake from her hands. Then the three of us began making our way into the park. Of course, the first person running full speed ahead to greet us was Sarah. Her long ponytail was just swinging as her arms stretched out wide for my mother. I wouldn't take anything from Sarah. She was a beautiful woman and even looked nice today in ripped jeans and a floral-print top. I just prayed she wouldn't start anything with Imani.

"Oh my God, Ma." Sarah huffed, catching her breath as she embraced my mother.

"How long y'all been out here?" my mother asked.

"About an hour," Sarah replied, then her eyes cut over to me and the cheesecake I was holding. "Please tell me that you made this cheesecake, Ma. You know that's my and Noble's favorite."

"Of course, Sarah."

As soon as my mother called her name, I could feel Imani's body grow stiff standing next to me. I looked down to see that her catlike eyes were now fixed on Sarah.

My mother must have felt the sudden tension as well, because she said, "Oh, Lord, please forgive me. I'm being so rude." Looping her arm through Imani's, my mother pulled her in close. "Sarah, this here is my future daughter-in-law, Imani."

Although it was subtle, I could see Sarah's neck tug back and her eyes blossom in shock. Her lips momentarily parted, further indicating her being dumbstruck by my mother's words. And while my mother was laying it on pretty thick, hinting at us being engaged, I'd be the first to admit it was quite amusing seeing Sarah's reaction.

"Imani, this is Noble's ex-wife, Sarah."

I could feel the exact moment Imani's gape left Sarah and began searing into me. I never told Imani that I'd been married before. She'd only known of Sarah from my last visit to New York when I had to assure her that there was nothing going on between the two of us. I knew that Imani's knowledge of Sarah still being partially present in my life would be no easy pill for her to swallow, so I never gave details on the matter, which now, looking at Imani's menacing eyes, I knew was wrong. She was still insecure from her past, so this, no doubt, caught her completely off guard.

Sarah reached out to shake Imani's hand and to my surprise, with a tight jaw and closed-lip smile, Imani accepted.

"I take it the big guy didn't tell you about me," Sarah said sweetly, sensing Imani's discomposure. However, Imani didn't even respond to Sarah's probing, she just gave another forced smile and batted her eyes.

As the three of us headed over to join the rest of the crowd, Sarah took off toward the parking lot, spotting someone she knew. The first person I spotted was Rashad, sitting at a picnic table with his pregnant wife, Matisse. Inadvertently my eyes scanned across the yard to find their four young children all running amuck. I considered the four of them to be my nieces and nephews.

"What's up, boss?" Rashad acknowledged while his wife struggled to get up on her feet. I chucked up my chin since my hands were full.

"Hey, Ma," Matisse said, hugging my mother. She looked over at the cheesecake in my hand. "Thank you, Jesus. I was hoping you made your strawberry cheesecake."

"I might let you have a piece since you pregnant," I teased, setting it down on the table.

Matisse slapped me on the arm. "Boy, shut up. You already know I'm getting me a piece of this cheesecake."

"Yes, you will. I'll make sure of that," my mother said, rubbing Matisse's swollen belly.

"Rashad, Matisse, this is . . ." I looked back at Imani, who was standing slightly behind me, and I reached for her hand to pull her up next to me. "This is my lady, Imani."

This was the first time I'd actually introduced her with a title next to her name, and truth be told, it felt good to finally claim her as my very own. Imani had become just that precious to me. While Rashad reached out to shake her hand, Matisse and my mother squealed like little schoolgirls. I wasn't surprised though, being that I hadn't brought another woman to meet my family since my divorce. In fact, Sarah had been the only woman in that capacity to meet my mother before today.

After Rashad released Imani's hand, Matisse reached out to hug her.

"So nice to meet you," Imani said. Then her eyes dropped down to Matisse's stomach. "Oh, and congratulations. Is this your first?"

Matisse and my mother laughed. "No, dear, this will make baby number five for them," my mother corrected.

Imani's eyes widened, making me chuckle. "Oh, wow, that's beautiful," she said with an elevated voice.

"That's too many damn kids," I muttered, causing Matisse to mush me in the arm.

"Well, they're all your godchildren, so what you saying? "Matisse rhetorically asked, rolling her eyes.

When Imani's eyes cut over at me at that revelation, I simply shrugged with a smirk. Rashad and Matisse had been married for over ten years and had been together since high school. And while I could never imagine myself with five children, I'd always admired their union. When they asked me to be the godfather to their children it was an easy yes. They all called me Uncle Noobie, and I assumed that the little one in her belly would most likely do the same.

Matisse grabbed Imani by the shoulder and turned her around so that she was facing the many children out playing in the field. "That one right there is my oldest, Jamar. He just turned nine. And right next to him is my baby Josh, he's seven." Matisse then pointed toward the other side of the yard where the swings were. "And see those two right there? Those are the twins, Mischa and Mikayla. They're both four."

"Wow! You definitely have your hands full," Imani said with a smile.

"Girl, you ain't lyin'. But it's a blessing."

"Come on, y'all. Let's go on over here and say hey to your brother," my mother cut in and said, looking over at me. I clenched my jaw at the mere mention of Kells, because at some point before the night was over, I knew I'd have to address Monica stealing my money.

Imani, my mother, and I all started making our way over to my brother, who was manning the grill with our uncles, Li'l Bill and Larry, standing next to him. Along the way, I made sure to acknowledge a few people from the old neighborhood who were present, as well as other extended family members who came. When we approached, Kells had his head down over the grill, flipping meat. But even from behind, I could tell that he was listening to the conversation my crazy uncles were having, because he was shaking his head.

"That shit don't work, Bill. I done tried the Niagra, and what's the other one?" I could faintly hear Uncle Larry ask as he snapped his fingers, trying to remember.

"I take Cialis. That one works real good for me." Uncle Li'l Bill started moving his hips in a humping motion. "Shiddd, Betty and Delores don't have no complaints for me."

I shook my head, realizing that they were actually discussing which erectile dysfunction medication worked the best.

"Well, all I know is that blue pill is some bullshi—"

"Li'l Bill, Larry, I want y'all to meet someone," my mother said, interrupting Uncle Larry's commentary.

My two uncles turned to face us, immediately gawking at Imani like two predators staring at a prime cut of meat. However, Uncle Li'l Bill was the most obvious, with his head down low, peering at Imani over the shades on his face. His eyes slowly wandered down her body as he licked his crusty lips. Meanwhile, all you could hear was Uncle Larry mumbling "Umph, umph umm," under his breath as he shifted the toothpick from one corner of his mouth to the other.

"Ahem." I cleared my throat, somewhat gaining their attention. "Uncle Li'l Bill and Uncle Larry, this is my lady, Imani." Both of my uncles immediately recognized my hardened glare and stood up straight, attempting to be on their best behavior. I knew the old, horny geezers didn't mean any harm, but I'd be lying if I said I didn't feel a twinge of jealousy seeing the way they were looking at her.

Imani sheepishly raised her shoulders and smiled. "Hi."

Uncle Li'l Bill removed the black Kangol hat from his head and tucked it under his arm before stepping forward. "Welcome to the family, sweetheart. I'm Uncle Li'l Bill," he said, reaching out for a hug.

When Imani went to hug him, she only wrapped one arm around him and gave him a few soft pats on the back. I let out a small chuckle when I noticed that she even had her butt pushed out to keep as much space between them as possible.

"And don't forget me," Uncle Larry chimed in. "Lawd, please don't forget me," he muttered under his breath.

I looked at him with a knowing scowl on my face. "Aye! Don't get fucked up out here, Unc."

He held his hands up in surrender and laughed it off. "I'm just welcoming her to the family is all. I know this your lady."

Imani then gave Uncle Larry the same churchly hug she'd just bestowed upon Uncle Li'l Bill, before Kells stepped up and offered her his hand. "Hey, nice to finally meet the lady who's making my brother go soft on me," he said.

That statement immediately pissed me off. My mind started to race, wondering if he and Monica had been in cahoots, stealing my money together. Did he really think I was going soft? Did he not think I would choke the life out of his ass if he betrayed me? Suddenly my body turned rigid at the thought. However, Imani didn't seem to notice the tension, because she shook his hand, smiled, and said, "Oh, he's not all that soft."

Uncle Larry and Uncle Li'l Bill doubled over laughing like it was the funniest thing they'd ever heard. "Well, I guess somebody don't need Niagra," Uncle Larry said.

Even Kells joined in on the laughter this time, finally getting the joke. But Imani just stood there clueless as to what that even meant. "Come again?" she asked.

My mother sucked her teeth and waved her hand at the three of them. "It's Viagra, you old dog. Now leave this girl alone. She doesn't need to get wrapped up in your and Bill's foolishness," my mother scolded.

I leaned down and whispered in Imani's ear, "Sorry about that."

She just gave a little smile and shrugged her shoulders, letting me know it was no big deal. I was appreciative of that because it let me know that she'd fit in with my crazy family. She was a bit uptight in Jamaica around my friends, so I really didn't know how today was going to play out. After all, I wasn't expecting for us to attend a family barbecue.

"Kells, where's Monica? I need to talk to you two after this shit is over," I told my brother.

After the look of confusion faded from his face, he created a hood over his eyes with hand and searched around the park. "I'on know, man. She was just standing here a few minutes before y'all walked up. She's out here somewhere," he said.

Suddenly I felt something tugging at my legs. I looked down to see my twin nieces, Mischa and Mikayla. They were adorable standing there in their matching pink outfits, each with two long pigtails apiece. I reached down and started tickling Mischa first.

"Uncle Noobie!" she squealed. Then I reached for Mikayla, allowing her to join in on the fun.

I scooped them both up in my arms and held them on each side of me. "Who is she?" Mischa asked, pointing at Imani.

"This is Uncle Noobie's lady, Ms. Imani," I told her.

"Is that your girlfriend?" she asked with a giggle before burying her face in my neck.

"Yes. That's my girlfriend." I cut my eyes over at Imani, seeing that her brown cheeks were now flushed.

"Come on, y'all, let's go get something to eat," my mother suggested.

After putting the girls down, we all followed my mother over to the food table. When my mother and I got in line to fix our plates, the girls pulled Imani by the hand toward the field that a few other children were playing in.

As I got food for us both, I kept glancing back at the three of them. The girls had Imani kneeling down in the grass on her dress, picking dandelions and putting them in her hair. The natural beam on Imani's face seemed genuine, and that gave me a warm feeling all over.

"She'd make a good mother for your children someday," my mother leaned over and said.

I kept my eyes fixed on Imani and the girls. "How you know, Ma? You just met her."

"Because a mother knows. And I also see the way you look at her. It's different this time around."

Turning our focus back on the table of food, the two of us moved a bit down the line. "How you figure?" I asked.

"You and Sarah always cracked jokes with each other and hung out in groups with your friends, like the two of you were still in high school or something." She shook her head like something was wrong with that. "With you and Imani, I can see that you're actually in love. Romantically connected."

"But I thought friends made for the best relationships," I said, scooping a dollop of potato salad on my plate.

"Well, would you consider Imani a friend?"

For a brief moment, I pondered my mother's question. "Well, yeah. I guess I would."

Chapter 19

Imani

As soon as we finished eating, I looked up to see the roving clouds turning dark. Even the temperature had dropped, and a chilly breeze had consumed the late April air. Noble wrapped his arm around me, allowing me to snuggle up against him to keep warm. He tilted his head down and affectionately kissed me on the top of my head.

"You ready?" he asked.

I nodded. "Yeah. It looks like it's about to rain."

"Let me go over here and get my mother. I'll be right back," he said, easing me from underneath him and standing.

"Can you please get me a slice of that cheesecake to go?"

He let out a small snort of laughter. "If there's any left. I think Matisse probably polished the rest of it off."

After he went and got his mother, we all loaded up in the car. Thunder roared the entire drive to Ms. Charlene's house, but not a single drop of rain fell from the sky. When we pulled up to her brownstone, I stepped out from the back seat and stood on the sidewalk, awaiting a warm hug goodbye. Like the true gentleman he was, Noble opened up his mother's door and helped her ease out of the car.

As she walked over to me, her arms were already open wide. "You make my baby so happy, Imani," she whispered, giving me a tight squeeze.

Hearing her say that caused an emotional lump to form in my throat. "He makes me happy too. Happier than I've ever felt." My voice unexpectedly cracked at the revelation. Tears all of sudden formed in my eyes.

Ms. Charlene smiled and fanned my face with her hand. "Shh, chile, don't you start that mess," she whispered. She didn't want me to cry, most likely because it would've made her cry too. "Now make sure you two come back by here and see me before you leave, ya hear?"

"Yes, ma'am. I'm sure Noble wouldn't have it any other way," I said.

I glanced over at Noble, who was leaning back on his Range with his muscular arms folded against his chest. The endearing smile in his eyes couldn't be missed as he watched the two of us interact. After Ms. Charlene and I wrapped things up with a kiss on the cheek, he opened up the passenger door and let me in. I gave one more good-bye wave through the window before he began walking her up the stairs to her front door.

When he got back in the car, he leaned over the console and said, "Kiss me."

For just a second, I gazed into his dark brown eyes, feeling that familiar pull of energy drawing us near. Gently, I placed my hand to the side of his face and felt his soft beard beneath my palm. And when I moved in to close the space between us, positioning my lips right up next to his, I sealed my eyes and inhaled his scent. God, I was crazy about this man.

Noble slid his tongue into my mouth and kissed me so deeply I had to fight to save my own breath. And when he released my mouth altogether, all I could do was think about how I desperately craved to have him inside of me. The entire way over to his SoHo apartment I had to squeeze my thighs together to calm the inner aching of my core. Shit, I even had to look out of the window for fear that if our eyes met, I'd let out a sensual moan.

Just after Noble parked the car in his parking garage, we headed up to his apartment, him quiet on one side of the elevator with me tormented on the other. Both of us burned with so much desire you could practically smell the lust oozing from our skin. As soon as we entered his place, I kicked off my shoes and rushed over to the bar to pour me a glass of wine. That's how bad I needed something to calm my hot ass down.

"Imani," I heard him call for me. When I peeked over my shoulder into the living room, I saw that the sliding glass door was open. He was standing out on the balcony with his back facing me.

I took a generous gulp of cabernet before placing my glass down on the counter. As I toed near the balcony door, I could see cracks of lightning flickering in the background. Noble didn't even flinch as he stood there looking over the rail. I licked my lips, taking in his thick neck and muscular back in the white T-shirt he wore. Then down to that tight ass of his, recalling just how good it felt when he pumped in and out of me. *Geez.*

"Did you need me?" I asked, trying to compose myself.

"Come here," he said, not even turning back to look at me.

I walked up and stood next to him, placing my hand on his back. I could feel the fast beat of his heart damn near breaking though his skin. When he turned to face me, he grabbed me by the face and forced me to gaze up into his eyes. I thought he was going to kiss me again, but he didn't. He just stared into me, making it that much harder for me to breathe. The next thing I knew, Noble took a step back and sat down in one of his patio chairs.

"Take your clothes off," he demanded.

My eyebrows instantly gathered at that. He'd caught me completely off guard with his request, because not only was it about to storm, but I was pretty sure his neighbors could see us.

"Noble," I breathed.

"Take that shit off," he demanded. He ran his tongue across his full lips as he sat back with drunken eyes and his legs cocked out wide.

Slowly, I pulled my dress up over my hips, feeling the cool air immediately hit my skin. Once I got it over my head, I tossed it in the corner. I was standing there completely wet for him as I shivered in nothing but my bra and panties.

"The bra," he said, looking me over.

"Noble, can't we just—"

He shook his head. "Take off the fucking bra, Imani."

As I reached behind my back, unclasping my bra, Noble kept his dark, hooded eyes fixed on me, penetrating me deeper with each second that passed. And although I was cold on the outside, with goose bumps and nipples hard as stone, the inner part of me was torrid. My heart thumped wildly in my chest as my clit pounded relentlessly between my thighs. Slowly, I peeled the bra straps off each of my shoulders and slid it down my arms, showcasing myself to him. All of a sudden, I didn't care about who else could see us, because in that moment all I wanted was him. I needed him.

"Mmm," he groaned, shifting in his seat. More bolts of quiet lightning flashed across the sky as his lust-filled eyes perused every inch of me.

Wearing nothing but a lace thong, I sauntered toward him on the balls of my feet. I could see the tent magnifying in his pants as I drew near. When I got right in front of him and stood between his legs, he sat up and ran his large hands up and down my thighs.

"Damn," he muttered, gently pulling my panties down over my hips.

I could barely step out of them before he propped my foot up on the arm of his chair, exposing my thrumming sex. As soon as I felt the tip of his wet tongue sliding down the length of my parted lips, a single clap of thunder sounded off in the distance.

"Ohh, God," I cried. The moan I had been holding hostage freed itself all at once. I sealed my eyes tight and allowed my head to fall back lazily while holding on to his big, brawny shoulders.

His warm hands cupped my ass, pulling me in even farther as he invaded me with his stiff tongue, plunging it in and out of my center like some sort of starved savage. That shit had my body bubbling over with a profusion of pleasure.

"Ohh, pleaasse," I moaned. Already I felt my body start to quake as he suckled on my clit.

With his face still buried between my thighs, I heard him mutter, "You just taste so good, baby."

That's when I felt that buildup of pressure reaching its breaking point and I lost it. "Oh, God, Noble," I cried. My eyes suddenly rolled to the back of my head as I exploded, screaming out his name. "Nobbbllee!"

I trembled when his flat tongue washed over me just a few times more. Then he placed sweet kisses to the inner parts of my thighs before leaning back and lifting his shirt over his head. The muscular flanks of his chest flexed as he flung it to the other side of the balcony. I dropped down between his legs, instantly feeling the concrete beneath my knees as I unzipped his pants. He lifted his hips, just enough for me to pull them down mid-thigh. Seeing that his erection was throbbing and already wet at the tip, I greedily took him in my mouth.

"Fuck, bae," he hissed, immediately palming the back of my head.

I didn't waste time teasing him like I normally do. I eagerly pushed down as far as I could, creating that subtle gagging sound from the back of my throat. As I began working my tongue up his shaft, I could hear him murmuring all sorts of vulgarities. Just hearing that had my center aching all over again.

"Suck that shit," he groaned low, digging his fingers deeper into my scalp. That garnered another moan from me with him still in my mouth.

As I began adding my hands, twisting them around his girth, I looked up to see his dark eyes watching me. I continued sliding him in and out of my mouth, making sure to keep my gaze locked in with his. Feeling my own saliva seep from the corners of my mouth and dribble down onto my breasts, I went in for the kill. I sucked the tip of his head nice and slow as I watched him unravel before my eyes.

"Baby," he panted out in a deep, husky breath. I contracted my lips around him again and softly moaned. "Oh, shitt," he breathed. He tossed his head to the back of the chair.

And just when I could feel his body start to tense, he sat upright and grabbed me by the sides of my arms. "Come ride me," he demanded.

I got up and straddled his lap, allowing him to take my left breast into his hungry mouth. As I eased down onto his length, my mouth hung ajar, and I could feel his teeth and beard lightly grazing at my skin. I began working my hips in a circular motion, wanting to fit more of him inside of me. That's when Noble grabbed me assertively by the waist and guided me down real slow. "Damn, baby. You wet as fuck," he whispered against my ear.

He gently squeezed my behind and thrust me down onto him. "Ahhh," I moaned. He did that repeatedly, and once we got into a steady motion with our bodies completely in sync, I began reciprocating. I crashed my hips against his as my hands locked tightly behind his neck. At this point, the sounds of thunder and the bursts of lightning had intensified, and my body could no longer hang on.

"Ohhh, Noble!" I cried out loud. I climaxed so hard that fresh tears literally spilled from my eyes. And Noble came too, releasing deep inside me. As crazy as I know this sounds, would you believe that's when the rain finally began drizzling down on us?

As I descended from my high, whimpering into his shoulder, Noble held me real close. Our bare flesh was pressed up against one another's, and I could hear the rapid beats of our hearts going crazy. We stayed like that for quite some time, just listening to the rain. Then he gently lifted me up off of him and pushed my wet hair back from my face. He leaned in close and kissed my lips so passionately. The blended taste of both of us, coupled with the rain, was sheer perfection. When our lips finally broke apart and he peered deep into my eyes, I felt like he was damn near looking into my soul.

"I love you, Imani," he confessed. He didn't even give me a chance to tell him how much I loved him too. He just placed a few simple kisses on my dampened shoulder, stood up with me still wrapped around his waist, and carried me inside.

Later that night as I lay asleep in bed, I woke up to the sound of movement around the room and the slight tapping of rain against the window. I cracked one eye open, and from the faint light entering through the blinds, I could see Noble getting dressed in the dark. "Where you going?" I asked groggily.

"I've got some business to handle. Be right back."

I glanced over at the nightstand, seeing that the digital clock read 12:48 a.m. "At this time of night? Is everything okay?"

Noble came over to me and kissed me on the forehead. "Everything is fine, baby, it's just business. Go back to sleep, and I promise by the time you wake up, I'll be right back in your arms."

Chapter 20

Noble

Boom! Boom! Boom!

"Nigga, why you banging on my door like that?" Kells pulled the door open and asked. He was standing there bare chested with a grimace on his face.

My eyes narrowed as I cocked my head to the side. "Nigga? The fuck you think you talking to?"

He dragged his hand down over his face like he was trying to get himself together. I didn't wait for a response before I pushed my way past him into his dimly lit apartment. I hadn't planned on addressing this shit about Monica at this time of night, but I just couldn't sleep. My mother, the family cookout earlier, and then sexing Imani out on the balcony, all caused a slight change in my plans. So now here I was at my brother's apartment a little after one in the morning ready to address this bullshit.

Not giving a fuck, I charged down the dark hallway that led straight to my brother's bedrooms.

"Man, where you going?" he asked, hot on my heels.

"Where the fuck is Monica?"

"Monica?" I could hear the surprise in his voice. "Why you gotta speak with Monica?"

Ignoring his question, I reached for the doorknob of his master bedroom.

"Aye, man, just wait! She ain't got no clothes on," he said. Panic was evident in his tone.

With my hand still on the doorknob, I glared at him in a warning fashion. "Fine. Go wake her ass up."

While I stood out in the hallway, he went in, shutting the door behind him. I could hear his deep voice reverberating through the walls.

"Monica, wake up! Why is my brother over here at this time of night asking to speak to you? What the fuck did you do?" he yelled at her.

After a few more minutes, the door finally opened with Monica standing there in what appeared to be one of my brother's oversized T-shirts. Kells stood behind her wearing the same grimace on his face from earlier.

"Now what is this about?" he asked, obviously confused.

I swear I had to clasp my hands together in front of me just to keep from choking the shit out of that bitch. I lifted my chin and cut my steely eyes down at her. "Tell my brother how you've been stealing my fucking money for the past five months."

She instantly closed her eyes and dropped her shoulders.

"Monica, what the fuck is he talking about?" my brother stepped up beside her and asked with a look of confusion on his face.

She shook her head but didn't speak, just kept her eyes closed.

"Man, she wouldn't steal," my brother said, trying to defend her.

"She's on the fucking tapes, Kells. She stole a total of $118,000 from the club."

His eyes ballooned before looking over at Monica. "Monica, what the hell is he talking about?" he asked her again.

She covered her face with her hands and started to cry.

"Answer me goddammit!" he yelled.

Startled, Monica flinched from the elevation of his tone. "I did it for you, all right?" she finally let out, revealing her face, which was wet with tears.

His neck snapped back. "For me?"

"Yes! You owe Lonzo that money, and he's not gonna stop coming after you until he gets it."

"Fuck," I muttered low. I fell back on the wall as I ran my hand over my head. I knew Lonzo, the local loan shark from Brownsville. But what I didn't know was what business he had with my brother.

My brother looked at me with guilt written all over his face. "Monica, I didn't tell you to do that. You don't steal from family, baby," he said, now with a softer tone to his voice.

I released a deep sigh. "How much you owe him?"

He shook his head. "Nah, don't even worry about it," he said.

"Baby, please! I've been begging you to ask Noble for help, and now that he's here asking . . . I can't keep living like this. I'm scared for you."

Monica had every right to be scared, because Lonzo was a very dangerous man. He would loan you money with 50 percent interest, and if you didn't pay up in the time frame he gave, then that might very well be your life. Lonzo also liked to prey on the desperate and weak-minded, traits he seemed to have sniffed out in my brother.

"How fucking much?" I asked again through gritted teeth.

Kells closed his eyes and blew out a heavy breath. "A half a mil," he replied.

I felt my jaw instantly clench as I pinched the bridge of my nose. "And what the fuck would you need a half a million dollars for?"

He sighed and ran his hand down over his head. "I was trying to invest in some shit. You know., like you did after you opened up the first club."

My face scrunched with bewilderment. "Invest? Invest in what?"

"Tommy's flipping houses on the other side of the bridge now. Asked me to go in with him," he explained.

Tommy was a fucking joke, and I couldn't even begin to understand why my brother would want to do business with him. In fact, I wasn't sure why my brother would want to do business with anyone other than me. I released a sarcastic snort of air from my nose. "Why the fuck didn't you just come to me?" I asked.

"Yo, you been taking care of me all my life, getting me out of shit." He shook his head. "I mean, at first I just wanted to make you proud. Thinking that if I could make a smart investment, you would see me differently."

"See you differently? Kells, I trusted you with my baby: the first nightclub I ever opened. If I didn't think you were capable, I wouldn't have left my shit in your hands. So tell me this, why didn't you just ask me for the money when Lonzo started flexing?"

He shrugged, letting his voice trail off. "I just didn't want to let you down, man. I didn't want you to think I couldn't handle shit on my own."

I just stared at Kells, listening to his stupid-ass rationale, and once he was done, I said, "I'll handle it." Then I cut my eyes over at Monica, who was now holding onto Kells's arm. "And you, if you ever steal from me again, I don't give a fuck if it's a single stick of gum, I will break your fucking fingers!"

Satisfied with the dumb, petrified look on her face, I charged back toward the front of the apartment and left.

The very next day, after I paid off Kells's debt, I took my mother and Imani out for brunch before we had to hit the road. We went to Jean-Georges over on Central Park

West. It was expensive as hell, but because I knew it was one of my mother's favorite restaurants, I made a habit of treating her every time I came into town. After all, my mother was my heart.

"I just may have to come down to Baltimore for a visit. See what all the talk is about," my mother said, taking a sip of her mimosa.

"I would love that, Ma." I glanced over at Imani, gently squeezing her hand underneath the table. "Wouldn't we?"

Imani offered a closed-lip smile. "Absolutely, Ms. Charlene. We would love that. You've been to Noble's place before, right?"

"Nope, but I'm looking forward to seeing you all's place."

"Oh, I have my own apartment. Noble and I don't exactly live tog—"

"Yes, we do," I cut her off.

"Noble," Imani whined.

"Well, do you all live together or not?" my mother asked, trying to clarify. She cocked her head slightly to the side as her eyebrows knitted together.

"I don't know if Noble told you the story of how we met, but—"

"He did," my mother said, nodding her head.

"Well, once I got on my feet, I was actually able to get my own apartment. Just so happens that all of that came when Noble and I started dating more seriously," Imani explained.

"I see."

"Plus, we still have a lot to figure out." I knew right away that Imani was referring to Brittani and the baby.

"Hmm, I see."

My mother was very observant, so there wasn't a doubt in mind that she knew something was holding Imani back from me. I didn't want to tell anyone about the baby until I was sure it was mine. This would be my mother's first grandchild, so I didn't want to even get her started. Plus, I'd have to tell her about the extent of my relationship with Brittani, which is not exactly the kind of conversation you want to have with your mother.

Just as I was getting ready to change the subject, I saw Sarah coming through the door of the restaurant.

I looked over at my mother. "Ma, please tell me you didn't invite Sarah."

My mother pursed her lips and raised her chin. "I did. I think it's important that Imani knows she's not a threat to her."

I could feel Imani's body turning stiff as I released a deep sigh. As Sarah waltzed toward the table, I had to admit that she looked nice today. She had on simple black dress pants, a long-sleeved white blouse, and some black peep-toe booties. Her hair was pulled up in a simple bun. My attraction to her never was our problem. It was the lack of time we actually spent together working on our marriage and being in love with one another.

"Sarah," I greeted her, standing up from the table. I gave her a half hug and pulled out her chair, which was next to my mother and across from me.

"Hey, guys. It's good to see you again, Imani," she said cheerfully before sitting down. Imani gave a small smile and held her hand up, just giving a partial wave.

After I took my seat, my mother leaned up and rested her elbows on the table. "So look, now that I have all three of you here, I just want to clear the air."

"Ma," I groaned, leaning back in my seat.

"No, this is serious. It was only yesterday that Imani even learned that you had an ex-wife. I could tell by the look of shock on her face when she was introduced. That was wrong of you, Noble, not to tell her beforehand, 'cause you know I raised you better than that," she scolded.

"I know, Ma. I know."

"Imani, I just invited Sarah here because I wanted to let you know that she is not interested in Noble in that way, nor does Noble look at her like that anymore. We have all known Sarah and her family since she was a little girl, so I've always considered her to be like a daughter, even before her and Noble started dating. However, with that being said, it doesn't mean that I don't already love you too. I have room in my heart for both of you. And seeing as how you will be the future Mrs. Noble Shaw—"

"Oh, no, Ms. Charlene," Imani said, trying to correct my mother.

My mother's neck snapped back as though she were offended. "What? You don't see yourself marrying my son?"

"Oh, no, ma'am, it's not that at all. It's just, well, things are still pretty new between Noble and me." Imani's gaze shifted over to me, and her eyes softened a bit. "I would love to get married one day. When the time is right," she said, batting her innocent eyes.

"Well, either way, you two make one cute-ass couple. That's for sure. I always give Noble a hard time about the women he dates, but this time he seems to have gotten it right. I think this is probably the happiest I've ever seen him, and well, that says a lot," Sarah chimed in.

"Thank you, Sarah," I said. It was nice actually to hear that coming from her. I leaned back in my chair a bit and scratched behind my ear. "It's true, we do have a few things to sort out, but make no mistake, this woman right here has my heart," I assured, giving Imani a little wink.

Chapter 21

Imani

"Are you sure you're all right?" Noble looked at me and asked.

I was sitting on the edge of the bed in my silk night-gown, watching him get dressed across the room. It had been three weeks since we'd come home from New York and today was the first doctor's appointment of Brittani's that Noble would actually be attending. I'd be lying if I said I didn't feel a little hurt and jealous by all of this. He was sharing some of life's most precious moments with another woman while being in a relationship with me. Not only that, he was looking damn good today in his blue suit, sporting a fresh haircut and smelling better than ever. *God.*

"I'm fine," I lied. I stood up from the bed and sauntered over toward him before grabbing him by the shoulders. "You'll have to hurry up if you're going to beat the traffic," I said, masking all traces of disappointment on my face. I stood on my tiptoes and straightened out his blue silk tie then ran my hands down the lapels of his jacket.

"Kiss me," he said, leaning his face down to meet mine.

I placed my hands on the sides of his beard and crashed my lips against his. I was expecting a quick peck on the lips, but Noble parted my lips with his tongue. "Mmm," he groaned into my mouth as we kissed. His large hands traveled up, caressing my nude body beneath the nightgown. "How much time did you say I had?" he pulled back and asked.

I look down at the massive bulge in his pants and instantly knew what he was thinking. I shook my head. "No, you don't have time for that, but tonight, tonight after dinner, I'll let you have me for dessert."

He gave me a little wink. "Now that sounds like a damn good plan," he said with a soft smack to my ass. Noble pecked my lips once more before going over to grab his cell phone and watch from the nightstand. And just as he walked out the bedroom door, he threw over his shoulder, "Love you, baby."

"I love you too," I said low, crawling back in bed.

An instant wave of sadness washed over me as I heard the front door slam. Right away I knew I needed to get myself together. Luckily Karen had asked me to meet her for lunch later, so that would definitely take my mind off things for a while. I hadn't seen her in a few weeks, so I knew we'd have a lot of catching up to do.

After another thirty minutes or so, I slowly pulled myself out of bed and padded down the hall to the kitchen. I made myself a quick bowl of oatmeal and raisins before going back and jumping in the shower. Since it was now May and fairly nice outside, I put on one of the sundresses Noble bought me from Jamaica and paired it with a pair of tan wedge sandals. I flat ironed my hair and added a sheer coat of gloss to my lips before heading out the door.

In exactly twenty minutes I arrived at Watertable, and after having the valet park my car, I entered the restaurant in search of Karen. I wasn't shocked when I caught her at the bar, flirting with the bartender. Laughing on the inside, I shook my head and made my way over to her. "Hey, girl," I said, greeting her with a hug.

"Since when do we do lunch at Watertable, Miss 'I'm too good for Applebee's now'?" she asked, hugging me back.

I lifted my sunshades off my face and propped them up on the top of my head and shrugged. "Well, you know, thought I might expand your palate today."

"Umm huh. You come here with Noble, don't you?" she asked, narrowing her bright green eyes as her lips twisted to the side.

I smiled. "Yes, I do, and their crab cakes are to die for. Now come on."

As we started walking to the table that Karen had already gotten for us, I heard her muttering behind me, "I see now I'm gon' have to step my game up. Can't be hanging 'round bougie bitches with no money."

I laughed. "I told you I got you, Karen."

"Umm-hmm, I'm just saying."

Watertable was an elegant restaurant. Each table was draped in the finest white linens, while a single pink rose and tea light candles sat on top. Providing a grand view of the inner harbor were floor-to-ceiling windows that framed more than half the space. And although it was a bit expensive, their food was divine. Thanks to Noble, Watertable had quickly become one of my favorite restaurants. Once we took our seats and ordered our drinks, we both got quiet, looking over the menu.

"So, how are things with you and that fine-ass Mr. Blue Suit?" she finally asked.

Pulling my eyes up from the menu, I parted my mouth to speak, but nothing came out because I really didn't know how to answer that question. Instead, I swallowed back my words and tucked my hair behind my ear.

"What's wrong? Y'all having trouble already?" she asked, looking concerned.

I shook my head. "No, not really. Things between Noble and me are great actually. After we spent that week in Jamaica, he took me to New York to meet his family." I beamed.

Karen cocked her head to the side with her green eyes just fluttering. "So then what's the problem? I know you, and something ain't right."

Dammit! Was I that easy to read? "Well . . ." I tucked my hair behind my ear once more and cleared my throat. "When we got back from Jamaica, there was a woman at his door."

"Ahh, shit!" Karen exclaimed, rolling her eyes. "Don't tell me this nigga got a bunch a side bitches."

"No, not exactly—"

"Not exactly!" she shrieked, cutting me off.

I put my hand up to stop her. "Just wait and let me finish the damn story!"

"Fine," she said, giving me a skeptical look with her arms folded across her chest. Her green eyes batted away as she pursed her lips for effect.

"When we got back from Jamaica, there was this lady there, and she said she's pregnant with Noble's child."

Karen's mouth fell open, and her eyes doubled in size. "And what did he say?" she asked.

"He doesn't know if it's his, but if it is, he's going to take care of it. It happened before me so . . ." I shrugged.

"So then what's the problem?" she asked, sensing my apprehension.

"I know I shouldn't feel any kind of way about it, but I feel . . . I just feel like someone is taking away my fairy tale with this man. I mean, hell, I don't know how to be a stepmother to a child, and I damn for sure don't want to deal with any baby mama drama." I shook my head.

"Well, it may not even be his, Imani."

Pressing my fingers into my forehead, I sighed. "You remember that day when we walked over to the club and I was going to ask Noble out to lunch?"

Karen nodded. "Yeah, and you stormed out all huffy and shit. Wouldn't even tell me what happened."

"Well, he was with her that day in his office. She was . . ."

"She was what?"

"On her knees, giving him—"

"Ohh, shit!" she gasped. "She was giving him head and you walked in on it?"

I nodded. "Something like that."

"Damn," she muttered, shaking her head. "So then you think the baby is his, don't you?"

I nodded again.

Just as she was about to delve deeper into the conversation, the waiter came over so that we could place our orders. As usual, I got their famous crab cakes with a Caesar salad, and Karen got the same. Over the next hour or so I poured out all my concerns to her. I confessed that I was now deeply in love with Noble, but I didn't know if I could deal with him having a baby. We were barely six months into this thing, and I didn't want to set myself up for another heartbreak if I could help it.

Karen just sat back and listened while eating her meal, only asking questions from time to time. I didn't have any friends outside of her and didn't have any real family I could turn to, so I appreciated her being there for me. When I was all out of words, Karen slid her arms across the table and reached out for my hands. I placed my hands in hers and released a deep breath.

"Imani, I've known you for a few years now, and I swear I have never seen you this happy with a man. Now, I completely understand that him having a baby with another woman is not ideal. And hell, it's probably scary as shit, but hey, there are plenty of women out there who do the stepmother thing on a daily basis. Just sit down with Noble and see exactly what it would mean if the baby is his. Like, how often would he get the baby? What role would you play in the baby's life? What would the relationship and interaction be between him and ol' girl? You know, shit like that."

I smiled. "You're smarter than you let on, you know that?"

Karen popped her imaginary collar and said, "Yeah, bitch, I know."

I let out a little laugh and shook my head.

"But for real, everything is gonna work out for you guys. I can just feel it," she said.

Later that evening, while I was in bed going over some paperwork for school, I heard the front door opening. I knew it was Noble because he'd texted me earlier while he was at work, stating that he'd be home around six. I already had our lasagna cooling on the stovetop and a nice garden salad chilling in the fridge. All that was left to do was pull out a bottle of wine and put the garlic bread in the oven.

Before Noble even made it back to the room, I could smell his expensive cologne and hear the sound of shoes clacking against the hardwood floors. As soon as he appeared in the entryway, our eyes met, and he gave me a half smile. Through his already-hooded eyes, I could tell that my man was tired. So much so that he'd already loosened up his tie.

"Hey, baby." He ambled over toward me, taking a seat on the edge of the bed.

Standing up on my knees behind him, I gave a quick, gentle massage to his shoulders. "Here, take your jacket off," I said, helping him out of his suit.

"How was your day, baby?" he asked, leaning down to take off his shoes.

"It was good. I just met up with Karen for lunch."

"Nice. Where'd y'all go?" he turned around and asked before lying back on his pillow.

Wearing boy shorts and a thin cami, I straddled his lap and undid the rest of his tie for him. "Watertable."

He smirked. "Hmm, that's your spot now huh?"

I cracked a little smile and nodded my head. Taking in a deep breath, I prepared myself to ask the one question I didn't want to, but I knew I needed to. "So how was your day? How was the appointment?"

Noble's dark, heavy set of eyes all of a sudden lit up. "It was good. He's got a strong heartbeat."

"He?"

"Yeah. " He swiped his hand down over his face before a faint smile took hold of his lips. "It looks like I'm gonna have a son."

Chapter 22

Noble

That night a few months ago when I told Imani I was going to have a son, I'd felt her body immediately go limp. Although she tried her best to hide her sadness, the evidence was written all over her face. Over the past couple of months, she had been taking this whole baby thing pretty hard, while I, on the other hand, had been finding it difficult to fight back my excitement. I mean, when Brittani first told me she was pregnant I was completely stunned and angry, more at myself than her though. But from the first flutter of his heartbeat during that initial ultrasound, I could no longer deny the joy I felt. I was already claiming the baby as my own because the dates the doctor gave were on point, matching the one and only time I'd ever slipped up and fucked her raw. Plus it was something I felt in my gut.

I was trying my damnedest to be sensitive to Imani's feelings, but the further along Brittani got with her pregnancy, it was tough. Now don't get me wrong, my contact with Brittani was still minimal, only going to her doctor's appointment and checking in on her a few times a week, mostly by text. I would never disrespect Imani or add to her insecurities by interacting with Brittani any more than that. But what got to be uncontrollable was that I couldn't stop talking about my son-to-be, Noble Jr. I had even gone so far as telling my mother and brother about him because I was just that excited. I could tell that Imani felt some type of way about it, and her way of dealing with it all had become to emerge herself in her studies. She was now in her culinary arts program full time, and for that, I was truly happy.

It was now the Fourth of July, and we were throwing a big bash at my club for the holiday. It took all of spring and this first part of summer for us to get the rooftop prepared, but things at the club were now in order and ready for tonight. Imani had been in the shower for over twenty minutes, so after stripping down to nothing, I pulled back the glass shower door and stepped inside. I immediately smelled her apple shampoo. She had her hair all lathered up with suds cascading down her beautiful brown body.

Wrapping my arms around her waist from behind, I immediately pressed myself against her. My dick was already hard and throbbing from the mere sight of plain old water and bubbles flowing over her naked frame. She was just that beautiful to me. I set my chin on top of her shoulder and spoke directly in her ear. "Why didn't you just go get your hair done? We don't have time for you to be washing and blow drying your hair, ma."

She craned her neck and pecked my lips. "It won't take long, Noble. I promise," she said.

My erection jumped on her back as I placed a few kisses on her shoulder. That led to my tongue swirling up the curve of her neck. "Noble, we don't have time for that either," she said with a hint of laughter in her voice.

"Well, let's make it quick then." I slid my mouth across the top of her back, then allowed it to travel down the length of her spine. Even though the water was warm, I could feel her body shivering against me. When my mouth got to the top of her round ass, I kneeled down and slowly sucked on each of her cheeks, leaving light red blemishes behind.

"Ohh," she softly moaned.

I parted her legs with my hands and reached up between her thighs. Although her mouth said that we didn't have time, her actions were saying something else. As my fingers began playing inside of her, I looked up to see that her eyes were tightly sealed and that she was fondling her own breasts. That field of vision, seeing her like that, made my dick instantly ache, craving to be inside her.

After removing my fingers, I put my hands around her hip and pushed her forward a bit, creating a smacking sound as her hands hit against the tiled shower wall. With me still on my knees behind her, I felt the warm water streaming down on the both of us. I reached up between her legs again, only this time, spreading her apart, strumming her swollen clit. The sound of her panting and moaning from anticipation had me throbbing irrepressibly. *Fuck.*

Burying my face in her from behind, I slid my tongue up and down her folds. "Ohh, Godd," she moaned with a natural arch in her back.

"Uumm, you taste so good, baby," I muttered, flickering my tongue against her clit.

From the way Imani had begun to squirm and moan, I knew it would only be a matter of time before she came. Holding her ass with a firm grip, I spread her even farther apart and plunged my stiff tongue inside of her. That must have sent her over the edge, because she leaned back and gripped my shoulder for support. The echoes of her loud cries reverberated throughout the entire bathroom, and before I knew it her orgasm had hit like a hurricane, causing her body to jerk uncontrollably. I continued to softly feed off her body, allowing her just enough time to come down from her climax.

Then I stood up behind her and slid the head of my erection up and down the crevice of her ass. "Noble?" she panted, knowing exactly what I was preparing to do.

"Baby, I want to feel every part of you. I don't want there to be a single inch of you that I haven't explored," I explained.

Nodding her head, she reached back behind my neck and pulled me in for a kiss. This would be my and Imani's first time at anal play, but there was no doubt in my mind that she'd enjoy it. In an attempt to relax her, I ground myself on her, sliding up and down between her cheeks, all the while kissing on her neck. Gradually, with the water still coming down over us, I was able to inch my way inside. She whimpered all the way up until I was fully in and standing completely still. Then slowly, with my hands planted firmly on her hips, I began to sink in and out of her. Immediately I felt her tightness squeeze around my shaft with every deep thrust I gave. I closed my eyes and bit down on my bottom lip, because I swear Imani's body felt like heaven here on earth.

"Fuckk," I hissed low against her neck, feeling my strokes pick up speed.

Slowly, her whimpers progressed back into full-out moans of pleasure, and her hips began to buck against me. She reached around to press her fingers into my sides as a means to keep us close. Then all of a sudden, I could feel that familiar tightness stirring in my groin. Without a second thought, I grabbed a fist full of her wet hair and yanked her head back for deeper access.

"Ahhh, Noble," she moaned.

"Feel good, baby?"

"Ohh, myy," she moaned again. I took that as a yes.

With my heart thumping like crazy in my chest, I pummeled into her over and over while strumming my finger across her clit. I swear the sounds of our bodies clapping against one another's beneath the water and her sensual moans was all it took. Within a matter of minutes, both Imani and I were cumming simultaneously.

***

Later that night, Imani and I had finally found our-selves on the rooftop party at The Heat. We were sitting in the VIP section with Karen and a few other acquain-tances, sipping on some Ace, just enjoying the music and the colorful fireworks bursting in the distance. Every-thing had turned out perfectly for my Fourth of July bash. The inside of the club was packed as well as the outdoor space upstairs, and it honestly felt good to have Imani on my arm, sharing the moment. I looked over at Kingston, who was managing the club for the night, and asked him to have another bottle of champagne sent over.

"Girl, Big Will would just die if he could see you now," Karen told Imani.

Imani had always been attractive in my eyes but these days she'd truly been stepping up her game. Tonight she'd styled her hair in big beach waves and wore just enough makeup to enhance her natural beauty. She wore a bright red Alexander McQueen romper that had three-quarter sleeves and showcased her smooth brown legs. On her feet was the pair of red five-inch Manolo Blahniks I'd bought her last month just because. Imani was my queen in every sense of the word, and on the rare occasions when she'd let me, I did my best to spoil her rotten.

"Ain't nobody paying Big Will's ass no mind," Imani re-plied, taking another sip of her champagne as she danced happily in her seat.

Suddenly something on the other side of the rooftop caught my eye. It was Brittani, sitting at the bar with her abundantly pregnant belly. She was there with two other ladies, laughing and seemingly having a good time.

I leaned over to Imani and whispered in her ear. "Ex-cuse me, I'll be right back," I said, then kissed her on the cheek.

Shooting up from my seat, I charged over to the bar, feeling Imani's eyes damn near searing into my back. As soon as Brittani saw me, she hopped down from the bar-stool and wobbled over to meet me through the crowd. I shook my head, seeing her in a little black tube dress and heels.

"Hey, Noble, what's wrong?" she asked all innocent-like.

What's wrong? She knew what the fuck was wrong. I took a deep breath to calm myself before I spoke. "Don't you think it's inappropriate for you to be at a club in your condition?"

Her neck instantly whipped back. "Condition? Noble, I'm pregnant, not terminally ill."

I pinched the bridge of my nose this time because I knew how I could get. "You know what the fuck I mean, Brittani. You're seven months pregnant with my son, and you don't need to be here."

Brittani rolled her eyes, scoffed, then glanced back over her shoulder at her girlfriends. When she turned back toward me, she let out a small sigh. "I can't leave, Noble. I didn't drive," she said.

Feeling completely fed up with her, I clenched my jaw. I grabbed hold of her arm, probably a little more aggres-sively than I should have, and spun her ass around.

"Noble, get off of me! What are you doing?" she shout-ed.

With a good grasp on her, I continued to walk toward the exit. That was until her girlfriends came over and blocked our path.

"What's going on, Britt? Where you going?" The tall, light-skinned one with a short boy cut said.

"Girl, this is just my baby's father. He don't want me at the club," Brittani explained. Then she jerked her arm out of my hold. "Oh wait, I left my purse and phone over there on the bar."

My eyes shifted over to where she'd left her things. "Go get your shit, Brittani, and let's go."

"Damn, that nigga sexy," I could hear the other girl mumble under her breath.

Just as Brittani stepped away to retrieve her things, I felt someone touch me on my back. I turned around to see Imani standing there with a look of confusion on her face.

"What's going on?" she asked, uneasiness apparent in her expression.

Fuck.

I sighed heavily, running my hand down over my face. "Baby, Brittani is here. She's seven months pregnant with my son and at the fucking club. Can you believe this shit?" Just hearing myself explain the shit out loud had me fuming. But that's when I noticed the scowl etching onto Imani's pretty face.

Then suddenly Brittani walked up and looped her arm through mine like we were a fucking couple. "I'm ready to go now," she said.

I knew she was only doing that shit to piss Imani off, so I quickly removed her hands from around my arm. Imani's eyes dropped down to Brittani's belly and slightly widened with befuddlement. She hadn't seen Brittani since that day outside my apartment door when we'd come back from Jamaica, and Brittani's stomach had quadrupled in size since then. Seeing her like this only made our situation more of a reality for Imani.

"I gotta go and take her home, baby. I'll be right back," I said, trying to give Imani the reassurance she needed.

Imani's eyes turned to slits as she let out a little snort. "It's fine, Noble, don't worry about me. Go handle your business," she said. I could hear a mix of sarcasm and anger dripping from her voice.

I walked up close and took her by the elbow. "I'll be back, Imani," I whispered sternly into her ear.

Not even giving her a chance to respond, I turned around, snapped my fingers, and motioned with my head for Brittani to follow me.

Chapter 23

Imani

A month had now passed since the whole Fourth of July debacle. And as we neared the birth of Noble's alleged son, things between him and me seemed to have gotten a bit more tense. For the first time ever in our relationship, we actually argued that night after the party. I was just so hurt seeing him care for another woman like that, and while I knew it was his unborn child he was genuinely concerned about, the visual of it all was just too much for me. I found myself totally out of sorts, and actually accused him of cheating on me with her, even when deep down I knew that wasn't the truth. For the rest of that week we barely said two words to each other, and to make matters worse, we didn't even make love.

I found myself focusing more and more on my studies these days, trying to cope with everything I knew was coming. In fact, things were going exceptionally well at school. I made a few new friends and had even passed every test with an A. Noble would help me study most nights and allow me to make some of the more difficult dishes from class for him over the weekends. He was great like that, always super supportive and reassuring me that this baby wouldn't get in between what the two of us had together.

Although there were many nights I wanted to, I never did muster up the courage to have the mature adult conversation we needed to have. I swear, Karen had given me the perfect blueprint that day at lunch, but I just couldn't. There were too many unknowns and uncertainties in our relationship for me to start rattling off questions to the man. For one, I wasn't his wife. I was just his live-in girlfriend. For two, we didn't even know for sure that the baby was his, although he was adamant that it was. You don't know how bad it hurt me when he told his mother that he was going to be a father over the phone, only to hear her happy voice come through, asking how far along I was in my pregnancy.

Every day, several times a day, I thought about just what this would do to us. I worried that eventually, he would want to be with Brittani after the baby was born so that they could have a traditional family. I worried that when things got complicated among the three of us, he would side with her because, well, she was the mother of his child. And the worst thought, which I'd admit was the most selfish, was that I worried Noble would love his child more than me. That all of his time and attention would be with his kid, leaving me completely out of the picture. *Damn.* That was hard to admit.

As I stood out on the sidewalk waiting for Noble to pick me up from school, one of my classmates, Jarritt, walked up to me. He was a nice guy. Young, could've only been about 21 or 22 years old.

"What's up, Imani?" he asked, walking over as he pulled his sagging fitted jeans up on his waist. His backpack hung off one shoulder, making him look like a real college kid.

I smiled. "Hey, Jarritt."

He scratched behind his ear and gave an apprehensive look. "So check it. You know for this next assignment we gotta partner up. And since you be doing your thang in class, I was wondering if you wouldn't mind partnering up wit' a nigga?"

"Ummm," I stalled. I mean, don't get me wrong, Jarritt was a cool guy. He always made us laugh in class and whatnot, but when it came down to it, I was very serious about my work. I didn't want to be just a regular chef at a regular old restaurant. I wanted to be an executive chef and possibly own my own restaurant one day.

Jarritt pressed his hands together as if he were saying a prayer then said, "Pleeassse."

I rolled my eyes and sighed, giving in. "Jarritt, if you don't take this serious, I swear I will—"

Before I could even get it all the way out, Jarritt reached over and hugged me. Stunned by his gesture, my body went stiff. I kept my arms down by my sides as he wrapped his completely around me. And just as he let me go, I heard Noble call out my name. "Imani!"

I turned to see him leaning over the passenger seat of his Bugatti with the window rolled down.

"Oh, hey, babe. Uh, um, this is Jarritt, fr . . . from my class," I stuttered. Believe me, the grimace on Noble's face was enough to make anyone stammer.

"Oh, hey, wassup, big dog," Jarritt said, taking the baseball cap off his head before giving a little nod. "Nice wheels, man."

Of course Noble completely ignored him. He just looked at me and said, "Come on, let's go!"

I sent a quiet wave over to Jarritt before getting in the car with Noble. He pulled off so fast that his engine roared and his tires screeched, burning up the road.

We didn't even make it down the block before he cut his eyes over at me and asked, "Who the fuck was that?"

I looked at him like he'd just lost his mind. "Just a classmate, Noble, geez. He just wants us to partner up on this next assignment," I tried to explain.

"So in order for y'all to do an assignment together, he's gotta hug all up on you like that?"

I rolled my eyes and let out a little laugh. "It was harmless, Noble. I promise."

He just scoffed and inclined back farther in his seat, driving all fast with that one hand at the top of the steering wheel.

"Look at you, acting all jelly," I teased, poking at his side.

He smirked. "I'm not jealous. Just don't like anyone getting all touchy-feely with my woman."

I started laughing, and the next thing I knew, Noble started laughing too. He knew just how silly he was acting over me, and to be honest, it actually felt kind of good hearing him say that I was his woman. After a few moments of silence passed between us, Noble turned down the radio.

"So, um, you know Brittani is due in about four weeks, right?"

"Yep," I said, now staring out of the window because he had suddenly dampened the mood.

"We haven't really talked much about it, and I think we should."

"I mean, what's there really to talk about?" I asked. Yes, I knew I was being completely childish about the situation, but in that moment it was like I was channeling my inner 12-year-old and just couldn't help myself.

Just as the light turned green, he released a soft snort of frustration. "Well, I just want to know if you are willing to be a part of my child's life. Will you help me raise him?"

I swear I didn't know what came over me, but I suddenly snapped. I turned to him with a sharp look in my eyes. "Noble, you don't even know if that child is yours. You're running around here telling everybody who'll listen that you have a son on the way. Get a DNA test, and then we'll talk." I pushed myself back in the seat and folded my arms across my chest. I felt an ugly frown take over my face as my chest heaved up and down. I was literally sulking like a spoiled brat.

"Now you listen here, because I'm only saying this shit once. I'm very certain that the child Brittani's carrying is mine. I understand that this is hard for you, and I've been doing my best to be sensitive to that but . . ." He blew out a deep breath then shifted his eyes over at me in the passenger seat once more. "You have got to come to terms with this shit or else we won't last."

My eyes immediately closed when he said that, as though they were trying to hold back tears. He'd finally said it. He'd finally admitted that it would always be his child over me. And I guessed that was to be expected, because Noble was truly a standup guy. Any woman would be lucky to have him as her child's father. I guessed I was just jealous that I wasn't the one given the honor.

"Talk to me," he said.

As soon as I opened my eyes up, the tears started spilling out. *Shit.* "I'm scared," I admitted through a whisper.

Noble pulled the car over to the side of the road and tenderly swiped his finger down my cheek. "Scared of what, baby? What are you scared of?" he asked.

"A lot of things." I sniffed, thumbing away my own tears.

"Like what?"

"Well, for starters, what role will I play in your child's life? I'm just your girlfriend, Noble."

He closed his eyes and let out a small chuckle. "Imani, you won't be my girlfriend forever. I do plan on making you my wife at some point, you know."

My eyes widened a bit. "You do?"

"Of course. I love you, baby," he said low.

"I love you too. Well, then I guess the next question I have is, have you and Brittani come up with a schedule? Do you know how often you'll be able to get him?"

"Imani, my father helped raise me. He was in my life, and I plan on doing the same for my son. I want fifty-fifty custody. Brittani's already agreed."

"So then, like every other week?"

He stroked his beard, thinking for a few seconds, then he said, "Well, probably not at first, but yes."

"I mean, we don't even have a nursery set up or anything."

"Will you help me get it together over these next few weeks?"

I gave a closed-lip smile and nodded my head before Noble took me by the hand and softly kissed the back it. "We'll be fine, baby, I promise."

I hiked my left eyebrow up. "Does Brittani know how you feel about me and that you want me to be a part of the baby's life?"

"Of course she does. You have no worries where she's concerned. That's already been taken care of, ma."

I didn't know exactly what that meant, but between the sincerity of his voice and the love he held in his eyes, I believed everything he was saying.

Freeing a huge breath of relief, I gently squeezed Noble's hand. "Thank you," I said.

"For what?"

I shook my head and closed my eyes. "For including me in your world. For everything."

Chapter 24

Noble

Over the past few weeks, things between Imani and me had been running smoothly. We decorated the nursery in a pale shade of blue and had gotten everything my son would need while staying with us. Imani would probably never admit this shit, but I swear she was now just as excited as me. The way her eyes would light up at the mere mention of his name, and that wide smile that would spread across her face was priceless. She was no longer on that jealousy hang-up, making it seem like there wasn't enough room in my heart for both her and my son. Finally, I think she got it. I was undoubtedly in love with her.

It was now the Saturday morning after Labor Day, and Imani and I decided to eat breakfast out at Miss Ruby's diner. Ever since she quit—well, I quit for her—she hadn't stepped foot back in the place. Surprisingly, other than a few of her old coworkers speaking, no one said anything out the way, and that included Big Will. While I ordered the steak and eggs, Imani had strawberry pancakes, and of course, Karen insisted on waiting on us. She was a trip.

"So what are you two getting into today?" Karen asked. She was over here socializing with us knowing she had other tables to tend to.

I looked across the table at Imani. "Well, I'm probably going to head on over to the club and get some work done when I leave here," I said.

Imani gave me those puppy-dog eyes. "How long are you gonna be?" she asked.

"Just a few hours. If you want to come, you can and just study up in my office."

"I hear that office of yours is a dangerous place," Karen interposed with a silly smirk on her face.

Imani gasped. "Karen, don't you need to be checking on your other tables?"

Karen looked around the crowded restaurant then turned back to us and said, "Yeah, but they'll be all right."

I shook my head. "So are you coming or do you want to just take my car?"

"I guess I'll come. You know I don't like driving your cars."

We sat there for another thirty minutes or so just talking with Karen and eating the rest of our food. When it came time to pay the tab, which was no more than a total of $20, I pulled out a crisp $100 bill and told Karen to keep the change. As soon as I stood up from my seat and went around to help Imani out of the booth, Big Will walked over. He had a wet, dingy towel draped across his left shoulder and a white tub in his hands, I assumed to bus the tables with.

With a little head nod, he looked over at Imani. "Morning, y'all."

Imani tucked her hair behind her ear and gave a little smile, indicating that she was a bit uncomfortable. "Good morning, Big Will."

No more words were exchanged between the two, so after she gave Karen a hug, we headed out of the diner. As we walked up the block with Imani's arm looped through mine, I felt my cell phone vibrate in my pocket. I pulled it out and saw Brittani's name flash across the screen.

"Hello."

"N . . . Noble, it's time!" she said in a panic.

"It's time? You're going into labor now?" With the phone up to my ear, I stopped midstride and looked over at Imani. Her eyes were widened with apprehension as she looked up at me.

"Yes. Sssh ssshh," Brittani panted.

"Is your mother with you? Is she taking you to the hospital, or do I need to come get you?" I asked all in one breathe.

"My mom. I'm on my way." I could tell just by the way Brittani was talking that she was already in pain.

"Okay, I'm on my way. I'll meet you there."

After ending the call, I grabbed Imani's hand in a hurry. "We gotta go, baby. It's time."

We rushed back to the car, and after a twenty-five-minute drive in downtown traffic, we arrived at Johns Hopkins Hospital. As soon as we entered the labor and delivery unit, I rushed over to the nurse's station while Imani stood behind me.

"Um, my, uh . . ." Shit, as a man who always prided myself on my composure, I was embarrassed that in that moment I didn't know what the hell to say.

Imani stepped up beside me and gently rubbed me on the back. "We're looking for Brittani Harris's room. We believe she's in labor, and he's the father," Imani calmly explained to the nurse.

The nurse looked down on her computer screen and clicked a few times with her mouse. "Oh, yes, she's in room 214. You must be, Mr. Noble Shaw?"

"Yes," I answered.

"It's down the hall and to the right," she pointed.

As Imani and I headed in that direction, I took in that hospital smell and heard random women hollering out in pain. Imani gave my hand a gentle squeeze and looked up at me. She must have sensed that I was nervous, because she smiled and said, "Everything's going to be just fine. You're going to be a great dad, Noble."

"Thank you, Imani. I appreciate you saying that, baby." I leaned down and gave her a quick peck on the lips.

When we finally reached the door to Brittani's room, I took a deep breath. It was my last attempt to shake off my nerves.

"I'll be out here in the waiting room. Just call me if you need me," Imani said, holding up her cell phone.

As I watched her walk back down the hall that we just came from, I ran my hand over my head then down my face.

"Ahhh!" When I heard Brittani wail on the other side of the door, I knew I had to get in there.

When I stepped inside, I saw her lying on her side with a wet washcloth folded up on her forehead. Her mother, whom I had only met once, was at her side and there was a nurse moving about the room.

"How you holding up, Mama?" I said, making way over to Brittani and hearing that constant beeping sound from the machines throughout the room.

I could see instant relief on her face as soon as her eyes landed on me. After saying hello, I went over next to her mother and took Brittani by the hand.

"How far along are you?" I asked, stroking the back of her hand with my thumb. It was a small gesture, but I was hoping that it would provide her some amount of comfort.

"She's seven centimeters. The doctors said it won't be long," her mother spoke up and said.

"How far apart are her contractions?" I asked her mother with my eyes fixed on Brittani. She was quietly wincing in pain.

"They coming every minute, minute and a half."

Just as soon as the words left Brittani's mother's mouth, a hard contraction hit. Brittani gripped my hand and hunched over in agony. When the contraction was finally over, Brittani inhaled through her nose and released small breaths from her mouth. Seeing that she was trembling, I reached over and gently rubbed her on her back. "You doing good, Britt. Hang in there."

I hated seeing her in pain like that. Glancing over at her mother, I asked, "Did she get an epidural?"

She shook her head. "No, she said she didn't want one."

Those hard-hitting contractions went on for another couple of hours before the doctor finally came in, checked her, and told us it was time to push. I was scared, nervous, and excited all together but I did my best to appear calm from Brittani's sake. I held up one of her legs while her mother held on to the other as Brittani bore down and pushed over and over again. After that, it wasn't long until my little man was coming out crying.

I literally had tears in my eyes seeing him for the first time as I cut his umbilical cord. Once he was all cleaned up, I cradled him in my arms and peered down into his sleeping face. He was already the spitting image of me. As I stood there with him at Brittani's bedside, I was overjoyed, overwhelmed with so many new emotions, love like I'd never felt it before. I leaned down a bit and brushed my hand over her curly black hair, applying a simple kiss to her forehead.

"Thank you," I told her.

When I stood up, I saw Brittani's eyes widening at something behind me. By the time I turned around, I only caught a glimpse of Imani's back as she headed back out the door. I gently passed Noble Jr. over to Brittani and left, hoping that Imani hadn't gotten too far. As soon as I stepped out the door, I looked to my right and saw Imani walking back toward the waiting room. I rushed up behind her and gently grabbed her by the arm before turning her around to face me. She was teary-eyed.

"Hey, is everything okay? Are you all right?" I asked.

She nodded. "I'm just happy for you, Noble. You deserve this and a . . . a whole lot more." She was choked up and could barely get the words out.

"You know that back there was nothing, right? Nothing but me thanking Brittani for birthing my son?"

She nodded again. "I know. I trust you," she said, still with a glossy set of eyes.

Lifting her chin with my index finger, I leaned down and kissed her lips. "I want you to come in and meet him."

Her eyebrows raised. "You do?"

"Of course, ma. Como on."

I took her by the hand and walked back down toward the birthing room. When we entered, I led her over to the bed, where Brittani was still holding Noble Jr. in her arms. As we neared, I could see Imani's eyes studying his tiny little features. She pressed her hands against her mouth in awe. "Oh, he's beautiful. Congratulations, Brittani," she said.

Brittani smiled. "Thank you, Imani. Would you like to hold him?"

Imani's eyes immediately lifted up to meet mine as if she were asking for permission. I nodded and gave her a little wink. After she went to the sink to wash her hands, she came back over so that I could place him in her arms. She took to him right away, her face softening up and her eyes filling with adoration and wonderment. Just seeing the two of them together like this consisted of what my hopes and dreams had been filled with over the past six months. And now the time was finally here, a beautiful reality.

Epilogue

Imani

Almost Two Years Later

It had been exactly twenty-three months, eight days, and eleven hours since the day Noble Jr. was born. I swear he was the perfect little boy, and I honestly couldn't have asked for a better relationship with him and even Brittani for that matter. That day when Noble told me he'd taken care of Brittani and that we had no issues where she was concerned, boy was he right! I only saw her on assigned days when she'd either drop off or pick Noble Jr. up. And a lot of times, rather than calling Noble directly, she would just call or text me instead. Now, I don't know what he said or did to make our lives "baby mama drama free," but so far it seemed to be working. It's like the three of us together always strove to be the most mature and cordial parents ever, always keeping the baby's best interest at heart. And, man, was I grateful!

The very next night after Noble Jr.'s first birthday party, Noble proposed to me. It wasn't any grand gesture that you might see in the movies or even read in a book, just him and me lying naked in the bed.

We were there in the dark speaking out our dreams that night, me nestled against his chest with his strong arms wrapped around me. I told him how eventually I wanted us to move out of the city and get a traditional house, especially now that we had Noble Jr. He instantly agreed. He then shared that he wanted to open up another nightclub out of the country, maybe in the Dominican Republic this time. The excitement in his voice when he described his vision gave me chills. And then suddenly things got quiet with him slowly caressing my arm. Just the soft sounds of our breathing, as though we were either thinking or taking it all in. Then all of a sudden, he cut through and said, "You know I love you, Imani."

I looked up at him, seeing only the white of his eyes peering back at me. "I love you too, baby."

"No, I mean, I really, really love you, Imani."

"Aww, Noh—"

He wouldn't even let me get it out. "Baby, you make me so proud to be your man. The way you're sticking it out with this school thing and the way you've been helping me take care of Junior . . ."

"What about you? Do I take care of you?" I asked knowingly.

He let out a little snort. "You know you do, baby, you always take care of me. Hell, some days I ask myself if I'm doing enough to take care of you."

"Of course you are!" I blurted out because I didn't want him to think otherwise. He'd been the best thing that ever happened to me.

"Baby?"

"Yes," I said, placing my hand on his chest before looking up at him again.

"Will you marry me?"

I was stunned to silence. A lump instantly formed in my throat, and tears suddenly filled the lower lids of my eyes.

"Say something, Imani. If you don't want to—"

"Of course I'll marry you," I croaked, now feeling the hot tears roll from the corners of my eyes. He lifted my chin and kissed me so deeply I could hardly breathe.

That night we made love like never before. Over and over, until we reached new depths I didn't even know existed. And then, just three short weeks later, we found ourselves out on the beachside of Montego Bay, Jamaica. Noble stood barefoot in the sand, dressed in an all-white linen suit, waiting for me to join him. I toed the rake-made aisle with nothing but him in my view. I heard the sounds of waves crashing against the shore and eagles squawking high up in the skies. And in front of God, his mother, Kells, our dear friend Rashad and his family, and even Karen and Sarah, we committed an eternity to each other and said our vows.

With our one-year anniversary just around the corner, things between us were better than ever. I still had four more semesters of school, but nevertheless, I was enjoying the learning aspect of it all. Noble would still help me study some nights, and I'd cook special dishes for him on the weekends. His nightclub in the Dominican Republic was now in its final stages, and in just two days we would be moving into our six-bedroom home. Noble had it built from the ground up, out in Anne Arundel County, and it was absolutely beautiful.

As I carried a sleeping Noble Jr. to his room for a late-morning nap, I passed by my husband in the hallway. He was dressed to kill as always in a tan Giorgio Armani suit and clay-colored Ferragamos on his feet. His hair and beard were lined to precision, and he smelled amazing, like the perfect blend of virtue and sin. *God.* I swear, I didn't think I'd ever get used to how attractive this man was or how, even now with our son in my arms, he made me moist between the thighs.

After laying Junior down, I went back out into the kitchen where Noble was sitting across from his mother at the table. Ms. Charlene was staying with us for a while, helping us pack and keep the baby while we moved into our new house. She and I had become very

close over the past couple of years and I no longer considered her to be just Noble's mother, but mine as well.
I went over to the sink and started to clean a few dishes from breakfast when I felt Noble's big hands slide
around my waist.

"Mmm," he groaned. His meaty member pressed up
against my ass as he lightly nibbled at my ear.

I blushed and rolled my eyes.

"What time is dinner?" he asked.

"Six? Will that work?"

With his chin resting on the top of my right shoulder,
he nodded. "Yeah, that's fine, baby. I'll call you if I'm gonna be any later."

When he kissed my neck, swirling the tip of his wet
tongue across my flesh, I couldn't help but close my eyes.
My head fell back against him as I bit down on my bottom lip, stifling a moan.

"Ahem." His mother cleared her throat.

Almost instantly, I could feel my cheeks flush as I
straightened up my stance.

"You know, your aunt Debra called me last week, talking
about she dreamt of fish. And of course, my mind went
right to Rashad, but now I see," she casually said before
lifting her coffee cup up to her mouth for a sip.

I turned to her with wide eyes but kept my mouth shut.
No one knew that I was pregnant, not even Noble. With
Junior being so young and us not even being married a
whole year, I didn't exactly know how he'd react. We had
so much going on already with me being in school, the
new house, and even his new club. I already knew this
was going to be a lot for us. Either way, my plans were to
tell Noble after we settled into the new house, just in time
for my first doctor's appointment.

"Let me talk to you for a minute," he said, pulling me
by the hand.

I cut my eyes over at his mother, who was reading the morning paper, and dried my hands off with a paper towel. "We'll be right back, Ma."

"Umm hmm," she said, keeping her eyes fixed on whatever she was reading.

Once Noble and I reached our master bedroom, he quickly shut the door and locked it. I was headed over to the bed to sit down when he pulled me back and pushed me up against the wall. His body instantly pressed against mine, forcing a yelping sound to release from my lungs. Within just a matter of seconds, his hand was wrapped around my neck, and his lips were locking in with mine. I could feel his hand slipping beneath my silk nightgown as our tongues played. His hard dick relentlessly poked at my stomach while his other hand explored my lower half. By the time his fingers reached my aching pussy, I was already moaning into his mouth, clawing desperately into his shoulders, and hiking one leg up to wrap around his waist.

"You wet as fuck, baby," he whispered against my lips.

Nodding, I closed my eyes and kept sucking on that bottom lip of his because I just didn't want him to stop. Once he finally got my gown up over my hips, I heard the unzipping of his pants. I looked down to see him lower them just enough to free his erection. And then without warning, Noble picked me up and slid into me with ease. My back pressed up against the wall as my eyes fluttered and my mouth hung from the intense pleasure of it all.

As he swelled inside of me, pressing the side of his face up against mine, I could feel his beard lightly grazing at my skin. "Gah you feel so good," he breathed, his hips thrusting in an upward motion as he sank in and out of me with fervor.

I wrapped my legs tighter around his waist and squeezed my pelvis, crashing down to meet his hips, simply feeling like I wanted to implode. "Noble," I panted.

He tightened his grip around my neck and kissed me again, still thrusting inside of me and picking up speed to where I could feel my breasts bouncing between us. "Oh, Goddd," I cried, my eyes rolling to the back of my head as I slid down on him in a rhythm.

He pulled back from me and covered my mouth with his hand. "Shh, you making too much noise, baby," he said, now slowing the stir of his hips into a sensual grind. "So this is what I'm going to get for the next nine months?" he whispered, still going in and out of me as he looked me square in the eyes.

He knew.

He removed his hand from my mouth, and with his eyes still open and locked into mine, he kissed me again. "I love you, Imani," he pulled back and said. His eyes silently told me that I was his everything.

"I love you too, Noble," I moaned lowly.

We shared only a few more minutes like that, him driving into me, until the point of no return. And after we both cleaned ourselves up and I sent him on his way to work, I found myself lying in bed just thinking. Thinking about how my life had instantly changed that cold day in December as I walked to the bus stop from Miss Ruby's diner. How I'd gone from getting evicted to finding the love of my life. Being heartbroken and single to actually being a happily married woman. Smiling, I closed my eyes and said a quick prayer, giving thanks to God, for meeting Noble Shaw.

The End

Better Man, Bitter Man

by

Sherene Holly Cain

Chapter 1

"Damn, baby," Jayce moaned. "This pussy is so good, I can't get enough of you," he stopped licking me long enough to say while simultaneously using it as an opportunity to come up for air.

"Shut up and eat everything on ya plate," I ordered as I scooted to the edge of the bed and allowed him to get better access to my goodies. Jayce was such a freak he would be happy if I only let him smell the pussy. Today was his lucky day because I was allowing him to get a taste of it as well. After the week I had, it was a must that I cum as hard as possible, and Jayce was just the man for the job.

What Jayce didn't know, and I would never tell him, was Nero's fine ass was the one that had me horny all week. I was saving myself for him, and I wasn't going to let anyone or anything penetrate me: not the fine-ass deliveryman who frequented my building, not my ex, Alan, with the delicious dick that could fuck me like a God, not the huge dildo I kept in the top shelf of my closet, and definitely not fine-ass Jayce Reynolds. I was, however, willing to let him feast on me until I released all of my juices on his amazingly talented tongue.

I thought I had hit the jackpot the night Jayce walked into my salon. Me, Marla, and Precious were all working late. It was the end of the month, and we had booked clients on top of clients so we all could make enough money to pay for our booth rental and still have something left over to splurge with.

I was finishing up a weave, and Precious was curling his customer's hair when Jayce came breezing in.

"Oh my Gawd, here comes the rain."

"What are you talking about, Precious? It's been raining all day," Marla said, looking up, confused.

"I'm talking about the moisture between my thighs."

We all busted up laughing because Precious is gay, and as far as we knew he hadn't had any type of sex change operation. The thought of any moisture forming between his thighs would surely be a sight to see.

Jayceon walked toward me looking sexy as sin, his tall, dark frame hovering over me like a tree. I looked like an ant compared to him, and it seemed like all he had to do to stomp me was raise his foot two inches.

"Can I help you?" I asked.

"You sure can," he said.

Now it was my turn to look confused. The thing was, this was a hair salon, and he was bald. The only thing we could do for him was condition his scalp. We all sat quietly, wondering what type of service we could possibly offer him, when he began to ramble about everything under the sun. I kept changing the subject to steer him in the direction of why he came into the shop, but it was all for naught, because he kept finding other things to talk about instead. I didn't stop him. The next thing I knew, I had finished weaving one head and shampooed, blow dried, and flat ironed another. Jayce invited me to dinner, and after we ate, we ended up at a hotel. The rest, as they say, is history.

Jayce was fine, and I had no doubt he would make somebody a nice boyfriend, but Nero Cumin was the man I wanted. He was tall, caramel creamy, and had emerald green eyes I could get lost in forever if I wasn't careful. His fine ass had the nerve to be bowlegged with so many muscles he could model for a magazine and a delicious-looking dick print that strained against his scrubs. But what I loved most about him was the sexy, neatly trimmed reddish brown beard he sported. Although I'd never been remotely close to him, I imagined it was him eating my pussy until my juices squirted all over that beard. I was sure I could bag him. I just needed to find a way to get in his presence to work my magic.

"Ummmmmm, Jaaaaaayce, yesss, right there. Oh, my God, I'm about to cum." He knew better than to stop to say anything, but just to be sure, I held his head in place with both my hands and tooted my crotch up to silence his hot, wet, tantalizing tongue. Jayce was the truth. He ate me until it felt like I was dying a slow and pleasurable death, and the next thing I knew, my eyes were rolling to the back of my head. I screamed to let Jayce know I was about to succumb to the mind-blowing pleasure he was giving me.

"Fuuuuuuck," I yelled loud enough for half the people in the complex to hear me. I couldn't care less. I was now shaking like a leaf and squirting like a faucet all over his lips. He opened his mouth to let out a moan and catch my stream of sweet cum at the same time. There was plenty of it to make him full.

Once I was sated, I looked over at Jayce. I wasn't the type of woman who kicked a man out after I got my rocks off, even though at this point I was sure he knew I wasn't going to let him penetrate me or get down on my knees and suck his dick. But I was going to try my best to bring him some type of pleasure even if I had to get up and cook dinner. I propped my pillows up, pulled my panties on, and lay on my back.

"Come here," I beckoned him. The smile on his face was priceless, and he wasted no time lying on top of me and grinding me. As he did so, I realized how stupid I was to do that. He could've easily yanked the flimsy under-

332 Sherene Holly Cain

garment off my ass and fucked me silly. Lucky for me he didn't.

Jayce had a nice-sized dick. It was long and thick, and had I not been so in love with Nero, I would have fucked him from sunup to sundown in a heartbeat. Jayce caressed my hair and took in my scent, and then he grabbed my long locs and wound them around his fingers as he slowly started dry humping me. His dick grew stiffer as he moved against me, and I got turned on all over again. Don't get me wrong. Jayce was drop-dead handsome in his own right with some beautiful light gray eyes to match. It was just that when it came to Nero, I had to draw the line.

My thoughts of my crush, the friction from the pillow beneath me, and the hot, thick flesh pressing against my hot box enticed me to no end. It was at that point I knew I was going to explode again.

"Ummmm," Jayce moaned. "Oh, T, ah, baby. I'm about to cum."

"Come on," I urged as I gyrated myself against his dick. Juices trickled out of my pussy, and I felt the beginnings of my own orgasm start to take over. "Fuck, Jayce, I'm about to cum."

"Come with me, baby," Jayce announced. I could tell he was getting ready to release his load. In seconds, I felt his hot jism trickle on my lace undies, and it turned me on so much, I came for the third time. I jerked and shook until it was over, then fell asleep in Jayce's arms.

I woke up to the smell of bacon and wondered if I was dreaming. Not only had I not been shopping, but if I had, I wouldn't have bought bacon, at least not the traditional pork version. It would have been more like turkey.

"Wake up, sleepyhead," I heard Jayce say as he handed me a cup of coffee. His eyes were so sexy with the sun shining on them from the window.

"Good morning and thank you."

"I hope you don't mind. I took the liberty of making you breakfast."

"You didn't have to go through all that trouble."

"It was no trouble at all. I enjoy cooking just as much as I enjoy eating." He laughed at his pun, licked his lips, and smiled. "Hold up," he said before I got a chance to answer.

The next thing I knew, he was bringing in a tray of food, had set it down on my lap, and started feeding me a strawberry. I grabbed it from him and fed myself.

"Maybe I didn't make myself clear that I'm not looking for this."

"Looking for what?" he answered nonchalantly as he began to eat his food.

"I'm not looking for the type of relationship that you think this is going to turn into."

"I know," he said as if I'd told him something as simple as, "I have a few clothes in the dryer."

"And," I added, "I'm not exactly going to pursue this sexual thing we have either."

"I knew you were going to say that the moment you refused to let me put it in you. You obviously don't know what you're missing. Won't you let me show you how good it can be."

"Let me put it this way: I'm only interested in friendship."

"I wouldn't call what we did last night 'friendly.'"

"But you can't say we went all the way, either. I say we throw the whole affair away and start over fresh."

"How do we do that?"

"Hi, my name is Tekhiya Fields, and I'd like to be your friend." I put my hand out for him to shake. He took the hint.

"Hi. My name is Jayceon Reynolds, and I would love that."

"So you're good with it?"

"I'll have to be. It is what it is. I'd rather be something than nothing at all."

"Then it's settled."

"Okay. Enjoy your breakfast. I have a couple of errands to run," he kissed me on the forehead and said.

I smiled as he walked away, noting how long it'd been since I had a man cook for me and even longer since I had one to show me love like he had, mostly because I was on some independent shit and partially due to the fact that men like him were very hard to come by.

I could only hope that Nero was the cooking kind. I had been picking some real duds lately, or I should say they had been picking me. It just so happened that I found Nero at a local deli while I was grabbing lunch for me and a coworker. He was walking out, and I was walking in, and he managed to pause long enough to smile at me. Then, as an afterthought, he reached in his pocket to grab a business card to throw in the "win a free sandwich" bowl. In the few moments our eyes met, I fell in love.

There had to be at least twenty cards in that bowl, and I didn't know which one was his. Why did my crazy ass wait until the restaurant was damn near empty, grab a handful of cards from the top, and stuff them in my bag? I sorted out every card when I got home, discarding the ones from women and weeding out the unisex and men's names. The sandwich maker had called him "Doc," and for that, I could've kissed him. There was only one doctor in my pile of cards, and Nero Cumin was it. It was then that I became obsessed with becoming his woman.

***

"You're slow as Christmas," I told my sister, Genyja, as we walked up the stairs of the medical building. The elevator was broken, and we had to walk three flights to the office where Nero worked.

"That's easy for you to say," she huffed.

"I'm glad you're wheezing. You're supposed to be getting checked for asthma. Walk a bit faster and it might increase your symptoms and make your visit more believable."

"Your skinny butt ain't the one carrying forty pounds of extra weight on you. I can barely breathe, let alone walk," she spat. "I'm risking my health and my reputation, all because you want to see your crush. You're lucky I'm even helping you."

"I'm sorry, sis. You're right. I appreciate you looking out for me," I added. Actually, she was perfect for the job. With her condition, Dr. Cumin was not about to turn her away if you paid him to. He was dedicated to every patient who walked into his office, and I was going to be just as dedicated to seeing that my poor asthmatic sister had the best of care.

I had already peeped Nero out. He was the best physician in Norobosco County, highly intelligent, single, and in demand. He had two girlfriends in his lifetime: his high school sweetheart, Layna, and a woman who was almost his baby mama, Marina. I say almost because she tried to pin a baby on him but got caught fucking her real baby daddy instead. I heard she got an abortion because she couldn't handle dealing with the two men while she waited to see if it was Nero's.

Layna turned out to be a gold-digger whose only claim to fame was spending money like it was water, even though things were extremely tight for them in the beginning. Nero didn't mind providing for her if she really had

the need for the stuff, but it turns out she was binge shopping during the mania phase of her manic depression,
and half the purchases she made were bullshit trinkets
she didn't even need.

Now me, I'd had my share of sexual partners, but I was
selective about who I fucked. As good as my pussy was, I
made sure I closed my old chapters before starting new
ones. I didn't have any mental illnesses for him to worry
about either, unless you called the hallucinations I had
about him wanting me so bad he could almost taste the
nectar dripping out my pussy a reason to call up a shrink.

"What are you daydreaming about now?" Genyja asked,
snapping me out of my thoughts.

"Sorry, sis. Right this way." I motioned. She followed
me down the hallway, and I opened the door, made my
way in, and signed her in at the reception desk. We were
told to have a seat and sat quietly until her name was
called.

"Genyja Waterman," a nurse yelled. I stood up, grabbed
my sister's hand, and led her down the narrow hallway to
the exam room. My heart started beating a mile a minute
when I smelled Nero's cologne. I knew it would only be a
matter of seconds before I would be face-to-face with his
fine ass.

"Hi, I'm Dr. Cumin," he walked in and introduced himself. My sister shook his hand, and I was almost jealous
she was the first one to touch him.

"Nice to meet you, Dr. Cumin," she said. "I'm Genyja,
and this my sister, Tekhiya."

"Hi, Tekhiya." He smiled, parting those luscious lips I
was dying to kiss. I almost forgave him for not shaking
my hand first.

"Hi," I answered sheepishly, my eyes travelling from
his eyes to his lips to his big, beautiful dick. He shifted
and put his clipboard in front of him.

"So what brings you here to see me, Genyja?"

"My asthma's been acting up lately."

"I see. Do you take anything for it?"

"Yes. But it doesn't seem to be working."

"It's not uncommon for asthma sufferers to experience flare-ups during the springtime. I'm going to change your inhaler to a stronger dosage and give you Prednisone for about four days. Make sure you take it as directed, but no more than the prescribed amount. It's a very strong steroid."

"Sure thing, Doc." She nodded.

He was absolutely beautiful. I found myself imagining he had me on the examining table naked while he sat on the stool eating me out, his tongue hot and wet, making me scream and writhe in ecstasy. It was only after he yelled my name sternly that I realized my fantasy had gotten way out of control and I'd once again delved into the world of Nero Cumin.

"Tekhiya," they yelled simultaneously.

"Huh?"

"You okay?" Genyja asked.

"Yes."

"The doctor asked if you have any questions."

"None that I can think of. Perhaps you should give me your card in case I think of something later," I told him.

Nero reached into his pocket, pulled out two cards, and handed one to both of us.

"No need to waste two cards. Just give one to Tekhiya," G shook her head back and forth and said.

Good girl, I silently praised her.

"Here you go," he said, handing it to me and gazing deeply into my eyes.

"Thank you," I whispered.

"Great. Nice meeting you ladies. Take care of my patient," he said to me.

"Yes, Doctor." I grinned.

Before we made it out of the room, he was bombarded with questions from the same nurse who led us in. She spoke with a syrupy voice, unlike the one she used with us, and batted her fake lashes so hard I thought they were going to fall on the ground.

You don't stand a chance, fool, I challenged her in secret. He smiled at her in a professional way but otherwise didn't seem the least bit interested.

Meanwhile, the receptionist chattered on the phone while we walked out, and she was oblivious to the fact we were standing there. In fact, she was so distracted we had to wait until she finished with her rant to get some help.

"I told you Dr. Cumin isn't up for grabs," she whispered to somebody on the line. "I tried, Dr. Foray tried, and his nurse is still trying. Half the women who come in this office try to date him, and he turns them down cold. I gotta go, girl. I'll talk to you later," she said once she finally looked up and saw us waiting.

"Dr. Cumin wants you to follow up with him in a week." She smiled. "Here's your appointment and prescription."

"Thank you," Genyja said. I didn't say anything to the receptionist, because as far as I was concerned, she was yet another female who thought she could steal my man but didn't stand a chance.

Chapter 2

The upcoming week was rough for me. I couldn't concentrate on anything but Nero. It seemed like I smelled his cologne everywhere I went and woke up from having dreams of him every night. Somewhere between checking myself in a mental institution and going to his job to beg for a date, I realized how much I needed him. Saving myself for him was one thing, but it would all be for nothing if I didn't do something to get his attention. I needed to find a way to do that before the rest of the vultures started coming out to feed.

It was now 5:30 on a Friday. His office closed at 6:00. Since I was already done with my last customer, I grabbed my keys, determined to catch him while he was on his way out to his car. At this point, the thought of begging for a date didn't sound half bad.

I drove to the parking lot of his workplace, waited for about five minutes, and then called an Uber, praying like hell one would show up fast. It did. I was climbing in it at 5:59, and by 6:03 Nero was walking out the building and getting into a black Navigator. My heart started beating wildly, and I almost got cold feet. That's when I knew I had to carry out the plan I had thought about many times in my head. The Uber driver was just about to pull off to go to the destination I'd chosen on the app when I instructed him to follow Nero.

"I thought you were going to the mall," he said.

"Can you please just follow him? At a safe distance, of course. I'll pay you for your troubles when we get there."

"Fine," he said and took off behind Nero, who was driving like he was auditioning for NASCAR. After about seven minutes of mad speeding, Nero parked in a bar lot and got out. I handed the driver a crisp hundred-dollar bill, and he smiled and thanked me profusely.

"You're welcome. Just let me out on the street. I can walk from there," I said, all the while praying this was Nero's final destination. I didn't want to be stuck at the bar looking stupid.

I waited outside for about five minutes, and then I walked in and looked for my man. He was sitting at the bar, looking like he just finished doing a photo shoot for *Sexy Men Weekly,* and lo and behold, there was an empty seat right next to him.

"Is this seat taken?" I walked up and asked as if I hadn't the slightest idea who he was.

"No," he said without looking up.

"Thank you," I said.

"No problem," he told me then went to take another sip of his beer. Curiosity must've gotten the best of him, because he looked out of the corner of his eye, then slightly turned to get a better view of me.

"Don't I know you?" he asked.

"I probably have one of those familiar-looking faces." I smiled.

"Not hardly, beautiful. That smile is unforgettable," he said.

"Thank you." I blushed.

"What are you having?" he asked.

"Kiss Me Quick."

Without hesitation, Nero leaned over and kissed me. Kiss Me Quick was the name of the drink I wanted to order, but he actually thought I wanted him to kiss me, and

I wasn't about to be the bearer of bad news. We tongued each other down for about two minutes, but it wasn't long enough. The shit was good. So good, in fact, that I was ready to fuck the shit out of him right there on top of the bar. If it hadn't been for the next chain of events, I probably would have.

The water I'd guzzled down earlier was suddenly killing my bladder, so I excused myself and made a mad dash for the ladies' room, getting there in the nick of time to relieve myself. I washed my hands, fingered my hair, and freshened my lipstick before heading back out to Nero. As soon as I rounded the corner, I ran smack dab into Jayce.

"So this is where you spend your free time," he said.

I was speechless. I didn't even know Jayce hung around in this part of town, let alone frequented the bars here. "I'm just here to meet up with some friends," I lied.

"Oh," he said, obviously having egg on his face after confronting me. "Female friends?"

"What difference does it make?" I blurted. "It's not like you're my man or anything."

Jayce looked a little hurt about what I said, and he made no secret of it. "I can't handle the thought of you with another man. We can change your status from single to taken anytime you're ready, ma."

"It's not that type of party, Jayce. You and I both know we help each other out from time to time, but other than that, we don't have anything special going on."

He looked at me as if to say, "You damn skippy, bitch, because you ain't letting me fuck but you sure as hell got me eating the pussy," but he must've thought better of it and said the next slick thing that came out of his mouth.

"Shee-it. You don't know it yet, but I'm your man, and one of these days you're going to have my last name."

"I have to go," I said, wrestling my arm away from him and walking toward a crowd of women I hoped to blend in with. I damn sure didn't want Jayce to know who I was entertaining. It wasn't any of his business, anyway.

I watched Jayce walk out the bar and breathed a sigh of relief.

Thank God, I thought before walking back over to Nero. To my horror, he was talking to a very attractive woman. I didn't let that stop me though. I went over to introduce myself.

"Hi, I'm Tekhiya."

She rolled her eyes defiantly and left my extended hand hanging in the air. She was obviously in her feelings about Nero being out with me.

"When you're ready to talk, we'll be waiting," she told him.

He didn't say anything, just watched her walk away.

"What was that all about?" I asked.

"A bunch of bullshit," he replied then downed his beer, which turned out to be the third one since I'd left. He had also added a few shots of tequila to the mix. Now it was his turn to be evasive.

"Let's get out of here," he said, automatically assuming I would want to. He was right. I got up without hesitation and followed right behind him.

"Where's your car?" he asked.

"I, um, walked," I told him, all the while hoping he wouldn't question me further. He hunched his shoulders and led me to his car.

Once we were inside, he turned up the music loud. I wanted to reach over and turn it down but decided that would be rude. I loved the artist maybe even more than he did, but I didn't really see the need to bust any ear-drums to listen to them. Besides, I was hoping to get to know Nero better, and this would've been the perfect opportunity for us to talk.

It didn't take a rocket scientist to figure out the good doctor liked living dangerously. Not only did he play his rock music loud, but he had an unwavering need for speed. I looked over at the speedometer. He was driving so far over the speed limit, I grabbed my chest to double-check if I had my seat belt fastened securely then held on to the handgrip as tight as I could.

I was almost about to curse myself for being stupid enough to get in the car with a speed demon behind the wheel when he made a complete stop in front of one of the most immaculate buildings I ever saw in my life. It was a restaurant I never thought I'd visit in my wildest dreams.

"Welcome to Che L' Dore," a valet opened my door and said. He put his hand out to lift me out the seat, and I almost forgot about the seat belt that moments earlier I'd checked to see was fastened.

"This is absolutely beautiful," I cooed.

"I'm glad you like it," Nero said, grabbing my arm to escort me in.

By the time we emerged from the restaurant, we'd stuffed ourselves with so many entrees and desserts it had to be a sin. Nero paid the bill, which cost more than my rent and car note put together, and we headed to his house where I was sure the fun was about to begin. I still hadn't learned a thing about this man aside from what I already knew because he had yet to open his mouth to share anything with me. Sure, I wanted the passionate kisses and mind-blowing sex I had dreamed he could give me, but I also wanted to know what made Nero tick.

He parked in front of a sprawling estate that made the restaurant look like a juke joint, and I couldn't wait for the tour. However, as soon as we got there, Nero got on the phone, went into another room, and left me in the living room watching TV for thirty minutes. When he came out, he didn't apologize or show me around. He just talked about his patient who needed his "help" and how he needed to make that happen. I thought he was going to drop me off at home while he handled his business, but he opted to leave me in his house until he returned. Of course, I took it to mean I was special. Why else would he leave me in his house?

"Make yourself at home. I'll be back as soon as I can," he said and kissed me on the cheek. I acquainted myself with the luxurious house to the best of my ability, making sure to take myself around to every room and marvel at each one's exquisite beauty.

After I accomplished that, I went into the kitchen and prepared myself something to eat, not because I was hungry—God knows I felt like a pig after eating all that food at the restaurant—but more so I could get some practice cooking in the state-of-the-art kitchen I was sure would someday be mine. With that mission handled, I sat down on the comfortable sofa to watch TV, imagining myself living in his house and hosting and having parties with all our family and friends.

It was taking Nero a long time. I was bored and had run out of fun stuff to do by myself.

Oh, shit. I haven't checked in with G in a while. She's gonna kill me for sure. I laughed, grabbing my cell phone to call her up.

"Guess where I'm at?" I blurted into the phone as soon as Genyja answered.

"Tell me," she said.

"Nero's."

"Dr. Nero?"

"The one and only."

"How'd you manage that?"

"It's a long story."

"Y'all do it yet?"

"Damn, nasty. Give me a chance."

"You're the one who's always talking about jumping his bones."

"When he gets back, I plan to."

"Where'd he go?"

"To see a patient."

"He makes house calls, too?"

"Apparently."

"Well, enjoy and keep me posted."

"Sure thing, sis," I said and hung up.

I tried to keep myself busy in the extraordinarily huge house, but despite my best efforts, it proved to be difficult. An hour passed and my eyes were getting heavier by the minute. I ended up falling asleep on the sofa, and I gasped when I felt a pair of arms scoop me up. To my relief, it was Nero. He was looking at me like the world started and ended with me, and I couldn't be happier. I watched him take me to my destination, his bedroom, lay me down on his huge California king, and kiss me passionately while he rubbed on my breasts. He took one of them out and sucked on it until it became a swollen peak in his mouth.

"Ummmm, baby. That feels so good."

"You like that?"

"I love it, baby. Don't stop."

He did exactly what he was told, only stopping to give my left breast the same attention he had given its twin, and I was in ecstasy. My pussy was soaking wet.

"Fuck me, Nero," I begged.

He smiled and took off his shirt. He was ripped with muscles everywhere. Most men who worked out had a small package, but I had already seen a glimpse of what he had to offer. He removed his pants then his boxers, and I saw the monster my pussy was now dying for. I took him in my hand, resisting the urge to suck the skin off his dick. He looked delicious, and I almost begged for a taste.

The next thing I knew, Nero was kissing a path from my breasts to my abs to my pussy. He flicked his tongue in me and tasted the juices that gathered along my clit, trying to catch most of it before it trickled onto the bed. He ate me like there was no tomorrow, moaning like it was the best-tasting juice he ever had the pleasure of lapping up. It was so good that I came in his mouth almost instantly and reached several orgasms just from oral sex alone. I wanted to return the favor, but he stopped me.

"Not yet," he said. "Touch your breasts." I quickly did as ordered, and he jacked off while watching my show, exploding on my D cups and rubbing his juices into my skin. It wasn't long before we succumbed to the alcohol, the food, and the events of the night and fell asleep in each other's arms.

When we woke up the next morning, I was a little disappointed that we didn't have sex. I thought we were going to make love, but we didn't. Again, I thought myself special for being able to make a man respect me enough to not make love on the first date, but I quickly grew to learn that Nero wasn't thinking about having sex with me. For weeks he didn't penetrate me, and I was beginning to wonder if something was wrong with me, or worse, something was wrong with him. We spent a lot of time together, so of course, I assumed we were an item.

Nero took me everywhere, flaunting me, showing me off to his friends, even letting me meet his family. But I had yet to taste his dick or feel him inside of me. I was ashamed to admit this to my sister. What woman in the world would tell her bestie that the man she loved and saved herself for didn't want her sexually?

Chapter 3

"Hey, bitch," G yelled over my phone line. "Where have you been?"

"Hanging out with Nero."

"You guys are getting really close, huh?"

"Yes." I smiled.

"When's the wedding?"

"What do you mean?"

"That's your mission, right? I mean, you guys are spending all this time together. I know you fucked the shit out of him, and I know it will only be a matter of time before he proposes."

You don't know the half of it, I thought. "No, ma'am. No wedding yet, but I'm working on it. What did you want to tell me?" I asked.

"I want to spend a little time with my sister. I'm not too far from your house, and I was going to come over."

"Come on. I'm just driving up. I'll wait for you outside."

"Okay, I'm on my way."

It only took G five minutes to get here, and I hugged her and led her up the stairs to my apartment, telling her about my lack of sex with Nero on the way. She was speechless, and that spoke volumes, because all she did was talk. I went to put the key in my door only to discover it was already unlocked.

"What the hell?" I yelled.

I lived in a pretty good neighborhood and didn't think anyone would break in, especially with my nosy neighbors around, but I was horrified.

Nevertheless, I opened my door with caution and proceeded to walk into the living room. I heard the television on and got suspicious because I knew good and damn well I turned it off before I left earlier. There was an arm and two feet sitting in my La-Z-Boy chair as we walked in the living room.

Now I was fighting mad, and I picked up the bat I kept by my entry way before storming over to my "guest." I was in the midst of swinging at his head when I saw who it was.

"What the hell are you doing in my house?" I asked.

"I missed you," Jayce answered nonchalantly. "You haven't been returning my calls."

"I don't give a fuck if the Pope didn't return ya calls. That don't give you a reason to break into my house."

"You haven't been with another man, have you?"

"What business is that of yours?"

G was horrified. She had been looking back and forth from me to Jayce, watching our heated exchange and trying to figure out what the hell was going on.

"Aren't you going to introduce me?" he asked.

"Not after you broke into my apartment."

"You keep saying I broke in, but it didn't exactly go down like that."

"I'm dying to hear this one," I folded my arms across my chest and said.

"I kind of told the landlady that I was a family member from out of town, and she let me in."

"I'll have to talk to her ass," I yelled as I went over to turn the television off.

"Excuse her rudeness," Jayce said. "My name is Jayceon. And yours?"

"Genyja," G told him, smiling from ear to ear. "She's been hiding you," she said, licking her lips and looking him up and down.

I was a little bit unnerved to see Genyja flirting with Jayce even though I wanted him only as a friend. I couldn't believe the jealousy I felt from her sizing him up. I would have been even more upset if he had looked at her with the same intensity, but he didn't because he was in love with me. I could see it in his eyes, hear it in his voice, and feel it through his touch.

"What is that smell?" I asked.

"I cooked dinner for you. I told you I missed you."

As much as I wanted to tell him, "Hell no, you didn't have to cook for me, and this is some bullshit," I didn't. The food smelled damn good. I ran into the kitchen to find out what it was. I had to wait in line behind G's greedy ass, but once I did, I saw that he had cooked me a pasta dish. I wanted to dig into it immediately. I hadn't eaten all day, and my stomach was growling something terrible.

He pulled out the chairs for both me and my sister and brought the food to the table. We ate like we hadn't had a meal in weeks, and when we were done, G was so enamored she couldn't even see straight.

"I love a man who can cook," she said. "That's the way to my heart. Jayce, are you married?"

Jayce looked at G like she was crazy, because he couldn't even fathom trying to talk to my sister when he was trying his best to get into my panties. So did I, because my sister was so straightforward about what she wanted. If I didn't know any better, I would have thought she was trying to get some of Jayceon's dick. I wasn't about to let that happen whether he was my friend or not. Yes, I was being territorial about J, especially since he was catering to me like I felt Nero should've been doing.

"No, I'm not," he chuckled then did something a lot of men wouldn't do, especially when they had a chance to make their crush jealous. "I'm actually hoping to become your sister's husband."

"What sister?" G said, knowing that I was with Nero and wanted to marry him. She also knew good and damn well I was the only sister she had.

"Tekhiya doesn't know it yet, but I'm her man."

"Well, I guess you told me," she said, looking offended.

"Sorry, G. I didn't mean to hurt your feelings. It's just that she has my full and undivided attention."

"My bad," she said.

Jayce reached over and wiped the sauce off my chin, and G almost lost it. She had never seen an exchange between me and a man this way.

"Can I talk to you for a minute?" she said, pulling—no, yanking—me into the next room.

"What the hell is wrong with you, T?" she wasted no time asking.

"What do you mean, G?"

"This man obviously worships the ground you walk on, he's fine as hell, can cook like a chef, and I know you fucked him. You're over there playing with Nero's crazy no-sex-having ass."

"Why you gotta call Nero crazy?" I said, secretly hoping she wouldn't harp on the sex part.

"You told me he's not hitting it. I'm just saying, what's up with Jayce?"

"Jayce and I are friends, which doesn't mean you can flirt with him. I'm not ready for him to talk to anyone yet, at least until I'm ready to let him go."

"Well, damn, greedy."

"Don't judge me."

"This man doesn't look like he's going anywhere, and he's talking marriage. Isn't that what you wanted?"

"Yes, with Nero."

"You think you're in love with Zero—I mean, Nero—but it's obvious you have feelings for Jayce. Why don't you give him a chance? Date both of them if you have to. It's your life, your decision."

"I've already made my decision, G. I want Nero, always have, always will. Leave Jayce out of this and stop flirting with him."

"Fine. I have to go. I love you, and I hope you pick the right man."

"Thank you. I love you too, and I'll keep you posted."

G left, but not before giving Jayce a wink and thanking him for the meal. I shook my head. My sister was a lost cause.

I had never been the type to let my body be deprived of sex. My motto was, "If it feels good, do it." Besides, as beautiful as I was, I had my choice of men whom I had to beat off with a stick. I wanted Nero so bad I stopped even looking around for anyone else. I was willing to suffer in silence instead of giving up something I wanted so much. I'm not saying it was easy. God knows it was hella hard, especially with Jayce's sexy ass trying me every chance he got.

In addition to him, one of my temptations in the form of a deliveryman was always coming into my building. One day, I looked out my window just as he was walking into the complex. He must've been psychic or something, because he looked up and winked at me right on cue. I wondered who he was delivering to today but didn't have to wonder long because my doorbell rang. When I looked out the peephole, he was standing there in the flesh.

"I have a package for you."

"What is it?" I asked.

"I'd have to be psychic to know that. Can I come in?" he said in one jumbled sentence.

I wasn't crazy. I knew most of the time the deliveryman didn't have to come in. He simply rang your doorbell, had you sign for the package, and went on about his business.

Since he had such a big box, I assumed he had to bring it in, put it down, and assemble it if that was permitted. I waved my hand to indicate that it was okay to enter, and he smiled and did just that. I opened it to find a KitchenAid appliance from Nero.

"Somebody must love you," he said.

"I don't think love has anything to do with it."

"I know if you were my woman, I'd treat you like a queen."

"Would you?"

"Yes."

"I'll keep that in mind, mister. What is your name anyway?"

"Paul."

"Nice to meet you, Paul. My name is Tekhiya."

"Beautiful name, beautiful woman."

"Thank you."

"So tell me, Tekhiya, is there anything else you need from me?"

"I can't think of anything at the moment."

"Well, I need something from you," he mumbled.

"And what might that be?"

"Well, I'm having a really rough day, and a hug from you just might make it better."

"Oh, yeah?" I smirked.

"Yeah."

"Okay, Paul. A hug is pretty harmless, right?"

"As far as I'm concerned," he agreed.

Without hesitation, I came closer to hug him. He grabbed me tightly, placed a big kiss on my cheek, and let me feel the package between his thighs. It was long, thick, and hard. My pussy juices started rolling down my thighs, and I wanted to scream.

"That was a good hug, Paul." *Just not good enough to make me cheat.*

"Yes. I knew you'd be soft and smell like fresh roses."

"Thank you," I said.

"Did you feel how excited I am for you?" he asked.

"Very much so." I nodded.

"Can I come over for lunch sometimes?"

"I'm in a relationship right now, Paul, but if I'm ever free, I'll look you up."

"I'll be around," he said. "And I'll be looking forward to that lunch, too."

I smiled, opened the door for him, shut it, and leaned up against it. That huge toy in my closet was calling my name.

I managed to make it through the night without using the toy or my fingers. God knows that was a challenge. I woke up to a ringing phone and wondered who it was. I hadn't heard from Nero, nor had I answered any of Jayce's calls. I didn't need any more distractions.

"Hello," I said sleepily.

"Hello, sunshine," my ex blurted into the phone. "You didn't think I'd forgot about you, did you?"

"No, but I was hoping you would go on about your business. You know I'm not getting back with you, so you need to leave me alone."

"Who said anything about getting back with you? I respect your decision, scaredy-cat."

He was referring to the fact that I'd broken up with him despite the fact that he was damn near perfect. He was handsome, rich, and could fuck like a god as I indicated before. What woman wouldn't want him? I was afraid of love, and he was giving it out so freely, it made me get cold feet. I asked if we could take a breather for a while. He agreed, knowing that I probably wouldn't want to get back together again because of my fears. It didn't stop him from trying though.

"Won't you let me come over?"

"That won't be a good idea."

"So you can see that new motherfucker, but you can't see me?"

"I thought you agreed we needed this break."

"I agreed to a break, but I didn't think it would be this long. I damn sure didn't think you'd get with somebody else while we were on it."

I couldn't answer.

"Fine then," he continued. "But I do miss you something terrible, and I want to make love to you."

"What?"

"Yes. I want to fuck, make love, do the nasty, whatever you want to call it. I miss coming inside you. I'm not giving up on you."

"I can't."

"Think about it," he begged.

I hung up the phone, and it rang again. I thought it was him, so I let that call go to the voicemail. He didn't know it, but the mere thought of his voice made me want to put my fingers in my pussy and work them until I had a powerful orgasm.

I didn't do it. I wanted—no, needed—to be faithful to Nero. I knew that sooner or later he was going to fuck me, and when he did, everything about us would be straight. He was playing hard to get, and I let him because I knew that when he did fall, he was going to fall hard.

I lay in bed for what seemed like hours when I got Nero's call, and I was more than eager to talk to him. I could tell by the tone of his voice he had the good news I was waiting for.

"You want to go out tonight?"

"Yes," I blurted out.

"I'll see you at seven," he chuckled and hung up.

That night, I almost broke my neck trying on the skimpiest, sexiest outfits in my closet, finally settling on one that was tasteful and provocative.

"I know you won't be able to resist me in this," I looked in the mirror and said. Then I added, "Tonight we seal the deal on our relationship."

I had just pulled my hair into a sexy bun when Genyja called.

"Did you fuck Jayce's fine ass yet?"

"Hello to you too, sister."

"Shut up with the hellos. Did you fuck him is all I want to know."

"Genyja, I already told you, me and Jayce are just friends. I haven't heard from him."

"First of all, you're not fooling anybody with that bullshit. Nero is not giving up the dick, Jayce is more than happy to give it to you, and you're ignoring his calls because you know that. If you call him up right now, I'm sure he'll be happy to come over and end your dry spell. He's more than capable of fucking the shit out of you."

"So is Nero. I have a date with him tonight, and I think this just might be the night we taste each other."

"How can you be so sure?"

"That man is not fooling me. Every time I'm around him, his dick gets rock hard. He's ready."

"Okay, girl. Keep on playing and you're going to lose a good man. I know you been flirting with your delivery guy and your ex, but I'm telling you they're all full of shit except Jayce. He's a real one."

I was going to ask what made her an authority on the subject since she didn't have a man and none lined up, but I knew that would start an all-out war I wasn't prepared to fight.

"I love you, sis, but I have to go. I'll let you know if there are any new developments."

"Please do," she said. "I live vicariously through you. You know I don't have a life or a man."

I giggled and hung up the phone. G was definitely Team Jayce, and I hated to disappoint her, but I knew what I wanted.

Chapter 4

Nero had a chef prepare us dinner at his house, and I couldn't be happier. The fact that we were alone together meant there was a greater chance that we would make love tonight. He literally fed me every morsel of my food from the appetizer to the dessert. Feeling his fingers in my mouth was sexy as hell. I tried to feed him, but he wouldn't have it, so I left it alone. He seemed deep in thought, and I wondered if he was thinking about getting me in bed.

"So what do you want to get into tonight?" I asked.

"You," he said. "I want to get into you," he reiterated, emphasizing the "you" so I would fully understand.

"Are you serious?" I asked.

"Very. Take your clothes off," he commanded. I wasted no time following orders. Nero threw everything off the table and hoisted me up on top of it. I imagined how mad the maid was going to be when she came in and saw the big mess we had created. Spaghetti sauce splattered the walls, wine fell on top of the chair cushions, and chocolate cake landed as far as the china cabinets. Neither one of us cared. We were too engrossed in what we were doing.

Nero pulled his dick out, and it looked so delicious I wanted to taste it on the spot. He was being stingy with it, of course, because his only desire was to push it as far into me as possible. I let him. He raised my legs up over his shoulders and plummeted into me so good and hard

I cried out in ecstasy. After so many weeks of pent-up passion, we both came instantaneously. I felt a little empty afterward, and I thought it was because it was such a short session, but at that point in time, I couldn't really put my finger on the exact reason I felt so low.

Next time will be better, I thought as I fell asleep from exhaustion. I spent the night with him but left early. I wanted to reminisce about our night.

Jayceon finally got the picture. He kept his distance while still keeping in touch. Instead of pushing the issue by showing up at my house, begging me to go out, or trying to seduce me into letting him hit, he had taken to texting me good morning or to ask about my day. He seemed really determined to do the friendship thing, or so I thought.

It was late on a Friday night, and I was sitting in my PJs and head wrap when I heard a frantic knock on the door. I had just gotten comfy on the couch with one of my favorite movies, a tablespoon, and a quart of French vanilla ice cream, and the last thing I wanted was an interruption.

The person apparently knew I was home as they laid on my doorbell with all their strength, sending a message that ignoring them in the hopes they'd get a life and walk away was definitely out of the question. I assumed it was probably somebody who was lost and needed directions, or some kid selling candy for a prize knowing full well the school told them to only sell to friends and family, not knock on the doors of strangers. I could be a serial killer for all they knew, but anyone that selfish and greedy had no qualms about breaking the rules, let alone losing their lives. Instead, they were bothering decent, hardworking people who only wanted to pamper themselves after a long day of work.

The more I thought about it, and the more they knocked, the madder I got. I angrily got up to march over to the door and yank it open, determined to make them feel my wrath, kid or not, when the knocker suddenly stopped. I peeked out the peephole and saw no one then slowly opened the lock and turned the knob. Jayce rushed me and grabbed me by the waist, scaring me so bad I almost peed on myself.

"You scared the hell out of me," I screamed.

"I'm sorry, baby. I missed you. You want me to come back another time?"

"I'm good. Come on in."

A look of relief spread across his face when he realized I wasn't going to turn him away. Then he smiled. "Nice pajamas."

It suddenly occurred to me I must look a hot mess in a way he had never seen me before. I couldn't do anything about the pajamas, but I did yank the rag from around my head and fluffed out my hair so I would look halfway decent. "Excuse my appearance."

"No problem, ma. You always look beautiful to me. Besides I'm invading your space. I hope I didn't wake you up."

"No. I was about to watch a movie."

He walked into the living room and peered at the TV. "I love *Imitation of Life*," he said.

"You don't know nothing about that."

"Shee-it," he sang. "I grew up on these classics."

"Let me find out you have an old soul." I smiled.

Jayceon sat down and got into the movie. At least, he pretended that he did. But I stopped any games he was about to play.

"What did you need from me?" I asked.

"Huh?"

"What's the nature of your visit?"

"It's a little embarrassing."

"Try me."

"I locked myself out of my apartment."

"Sorry, but I can't help you. You never gave me a spare key."

"I know that. I was wondering if I could crash here for the night."

"Ummmm. I think you should rent a room."

"You want me to pay for twelve hours? That would be highway robbery. Let me sleep on your couch, and I'll bounce as soon as my landlord opens up his phone lines."

"As you can see, the couch is occupied right now." I pointed to the covers and the ice cream sitting on my sofa.

"I won't take up that much space," he promised.

"Okay. But don't talk during my movie."

"Bet."

What started out as a fun movie night soon ended up being a mini pamper party as Jayce spotted my old pedicure kit and some nail polish. He filled the bucket with warm water and massaged my feet until they felt like a piece of putty. It felt so good to have a man touch my erogenous zones I thought I had died and gone to heaven. He enjoyed watching me squirm as I went out of my mind raving about the job he was doing. He placed my toes in his mouth and sucked them so good my panties got soaking wet, and I was on the verge of cumming.

"Damn, ma. If I had known this, I would've run some bath water and massaged you while I bathed you."

My eyes flew open at the thought of that. I almost ran in there and turned on the water myself. He had some magic hands, and I already knew what his tongue could do. "You'd do that for me?"

"I'd do anything for you. You already got me cooking and washing and licking your feet, and I damn sure never did that before. If my boys knew that, they would clown me for sure. But I don't care. I know a good thing when I see it."

"Ummm hmmmm," I groaned.

"You don't believe me?"

"No. Not as good as you suck toes."

"Girl. You got me open."

He got up before I had time to answer, went into the bathroom, and started running the water. I was going to stop him, but there was no reason to be shy now. He had already seen me naked.

I walked in, started undressing him, and allowed him to undress me.

"Are you sure, ma?"

"Yes. It won't be fun unless we're both naked."

Jayce didn't wait for me to change my mind. He helped me into the tub and got in behind me. He had turned on some music on his phone, and we listened to the soft jazz of Najee. I was so relaxed, and it felt so good to lean on a nice strong chest, I almost went to sleep. Jayce sensed it and pushed me forward, washing my body as promised and focusing on my breasts, which got hard as soon as he touched them. Somehow his long arms managed to scrub all the way down to my ankles without me turning around. So many times I wanted to stop him, but this just felt so right.

He stood me up under the pretense that he was going to wash my pussy, only he dropped the washcloth and started rubbing me with his fingers. I felt his dick poking my back and immediately got turned on. I turned around to look at it for the first time. It was beautiful. I resisted the urge to take it into my mouth as he planted kisses on my breasts and stomach, then slid down to my dripping wet love tunnel.

There he was, on his knees, darting his tongue in and out of me, and I knew exactly what that tongue was going to accomplish. I threw my head back and prepared to be dazzled by his sweet, thick tongue, and he gave me exactly what I knew he was capable of giving. This time, when he knew I was about to cum, he stopped and lifted me into his arms, effortlessly carried me into my room, gently laid me on the bed, and entered me. I didn't stop him. I was dying to feel his thick flesh inside me and let him, as G would say, fuck the shit out of me. He didn't disappoint. In fact, he had me climbing the walls.

"Fuuuuuuck, Jayce. You feel so good."

"So do you, baby. I'm trying my best not to cum."

"Me too," I said.

"Go ahead."

He didn't have to tell me twice. My pussy was having the time of her life, and she was about to cream all over him.

"Oh, baby, I'm about to cum."

"Don't hold back, love. Give it to me."

Before he got those words out, I came so hard I thought I lost all my fluids. I screamed loud enough to wake the dead, and I was creaming everywhere. My body was shaking so hard I thought I was having a seizure, and I wanted to tell him to never stop fucking me. But I couldn't do that.

"Did you enjoy that, baby?"

"Hell yeah."

I was so satisfied that all I wanted to do was curl up in a ball and sleep, but Jayce had other plans. He worked the hell out of my pussy, giving it a lashing it had never had in life. Not only did he not cum fast, but he also showed no signs of coming anytime soon.

"Dayum, man," I moaned when he turned me on all fours. "You're insatiable." He had already had me missionary style, with my legs on his shoulders, made me ride him, and fucked me in a wheelbarrow position. Now he was plowing his big dick in me from the back. He must've made a vow to himself that if I ever in life let him hit, he was going to tear my pussy up.

"I can't get enough of you."

"Jayceon, please."

"You begging now?" He smiled.

"Yes, baby. I can't take it."

"Take this dick."

"This is too much."

"You ain't seen nothing yet."

The fact that he went harder told me he had no empathy and he damn sure wasn't thinking about stopping. He pumped all ten inches of his meat in me, and he was determined to make me take it. At one point, he fucked me so hard I thought he was trying to kill me. My ass didn't try to beg him to stop anymore because it didn't help my situation in any way. By now my voice was gone, and all I could really do was moan.

"Jayceon," I screamed. If he heard me, he was ignoring my ass, because he had turned into a madman whose only mission was to fuck me into oblivion.

"Almost there, ma," he finally said. I had gained some of my composure, and I fucked him back. I don't know where I found the strength, but I even squeezed my PC muscles.

"That's it, ma. Squeeze that dick. Own it. Talk to me."

I decided to take him up on his offer. I knew if I wanted him to stop, I better open my mouth and say something. "Yes, Jayceon. Fuck me good," I said as I fucked him back.

"You want me to fuck you?"

"Yes, baby. Fuck me like I never been fucked before."

"Oh, yeah," he moaned. "I'm about to give you this cum, baby."

"Come for me, baby."

"Where you want it at?"

"On my breasts."

"I'm going to splash all over your big, beautiful breasts."

"Yes, baby. Cum all over my breasts."

I couldn't believe it. The dirty talk was turning me on as well, and I was about to cum again. I was just finishing up when Jayce yanked his dick out of me and came all over my breasts. Feeling his hot, thick fluids on my nipples took me to an all-time high. I rubbed it in and felt them tingle.

"Damn, baby. You are the truth," he said.

"So are you," I said as I watched him get comfortable beside me. This man had the nerve to cuddle me and plant soft kisses on my head and neck, unlike most men who fell asleep immediately after sex. Who the hell was he, Superman? My ass was asleep before him.

"What are we doing tonight?" Jayce asked after he had fed me breakfast and gave me a real bath. He looked sexy as hell with his wet, bulging muscles and dick bouncing under the towel.

"I have to let you know later."

"I see," he said disappointedly after he realized that I needed to check in with my man. I guessed after the night we had, he thought I was just going to leave my relationship and be with him. It didn't exactly work like that all the time, but I was sure he knew that.

Shortly after that conversation, Jayceon got dressed and kissed me on the cheek. "I hope you can come out and play. I want to take you out."

"I'll let you know later, okay?"

"Fair enough," he said before walking out.

I let out a deep sigh and wondered how I got myself into a mess like this when my only goal was to end up with one man. A man whose schedule was so busy, he hadn't called me all night, but if he did, I wouldn't have answered because I was letting Jayce blow my back out. I got dressed and prepared to go shopping when my phone rang.

Chapter 5

"Hey beautiful," Nero said.

I perked up as soon as I heard his voice. "Hi, baby. What's up?"

"Not much. I'm sorry I didn't call. I had a late shift last night. One of my patients had surgery."

"Sorry to hear. Are they okay?"

"Business as usual, baby. I was wondering if you can come over early today, for lunch. I have to work another late shift at the hospital tonight."

"Sure. I'll see you in a few."

"Cool. I can't wait. I miss you."

"I miss you too," I said and hung up.

I missed you so much I fucked the living daylights out of another man, I thought, shaking my head at my behavior. The sad part about it was I didn't understand why. Was I just horny as hell because I had deprived myself so long, or was I just unsatisfied? Maybe I just found it hard to resist all the fine-ass men in my circle.

I tried to make some sense of it the whole ride to Nero's house, but it was a lost cause. I didn't know what was wrong with me, but I hoped to find out soon.

When I arrived to Nero's house, lunch was served on fine china, there was plenty of food, and he looked like new money. There was no doubt I was a lucky woman who had a man most women would die for. But talking to Nero made it painfully clear that we were not on the same page. In fact, from our conversations and exchanges alone, it seemed like we were like night and day and I was nowhere near his speed.

Still, I did what most women do. I tried to change my man. Nero appeared to be doing a damn good job making me happy instead of actually accomplishing the task, and I did a bang-up job ignoring all the signs.

"How come you never cook for me, baby?" I asked.

"I can't cook a pot of water without burning it. Besides, who needs to do that when you have the money to hire a chef?"

"I'm just saying, I think it's romantic."

"What's romantic is having the luxury of giving your woman the attention she needs without all the mess and cleanup."

"Would you give me a pedicure after a hard day of work?"

"Eww, hell no. I don't mess with feet, baby."

"Are you saying my feet are crusty?"

"Nope. I'm saying they got nail salons for that, sweetheart. I'm not the type to take baths or showers with you. Who has time to do that anyway? I say we each choose a bathroom, take separate showers, and get right to the lovemaking. Come here, woman."

All I could do was shake my head. Nero just didn't get it. I tried to keep an open mind with him. It's just that Jayce had shown me the finer side of life, one that money couldn't buy, and I couldn't wrap my mind around anything else.

I did as I was told, warming up to the idea of making love to my man despite the fact that I'd just fucked Jayce's brains out hours before. Even though Nero was dead set on going against me, I still believed in us and was determined to work through it. I kissed him passionately and followed him to his bedroom. Now that was one thing we did agree on.

Making love to Nero was satisfying, but again there were no bells and whistles. He didn't overexert me or demand that I talk dirty, nor did he require me to get in all kinds of positions or perform oral sex. For some reason that disappointed me but didn't turn me off to him. He simply wasn't the type to jump through any hurdles when it came to sex. I finally came to the conclusion that this simply wasn't the important part of our relationship. I just had yet to find out what was. I left his house a little after ten and drove home silently, thinking about the last twenty hours.

When G called me, I didn't have the guts to tell her about Jayce's visit, nor did I elaborate about Nero's lack of participation in any of my suggestions. I laughed at her because she was still on a mission to hook me up with Jayce, and that's exactly why I didn't indulge her.

I walked into my place and noticed flowers filled every room. There was no guesswork as to whom they were from. If this were a race, Jayce would be winning. I just didn't know how to let go of Nero or what to tell him if I did. Sure, Jayce was exciting, but could he fulfill my needs in other areas? I picked up the phone to call him as promised, somehow knowing he would have the answer to that question tonight.

The club was popping, and everyone who was anyone was there. I even saw a few celebrities walk in with their entourages. Jayce walked me straight to VIP, and we popped bottles like it was going out of style.

"Can we afford this?" I asked in disbelief.

"Why don't you let me worry about that, beautiful?"

I was getting a little nervous. Jayceon had forked over a sick amount of cash to supply me with an outfit I probably would never have worn if he hadn't bought it. First of all, it cost more than six months' worth of groceries, and the shoes alone cost more than I made in a month. Secondly, it was so short and tight I was sure my ass was going to catch pneumonia or a cold in my coochie, as Mama used to say. Now I was looking at the $5,000 bottle of wine in his hand, and I thought he had gone stark raving mad.

"Damn. What the hell do you do, rob banks for a living?"

Jayceon chuckled, but of course, he didn't answer me. He had more pressing matters to tend to. Everyone seemed to know him, which told me that he frequented the club quite often, and women came in droves trying to get close enough to him to say hello. At one point, or maybe two, a woman looked at me with disdain, like I had a lot of nerve to make him bring me here. If only they knew.

"Relax, baby," he said, sensing how uncomfortable I was. "I got you."

"I hope so, because I can't afford to buy the dishes in here, let alone wash them."

Jayce fell out laughing, but I was serious as a heart attack. I had managed to breathe a sigh of relief when the waitress came up and asked if she could bring us anything else. That alone told me he wasn't new to this.

"You all right, man?" one of his boys asked, eying me suspiciously.

"Don't be rude. Say hi to Tekhiya."

"Hello, Tekhiya. I'm Flip. You fine as hell. I can see why my man J been hiding you, and the fact that he got you up in VIP, that's a first for him."

"Hello, Flip, and thank you for the compliment, I think."

Two more friends followed Flip, and they had the same reaction. They introduced themselves as Carter and Radical. I didn't trip about the nicknames because I figured their real ones were either none of my business or not important for me to know.

"So this the bitch you left me for?" a short, light, bright, and damn near white woman screamed.

His friends tried to keep her out, but she was fighting and scratching them. Jayce told them to let her through. I got up and got ready to say, "I got your bitch," when Jayce intervened.

"G'on somewhere with that, Mageela. It was over a long time ago."

"Fuck you, J. I gave you everything."

"You mean the baby you got rid of? Yep. You gave me something all right: a fucked-up head for months."

"I didn't mean it, baby. We can make another baby. Take me back, please."

"Not going to happen, Geela. I suggest you move on with your life."

"I love you, J."

"Bye, Geela," he said and turned back to me like they never even met.

I felt kind of sorry for her but more so for Jayce. He seemed really hurt about the baby. "I'm sorry," I told him.

"It is what it is," he said. "Can I ask you something?"

"Sure.

"If you were pregnant by the man you loved, would you get an abortion?"

"I couldn't imagine killing a baby even if I was pregnant by my worst enemy. I want a baby more than anything in the world."

"Really?"

"Yes."

"I would love to give you some babies."

I smiled. It was a nice gesture, but I knew it would never happen. I didn't bother explaining. It wasn't important at the time. My response alone seemed to cheer him up. He kissed me passionately despite the fact that we were being watched like we were the hottest item in the place. I opened my mouth to accept his tongue.

It felt hot, wet, and exciting. My panties were getting wet for him, unlike the way I responded to Nero. Jayce put my jacket over my lap and let his fingers glide into my pussy. I closed my eyes and moaned. He smiled when he felt me drench his index finger and pulled it out for a taste. Something about the way he savored my juices turned me on to no end, and I whispered in his ear that I wanted him. "I want to fuck you."

"Let's go," he said without hesitation.

We shook the spot, as they say, much to everyone's disappointment, but we didn't care. We were on a mission, and that mission was to see who would have an orgasm first. I was dying to get some of Jayce's dick, and at that point, I knew if he could make me feel that sense of urgency for his touch, then he was the man I needed to be with.

Jayce pushed me onto the seat of the limo, dived in, and barely got a chance to close the door before I clawed at his pants.

"You want it bad, don't you?"

"Take those pants off so you can find out."

"You done got feisty overnight."

"What can I say, baby? You dick whipped me."

"Yeah?"

"Yes."

"Show me just how much."

I ripped off my panties, straddled his dick, and started riding him like a cowgirl. This time he had to keep up with me, as I was so determined to have him inside me, I took the dick with ease. I tried my best to fuck the living daylights out of Jayce, and he was enjoying every minute of it. Of course, he got back on his game and flipped me over so my ass was in his face. He licked my pussy and asshole until I had to beg him to stop making me cum like crazy. I was amazed at his skills.

"I had to do something. You had me screaming like a bitch," he said.

I smiled and allowed him to maneuver himself over me and fuck me until we both came harder than we ever came before. Then we lay in each other's arms until the limousine came to a complete stop in front of my house.

"I would come in, but my friends are blowing up my phone. I'm sure they're worried, or something happened at the club."

"I understand. I'll see you later."

"Yes, you will, beautiful." He kissed me and motioned for the driver to drive off.

After taking a long bath and thinking about the events of the last few days, I found myself to be incredibly tired and went to bed. I woke up around three o'clock in the morning to frantic knocks at my door. Forcing one eye open, I looked at the clock and confirmed that it was much closer to four o'clock. Nevertheless, curiosity got the best of me, and I made my way to the living room, looked out the peephole, and saw that it was Nero.

"Baby, what's wrong?"

"I need you," he said.

"What?"

"I'm sorry to wake you. It couldn't wait until morning."

"What? Why?"

"I don't want to be without you."

"Nero, I—"

"Marry me," he said, dropping to one knee and fumbling with a ring box. The rock he pulled out was shining even in the dark moonlit living room, and it looked to be about five carats. Even though a few hours earlier I had decided to be with Jayce, I just couldn't form the word no.

"Yes, Nero. I'll marry you."

"Yeah?"

"Yes."

"You just made me the happiest man in the world," he said as he slipped the ring on my finger.

I wanted to say something back, like "I'm so happy too" or "This is the moment I've been waiting for all my life." But I couldn't because I knew something wasn't right. I just couldn't put my finger on what it was.

Nero spent the night with me, and of course, we made love. It was just as plain as always, which should've alone sent the message that I was with the wrong man, but there's something about a five-carat ring from a rich, handsome doctor that can make a woman do strange things. I woke up with a new determination and willpower, but this time it was to call my family and friends and tell them it was time to plan a wedding.

I contacted G first, and she was about as excited as a new mother finding out she was giving birth to a monkey. She had always contended that it was Jayce I needed and today wasn't any different. I then called Jayce and broke the news to him. He was beyond livid.

"T, please don't do this. I can make you happy. He's going to drag you through the mud."

"I thought we agreed you're my friend before anything."

The silence on the other end of the line made me look at the phone to make sure he was still there. I saw the cell phone time clock moving and heard him breathe a few exasperated sighs, so I knew he was still with me. I almost thought I heard him crying but dismissed the thought of that.

"You're right, T. I'm sorry. Congratulations."

"Thank you, J. Can we talk later?"

"You still want to talk to me?"

"Of course. I love you."

"I love you too, T. I just wish you knew how much."

"Thank you. Goodbye," I said, without allowing him to elaborate.

Now that I had told the two most important people in my life, I was happier than a kid in a candy store. I, Tekhiya Fields, was getting married.

Chapter 6

A few weeks later, I was walking into Nero's house when I heard voices. At first, I thought it was the help talking about their day of work as I'd heard them do so many times in the past. But when I put my ear to the door, I heard Nero, an unknown woman's voice, and a man I couldn't mistake if I wanted to. The man and woman appeared to have the same goal: trying to talk Nero out of marrying me.

"Please don't do this. I love you. I always have," the woman said.

"Shut up and get out of my house," Nero spat.

"You don't even love her. Why are you doing this?" the other man said.

Nero didn't answer him. He just asked him a question. "And you do? You knew what it was the moment you agreed to it. How much is it going to cost to get you to leave?"

"Go to hell."

"It's not my fault your ass got sprung."

"I may be sprung," the man admitted, "but I didn't want to do this from the start. 'One more lick,' you said. You've always been a selfish motherfucker, and you still are. There's not enough money in the world to pay me off. I'm just sorry I listened to you."

"You're just a sore loser, unable to admit that I'm the better man."

"Fuck you, man. She don't love you. I just hope she re-
alizes it before it's too late."

I busted through the French doors before anyone
could answer and every mouth in the room flew open.
The smudged makeup and tears on my face told them I
knew about their betrayal, but I still had no clue why they
had done it. All I knew was I had been a part of a sick
game that I didn't sign up to play.

"You motherfuckers know each other?"

Neither of them said anything, as if their silence alone
was going to make me back down. It only made me an-
grier.

"Sit down, T," Nero said.

"Fuck you. You invaded my life like I was a nobody.
Now you owe me an explanation."

"You're right," Jayce said as he looked at Nero. "Are you
going to tell her or shall I?"

Nero hunched his shoulders. "I'll tell her, and you can
fill in the blanks for all I care," he said like he was discussing the weather.

It was obvious this was something he had done before
and didn't give a shit about who he hurt, including me.
I sat down long enough to listen, although I was sure I
wasn't going to like anything they had to say.

"I saw you walking into the sandwich shop and knew I
had to have you," Nero began. "I used to see you all the
time when I came in to eat, but on that particular day, you
and I had both opted to call in and pick up our food. The
reason you never saw me before was because you were always deep in conversation with your coworker, and when
I passed you, I had my head down or pulled my hat down
and covered my eyes with glasses to conceal my features.
I had assumed you and your coworker either got too tired
or too busy to continue dining in, but I noticed you'd still
pick up your food from time to time and when I saw that

happening, I was afraid you'd grow tired of that soon and I'd lose you altogether. I wanted to approach you, but I knew a woman like you would be damn near impossible to pull, not because I wasn't capable of it but because I knew you were picky about your men. I also knew you had just gotten out of a long-term relationship and might not be receptive to a new one. I watched and studied you a long time before I decided to make my move, and when I did, I couldn't resist bringing my cousin in on the deal.

"Jayceon and I had always been close but lately had grown apart. One of our favorite pastimes was a game we made called Better Man, Bitter Man, where we would pick a woman and see who'd end up with her. We broke a lot of hearts, but the only thing important to us was seeing who would win. We were tied at six wins each, and not only did I feel we needed to break that tie, but I also thought delving into our rocky and mischievous past would resuscitate our dying relationship and bring back the closeness we lost. I just wish I'd known that the wedge that was driven between us wouldn't be easy to close. Still, I needed to believe that this new game we were playing came with a different set of rules."

"Let's hit a lick," I told Jayce. "One final run to prove who's the better man."

"We already proved we're both just as good," he protested. "We need to let this go. We're getting too old for this shit. It's time to settle down and find a good woman."

"Which we will, right after I beat your ass in that tie-breaker."

"In your dreams, man."

"Scared to lose?"

"Just to show you you ain't shit, I'll play. I'll even let you pick her."

"I already did."

"Who's the lucky woman?"

"Her name is Tekhiya Fields," I pulled out her picture and said. Jayce looked at it and shook his head.

"Damn," Jayce yelled.

"What, you don't like the way she looks or something?" I should've known something when I saw his reluctance.

"Naw, man, she's cool. Just shoot me her info later."

"Sure thing. I know you're a little worried because you're not used to dealing with women of her caliber."

"Sheeeee-it. She'll be like putty in the hands of a seasoned veteran."

"I hear you talking, man," I told him before hanging up and setting my plan into action.

"You seemed to fall for it, hook, line, and sinker," Nero told me.

I'd heard enough to know it was making me sick to my stomach. I made a mad dash to the bathroom, making it in the nick of time to throw up in the toilet. Jayce followed me and held my hair while I regurgitated all my lunch in the commode.

"Don't even think about it, Jayce. How could you do that to me without so much as telling me even once? I can expect it from Nero, but not you," I yelled at him in disbelief.

He reached over to help me up, but I pushed his hand away. "Don't touch me. I can't believe this shit," I spat.

"Please, Tekhiya. Don't shut me out, not now. You've heard Nero's side of the story. Now it's time for you to hear mine."

I looked at him like I wanted to kill him, and he looked at me like it was the end of the world. Unlike his cousin, Nero, it was obvious he was in agony about the whole situation.

"Go ahead," I said, waving out my hand to give him the floor.

"The night I ducked into your shop to get out of the storm was a game changer for me," Jayce began. "The first thing I saw when I walked in was your lovely body walking toward me, followed by your lovely eyes, then your beautiful smile, which made me feel like the sun was shining through the storm. I had never seen anything lovelier than you, and if I live to be a hundred years of age, I doubt I will ever meet anyone who can compare to your beauty. You greeted me with the sweetest voice any man could ever hope to hear, and I thought I was going to pass out in your presence.

"When you asked if you could help me, I could've sworn you asked if I could stay with you forever, and that's just what I planned to do. I didn't know what to do or say so I kept on rambling, saying anything to keep you talking, hoping you wouldn't dismiss me and walk away. I just kept talking through two of your clients and a lunch break. It's like you had me captivated, took over my heart and mind. Everything that happened after that, I had no control over. I think we must've talked for hours that night, and right now I can't even recall what we talked about. All I know is you saved me, and I will forever be grateful to you for that.

"I had just found out my ex terminated her pregnancy and had the nerve to beg me to come see her. What she didn't know was if I went anywhere near her, I probably would've terminated her ass. But you were so kind and understanding, and you listened to me vent even though you had no idea what I was going through."

"I don't know what I was thinking about when I let you take me to that hotel room. You could've been a serial killer for all I knew."

"I'm glad you did. Your lips were so soft, tongue was so sweet, and you had the sweetest pussy I ever tasted. I wanted it forever, even if oral was all you ever let me have.

What you considered booty calls, or rather, coochie calls, I considered investments, because I knew that no matter what it took, I was going to make you my wife."

"You must've thought I was pretty crazy when I said I only wanted oral sex and dry humping."

"No. I thought it was cute. Believe it or not, I got my rocks off pleasuring you. No matter what you decide tonight, just know you have my heart."

"If we met on a rainy night in winter and got together months before he presented you with the wager in the spring, why did you go through with it?"

"Nero likes to do shit to cover up for his shortcomings. He always felt like he had to measure up to me, when the truth of the matter is I love him like a brother. He didn't have to compete with me, but for some sick reason, he felt he needed to prove who's the better man. He tried to outdo me in school, in our careers, and in the love department. If you and I had consummated our relationship and ended up together beforehand, I would've told him to kiss my ass, but part of me believed I would win and I could end this stupid tie."

"Why didn't you tell me about the bet?"

"I wanted to come clean, but it never seemed to be the right time. I figured once I showed him I was the one you wanted, we could live happy and never have to deal with him again."

"I'm sorry, Jayceon, but I just can't trust you anymore. Goodbye."

"Tekhiya, no," he said to the back of my ass as I walked away.

"What about the wedding?" Nero said as I walked out the front door.

"Fuck you, Nero." I yanked the ring off, turned around, and threw it at him.

I was so done with both of them you could stick a fork in me. I couldn't believe anyone could be so selfish as to make a bet on a person's life as if they had no choice at all what was done to them. But here I was broken because I was chosen for a sick joke that two men had played to boost their egos.

Part of me wished I would've picked Jayce so Nero's sick ass wouldn't be able to boast that he had won, but despite the fact that it was Nero's idea, they both had admittedly been playing the game for years, and I had chosen his arrogant ass in the long run even when I knew I shouldn't have. I cringed when I thought about the fact that the only reason Nero asked me to marry him was because Jayce was winning with just his charm, his genuine spirit, and his bedroom skills.

Chapter 7

I was shattered, without a friend in the world and no one to turn to for strength. To top it all off, I hadn't had my period in a while and knew it was time to go see a doctor. I had chalked it up to stress because I knew I couldn't be pregnant.

After a botched surgery years ago, doctors had told me I would never be able to bear children. That's the reason I had unprotected sex with both men without any inhibitions. With the way STDs were being passed around, I knew it wasn't the smartest thing to do, but it was damn sure a cool idea at the time. I usually didn't trip about stress because I saw it as a normal part of life, but I was beginning to fear I had cancer or some other life-threatening illness, because I was pretty sure stress wouldn't cause me to throw up all the time. The strange thing was my breasts were tender, and I had gained a few pounds.

The doctor ran a lot of tests, and when she finally called me into a room and told me I was pregnant, I had mixed emotions. I was delighted I was having a baby but sick because of my potential baby's daddy. *Why did this happen now?* I wondered, thinking I would've been more accepting of it if it was my ex's child. At least he was honest, I rationalized. Now I had to deal with the cousins from hell until I carried this baby to term. Abortion was out of the question, because after all I'd gone through my baby was a definite blessing that I was unwilling to part with. The child growing inside me didn't repulse me. In fact, I loved it even more than I ever loved anything in my life.

Both Nero and Jayce tried to apologize profusely, but I made it no secret that I was done and gave them my ass to kiss. In addition to that, I had moved, changed my phone number, and quit my job. The thought of raising my baby alone was horrifying, but I knew it was something that I couldn't back out of.

My ex had offered to marry me and raise the baby as his. I thought it was a sweet gesture, but I couldn't take him up on his offer. Despite my situation, I couldn't see myself marrying a man I didn't love just to give my child a name. My baby was going to be raised in love by me and my sister, and when he or she was old enough, I would explain to them what happened in a way they'd understand even if I was married and had other children at that time.

"Hey, sis," G said into the phone.

"What'd you do now?" I asked.

"Why I have to be guilty of doing something because I'm calling to check on my niece or nephew?"

"You just have that 'I'm about to tell you something that will blow your mind' voice."

"Well, actually I did call to warn you."

"About what?"

"I kind of, sort of talked to your baby daddies."

"You what?"

"Calm your ass down. You're pregnant, T."

"You're the one upsetting me. I can't believe you would do some dumb shit like that when I told you I got this."

"Yeah, but T, they have a right to know, especially J, but I'll let you be the judge of that."

"What do you mean? You didn't give them my number, did you?"

"Not exactly. I gave them the address."

"What the fuck, G?"

"Sorry, puddin'. I know you hate me right now, but I promise you, you'll thank me later."

As soon as she said that, I heard a frantic knock on the door. I hung up on her ass to answer it, and to my horror, it was Nero. When I opened the door slightly, he pushed it open and walked in like he owned the place, no hello or nothing.

"What the hell is wrong with you, T? I hear you're pregnant with my baby. Why didn't you tell me? Do you plan to keep it? Because there's only a window of time you can have an abortion."

"I'm not killing my baby, and I don't want a dime from you."

"That's what they all say. Do you know what my net worth is?"

"'All'?"

"Yeah. You think you're the first woman who tried to trap me?"

"If I wanted to do that, I would have told you about it."

"You would have done exactly what you're doing now: holding on to the news until it's too late to do anything about it."

"I said it before, and I'll say it again: fuck you, Nero."

"I already did that, and now you're pregnant. We're taking a blood test, because I know you were fucking my cousin at the same time."

"Don't flatter yourself. You didn't do that great of a job."

"Did he?"

I didn't even bother to save his ego, especially when he was asking to see who had fucked me the best. Instead, I drove the knife deeper into his back. "You're so weak, it's probably not even yours."

"You can insult me all you want, but I had your ass screaming, climbing the walls, and ready to walk down that aisle in front of everyone you know."

"I'll get you that blood test as soon as possible. I'll even let you waive your parental rights. Like I said, I don't want anything from you."

"Good. I'll be in touch. Don't try to disappear again until I get those results."

"Did I hurt your feelings by calling you weak? Are you feeling inadequate about Jayce being the father instead of you? It's a baby, not a contest, you bastard."

He ignored me. "If I have to look for you again, I'm going to hurt you, bad. Do you understand?"

"I'm not going anywhere." I nodded.

He exited the room, and I breathed a sigh of relief as soon as I closed and leaned against the door. My heart was beating so fast I thought it was going to come out of my chest. Nero had me spooked. There was something about the way he was acting that had me ready to pack up and leave. He had threatened to hurt me, and I believed him.

Someone else knocked on the door. I wasn't going to answer it because I was afraid of what Nero would do to me if it was him. His behavior was off the chain, and I couldn't understand why I hadn't noticed it before. Jayce hadn't shown up yet, and that told me he either didn't care or had moved on with his life. The only other person it could be was G, and she damn sure would've given up trying and just used the spare key by now. Either way, I felt it was best that I not open the door.

The person was still knocking after I went to the kitchen to get a cold glass of water, turned on the television, and sat down in my favorite chair. I had just closed my eyes to pray that they would just go away when I heard somebody call my name.

"Tekhiya, it's me. Open the door," Jayce yelled.

"Go away, Jayce. I'm going to work this out by myself."

"Just let me in, T."

"I'm sorry I made a mess of things. I can fix it. I'll get the paternity test as soon as I can."

"Open up, T," he screamed, beating on my door to make his point. I was horrified. I didn't want him to hurt me. I just wanted to live.

What the hell? It can't be any worse than it already is.

I swung the door open, and Jayce almost fell in. He looked good as hell. He had lost some weight, but it looked good on him, and he had grown a beard. Not only did I want to wrap my arms and legs around him, I wanted to drench the sexy patch of hair under his chin with my juices.

"Why didn't you tell me, T? Why did you shut me out?"

"I didn't want you to think I was trying to trap you."

"It's just as much my fault as it is yours. I'm sorry about what I did to you. I wanted to tell you so many times, but I got tongue-tied. Somehow I thought I could make you fall in love with me and you would forget about Nero. You were so good to me. I never should've gone through with that stupid bet. I found out he had profiled you and knew I was seeing you when he decided to take matters in his own hands."

"Why would he do that?"

"Jealousy."

"He tricked me into wanting him under the pretense that he was a doctor who was looking for true love. That son of a bitch isn't even capable of love."

"He even got our cousin, Paul, the delivery driver, in on it to sweeten the deal. The fool knew what he was doing all along. Baby, I'm so sorry."

"Me too. I didn't mean for any of this to happen, especially now that an innocent child is involved. I really meant what I said about not trying to trap you. The doctors had told me I couldn't have any kids, so this is my miracle child. I can't get rid of it."

"Let me tell you something about Nero and me. I was the one who was going to school to be a doctor, but I gave up my dream when he went to medical school to copy me. I ended up going a different route, and now I own and run a pharmaceutical company. I also own the club I took you to. I can take care of my family just fine."

"It's nice of you to let me know how you feel about me, but I don't want to bring you any shame if the baby isn't yours. I'll take that paternity test as soon as I safely can. Like I told Nero, I don't want money, and you can sign over your paternal rights. I'll take my baby and get out of your hair for good."

"That's the difference between me and Nero. He can't be with you unless the child is his. I want you whether it's mine or not. I don't care about any of that. I just want you. I love you, T, and I meant what I said about family."

"Are you serious, Jayce?"

"As a heart attack."

"So many times, I thought about how good you were to me, how satisfied I was whenever I was with you, and I realized I love you too. I'm so sorry I didn't see it sooner."

"You have no idea how long I've waited to hear you say those words," Jayce sighed. "The important thing is you see it now."

We kissed, and it felt so right. It had always been right. Jayceon was my man, and it had taken all of this for me to figure it out. I was just glad I did.

Jayce picked me up and carried me to the bedroom, where we made love into the wee hours of the morning. I thought I was having a nightmare when I woke up to the sound of the door breaking down.

"What the fuck?" Jayceon yelled as we watched Nero point a shotgun at our heads.

"How could you let a bitch come between us, man?"

"What the fuck is wrong with you, man? Take that gun away from my woman's head."

"Your woman? You want to be with her? You know she still loves me, right?"

"You're talking crazy, man. You need help."

"This is not how it was supposed to go down. We were supposed to be playing these bitches. Make them fall in love with us, choose the better man, and then we leave them high and dry. But you had to fall in love with her ass. I ought to smoke her for taking my family away."

"You did that all by yourself. Leave her out of this. It's about you and me. I'll do whatever it is you want me to do. You want me to leave her? You want to start a new bet? You want me to leave town? Name it."

"They always want you. It's always you."

"What about your baby mama, your first love? They chose you."

"Those raggedy bitches, especially Marina. I was going to make her my wife until she admitted she wanted you too. If it hadn't been for you, Tekhiya would be mine as well. Well, I'm not going to let you have her."

"What?"

"I'll get rid of her, and we can start over, cousin. Just you and me, blood brothers."

Nero raised the gun toward me, and I was horrified. I had so much life left in me, and I didn't want to die like this. What had I ever done so wrong?

"Noooooooooo," Jayce yelled and jumped in front of me to cover the bullets.

I felt one of them pierce my right leg, and I looked up at Jayce's lifeless body. Blood was everywhere, and I heard myself screaming.

The next thing I knew, I was waking up in a hospital, hooked up to all kinds of machines.

"T," I heard G whisper, "I'm so sorry. I was only trying to help."

"Where's Jayceon?"

"He's going to be fine. The bullet pierced his lung, but he made it."

"My baby?"

"Your baby is fine."

When I locked eyes with Jayce, it was like God was giving me a gift straight from heaven. My one true love was going to live out the rest of his natural life with me, and I was never going to let him go.

As soon as we were released from the hospital, we were married by a justice of the peace. We were thinking about having a winter wedding in a church for all of our family and friends to witness after our baby was born. Everybody except Nero, that was. He was too busy running from the law. I prayed the police would find him soon. But I was so glad that Jayce was here to keep me safe in the meantime.

A man who would put your life before his is always the better man, especially one who wakes up every day and tells you that he loves you and can't get enough of you. Jayce told me that and then some. I believed him because that was exactly how I felt about him.

The End

Audacious Acts

by

Shantaé

Chapter 1

"Uhhnn," I whined as I arched my back slightly, attempting to find the perfect angle. Spreading my legs just a tad wider, I pressed Pinky harder against my clit. My legs immediately began to shake, and my heart rate soared when I finally caught that spine-tingling wave I'd been searching for. "Oh, God! Please let this be it. Pleaseee," I whimpered and pleaded to no one in particular.

The onslaught of sensations traveling throughout my body told me that this could be the one: the one that would be so electrifying and life changing that it'd knock me out instantly, subsequently erasing the violent thoughts of strangling my husband from my mind. I'd been duped by the first two, so I wasn't going to get my hopes up this go-round. Seconds after changing the vibration pattern, the orgasm I'd been chasing for the last twenty minutes ripped through me, causing my body to seize uncontrollably as a gush of fluids shot from my opening, saturating the sheets beneath me. Panting, I chunked Pinky across the room with what little strength I had, causing it to crash against the wall before it hit the floor and rolled around on the hardwood. I then closed my eyes and silently cried.

My weeping didn't stem from the jubilation I should have felt after letting go of three amazingly intense orgasms courtesy of my bullet. It was brought about due to frustration because it still wasn't enough. I still wasn't satisfied, but just like many nights prior to this one, I would go to sleep without having this nagging thirst of mine quenched. Before they could reach my hairline, I quickly wiped away the tears that trailed down the sides of my face. When I was able to breathe normally, I went to the bathroom to clean myself up before climbing back in bed.

With my back against the headboard and my arms folded across my chest, I kissed my teeth as loud as I could, hoping to disturb the sleep of the big log of a man stretched out beside me. If he didn't stir while I did all that whooping and hollering during my self-pleasure session, there was no way he would now. His ass was the reason I was in such bad shape, and I just wanted to punch him repeatedly until I could somehow get through to him.

Turning my head to the side, I admired my husband's face. Even asleep with his mouth hanging open and snoring like a savage, Moraiah Heard was hands down the most handsome man I'd ever been with. When I say that my man was fine, goodness gracious, I'm only speaking facts. It was agonizing, but I just couldn't help giving him a lustful, full-body once-over.

My baby was a sexual chocolate god. All six foot seven inches of him. He'd done away with his low-cut Caesar two years ago, and I immediately fell in love with his slick-shaved head and often rubbed it like a psychic would their globe. The thick black beard he sported was one of the most attractive things about him though. Mo was up on that Beard Gang shit before it became a thing and took social media by storm. His was full and healthy but was cut in a way that didn't cover up or take away from those juicy lips of his, which brought me so much pleasure. The length was perfect and never would you catch him without a fresh line up and trim. Just as I had my natural hair-care products lined up on my side of the counter in our restroom, he had his Uncle Jimmy beard-grooming essentials stacked neatly on his side. I whimpered thinking of how good it felt when the hairs of his beard grazed my inner thighs and pussy lips when he gave me mouth and lip service. I'd give anything to have that face of his between my legs right at this moment.

My eyes traveled lower to that sexy-ass chest of his, which rose and fell subtly as he dozed. It was brawny and appealing to the eye, with just the right amount of hair dusted across it, trailing down his torso and into his boxer briefs. Moraiah's biceps were huge just like him, and right now I imagined all the times he would use those same arms to lift my healthy ass up before spreading my legs wide to bring me down onto his impressive length. My pussy creamed just thinking about it. This man got off on tossing me all over the bed, twisting and turning me in all types of awkward positions, and I personally enjoyed every minute of it. By the time my peepers landed on that semi-erect growth that rested on his muscular thigh, I was done for, and both sets of my lips were salivating uncontrollably.

It was just a few minutes before midnight, and I lay there with this scorching fire burning down in my soul that had no chance of being put out before I closed my eyes to rest tonight. For a chick with a sex drive like mine, this **was** the worst form of torment. While Moraiah enjoyed what looked to be a peaceful slumber, I lay here overheated, aggravated, and in desperate need, which was pretty much the norm for me these days. It irked me to no end that my husband of six years seemed oblivious to my plight. My wants. My desires. My never-ceasing need to be close with him physically and emotionally. I'd tried everything I could to let him know how unhappy, lonely, and sexually frustrated I was, but my words continued to fall on deaf ears.

It hadn't always been this way with us. There was a time when Moraiah made me feel like I was the most beautiful female walking the face of the earth and he couldn't keep his hands off of me, groping, caressing, and kissing me constantly. His touchy-feely behavior took some getting used to, but over time I'd become accustomed to it. I'll even go as far as saying I craved it.

It bothered me terribly just thinking about it, but these days I wondered if he was caressing and kissing on someone new. I didn't want to believe it, but it was a possibility that there was another woman out there receiving the adoration and attention that was once reserved only for me. I prayed that I was wrong, but it was the only conclusion I could come to because lately, I was lucky if I could get a friendly peck on the cheek before he bolted out of the door for work in the mornings, and by the time he made it in most nights I was in bed already asleep.

I understood that we were both busy with very successful businesses, him with two vehicle repair shops and me with my salon, but I believed wholeheartedly in the saying that you make time for what's important to you. While I made sure to set ample time aside to cater to my man, he continued to fall short when it came to making me feel like an important part of his life. I lost count of how many times I'd planned a romantic evening for the two of us only to end up sitting at the dinner table alone for hours before realizing that he wasn't going to show up.

For the last few years, his life revolved around his job, and I'd become a nonfactor. It was all good though because I was slowly slipping into "fuck it" mode, and for Mr. Heard that was the worst state of mind for a woman like me to be in.

Something had to give, and it had to happen soon before I fucked up and did something I would later regret.

Chapter 2

"I think you're making a mistake, Dolce. I really think you should try talking to Moraiah again," Krissy urged.

"Girl, fuck that. She's been taking your advice for over a year now and look where it's gotten her," Neeka chimed in.

"But—"

"No-damn-where!" Neeka held her hand up in Krissy's face, shutting down the rest of her response. "I hate to say this shit, but do you, bitch. Mo my nigga and all. I mean, I've only known his ass all of my life. But he ain't handling up like he's supposed to."

"Exactly," I agreed.

"Neeka, shut up. You just want her to be like your friendly coochie-having ass," Krissy joked while Neeka stuck her middle finger up in response.

Reclining in my chair, I pondered deeply on my situation as they went back and forth with one another on the patio of Ojeda's, our favorite Tex-Mex spot. I met both Neeka and Krissy when we were students at Texas A&M. They were my closest friends so for years they'd been privy to most of my life challenges and struggles just as I was theirs, and I truly valued their opinions.

It was legit like having my very own devil and angel on opposite shoulders when it came time to make important decisions. While Neeka was constantly on ten and was always on some YOLO-type shit, my girl Krissy was our constant voice of reason, always encouraging us to do the right thing. She'd stopped both of us from making some dumb choices over the years, and I appreciated her. This time, however, I was leaning toward taking the advice of my free-spirited single friend.

Of the three of us, I was the only one who was married. Kristal, or Krissy as we called her, was in an exclusive relationship and had been for a number of years. Neeka, on the other hand, liked to walk on the wild side and didn't let the opinions and judgment from others stop her from living her best life. If that meant fucking a nigga she met at the club on the first night, then that's precisely what she would do. Mo's present movements were alarming to her as well, seeing as how she'd known him longer than I had and was the person credited with introducing my husband and me almost eight years ago. It was a crazy and very long story, but let me hit you with the short version.

When I met my man, he was nearing the end of a three-year stretch in prison on drug charges. You might say I was crazy as hell for getting involved with a known criminal, but I really couldn't care less about what people thought. We were all hanging at Neeka's place one evening while she made us her famous honey-barbeque wings. Her phone rang, and since her hands were full she asked me to pick it up, and from the moment I heard Moraiah state his name for the operator I was caught up. His voice was deep, and he sounded sexy as hell without trying. Of course, I'd seen pictures and heard stories, but I had never had the pleasure of meeting him. He flirted with me for a few minutes before my blushing ass passed Neeka the phone. Unbeknownst to me, she gave him my number, and he hit me up the following afternoon. From there we began talking every day, and before I knew it, I was hitting the highway to see him every other weekend.

I'd experienced so much heartbreak when it came to
the opposite sex that Moraiah was like a breath of fresh
air. Yes, even locked behind those walls, he became everything to me. Don't ask me how I knew but I could tell
off the top that he was one of the good ones. My ass was
so in love that I even offered to put money on his books,
but he wouldn't hear of it. Moraiah was a provider, not
a user. Plus, he had more money than he knew what to
do with so he didn't need mine. He had gifts sent to my
house regularly and made sure my phone bill was paid
every month so he could call whenever he wanted. Of
course, I eagerly accepted each and every collect call.

Moraiah got out of prison determined to change his
life, and that's exactly what he did. He opened his very
own car repair business and left the streets behind. He'd
worked on cars with his father coming up, and while he
was in prison, he received his business degree as well as
his certificate in automotive training. We lived separately
and got to know one another better over the first year of
him being home, and there was no doubt in my mind that
he was the man I wanted to spend the rest of my life with.
He felt the same way about me, so he proposed.

We eloped and signed the deed to our first home on
the one-year anniversary of his release. Since then we'd
been joined at the hip. Well, it was like that up until a
year or so ago. The last few months had been the absolute
worst. There was a definite disconnect between us that I
couldn't fix on my own. We went from being inseparable
and having sex several times a day to maybe having dinner together two to three times a week and sex maybe
twice in that same time span. Sometimes it was only once,
and I couldn't stand it any longer.

"So, Neeka, you're sure that this place is legit? My iden-
tity will be protected, and I won't have to worry about
my business getting all over Dallas should I decide to go

through with it?" I questioned, interrupting their verbal sparring. These two could go all day if you let them.

"Dolce, how many times do I have to tell you that you're straight? I've been a member for over a year, and as well-known as I am around town, nothing about my dealings at the club has ever been brought to light. You know for a fact they recognize me when they see me there, but they don't speak on it. I've seen niggas I fucked at the club days or weeks later in public settings, and both parties walked by like we'd never seen one another a day in our lives. We pay a grip for that anonymity, and everyone sticks to the code. I honestly don't think you're about this life though, so even if you decide once you're there that you don't want to partake, then you can just watch. Maybe learn some new tricks to entice that husband of yours. There's no pressure," she assured me.

"I can't believe you're actually considering this shit," Krissy sighed. "You're really going to cheat on Mo?" Her tone was distressed like she was the one about to get played.

"Damn, don't say it like that," I sighed, slumping down in my seat again.

"There's no other way to say it, Dolce. You two have been together for forever, and I swear that before I hooked up with Tristan, I looked to you and Moraiah as a relationship goal." She touched my hand supportively.

"That was the old us. The new us is more like a roommate situation instead of husband and wife, and I'm sick of it," I complained.

"I get that, but that's something that can be fixed, D. You love Mo, and he loves you. I want you to really think about what you're doing and what it would mean for the two of you if Moraiah got wind of this shit. You have a lot to lose, boo, and please let's not ignore the fact that your husband is loco over you. There will be all types of smoke

in the city if he finds out his precious Dolce has been allowing some random nigga to smash them fat-ass Puerto
Rican cakes of yours," she warned playfully.

"Shut up, Krissy. I'm blacker than your ass, and you
know it," I retorted.

My friends liked to tease me about my heritage, which
was funny as hell seeing as how I didn't speak a lick of
Spanish and my melanin was popping way harder than
the both of them. My mother was Puerto Rican, and
Papa was blacker than black. I was raised up around his
folks, so that's who I related to most. Mama's parents dis-
owned her when she got with my dad, whom they considered a hoodlum, so I never got a chance to connect with
that side of the family, and if they were as judgmental as
she said they were, then I was better off without them
anyway. They would surely disapprove of my marriage to
Moraiah, considering he was a convicted felon.

"Shit, you may be on to something. Mo has been so chill
over the years I almost forgot about his crazy side. Girl,
maybe you oughta take Krissy's advice and try counseling
or something." Neeka suddenly switched sides, making
me roll my eyes.

"Believe it or not I suggested counseling months ago,
and Mo promised that we were fine and that he'd try
harder. Shit lasted all of two weeks and he was right
back on the same shit. I'm not happy, and I haven't been
for a long time. Hell, that nigga swear he handling his
business, but for all I know he's out there doing the same
shit I'm only thinking about doing because the truth of
the matter is, he's definitely not doing me. I know something's up, and last night was the last straw, honey."

"Nah, D. Mo would never cheat on you, and I know that
for a fact, but tell me what happened last night," Neeka
requested as she dipped her stuffed jalapeno into the hot
queso that our waiter had just placed on the table.

"So, I came home from the gym last night and was surprised as hell to find him lying across the bed, watching TV already. I'm all excited because it was the first night in months that he'd made it home before I went to bed, so I just knew I was about to get some quality time with a good ol' side of dick. Nigga didn't say a word to me. Just tossed the remote, grabbed me up, and kissed me all deep and passionate like only he can. You already know my sex-deprived ass was ready for whatever. Was damn near humping his leg like a dog. Rushed in the bathroom to take a quick shower, but by the time I was done, he was knocked the hell out. I tried for about ten minutes to wake him up but that nigga was dead to the world, and I've never been more pissed at him in my life. If I would have known that he was that tired, I would have hopped on his dick as soon as I walked through the door. Musty pussy and all," I said sarcastically while they snickered.

"His dick was still a little stiff from our li'l make-out session, and I honestly thought about just taking that shit, but I shouldn't have to damn near rape my own husband to get my rocks off. I just said fuck it and pulled out Pinky." I paused my story to look at them, and these bitches were cackling away. "I'm glad y'all think this is funny. My marriage is slowly falling apart, and my best friends think the shit is a joke."

"Kill the dramatics, bitch," Neeka teased before I continued with my rant.

The three of us ate, drank, and talked for another two hours before we went our separate ways. Being around them always made me feel better, so by the time I was headed home, my mood had greatly improved, and I tried my best to put all plans of visiting Neeka's little sex club out of my mind. I was just going to have to work a little harder to get Moraiah's attention. He was working late as usual tonight, but I planned to wait up for him so that we could talk. Krissy was right. I had a lot to lose, and I loved my husband way too much to jeopardize what we had. I truly hoped that things would get better. All I needed was for Mo to meet me halfway.

"I'm not trying to hear that shit, Neeka. I know you just left your place and you'll have to pass me to get there, so come on," I hissed into the phone.

"Dolce, what happened to you trying to work things out? What the hell is going on?" she questioned.

"It's a long story that I'll be more than happy to share with you when you get here," I sighed as I raced around my room trying to find something sexy to wear tonight. I had no idea why I was rushing. It wasn't like Moraiah was going to be home anytime soon.

"Dolce—"

"Look, I'm going either way, Neek, so you may as well come pick me up. If not, I'll call the car service to come through and scoop me. Wouldn't you rather I be with you my first time?" I added when I noticed how quiet she had become. The last thing I needed was a lecture from her. She'd known my husband longer than I had, but she was my best friend now so her loyalty was to me.

"Fine, I'm on my way," she spat before hanging up in my face.

The concern in her tone made me feel bad for involving her in my problems with Moraiah. She talked her shit, but more than anyone knew, my friend wanted to see us win. My plan after lunch with my girls was to pass on the club and work on my marriage, but I was tired. It had only been a couple weeks, and it had already become too much being the only one in the relationship putting forth any effort. I mean, I'd only been doing it for the last year and some change, and I truly felt like our marriage would never get better. It didn't help that Moraiah blew me off anytime I tried to speak with him about what I was feeling. A bitch was fed up and horny as hell.

Now I wasn't sure I would be sleeping with anyone tonight, but I did want to go just to see what it was all about, seeing as how I would probably become a lifelong member of the club I was currently dressing up for when my marriage ended. There was a point when Moraiah was my best friend, and the bond we shared was unmatched. I doubted that could be recreated with another man, so I would more than likely remain single for the rest of my days. Besides, I was sure I wouldn't have a problem getting regular dick up in there, and that's what I needed in my life. Dick! Long dick. Short dick. Thick dick. Slim dick. Pale or dark dick. I wasn't about to discriminate. As long as it was exceptional dick. Shit, at this stage of my drought, mediocre dick didn't sound half bad.

Standing in the mirror, I did a quick assessment of my appearance. My size-fourteen frame looked damned good in the long-sleeved sequin button-down shirt dress that I threw on for tonight. It was hunter green, which was my favorite color and super sexy. Stopping midthigh, the final button was purposely left undone, giving a good glimpse of my juicy thighs when I walked. Turning to the side to get the view from the back, I fell in love with the way it hugged my ample hips and backside. Not too tight but snug enough for the men tonight to see what I was working with underneath. I skipped the panties, so my shit was jiggling just right as I moved. Topping off my look were my favorite above-the-knee satin high-heeled black boots. Not to toot my own horn, but I looked good as hell, so toot-toot! My blowout was popping, hanging down my back and stopping right before it reached my ass. I kept it light and cute with the makeup, and my accessories were on point.

While checking out the cute bracelet Moraiah had given me for my birthday last year, I couldn't help but notice my wedding ring. Seeing it had me second-guessing myself, but before the guilt of what I was about to do could sink in, I removed it and placed it in my jewelry box, snapping it closed with the quickness. I wasn't about to let the huge symbol of the commitment we'd made and a reminder of our love stop me from hitting up this place tonight.

Finally satisfied with my look, I grabbed my clutch and headed for the stairs. As soon as I made it to the bottom, my cell vibrated. It was a message from Neeka letting me know that she was just pulling up. I quickly locked up and strutted down the driveway to where she was parked. For some reason, her ass never pulled all the way up the drive, and it irked me to have to walk those extra steps, especially in heels as high as the ones I was rocking tonight. From what I could see she looked to be in the midst of a heated conversation but ended the call before I could make it to the car.

"I see your ass ain't come to play with these hoes tonight." Neeka smirked while looking me up and down as I sank into the warm leather seat of her Porsche Cayenne.

"When have I ever?" I playfully lifted a brow while side-eyeing her.

"Whatever, bitch. Where you tell Mo you was going?" she asked as she typed away on her phone.

"I didn't tell his ass shit. I've been calling him all day, but he acts like he's too busy to talk, so he'll see me whenever the hell he sees me," I replied defiantly as she pulled away from the curb.

No sooner had those words left my mouth than my phone began ringing and vibrating in my hand. A picture that Moraiah and I had taken on the beach in the Dominican Republic a few years back flashed across the screen. Seeing his number and a photo of us during happier times caused my heart rate to slightly accelerate, but instead of answering like I knew I should have, I declined the call and immediately turned the device off.

He had some nerve calling me when I'd been trying for weeks to get a moment of his time. Ass hadn't dialed my number in forever, but it was just like him to hit me up when I was pissed with him and on my way out to this club to get into some freaky shit. I'd been wanting to visit this place for the longest time, and now that I was finally getting the chance I wasn't about to let him ruin it for me.

"A'ight, Mo gon' get in that ass behind you ignoring his calls, Dolce," Neeka warned as she watched me place my phone in my clutch. "Next he'll be calling my fucking phone."

"Girl, he ain't about to do shit. He was probably calling to let me know he wouldn't be home until later tonight anyway. Nigga wasn't about to tell me shit I didn't already know, so he'll be just fine," I huffed and rolled my eyes.

I was putting up a good front, but I really wanted to take my phone back out of my purse, turn it on, and call him back. As much trash as I talked, I would much rather be with my husband tonight, but if Moraiah thought for one minute that us spending time together was only going to be on his terms or when he felt like penciling me in, then his ass was dead wrong. That wasn't how things were supposed to work, and I refused to continue allowing him to treat me as a second thought.

Chapter 3

About twenty minutes later, Neeka was pulling up to our destination. Looking around, I noticed that there was no activity in the parking lot like you might see at a regular nightclub. If there was music playing inside, it couldn't be heard at all outside the establishment. It was eerily quiet, and not one person was spotted moving about. Knowing that I was so close to one of my fantasies sent tiny shivers up my spine. From my peripheral, I could feel my bestie watching me, but I ignored her. Not wanting to appear overly anxious, I discreetly took a couple calming breaths to relax myself. I had my own personal reasons for being excited, but I didn't plan to share them with her. At least not right now. Neeka and I were both silent as we pulled down our visors to check our makeup and hair one final time before exiting the car.

The building itself was a huge single-level brick structure, all black with no signs or markings on the outside. I had probably passed this place hundreds of times but never gave it a second glance. It was out in the open but didn't stand out at all, and one would never know of the wicked mischief that went on inside those walls. Hell, I'd only heard stories from Neeka, but I was delighted as hell to be finding out for myself after all this time. If my original plan for the night fell through, I had no shame in buying one of the many toys they had on display while pleasing myself and watching the regulars do their thing.

I was very open sexually, and that was all Moraiah's doing. Before we met, I was considered somewhat of a prude, and I'd been cheated on by every single boyfriend I had before him because of that, for not being exciting enough and down to explore in the bedroom. All of that changed when Moraiah entered my life. His big, fine ass unleashed the freak hidden inside me and turned me out so bad that he could ask me to hop on his dick in the front row of a movie theater and I would do so without question. His sex had turned me into a fiend, and it angered me that he all of a sudden chose to stop feeding the ferocious appetite that he was responsible for satisfying. Shit wasn't cool at all.

"You sure you're ready for this?" Neeka asked once we reached the entrance.

"I wouldn't be here if I weren't," I replied confidently.

Shaking her head, she reluctantly opened the door and held it, allowing me to enter ahead of her. There was a podium-like stand with a pretty chocolate chick standing behind it. She was dressed casually in all black, and she greeted us with a warm smile when we walked in. I saw Neeka pull out her member card, so I followed suit. I'd filled out an application, had my background checked, and made my first payment weeks ago. I received my card by mail the following day. I honestly never thought I'd use it, but here I was having my ID and member card scanned.

"Enjoy yourselves, ladies." She grinned, handing us each our cards back along with a keychain. We had a key along with a single number on the ring. I was seven and Neeka had number two.

"That's it?" I whispered to Neeka's back, hurriedly moving behind her as she strutted down the dark hallway.

"Yeah, bitch. What did you think they were going to do? Pat you down, strip search you, and make you jump through hoops to get in or something?" she tossed over her shoulder.

"Nah." I played it off with a nonchalant shrug. Honestly, that's exactly what I was thinking. I didn't know why I was expecting some sophisticated high-tech shit where you had to use a palmprint or fingerprint to gain entrance. With a name like Privacy, I even imagined that they went so far as to use facial recognition for the members, but there was just that small open area that looked identical to any other front desk area at the club.

I was about to ask her about the key, but I remembered the part of the contract that I signed where it mentioned that all phones and personal belongings had to be locked up prior to entering the actual club area. Anything you needed to get down with the get down was available inside, so there was no need to keep anything on your person, and of course, they didn't allow phones, to eliminate the risk of the guests being taped while performing audacious acts with people they hardly knew.

I nodded my approval once we entered the locker room. It was brighter and much classier than what I'd seen upfront. The lockers were clean and spacey. I didn't have much on me tonight, but I for one loved to put on a show. Role play was a specialty of mine. If I became a regular, I could see myself bringing several different outfits and changing throughout the night, and I'd need that extra room to store my belongings. There were mirrors all around as well as various lounge areas. Women of all shapes, sizes, and shades of brown moved about, primping and priming themselves for the night. Shit actually looked like a fancy strip club dressing room, only cleaner and a bit more pleasing to the olfactory. No shade, but the few shake-joint locker rooms I'd been in to do hair didn't always smell fresh and tended to look a bit on the trashy side. This here was bomb, though.

"Shit," I heard Neeka groan, prompting me to turn around.

"What's wrong, Neek?" I asked after closing my locker.

"Nothing really. The dude that I'd made plans to fuck with tonight hit me talking about he just walked in the door. I tried texting him before we got here to tell him not to come but I guess he's just now seeing my message," she quickly answered while she typed fast as hell.

"Why'd you tell him not to come?"

"Duh, heffa. I wasn't expecting you to be here tonight, and there's no way I'm leaving you all alone your first time here. Mo is already going to ring my fucking neck when he finds out you came with me," she answered without looking up from her phone.

"Girl, fuck that. I don't need a damn babysitter. I'm grown as hell and perfectly capable of navigating through this place on my own. I actually prefer it that way. Besides, I'll probably only stay an hour or so before I call a service to pick me up." I shrugged.

"You sure, D? You know I ain't tripping on no dick. I can get that shit anytime," she told me, trying hard as hell to hide her hopeful smile.

"I'm positive. And you let me deal with Moraiah. If he had been taking care of business, he wouldn't have to worry about me having my ass up in here in the first place. I already told you I don't plan on hooking up with anyone anyway. I'm here tonight as a spectator only," I promised with my fingers crossed behind my back.

"Whew! Thank God, honey, because li'l buddy who's meeting me here tonight doesn't get to stop through that often due to work, and although I didn't want to cancel on him, I wasn't about to leave you hanging over no pipe. No matter how good it is," she added before slyly biting down on her bottom lip.

"Let me find out you feeling this nigga, Neeka." I side-eyed her playfully.

"Of course I'm feeling him. He wouldn't be getting this pussy if I weren't, but don't get it fucked up. He's not the only one I'm feeling, and he damn sure ain't the only one I'm fucking." She shrugged as she smoothed her hand down the front of her bandage dress while checking herself out in the mirror.

This girl was a trip, but I loved her to pieces. Not only was she beautiful but she was a wonderful person inside and out. Down to earth and full of life. Neeka was one of those people everyone enjoyed being around. She'd done a lot for our community, and just the mention of West Dallas Neeka was enough to bring the entire city out. As her friend, I did look forward to the day she found love and settled down though. She claimed she didn't want that, but I didn't know how true that was. We all wanted love, right? I'd experienced it on a level that I had only dreamed of, and hopefully she knew that same feeling one of these days.

"Well, do your thing tonight. Have fun and be safe." I kissed her cheek before turning to leave the dressing room.

"Same to you, and don't do nothing that's gon' have my homeboy going back to the pen, bitch," she called out behind me. I could do nothing but laugh and shake my head.

Following the signs, I made my way down the narrow hallway. I paused when I reached the bright red blinking sign that read ENJOY YOUR PRIVACY. After taking a deep breath I pushed on, but my eyes were not at all prepared for what I saw when I finally walked through the entryway without a door. Like, I knew exactly what I had signed up for, but to see it live and in living color was an entirely different thing. This was the sophisticated kinky shit I spoke of when I mentioned my expectations earlier. The outside of this establishment didn't match the inside at all, and I must say that was a good thing. It was sexy as hell in here. Not only were you witnessing sexual acts first-hand with your own eyes, but you could feel it in the air. It was a hard thing to describe, but there was this whole sensuous, carnal-like vibe flowing through here. From the design, the ambiance, and all the way down to the staff. Even the music was erotic. Did I mention that members of the staff were all nude? No pasties on titties, no covering of any private parts. They were literally letting it all hang out, and they walked around as if it were completely normal to do so.

Closing my mouth, I hid my devilish grin as best I could as I made my way over to the closest bar. There were three of them total, and from the menu I saw online, they served every drink you could think of at each of them. They boasted the best bartenders in the business, and I couldn't wait to try out a few of their concoctions. First on my list was the Pink Orgasm. It was made with Bacardí 8 Años, which was a favorite of mine, so I had to try it. From reading the reviews on the site, I determined it was the most popular and best-tasting drink they offered.

I felt eyes on me, so I paused midstride to look around. Unable to locate whoever was scoping me out, I continued. Taking the empty seat at the end of the bar, I observed members going in and out of the numbered rooms situated along the perimeter of the club. There were eight of them total, and from what Neeka had told me there could be just about any indecent, fetishtic deed you could think of going on behind those doors. I also learned that the four rooms with a letter behind the number were the rooms that allowed other members to watch the action that was going down inside, and I planned to get a little peek at some point tonight or maybe even put on a little production of my own. For now, I would enjoy the sexual encounters going on all around me. There was enough bumping and grinding happening to keep me entertained for quite some time.

Couples, groups, and singles could all be seen going at it, and the sight caused my nipples to swell and my core temperature to rise. I knew in my mind that the likelihood of it happening was slim to none, but my body flatout wanted in on the action. To my left there was a couple stretched out on a lounge chair in a sixty-nine position, devouring one another. To the right of me, there was a handsome Indian guy sandwiched between two pretty chicks, one Hispanic and the other African American, with his hands up both their skirts as they tongued each other down. They were in their own little world, loving, touching, and most importantly, not giving a fuck.

I swear I was digging the hell out of this place already and I hadn't even been here an hour yet. I also liked that there were just as many women here as there were men. Maybe even more. To see females who weren't afraid to speak up about what they liked and doing things that made them feel good was a beautiful thing. I understood first-hand what they were experiencing, because the moment I opened myself up to embrace my sexuality and power as a woman had to be the most freeing feeling in the world for me. I walked different. I talked different. I loved different. Hell, I even orgasmed different.

My eyes widened in realization the moment I noticed that there was a central theme for the men in attendance tonight. They were all bearded! I'm talking not one man in here with a bare face. I found myself in beard-lover's heaven, and like clockwork, my mind drifted to my husband. I wished he were here right now. I was biased, but no one was more attractive to me than my man, and his beard was shitting on every nigga's in here. I now realized why there were so many women in here tonight. Apparently I wasn't alone in my love for a sexy-ass bearded man. Sheesh.

"What can I get for you tonight, beautiful?" the bartender asked, his deep voice breaking me from my thoughts.

When my gaze met his, I was temporarily stumped by his beauty. Yes, beauty! This man was gorgeous with his long lashes, big, sleepy eyes, and straight white teeth. It seemed he was used to being ogled by women, because he said nothing. He just stood there smiling knowingly while I stared his light, bright ass down. I had no doubt that men gave his fine self a second glance as well. That's how good-looking he was, and let's not even get started on his body. It was immaculate. Glancing down though, I noted that his dick seemed a bit small, but it wasn't erect, and I could testify that looks could be very deceiving. That thing could very well grow to twice its length when he became aroused, but it was too bad that I'd never test that theory. Especially with those extra-large balls dangling underneath it.

I propped up on the bar with my hands folded under my chin and asked, "What do you suggest?" I flirted playfully for the hell of it as if I didn't already know what I wanted.

"For you? Let me see," he drawled out slowly before coming from behind the bar, little dick just a-swinging.

Before I knew what was happening, he was standing at my side, pulling me from my seat by my hand. Lifting it in the air, he twirled me around while he looked me over. I wasn't shy at all, so I let him do his thing, grinning and batting my eyelashes the entire time. Once he was done with that, he yanked me to where my body was flush against his chest, hand sliding sensually down my side before he let it rest on my ass. Palming it gently, he leaned his head down so that his mouth was close to my ear.

"For you, I recommend the Squirter," he proposed sexily, causing my breath to hitch and my eyes to slam shut.

When I opened them, he was no longer holding on to me. Shit happened so fast I thought I was tripping. I nervously licked my lips and pushed my hair behind my ear. Just as quickly as he had come around the bar, he had his naked ass back where he belonged, mixing my drink. Nigga didn't even give me a chance to say yes or no to his drink suggestion, but I honestly didn't care what the hell that cup had in it. I was drinking it the fuck up anyway. I realized in that moment that I'd fucked up by not wearing panties, because I was already feeling some slight dampness between my thighs. If things kept going the way they were I'd soon be crying a river down there, and I needed something to trap the wetness.

It was too early in the evening for this shit, and he was only the first of many men I was sure to encounter tonight. I guessed the fact that my sex life had been pretty blah these days was causing me to become aroused behind the slightest touch or sensual gaze. I was supposed to keep it PG with these niggas tonight, but at the rate I was going I was gon' have this dress of mine hiked up, getting fucked by some unknown man before it was all said and done. Or maybe I would take Biggie Smalls here on for a couple rounds on the floor behind the bar. If I was to step out on him tonight, Moraiah would have no one to blame but himself.

"Enjoy." Mr. Sexy winked and placed my drink in front of me before moving on to the half-naked lady seated next to me, displaying the same charm with her that he had with me.

Picking up my glass, I quickly spun around on my stool, slowly sipping my drink, which just so happened to be one of the tastiest cocktails I'd ever had. After observing the crowd for about fifteen minutes, I locked eyes with a gentleman watching me from across the room. He was at a round table with three other very professional-looking men, each of them attractive as all get-out. I smiled then quickly averted my gaze, but I could still feel his eyes on me. I didn't want to appear standoffish, but I also didn't want to come off as someone who was available, because I wasn't. At least not to him. I glanced his way again and saw that he was standing to his feet. *Shit,* I thought to myself as I turned where my back was now facing him. Hopefully, he would take the hint and stay where he was. I was too vulnerable to be turning down advances from a man as fine as that one.

"Is this seat taken?" someone asked, the voice all too familiar.

The glass I was holding threatened to slip from my hand, and my entire being became rigid at the sound of it. I hadn't even felt him walk up because I was too concerned about being approached by the man from across the room. This one here was the one I should have been on the lookout for. I shook my head no to answer him, but I refused to give him the courtesy of properly acknowledging him.

My clit pulsed in excitement when he finally sat down. I had to close my eyes and practice some deep breathing exercises to get myself together before I bubbled over at the fact that he'd actually shown up. I'd laid everything out perfectly hoping he'd take the bait and now here we were. If I could just steer clear of Neeka for the rest of night, I'd be good. Hopefully, she'd be too busy getting her back blown out to notice me and the beefcake sitting next to me with his energy on ten.

Following a few moments of silence, I gathered up enough courage to face him. I watched his facial expression closely as his eyes traveled all over my body before coming up to lock with mine. I was sure he could sense my uncertainty because that's exactly what I was feeling, but his expression remained unreadable. I hated that because I desperately needed to know what he was thinking. Whatever it was, I just hoped that he wasn't angry with me, but I didn't know what he expected. Desperate times called for desperate measures.

As a diversion tactic, I slowly gaped my legs open in my seat, causing his gaze to drift from my face and drop lower. My dress had risen just enough for this move to have the intended effect. At the point he realized that I was pantiless, I watched his eyes turn from light brown to a dark color, almost like coffee with no cream. Lowering his head, he rubbed his hand down the back of it several times before bringing it around to smooth down then tug on his beard.

With bated breath, I waited for him to speak. After a minute or so he placed his hands on my thighs, gripping them tightly before pulling me to the edge of the stool to the point our knees were touching. The scent of my arousal hit us both at the same time. He growled low with a quick shake of his head while I closed my eyes, embarrassed by the amount of wetness seeping from my center.

"How about you, baby girl? Are you taken?" he questioned after clearing his throat.

"No, I'm not taken. Free as a bird, baby." I chucked my head up confidently.

"Is that right?" he questioned with a lifted brow. His inquiry held an underlying threat, so I hesitated to answer, my cocky attitude diminishing by the second. "Grab your drink and let's go," he demanded then stood and walked away.

Unsure if I was ready for what was about to go down, I hesitated moving from my seat. It was like I was temporarily paralyzed. When he realized I wasn't behind him, he turned and shot me a look that put fire under my ass.

I jumped down from my seat, leaving my drink behind. On wobbly legs I obediently followed him, brushing past my admirer from moments earlier on the way. My eyes bucked slightly when we made eye contact, but I kept it moving and was thankful that he didn't try to stop me to talk.

I was experiencing all kinds of emotions as this man led me. Fear. Lust. Giddiness. Anticipation. However, my compulsive hunger for passion and penetration topped the list and motivated me to move swiftly behind him as he unlocked the door of room 2A.

Chapter 4

Opening the door with the key that was given to me upon my arrival, I turned to make sure she was still with me. She was looking so good that I found myself becoming pissed that anyone else had the privilege of seeing her tonight. Given our situation, I didn't have the right to feel that way, but it was real. She had those thick thighs out looking scrumptious as fuck, begging to be kneaded and nibbled on.

"Shit," I mumbled low when she walked past me to enter the room and I was able to inhale her heavenly scent.

The room I'd reserved online was the size of an actual bedroom, and the queen bed was just right for us to be able to do the damn thing comfortably. I just hoped she was ready for what I had in store. Everything I'd ordered for tonight was placed neatly on the bedside table. Oils, beads, bullets, dildos, and a few other necessities. It wasn't likely that we would use them all, but I was damn sure going to try to. Her eyes followed mine, and when they finally landed on the table, they widened in surprise as well as slick apprehension. On cue, she began to fidget and play with the charm that hung from the necklace around her neck.

"Why you acting so skittish? This is what you wanted, right?" I didn't understand what her hesitance was about, seeing as how she was the one responsible for my presence here this evening.

"It is, M—" she started, but I raised my hand to stop her. "Not tonight." I shook my head emphatically.

Confused, she asked, "What do you mean not tonight?"

"I'm not him. Not tonight. I'm just trying to give you the experience you wanted," I answered, tugging on my beard.

After a few seconds, she took a deep breath and nodded her head, signaling that she'd caught on.

"Have a seat." I motioned toward the bed before pulling off my jacket and placing it on one of the hooks near the door. Right next to it was a computerized panel installed inside the wall. The device performed a number of functions, including lighting and temperature adjustment, but I was in search of some music to set the mood. When I found what I was looking for, I made my selection then proceeded to get the lights and everything else just the way I wanted them. Having taken care of that, I went on to remove the rest of my clothing while commanding her with my eyes to remain in place, focused solely on me until I gave further instructions.

Like a good girl, not once did she take her eyes off of me. Finally, I made my way over to the woman of the hour and pulled her to her feet. I swear I'd never seen anyone as beautiful as her, and I'd never tire of staring at her. My intense gaze had her on edge, but that was my intention. My mode was on some savage shit, and it was clear that she detected it by the way her chest rose and fell from the rapid breaths she took. She suddenly began backing away from me and didn't stop until her back was against the door.

"Come here," I ordered sternly.

I smirked, because she was shaking her head no, but she obviously had no control over her body, because those sexy-ass boot-clad legs were moving my way at the same time. I loved the show she was unknowingly putting on for me. That walk of hers was cold as fuck and was definitely some runway-worthy shit. All I saw was voluptuous legs the color of cinnamon, and all I could imagine was having them wrapped around my waist as I pounded her pussy to oblivion and back. Catching a whiff of the fragrant scent between her thighs a few minutes earlier had me about to toss her on top of that bar and have my way with her. That that pretty thing wasn't covered by undergarments made my shit brick up even more. Shit pissed me off a little, too.

I don't want to give you the wrong impression
I need love and affection
And I hope I'm not sounding too desperate
I need love and affection.

Future's voice boomed through the speakers louder than expected, but he was right on time. Our eyes locked once again as I recalled that love and affection were what she claimed to be lacking in her life, and I was tasked with giving her all of that and much more tonight.

"Can I kiss you?" I whispered desperately in her ear once I had her in my arms again.

"Please," she requested barely above a whisper, causing me to sigh in relief.

I knew what this was. Just one night that was all about her and her needs, but I hoped that she would let me have her my way in some fashion as well. Fulfilling her fantasies was my top priority, but I really wanted her to grant me just a little leeway. I was an excellent multi-tasker in the bedroom, so I was positive that I could give her what she needed while taking a little for myself at the same time. If I'm being honest, I was in just as much need as she was, but I was going to have to place those needs on the back burner for one night.

Taking her pretty face in my hands, I looked deep in her eyes for a few seconds before my mouth descended upon hers, kissing her like it was the last kiss I'd ever receive, and I needed to somehow burn the memory of it into my brain to reminisce on it for years to come. Her lips tasted like cotton candy, and I had a major sweet tooth. I sucked and licked them sloppily, hoping to get a damn sugar rush from the flavor of her.

"Mmm," she moaned, throwing her arms around my neck when my tongue finally pushed past her thick lips.

Swear I tried to slither this long muthafucka all the way down her throat. Choke her ass with it as punishment for making me so crazy about her then threatening to take it all away. I felt convicted when I felt her trembling weakly in my arms. It was plain to see that she hadn't been touched or kissed this way in a good minute. If I hadn't been holding on to her, she would have surely tumbled to the floor. Gathering some control, I reluctantly pulled away from her.

"Your husband ain't been kissing you, baby?" I asked although I knew the answer. She'd already broken everything down for me.

"He hasn't," she panted with her forehead pressed against my chest.

Pulling back a little, I lifted her face by her chin. I needed her to look me in the eyes as I said what I had to say. "I'ma handle that for him, okay? I plan to kiss and lick every inch of you tonight," I promised as she blushed and lowered her head once more.

I removed the coiled key chain from her wrist and placed it on the table before going for her clothing. Her breathing became more labored with each button I released on her dress. Once I had it all completely undone, I pushed it off of her shoulders, letting it fall in a pile at her feet. I almost bent down to remove her shoes but thought better of it. They were super sexy, and I wanted to fuck her with them on. All she was wearing now was one of those sticky strapless bra things that pushed her titties up, and because I had no idea how to get it off, I let her do the honors. No sooner had she'd peeled it from her skin and tossed it than I had those plump, round globes in my hands, twirling her nipples like you would a volume dial. We hadn't even gotten to the good part yet, and she was moaning like crazy, and hearing those sweet sounds was all the motivation I needed. Walking her backward to the bed, my hands greedily moved all over her body.

"Yessss," she whimpered in appreciation.

I quickly laid her down and dropped lower until I was face-to-face with her yoni. I had a strict policy to always lick before I stuck, so I got right to it, giving her pussy a few soft kisses to start off. The smell of her alone was driving me insane, and it had been a minute since I'd been fed, so I was about to go in. Her folds were already glazed with her juices, so I made an attempt to clean up the mess she'd made, but no matter how much I sucked and licked it away, she continued to produce that sweet cream for me. It was literally pouring from her, and I'd never tasted anything so delicious. Dolce had been blessed with sweet-ass lips on her face and between her legs as well.

"Your nigga ain't been eating this pussy either, baby?" I asked before taking her obese clit into my mouth and sucking the life out of it. She tried pushing me away, but the lock I had on her thighs prevented it.

"Nooooo," she squealed while locking her thighs around my head. Soon after, she released a gush of fluid.

Not wanting a drop of it to go to waste, I quickly abandoned her love button and went lower to lap up my reward. "Fuck, girl! That nigga been missing out. If you were mine, I'd have to taste that sweet-ass pussy several times a day," I told her before cranking it up again. I made her come twice more before I finally let her legs go. Like dead weight, they plopped to the bed in an uncoordinated fashion.

"You good?" I asked, amused by the way her arm was draped lazily over her eyes.

She offered no response. Hell, she couldn't talk even if she wanted to, and that's what I liked to see. Her ass panted like she'd just completed the hundred-yard dash in nine seconds flat or something. Her body hadn't been properly cared for in a while, and it was showing. Looked like she was already prepared to tap out on me, but I wasn't having that.

Leaving her on the bed with her legs wide open and that pretty pussy exposed, I walked over to the panel and tapped the screen several times. While I waited, I moved over to the table to get a few things I'd need for this next phase. Although she didn't need it, I grabbed the strawberry-flavored liquid that doubled as a lubricant and massage oil. That tongue-lashing had her relaxed enough, so I planned to skip the massage and use it for the former.

A few minutes later the buzzer interrupted my preparations. I made my way over and opened the door up to accept my order. In all of her naked glory, a sexy waitress stood there with my tray full of treats. She gasped when her eyes landed on my dick that jutted out nine-and-a-half inches in front of me. I had no shame in my game, so I didn't bother covering up before coming to the door. The young woman, who looked to be no older than twenty-five, licked her lips and smirked sexily at me, but my face remained stoic. I had no idea what she was thinking, but I had nothing for her ass. Not taking anything away from her because she was definitely a cutie, but there was no one in the world more important or beautiful to me than the woman stretched out on the bed awaiting my return, still shivering in ecstasy from multiple orgasms. I felt movement behind me, so I looked back to see Dolce raised up on her elbows, watching us through hooded eyes, legs still spread wide. No shame or fucks given.

"Shit," the waitress tried to whisper, but it was loud enough for me to hear. I turned back to face her and chuckled low when I realized that she was just as turned on by the sight as I was. "So, umm, if you two are looking for a third, you know, a unicorn for the night, I'd be more than willing to come back. My name is on the ticket, so look me up on there if you're interested." She pointed hopefully toward the panel after handing over my tray.

"We're good, Treasure," I answered after glancing down at the ticket to find her name in bold letters. I placed my hand on the doorknob as a signal that it was time for her to leave. I wasn't trying to diss, but tonight was all about Dolce Marie, and extra parties were not required nor were they needed. I did my thing and was down with that freaky shit, but a nigga like me would never share that one. Ever. With any-fucking-body. Male or female.

Looking a bit disappointed, she shrugged. "Well, at least activate the mirror so that I can watch. I'm always down to see a good show, and you two look like you're about to cut the fuck up." She glanced at my dick again.

"That's the plan." I winked before closing the door and proceeding to tap a few buttons on the panel, activating the two-way mirror. With that taken care of, I picked up the green shot glass and walked over to give it to Dolce.

Chapter 5

"Drink this. You're going to need your energy, and this will help," I informed her.

Nodding, she took it down in one gulp then placed the empty glass back on the tray while I took the second shot myself. She was sitting up in bed now, so I handed her the smoky pink cocktail I'd ordered for her. For some reason, I felt like she would like it. Setting the tray down, I went about getting everything else ready, allowing time for the drink to work its way through our systems. It didn't look like I would be waiting long for that to happen, because I could immediately feel tingling throughout my body, and my dick, which had deflated some, was slowly coming to life again. After removing the drink I'd ordered for myself, the brownies were all that remained on the tray. Those would be for later though. At the end of the night when we were spent from multiple orgasms and intense rounds of lovemaking, we'd mellow out with those.

I could feel her watching me as I drenched the medium-sized butt plug and then the chocolate dildo with the lubricant. I'd brought these two from home just for this occasion. My heart rate sped up, and small beads of sweat suddenly covered my body when I looked over to find her running her palm up and down her pussy before making circles on her clit with her index and middle fingers. She had one of those fat joints that got hard and protruded out from behind her plump lips when she was aroused, and I couldn't get enough of sucking, nibbling, and slurping on it. The sloshy sounds of her playing in her wetness could be heard throughout the room, and it had me on the brink of losing my cool and forgetting my goal for tonight. Whatever they put in that shot was working its magic on both of us. It wasn't a scary feeling like I was drugged or anything. What it seemed to do was cause every single erogenous zone in my body to become hypersensitive. And warm. Shit! I was already horny and craving her before taking that down, but now I was feeling like a nigga who never had a shot of pussy in his life. Felt like I was about to nut on myself at the mere sight of her pleasing herself.

"Hurry, please," she called out, speeding up her finger movements.

"On all fours," I directed with urgency.

She eagerly did as she was told, expertly arching her back once she was in position. She groaned loudly when I inserted the butt plug into her ass and rotated it around some while she played with her clit. "Shiiitttt, I'm coming already," she whined pitifully while backing her ass up against the plug.

"I see, girl. Damn." I shook my head in amazement as I witnessed the thick white substance seep from her opening and onto her fingers. Her ass was nuttin' like a whole nigga up in here, and I loved it.

I couldn't help bending down to lick her clean. I'd long ago been labeled a pussy monster by my wife, and with this shit in my system, I was trying to suck the lining out of this muthafucka right now. I could hardly breathe due to the fact that I had my face stuffed so far up this girl's ass. Pushing her ass in the air with the palms of my hands, I stuck my tongue in her honey pot as far as it could go and got to swiping. Up down, left right, in a circle, then repeat. I did that shit until she was cummin' in my mouth again, which didn't take very long at all. I wanted to keep eating her out, but we had to move on, and I knew she was waiting on me to fill her other hole. "You ready for the other one, love?" I asked after running my tongue up and down her slit one last time. Her body convulsed as she came down from her sexual high while I sat on my haunches, watching her shake while her pussy juices saturated and dripped from my beard. Her essence on me was the most savory scent ever, and I never wanted to wash it away.

"I'm ready, baby, but instead of that one"—she motioned toward the dildo—"I want yours." This time she was nodding toward my dick, which just so happened to bounce up and down at hearing her request. Shooting me a naughty look, she began clapping her ass to entice me, and it worked.

"I got you, but we're definitely coming back to this one next," I informed her before placing it on the tray.

As soon as I was in position behind her, "First Fuck" by 6lack and Jhené Aiko boomed through the speakers right on time. The song and its timing were fucking perfect.

"*I bet you love me more after that first fuck,*" 6lack sang as my thick dick breached her sopping wet opening for the first time tonight.

> *I'm a make it mine*
> *Mine for the night*
> *Got me pulling on yo' hair*

"Ahhh, shit!" we moaned together.

"Fuck, I needed this so baadddd!" she added, backing her ass up on me with greedy force.

"Damn, ma, slow down! I take it your man ain't been fucking you either," I grunted, hitting her fast and hard trying to keep up with her bouncing ass.

"Ooohhh, nahhh! He ain't been fucking this pussy, but you doing the damn thing, daddy. Please don't stop!" she wailed, and of course, I was happy to oblige.

I gripped her ass with one hand, nails damn near puncturing her skin, while I wrapped her long, silky hair around my fist and pulled it tight before I began beating her pussy up even harder. I sped up when I felt her walls tighten and start to choke my mans up, and just as I'd anticipated, she was wetting up the bed and my abdomen moments later. I had long ago trained myself to hold off on my orgasms, so once she came, I pulled out, declining to go after a release for myself. When she was satiated, and I knew my job was complete, then I would get mine. Dolce was still bucking when I slowly slid the dildo inside of her. Once it was all the way in, I turned it on to the lowest setting so that we could work our way up.

"That feels so damn good," she groaned while backing that ass up frantically against the dildo. It was the same size and width as mine, which was why she loved it so much. Seeing her go ham like this prompted me to begin stroking my dick. When I saw her movements become faster, I upped the intensity two notches on the toy inside of her. On setting three, the device moved around inside of her in wild circles. That one there was her favorite, and within seconds, she exploded and howled so damn loud that I was sure people could hear her over the music on the other side of the door. As soon as she got hers, I stopped beating my dick.

Pace yourself, I coached inwardly.

"One more hole, daddy," she breathed heavily as she looked over her shoulder at me.

"Tonight is not about my pleasure, Dolce. I'm focused solely on your wants and needs," I explained. I knew what she was asking, but I had other plans.

"If that's the case, I want and, umm, I need your dick in my . . . in my mouth," she stuttered with a quick lick of her luscious lips.

She was having difficulty speaking due to the fact that the dildo and butt plug were still inside of her doing their thing. Normally after busting that many nuts she'd be exhausted, but with that drink in her system, she was on one, and I for one wasn't complaining. It was her night, so I decided to appease her. Leaving the setting as is, I moved to the head of the bed and got in position in front of her. She eagerly wrapped those lips of hers around the head of my dick and made an attempt at sucking my soul from my body. Her mouth was so fucking wet, and the suction of it was on a level of mastery I'd never experienced before her. Shit drove me mad but in a real good way. I was losing control, and there was nothing I could do to stop it.

Slurp. Suck. Slurp. Twirl. Slurp.

"Gaahh damn, girl," I grumbled, tossing my head back in pure pleasure. I wasn't sure how much longer I was going to be able to hold off. She was about to get this shit up out of me whether I wanted her to or not. Releasing me from her oral cavity, she spit on my dick nastily and began stroking the head with one hand while using the other to stuff both of my testicles into her mouth and suck vigorously. She knew exactly what she was doing. Always drove me wild when she did that shit. After she was done with that, she took me back down and deep throated my shit repeatedly until my toes were throwing up gang signs. Tears sprang from her eyes as my dick choked her out, but she didn't stop. She proceeded to perform some swallowing motions with her throat followed by her humming my favorite tune on my dick. Don't ask me what the tune was because I had no idea, but I swear that was all she wrote. My balls tightened up at the sound of her cries. She was busting yet another nut while simultaneously drinking down what felt like gallons of my babies. I hadn't nutted like that in a long-ass time, and the fact that I'd been stalling my release tonight only made it more intense and satisfying when I finally let it go.

When we were able to regain our composure, things took off, getting kinkier and nastier every round we went at it. Tonight I was supposed to be fucking her, but a few of those rounds she ended up taking control and fucked me instead. I didn't recall if we ever had a chance to try the edibles I'd purchased, but I wasn't tripping. What I did know was that we put on one hell of a show for anyone who had the opportunity to watch from the mirror. One of her fantasies was to fuck a stranger while a group of people looked on, and I made that happen for her tonight. We had to improvise on the stranger part, because like I said earlier, I wasn't into sharing. That pussy had Moraiah Heard stamped all over it, and that was something that would never change if I could help it.

I was glad that I'd paid to have everything recorded, because I knew she'd want to see herself on video. Tonight was definitely one for the record books and something we had to add to our archives. That way we could go back and watch it anytime we wanted or maybe reenact some of the scenes from tonight. At some point, my dick finally went down, and she cried out that she absolutely could not come again, so we fell into the mattress, prepared to pass the hell out. We had this room reserved until closing time, which was 5:00 a.m. That gave us time to get an hour or two of sleep.

Before I fully drifted off, I pulled her close to me and whispered, "I love you so much, Dolce. Please don't give up on me, baby."

I didn't know if she heard me, but I hoped and prayed she did and that she gave me a little more time to get things lined up the way I wanted. She'd confronted me several times asking if I was cheating on her, and I answered honestly each time. I would never betray her like that, and it hurt that she didn't believe that. That was my fault though, so I planned to work overtime regaining her trust if she gave me the opportunity. If she could hold out a just a bit longer, I'd have way more time to spend with her. For being so distant over the last year I had a lot of making up to do, and I planned to do it in a big way. I knew it wasn't going to be all peaches and cream, but I was confident that with time things would get back to the way they used to be between us.

Chapter 6

Dolce

"Aye, baby, where you going?" Moraiah's voice halted my movement.

It had been a few days since we engaged in that all-night sex marathon at Privacy, and surprisingly I wasn't feeling any better about our situation. Would you believe that he'd gone back to work that same morning like clockwork and come home hella late as usual? I had stupidly taken the day off believing that we were going to spend it together, but I was all kinds of wrong. We made it home at a quarter to six, and I sat at the foot of our bed and watched in utter disbelief as he rushed to take a quick shower. Soon after, he popped a quick kiss to my forehead and dipped out the door like the night before had never happened. I didn't even bother waiting up that night, but I did feel him when he slipped in behind me and pulled me to his side of the bed. As bad as I wanted to snatch out of his hold, I remained in place, relishing the feel of his warm body snuggled against mine.

"Out," I finally answered his question like that was all that needed to be said.

"The hell that mean, Dolce? Out where?" He looked me up and down angrily, clearly not feeling the skintight jeans, crop top, and heels I was wearing. I had his ass and titties all on display this afternoon hoping to get his attention.

Seeing this tall, gorgeous man standing there looking all disgruntled was distracting as hell. Jaw muscles flexing as he did that smooth-ass contemplative tug on his beard. Shit had my thong wet as fuck already. Snapping out of the trance I was slowly slipping into, I replied, "It means just what I said, Moraiah. I'm going out. What's up with you though? You haven't been worried about my comings and goings, so don't start that mess now. Keep working around the clock and doing you, and I promise to do the same," I sassed while trying to move around him, but he had me cornered against the door in the foyer of our home. "What are you doing?" I looked up into his eyes when I noticed that he wasn't trying to get out of my way.

"I'm trying to see who the hell you think you're talking to. The fuck is your problem, Dolce?"

"You know what my problem is, Moraiah!" I shouted.

"If I knew, I wouldn't be fucking asking." He clenched his jaw like he was trying to control his anger.

"I'm not going to keep spelling it out for you. I've done all the talking I'm going to do. What's the use when it's clear that nothing is ever going to change?" My voice cracked with emotion.

"I told you I was going to do better and I will. Why do you think I'm here today?" he asked.

"Hell, I don't know, but I guess I'm supposed to be happy about it. What about all the other days though? What about tomorrow or the day after? Will you be here or have time for me then? Probably not, so I'll believe that 'doing better' shit when I see it. Now move!"

"Nah, fuck that. I ain't moving nowhere." He got in my face, causing me to turn my face to the side. I knew he'd never harm me physically, but his tone and energy had me shook. Calming himself, he pulled back some before turning my face back toward him. "I thought we were good, D. Why you tripping on me?"

"Why am I tripping?" I snapped, pushing his hand away. "Did you really just ask me that shit? Why on earth would you think we were good, Mo? We haven't spent a minute together since that night," I pointed out. "Oh, I get it." I threw my head back in feigned amusement when something dawned on me. "You thought throwing me some good dick was going to shut me up long enough for you to go right back to acting like I don't exist? Nah, I'm cool on you, boo."

"What you mean you cool on me?" he questioned, voice full of panic.

"Quit acting like you're slow, Moraiah Heard. This question-and-answer business is really beginning to piss me off, but let me break it down for you so that we're clear. You've told me several times over the course of the last year that things would change, but nothing has. I still feel completely alone in this marriage, and you're not even trying to fix what's broken. So, what I'm saying to you is I'm not falling for your shit this time. What I'm promising you right here and now is that if you don't get your shit together, you're going to lose your fucking wife," I threatened while he looked on in defeat and disbelief.

My words seemed to have knocked the wind out of him as he removed his hand from my wrist and took a wobbly step back. His rubbing down the back of his head and saddened eyes did nothing to move me. Mo was all man, and there were few things that made him weak. I knew for a fact that one of those things was me, so I was sure hearing me say those things cut him deep. Of course, I didn't mean any of it and was only being hateful out of anger, but I needed him to realize that I was no longer playing games. Life without me could be his reality if his actions didn't start to line up with his words and promises.

It was mind blowing that my husband actually thought that lack of sex was the only reason that I'd been unhappy and complaining all these months. That had to be his line of thinking if he thought he could use his dick to pacify me. Sure, the infrequency of our lovemaking was partly the problem, but he was missing the point I'd truly been trying to get across. I missed my fucking husband, and I wanted him to do better. Making love to him on a more consistent basis would be amazing, but I needed his love, time, and attention even more. I wanted him to take me out every once in a while. Listen to me when I needed to vent about my day or business at the shop in general. Most of all I wanted him to allow me to be a wife to him again. Just like I wanted him to make me feel important, I wanted to do the same for him. Cook for him, cater to him, have him tell me about his struggles and what I could do to make it better. He was everything to me, and I wanted to be the same to him. When he offered no response, I rolled my eyes and brushed past him in frustration.

"Should have just fucked some random nigga at the club instead of your ass," I spat spitefully, shoulder checking him on my way out.

This time he allowed me to leave, and that shit hurt too. Why couldn't he go as hard for us as I was willing to? His lack of fight broke my heart, and by the time I made it to my car I was crying hysterically. Was this really how things were going to end for us? God, I hoped not, but I refused to remain in a one-sided marriage.

Moraiah

Dolce fucked my head up so bad with that threat that I couldn't even begin to formulate a response. Just stood there numb and terrified beyond words, thinking that this could actually be the beginning of the end.

A few weeks ago, I came across the composition notebook where she kept her poetry, so I knew how she felt. But to hear the same words I'd read off that paper flow from her mouth so freely and adamantly almost knocked me off my damn feet. Writing was a passion of hers that very few people knew about, and anytime she became overwhelmed she took to her notebook, unleashing her pent-up frustrations onto those pages. It had been a long time since I'd read anything of hers and I was curious to know where her head was at these days. As I flipped through the pages, I became overwhelmed my damn self. It killed me to find out how much pain my absence and denial of our problems had been causing her. Her most recent sonnets were raw, real, and transparent as fuck.

"Abandoned and disconnected from my lifeline." That one line almost made me shed a few thug tears. I considered her my lifeline as well, and her poems had the same effect on me now that they had when she would send them to me when I was locked up. Pages and pages of powerful words written on fancy pastel-colored paper were what got me through many rough days while I was locked down. I honestly fell in love with her mind and wordplay well before I fell head over heels for her heart, brains, and beauty. There was always an underlying message in her writing that spoke directly to me. It made me feel close to her, and she unknowingly inspired me to choose a different path once I was released from prison. She loved a nigga so much that she would have accepted me whether I chose to still be the dopeman, a plumber, or even if I had a job flipping burgers at In & Out. That realization alone made me want to be a better man. A man worthy of having someone so loving and selfless as my wife.

She never cared one way or another if I read the things she'd written, and I low-key think she wanted me to see that shit. Just like she wanted me to see the confirmation email she received from the club saying she had a reservation for the night I showed up at Privacy. I came in from work late one night and found her passed out with the laptop in bed with her. This was a nightly occurrence, so I did as I always did when I made it home, which was to shut it down and put it away for her. Afterward, I would tuck her in then kiss her face repeatedly before heading to the bathroom for my nightly shower.

Before I could close her laptop down that particular night, however, something on the screen caught my eye. Seeing that email had me boiling mad and ready to wake her up to question her, but I wanted to get more information before I confronted her. The following day I checked our account and saw where she'd made a payment to the club one day prior. Her bold ass knew I was going to see that shit, and right after I called the bank to confirm where the payment had gone, I picked up the phone and called Neeka. If anyone knew what was up, I knew she did. Well, I called her right after I submitted my own application to Privacy and paid all the necessary fees. My wife had to know that if she was going to be up in there, then so the fuck was I.

Neeka and I knew one another from way back and were really good friends, but my wife came into the picture and straight up took a nigga's spot. I didn't mind though because Neeka was good people. Her ass was no help when I reached out to her though, only confirming what I knew to be true. She was team Dolce all the way, refusing to give up the dirt on her buddy. I didn't care what she said, I knew she knew what was up because she'd told me when she first started going to Privacy a while back. I swear the moment I heard that shit, I gave Neeka strict instructions that my wife was to go nowhere near that place. I threatened the fuck out of her, and she acted as if she planned to respect my wishes, but I guessed she changed her mind. I understood that she couldn't control a grown woman, but I was hoping she would have looked out for her boy and given me a heads-up when Dolce confided in her about wanting to go. I wasn't upset with her though because she gave me some good-ass advice and basically told me the same thing Dolce had before she stormed out of the door a moment ago:

"All I'm going to say is you better get it together before you lose the best thing that's ever happened to you, Mo."

Although I already had some things in motion concerning my businesses that would allow me more time with my wife, learning about this club shit and reading her most inner thoughts on paper made me speed up the process. There was no way that I was going to allow Dolce to leave me. I would rather die than live without her. Today was the day that I was supposed to share the good news with her, which was the reason I was home on a day I'd normally be gone from sunup to sundown. She threw me off when she blew up on me, and I could hardly breathe when she spat those evil words my way. Would it really be that easy for her to walk out of my life?

Shit! Why am I still standing here?

I snapped out of it and flew up the stairs to get dressed. My wife had been fighting for our marriage all on her own for the last year at least, and now it was time for me to show her that I was just as invested in fixing things and making sure we lived out our happily ever after as she was. After throwing on some gray sweatpants and a sleeveless lightweight hoodie, I slipped on some retro J's, grabbed my keys, and rushed out the door. I stopped short when I came out to find Dolce's car still parked next to mine. It looked like she never even pulled out of the driveway.

Taking a deep breath, I prepared to go to her and pour my heart out, but the shaking of her shoulders caught my attention. She had tint on her windows so I couldn't see her face that well, but the closer I got to her car I could damn sure hear her. My baby was crying hard as hell, and hearing her bawl like that made me feel even lower than I already did. I didn't think it was possible for me to feel any worse, but I was wrong. I walked over quickly and pulled open the driver's side door.

"Baby," I called to her, squatting down between her and the open car door.

She was caught off guard by my presence initially, but she quickly fell into my arms and continued to sob. I carefully lifted her into my arms before closing the door and locking up her ride. Slowly, I walked with her into our home then secured the deadbolt and chain.

"I'm sorry, D. I've been hearing what you've been saying, and I swear to you that my talk of change ain't just words this time, baby," I whispered in her ear as I carried her up the stairs of the home we'd surely grow old in. I laid her down on our bed and sat at the edge, awaiting her response. She only cried harder at hearing my words, so I continued. "Over the last six months I've been training Casper for the manager position, and I feel like now is the best time to have him take over for me. He'll handle both shops, and I'll only go in three days a week to do the books and check on things. I would have done this sooner, but I had to pick someone I could trust to do the job. We've worked too hard building that business up to let someone run it into the ground, babe. That's the only reason I kept asking for a little more time. And just so you know, all changes are effective immediately. I know you feel like I haven't been paying attention, but I have," I told her in my sincerest voice.

"Moraiah, baby, I'm so happy to hear you say that!" she exclaimed before rising to toss her arms around my neck. I chuckled as she hugged me tight as hell. "All this time I've been thinking that you were sleeping with someone else because you were behaving like you no longer wanted me. Like I wasn't important to you," she stated sadly as she wiped the tears from her eyes with the back of her hand. "Why didn't you just tell me what was up?"

"I wanted to surprise you with the news. Plus, I didn't want to get your hopes up just in case things with Casper didn't work out, but I realize that keeping you in the dark wasn't the best idea," I admitted as I wiped away the remaining wetness from her face. "And one thing you won't ever have to worry about is me not wanting you or me being with someone else," I said before aggressively taking her mouth for a sensual kiss. "So are we good? You're going to give me a chance to make things up to you?" I asked with a kiss to her nose.

"Of course, Moraiah. Just promise me that you're serious this time. Actions speak louder than words, babe." She pulled back to look into my eyes.

"I'm very serious, Dolce. I love you more than anything, and I promise I won't let you down."

"I love you, Mo Mo." She gazed into my eyes adoringly.

"I know you do, but I need you to take back that shit you said earlier," I told her with my eyebrows furrowed.

"What part?" She smirked playfully.

"You know what part I'm talking about. That shit you said about fucking some nigga at that club. Just like I showed up last time, trust and believe I would show up again and set it the fuck off up in there if you try playing with me like that," I threatened while she laughed uncontrollably. "Think it's a game if you want to. Why do you think I have on these fucking sweats? You thought I didn't know it was Gray Sweatpants Night up in that bitch," I said as a look of guilt crossed her face.

"I was just upset, Moraiah. You know better than any-one that I'd never do that to you. I only said that to piss you off. I knew you would come for me today just like you followed the trail I left you the first time."

"So we understand each other then?"

"Yes, husband." She snuggled up closer to me.

"Just for clarification, this pussy may be between your legs, but it belongs to me. You hear me, Dolce? Don't ever threaten me like that again, understand?" I asked, palm-ing her hot spot through the tight-ass jeans she had on.

"Yes, husband." She smiled naughtily before moving over to straddle me.

"You sure you don't want to hit Privacy up tonight? I'm already dressed for the occasion," I joked.

"No, daddy. I'm good. This right here is all I need," she purred as she began to slowly grind on my dick.

"Cool, I can get with this any day," I said before pulling her face down to mine prepared to kiss her. "Wait, baby. I almost forgot that I have a surprise for you." I pecked her once before getting up from the bed.

"What is it?" she asked excitedly as I reached into the top drawer on my side of the dresser.

"You'll see." I shot her a lustful look before turning to insert the DVD into the player.

While it loaded up, I went back over to help relieve her of her clothing before doing the same. The video queued up the moment we got comfortable in bed. I watched as her eyes widened at seeing us enter our reserved room at Privacy a few nights ago. We cuddled, kissed, and ca-ressed one another as the video played. We usually gave our tapes our undivided attention when we watched it the first go-round, but this shit was so sexy and erotic that I doubted we'd make it through to the end.

"Damn, babe. You fine as hell," Dolce complimented me as we watched the part where she sucked my dick the first time that night. I remembered how good it felt once I was finally able to let that first nut go, and I needed her to suck me up like that again today.

"You the one, baby," I whispered against her face. "You're beautiful to me every day, but that night you was on some other shit. I couldn't get enough of looking at you. Them fucking sex faces," I recalled before blessing her with a deep, sensual kiss. "That banging-ass body." I sucked on her cheek hard enough to leave a mark. "And let's not forget that good-ass pussy, fuckkk!" I groaned, biting roughly at her chin as she moaned. "Shit, girl, you had my fucking head gone," I confessed.

"Mo Mo, please," she begged as she stroked my dick.

I figured we wouldn't make it through that entire video, and I was right. We stayed in bed for the remainder of the day and night, sexing each other crazy. We'd just come down from our final orgasmic high as the sun started to peek through the blinds of our bedroom. Neither of us was asleep, just tangled up in the sheets, lost in our own thoughts.

"D, I know it may be too soon seeing as how you just agreed to give me a second chance, but do you remember what you promised me once I got to a point that I wasn't working so much and could carve out more time to be home with you?" I inquired out of the blue.

"Yes, Moraiah. I told you that then and only then would I think about trying to start a family," she replied with her head on my chest while running her fingers through my beard the way I liked. Shit was soothing as fuck.

"I'm not being pushy, and I know it may take some time to prove to you that I'm serious about cutting back on work, but I want to put that on your mind so you won't act brand new when I bring it up down the line. I want them babies that you promised me. All eight of them," I teased before kissing the top of her head. We both just laughed before going silent again. Minutes later she spoke up.

"I trust you, Moraiah, and I believe you when you say that you're committed to working on our marriage so we can definitely make that happen." She grinned, giving me the best news I'd received in a while.

It felt damn good knowing that I still had her by my side, and I planned to make sure she never regretted giving me this second chance. I would stay true to my word and keep her and all eight of my future children as my main priority. Always.

The End